We Be Dragons

We Be Dragons

Michael Weitz

Rook & Rook

WE BE DRAGONS

For information:
michaelweitzbooks.com

Edited by: Kristen Corrects, Inc.
Cover design: 100 Covers
Chapter head art: Tam Thrift

ISBN: 979-8-9929701-0-4

For Jason Pfaff,
my best friend since 5th grade!
Here's to our many adventures, both imagined and real.
Thank you.

Other Books by Michael Weitz

Even Dead Men Play Chess
The Grandmaster's King
Till Tomorrow

Cast of Characters

John Brewer	*Dungeons & Dragons* (D&D) game Dungeon Master
Eric "Truck" Pinder	John's best friend and D&D player
Toff Hansen	friend and D&D player
Charlie Davis	friend and D&D player
Levi Pratt	friend and D&D player
Nick Meyers	friend and D&D player
Evie Brewer	John's mother
Earl Conklin	Owner of the Sam's 76 gas/service station
Jim Henley	Farmer
Patricia Henley	Jim Henley's wife
Blaine	Jim Henley's farmhand
Dale Kleinert	Combine driver for Jim Henley
Paul Statler	Jim and Patricia Henley's son-in-law
Wayne Phillips	Weston police officer
Paulette Dickerson	Member of the One Vision Bible Church
Aaron Evans	Member of the One Vision Bible Church
Lisa Martin	John Brewer's dream girl

ALCHEMIST'S BANE

Kryger (cry·ger)	A human fighter, played by Truck
Xan (zan)	An elf magic-user, played by Toff
Domo (doe·moe)	An elf thief, played by Charlie
Franco (frank·oh)	A human cleric, played by Levi
Bellator (bell·uh·tore)	A dwarf fighter, played by Nick
Jovar (joe·vahr)	The mayor of Sandole, a non-player character in the D&D adventure
Bohz Grauer (boze grau·wer)	A duergar warlord, a non-player character in the D&D adventure
Clavam (clay·vum)	A non-player character in the D&D adventure

Chapter 1

1986

John Brewer was in the Top Notch Café eyeing the menu—and the brunette behind the counter—when the first wail of the air raid siren pierced the calm afternoon. There were six other customers in the small diner, a family of four having lunch by the door and two men in gray overalls near the back.

"Decided yet, John?" That from Lisa, the brunette working the counter just as the alarm howled outside. Before he could answer, a second wail started and the two men jumped up and trotted toward the front door.

"Hold the check, Lisa," the man in front said. "I'll grab it later."

As the men pushed through the door, the parents in the booth stopped eating, Lisa stood, and John lowered his menu. They all stared at nothing. Waiting.

When the third siren confirmed their fears, Lisa dashed to the rectangular phone on the wall near the kitchen and started dialing, the handset cradled between her ear and shoulder. The parents dropped their forks and whispered to one another, their eyes wide; John slid out of the booth and made for the front door with an apologetic wave toward Lisa. He'd lost his appetite.

In Weston, the World War II-era air raid siren was used to call the volunteer fire department crew. One blast brought in a skeleton crew, fire and ambulance, for a non-life-threatening situation; two blasts meant a medical emergency and required a timely response; three blasts meant all hands on deck, a life was in danger, move your ass.

It was just before one on a Saturday afternoon in early June. In a town of fewer than three thousand people, everyone knew everyone. And one of them was in trouble.

Memories of his father and the three-siren wails that brought news of his death slowed John's pace as he trotted back to Sam's 76, the gas and service station he'd worked at since the previous summer. His boss was Earl Conklin, who'd bought the business from Sam Davis in 1981 and kept the name. "Easier, cheaper, and around here, people tend to like things to stay the same," he'd told John.

Earl was on the phone when John came into bay 1. Earl's hands were black with grease and his fingerprints covered the cream-colored plastic phone as if it had been dusted at a crime scene.

John stood beside the lift and peered at the underside of a K-car while trying to listen to Earl. His boss wasn't talking to a customer; after a three-siren call to the volunteer fire department, everyone near a phone was calling anyone who might know what happened and to whom.

He just noticed the oil pan beneath the car was missing its plug when Earl hung up the phone. "What happened?" John asked.

Earl shook his head and took off his cap. He swept his hair back and wiped his palm across his belly. "Don't know exactly." He tugged his cap back on and said, "Farm accident out near Henley's place is what I've heard so far. No tellin' what happened yet."

John nodded and moved to the back of the shop where he'd hung his own coveralls and stepped into them. Earl called from behind, "We'll hear soon enough. Meantime, switch out the filter"—he nodded at the car—"put the plug back in the pan, drop 'er down, and put five quarts of 10–30 in 'er."

John stepped under the boxy sedan and peered up under the engine. Everywhere he looked was what his boss called *oily-brown-n-black road shit*. That's what it was too; oil from the engine covered in dust and grime from the road. Everything was the same color, so John found the oil filter partly by shape and partly by knowing where to look. He swiped a finger through the oily-brown-n-black road shit to make sure and then fit the filter wrench around it and pulled. Earl rarely needed the filter wrench; all he did was wipe the oil filter off with his rag then twist it off. John's grip was good, but Earl's was like a boa constrictor.

John drained the oil, replaced the plug, and spun a new filter in place. He looked over at his boss while he lowered the car slowly to the ground, but Earl was back on the phone.

The car swallowed five quarts of fresh oil and John started it up. Crawling underneath, he made sure neither the oil filter nor the plug leaked. Satisfied, John turned the car off and inspected it once again for leaks. "Okay," he called to Earl. "She's good to go. Did you hear anything yet?"

Before Earl could emerge from behind the counter and come out into the car bay, the rounded nose of a '57 Chevy pickup screeched to a halt and darkened the light coming inside the shop. The rumbling V-8 roared once then fell silent as the driver turned off the engine and stepped out of the cab.

As he closed the door of his pickup, Eric "Truck" Pinder called, "Brewer!"

John glanced at his boss then answered, "Hey, Truck."

"Did you hear?"

"No," John said. "Did you?"

"I think it's Dave Carlson."

Earl grabbed Truck by the shoulder and spun him around. "How do you know?"

"Stu's brother called him at the café. He heard it from Dean."

The small-town grapevine, a telephone gossip and news network faster than any journalistic agency known to man.

"Damn," Earl said. He stuffed his rag into his back pocket and reached for the phone. "It was a three-alarmer too."

CHAPTER 2

A week later, Dave Carlson's funeral was the talk of the town. If it had been anything else, it would have been the event of the season. Half the town had been there to pay their respects while the rest talked about it with their friends and neighbors in somber tones and meaningful shakes of their heads.

That same afternoon John Brewer was in his garage with his friends getting ready to play *Dungeons & Dragons*. The six boys had been playing for years, and now that they were all seventeen years old, this would be the last summer before they graduated and "real life" began. John wanted this last summer of D&D to be memorable.

Second- and third-hand throw rugs hung like tapestries on the side walls of the garage; they insulated against the cold winter months and helped soundproof the small space. An old pool table light hung above the plywood table, two floor lamps leaned out of dark corners to provide more ambient light, and a small table lamp with a barrel-shaped shade stood on the corner at the head of the table. It was old and run-down, but it was theirs and they'd christened the garage the Council Chamber to make it sound more grandiose.

The boys sat around the table in mismatched chairs and spread their paper, pencils, and dice in front of them. "Did you guys hear they think there was somebody else with Carlson when he died?" Charlie asked. He pushed his glasses up on his nose and crossed his arms. He had a hatchet-shaped face with a wide forehead and a crater-deep dimple in the middle of his pointed chin. His walnut-colored hair was short, straight, and combed flat against his head. The black, thick-framed glasses he wore made him look like a 1960s-era NASA engineer.

"*May* have been there," corrected Levi.

Charlie shook his head. "Whatever."

"How do you know?" Nick asked. "Who's *they*?"

"I heard Gary talking in the break room at work." Charlie worked as a box boy at Weston Grocery, where Gary Carter, a volunteer firefighter, was the meat department manager. "He said they saw a footprint in blood."

"Big deal! Carlson was spraying blood everywhere!" Nick lashed out. Then he looked at Toff. "Sorry, dude."

For the past two years Toff Hansen had worked summers on the same farm as Dave Carlson. The boys still didn't know how to act around him, unsure how the death had affected him.

Toff shook his head and looked at the floor.

"Not blood *on top* of a footprint," Charlie went on. "A footprint on top of the blood. Like someone stepped in it."

Nick wasn't having it. He shook his head. "Yeah, it was probably *Dave's footprint*. I'm sure he was stumbling all over the place. Didn't they find him close to the road?"

"Well," said Charlie as he pushed his glasses up again, "I'm just telling you what I heard."

John smiled. "Are you saying you think he was murdered?"

"Not *me*," Charlie corrected. "*They*. And no one said murder, just that someone might have seen it happen."

John nodded. "Right. Well, murder or not, nothing that interesting happens in Weston."

Truck banged the table with his hands. "True words, right there! Let's play some D&D!"

Truck had taught them to play *Dungeons & Dragons* in sixth grade and became the de facto leader of the group. He didn't ask for that honor, it just happened that way. The game was their weekly escape from schoolwork, summer jobs, and the monotony of small-town banality. Weekends became havens for imagination, the sharing of ideas, and working together to solve problems. And it wasn't just about the game—D&D was social time. It's how they grew up together.

"Can we start over?" Levi asked. "I don't remember anything."

John finished organizing his things at the head of the table. He was the Dungeon Master, or DM, and had spent the last three weeks of school preparing more for this D&D adventure than his final exams. They'd begun the game a week earlier, but it ended quickly after John's mom came into the garage and told Levi he was needed at home. John adjusted his Dungeon Masters screen, a cardboard barrier between him and the players that hid DM-only information from the group. "Really? You want to start over?" he asked and looked around the table.

"No! Hell no!" Nick said, waving his hands. At 6'1", Nick Meyers was a hopeful recruit of the Weston High basketball team, but he was barely 140 pounds, refused to cut his unruly long black hair, and disliked anything organized, like team sports. He wore faded, threadbare jeans every day, even in the heat of summer, and topped them off with a beat-up black leather jacket over a T-shirt. He looked like he played guitar for the Ramones. "Come on, you guys," Nick went on. "We got hired by the mayor of Sandole, remember? What was his name?"

"Jovar," said Toff. "He wants us to go to some ruins, find a guy who's looking for an ancient artifact, and stop him. And bring the artifact back to him if we can." Toff was the brainiac among the group of friends. He'd gotten straight A's ever since first grade and was on track to be class valedictorian.

Levi shrugged. "I don't remember any of that."

"Okay, a quick summary," he said. "Like Nick said, your group was hired by Jovar, the mayor of Sandole, a small town near the ruins of a castle and old mine. Legend has it that an ancient artifact is lost somewhere in the castle ruins or in the mine. There's a duergar warlord, or mercenary, named Bohz Grauer who's taken over the ruins and is searching for the artifact. The problem is that he and his minions keep raiding the town. They steal food and supplies, but worse, they enslave whoever they can from the town and force them to search for the artifact. Jovar wants you to stop Bohz Grauer and, if you happen to find the artifact, bring it back to him."

Levi thought about it. "Okay. Two questions. Do we know what the artifact is?"

"Probably a magical amulet, but we don't know what it does," said Toff. "Which is why this Bohz Grauer may have a wizard working with him. Our Dungeon Master forgot to tell you that." He smiled at John.

"Yeah," Truck added, "but that's not our main goal. We're supposed to off that duergar." He chuckled and rubbed his hands together.

"That's my second question," Levi said. "What the hell's a duergar?"

"The duergar are an offshoot of the dwarven race," John said. He'd read all about this character in the module because he'd never heard of one either. He found more about them in *Monster Manual II* as well. "They're also called gray dwarves. They're basically an evil subset of dwarves."

"Can we just call them gray dwarves then?" Levi asked. "I'll never remember *doo-er-gar*. That sounds made up."

"It *is* made up," Truck said with a laugh.

"Come on," Levi pleaded. "You know what I mean." Levi was the shortest of the group and claimed it gave him a better shot at becoming a Hollywood heartthrob because all leading men were "of the non-tall persuasion." His reddish-brown hair would have been at home atop a Muppet and his rubbery countenance often landed him in hot water when he was a young altar boy making faces at the congregation.

John glanced at Truck, who shrugged. "Yeah, that's fine," John said. "You got it? Find and stop Bohz Grauer, get the artifact."

"Not necessarily in that order," Nick added.

"Got it," Levi said.

John nodded and looked around the table at his friends and thought of the characters they played. Truck's character was Kryger, the massive human fighter who led the group and carried an array of bladed weapons but favored a heavy broadsword that took two hands to swing with limb-severing accuracy; Charlie's character was Domo, an elven thief whose shadowy skills were extremely useful; Nick played Bellator, a gruff dwarf fighter who wasn't afraid of any contest regardless of his size; Franco was Levi's character, a human cleric with powers to both heal and wreak havoc; and Toff played Xan, an elf magic-user who practiced the arcane art of casting spells. John smiled. This was going to be a fun adventure. "Good," he said. "We didn't get far last time, but let's pick it up from there."

"A guide led us to the castle ruins, and then hightailed it back to the village, right?" Charlie asked.

"Right," Truck said. "We were left at the bottom of a hill but could see the ruins at the top." He looked at John and declared, "Kryger goes up the hill and stops at the rock wall." He looked around the table. "Are you with me?"

Everyone nodded and scooted closer to the table.

CHAPTER 3

Kryger took a deep breath and surveyed their surroundings. In the silvery early-morning light, he could see the ruins much better and scanned the outer perimeter of the ancient castle. With his sword, he pointed at a pile of rubble at the base of the wall. "We can go in there," he said. His voice was deep, as if his lungs were hollow tree trunks. "Domo and Xan, keep an eye out; they may be creatures of the night, but they'd be fools not to post sentries."

Domo was an elf, a thief by trade, specializing in stealth. His charcoal-black hair was curly and long enough to cover his pointed ears. He wore soft dark leather garments with an array of hidden pockets and pouches. His thin stature allowed him to hide and move about quietly and unseen, but it also served to hide his great strength. Xan was also an elf, but from the forested mountains of the north where he'd studied the mysterious arts of magic and had developed exceptional powers and an array of spells. He had the same sharp features as his kinsmen but wore earth-colored robes and a crimson, wide-brimmed beret atop his long blond hair. Both were well-honed in their individual crafts, and while Domo's keen senses were superior, it was their elven characteristics of sharp sight and hearing that made them both natural lookouts. Domo and Xan nodded at Kryger but said nothing, each looking warily about.

"How do we want to approach the ruins?" Franco asked. A holy man who dealt in the healing arts but also carried a mace the size of a boar's head, Franco wore an unpolished breastplate over a heavy rawhide jacket. Leather bracers protected his forearms and shins, and a long cloak the color of the midnight sky concealed his armor when he chose.

"I should lead," Bellator said quietly. "It's worked well before; if Xan must cast a spell, I won't block it." Bellator was a dwarf and a proud and storied warrior. His tallish 4'3" gave him the extra reach needed in battle. His bravery and strength were the things songs were made of.

The group picked their way through the tall weeds and scattered stones to the pile of loose rubble that was once a castle wall. They ducked low as they neared then slowly peered over the broken stones.

The ward was littered with the spines of walls that once held roofs and housed industrious people. The masonry had withstood ages of weather, though a few walls had fallen, or leaned in fatigue. Wooden doors and thatch roofs were gone, withered away with time, carried off by peasants in need, or eaten away by insects and vermin.

They stopped for a moment and surveyed the buildings ahead of them. On the far side of the compound the castle's great hall still stood. Only the uppermost floor of the tower looked somewhat damaged and open to the elements.

"It looks like the ground floor and next two stories could be in use," Xan said, pointing. "As long as the top floor has no cracks in the masonry."

"The tower, as well," added Domo, following the magic-user's gaze. "Its slate roof is there, but damaged. The lower rooms may still be usable. I see no movement either."

"Nor I," grunted Kryger.

"No guards?" asked Franco. "Is it arrogance, or simply unnecessary? Jovar made it sound as if no one has given Bohz Grauer any resistance."

"Perhaps we can use that to our advantage," said Bellator. He smiled at the cleric. "A passive army is half beaten."

"I never believe an enemy, army or otherwise, is passive," offered Domo with a condescending look. "Ever."

Bellator rolled his eyes then looked at Domo. "Nevertheless, there seem to be no sentries."

"Which means traps," said the elf. As a thief it was Domo's job to detect traps, tricks, and non-magical deceptions. And to set them too, if needed. "If the mercenaries this warlord is using to raid the town and mine the ore are truly nocturnal creatures, then the ruins must be protected by traps in the daylight."

Kryger nodded at Bellator. "I agree." Then he turned to the thief. "How do we find them?"

Bellator hefted a small boulder over his head. "I say we

start tossing stones and see what happens."

"No!" cried Xan, putting a hand on the dwarf's arm. "Setting off any trap could alert someone to our presence. We must find the traps and disarm them or avoid them."

"Can you cast a spell to see them?" asked Franco.

"No need," said Domo. "Bellator, you are mere inches from one now. Do not move or you will bring the wall down upon us."

Domo scampered over the toppled boulders as easily as a mouse and hopped cat-like to the ground on the other side. His thin form disappeared around the corner of the stone wall. "I am attempting to dismantle the device," he said, just loud enough to be heard. In a moment he came around again and held up a small pin. "Success. It's safe to come into the courtyard."

The small band of adventurers scrabbled over the ancient pile of stones that had once been part of the outer wall of the fortress and regrouped near the hooded thief.

"Xan, keep an eye on that tower," said Kryger as he pulled the map from his leather pouch. "This shows that the mine entrance should be over there, inside that low barracks." He pointed at a long rectangular building that had withstood the test of time but for a sheet of vines that had rooted themselves in the facade.

"What about the Great Hall?" asked Bellator. "If we go into the mine first, we could be attacked from behind."

"True, but if we make it into the tunnels without alerting anyone, and we don't allow anyone back out, we'll have the element of surprise. I don't see that happening if we run into trouble in there." Kryger pointed his chin at the larger building with the tower rising from the corner.

Franco nodded. "Having the advantage of surprise is important here; we are but five against an unknown number of enemies. If the numbers are overwhelming..." He trailed off with a sigh and shook his head.

"Always an inspiration, brother." The dwarf chuckled.

"Bohz Grauer's wizard, if there is one, is most likely in the tower," Xan observed. "Or on one of the upper floors of the hall. If we neutralize Bohz and possibly obtain the artifact, the wizard may not wish to fight."

"Unless he wants the artifact for himself," Domo said.

"True, my elven cousin," replied Xan. "However, as Franco said, if we attempt to secure the wizard first, there is no hope for surprise against Bohz Grauer, and he is our main objective. The enslavement of the townspeople must be ended."

The five adventurers nodded in agreement.

"Can you spot any other traps between here and the building, Domo?" Kryger asked the thief.

"The piles of ruined buildings are a hazard in themselves," Domo answered quietly. He scanned the ground before them. "I will walk ahead and see what I can find. Follow at a short distance, but do not lose sight of me, and walk only where I walk." Domo lowered his hood and squinted into the morning sun. He slid a long dagger from its sheath and started toward the low building against the back wall of the castle.

Kryger let the thief get twenty paces ahead then motioned for the rest of the party to follow. As they set out, they heard footfalls from behind the ruins of what was once a blacksmith's shop.

Domo motioned for the group to stop. He crouched then slowly looked around the ruined wall. A rock sailed past his head as he ducked, and the footfalls grew louder and faster. Whoever—or whatever—they were, they were running.

Domo trotted back to the party. "Skeletons,"[1] he said. "A patrol of eight."

Kryger drew his sword and Bellator hefted his mighty battle axe with a deep chuckle.

"These are undead creatures brought about by dark magic," Xan said. "Don't underestimate them."

The skeletons rounded the corner where Domo had first espied them and then charged. Seven of them gripped rusted swords and one held aloft a spear. The white bones shone in the morning sun and rattled as the creatures stumbled and twisted over the stony rubble. Their teeth clicked as they worked their mandibles, but they made no other sound as they hurried into battle.

The party spread out and advanced toward the skeleton guards more slowly. They watched and let their foe come to them.

The skeletons rushed forward, swinging their swords and gnashing their teeth. A spear flew through the crowd but missed its mark, clattering against the stones. Bellator stepped forward and with a mighty swing swept the two lead guards with his battle axe. Their lower ribs and spinal columns exploded in a shower of calcified splinters as the

[1]Skeletons are magically animated undead monsters enchanted into servitude by a powerful magic-user or an evil cleric. *Monster Manual* (Lake Geneva, WI: TSR, 1979), 88.

weapon cut them in half.

Kryger roared as he stepped into the battle. He slashed down at the skeleton closest to him and shattered the creature's shoulder so that the sword arm and hand bones all fell to the ground. But the skeleton kept advancing, reaching out to grab hold of Kryger's neck with its other hand.

On the other side of Bellator, Franco raised his mace and smashed the skull of the skeleton in front of him. The power of the blow went through the undead body and the bones blew apart.

Behind the company, Xan was readying an incantation that would allow him to engulf the enemy in a ball of flame, but it would take him another few moments to recite the spell.

Domo stood nearby, guarding the magic-user while he concentrated. But that didn't mean the thief couldn't join the battle. Domo chose a fist-sized rock and threw it at a skeleton that had raised its sword toward Kryger. The stone hit the target and knocked the creature back a step, but once it regained its balance the skeleton advanced again.

Only one of the skeletons was destroyed, the one that had suffered the wrath of Franco and his mace. The torsos of the two halved by Bellator crawled about the melee and grasped at the ankles of the combatants, and the one that Kryger had hacked the sword arm from still harried him with attempted grabs and swings of its bony knuckles.

But there were still four other able-bodied guards to contend with. These pushed forward, swinging their swords, their eerily quiet charge punctuated only by the clicking teeth and cracking joints.

Bellator swept the legs out from under one guard then cleaved the skull in two with his axe. Kryger skewered the single-armed skeleton through the ribs then swung the creature at one of the advancing guards. The two fell in a tangle of bones and Kryger used the opportunity to crush their two skulls with the hilt of his sword as if they were giant walnuts.

Franco rushed forward and with a powerful blow knocked the lower jaw and left collarbone from one of the two still-standing skeletons. He didn't see the other guard advance toward him, sword raised, but Domo knocked it back with another well-placed stone and Franco smashed its skull with a jarring hit from his mace—his holy roller, as he called it.

Bellator picked up a rock and smashed those skulls still working their jaws and clicking their teeth. Domo used the bones of one skeleton to pry apart the forearm of another that still crawled on the ground, and Xan discontinued his now-unneeded chant.

"Back to dust with you all and may your poor souls now rest," Franco muttered under his breath.

"I hope," said Kryger, "that's the strength of all the adversaries we may come across."

Xan shook his head. "Only an evil wizard can animate skeletons and set them to guard the grounds. These were not a difficulty for him, I'm sure of it, but they're fairly capable guards to frighten off any locals who venture inside these walls. We must be wary; the truly evil creatures I fear this wizard may have brought forward await us yet—those that do not dally in the sunlight and will not attack with mindless abandon."

"Do you think the battle was overheard?" Franco asked, nodding toward the Great Hall.

Domo shook his head. "I do not believe so. I have been watching and have seen no movement."

"Does everyone still have all their fingers and toes?" Kryger asked. "Good. Let's continue then."

Once again Domo moved ahead of the group. Several times the elf stopped and inspected the ground, or the piles of fallen stones, but kept moving forward without a warning to the others.

When they reached the building marked on the map, they saw the main entryway beneath a curtain of vines: large iron doors, barred, chained, and locked.

"This metalwork is not ancient," Domo said, motioning to the security measures. "The doors are probably locked on the inside as well."

"Then how does anyone get in or out?" asked Bellator.

"I am sure there are some who dwell inside and some who do not," Xan said and pointed toward the great hall. "There must be a set time, perhaps sunset, when someone on each side of the door unlocks it."

"We must find another way in," said Kryger. "Spread out but be careful."

The group separated and inspected the structure, feeling the stonework, their eyes roaming over the surfaces, one hand gripping their weapon of choice.

Xan wandered around the corner and spotted what they were looking for. "My friends!" he called softly. "Here!"

Toward the back wall and mostly hidden by overgrown weeds and vines, a small door was set into the stone. It was only four feet tall and almost as wide. "A service door," Franco remarked. "Probably to pass food or supplies through without blocking the main entry."

The wooden door was gray with age and braced with thick iron bands that had rusted over the ages, but was nonetheless solid. "Domo," whispered Kryger, "can you open such an old lock?"

The thief knelt in front of the door and slid his sensitive hands over the surface. "Very old. Thick. This door is still solid. Good craftsmanship."

"Yes, yes," Bellator grunted. "The door is a work of art. Can you pick a rusty lock or can you not?"

Domo ignored the impatient dwarf and set to work with the tools of his thieving trade. "Yes, Bellator," he said after a few moments. "I can. But the hinges need oil, lest we alert the entire mine." He held up a finger to silently ask them to wait a moment. Then he pulled a vial of shimmery, almost glowing viscous liquid from his pouch and poured just a drop upon each hinge and the lock itself. "We must wait a few moments for the oil to coat the pins."

"That's not like any oil I've ever seen," said Bellator. "And you use so little. Is it magic?" The dwarf was the newest member of the adventuring group and hadn't had the opportunity to witness all the skills of the others.

Domo shrugged. "Perfect for just such an occasion," he

said with a smile. Then, with his tools held nimbly between his fingers, he set to work on the lock. After a few moments he stood up and nodded.

Kryger got down on his knees and applied steady pressure to the door until he was able to push it open far enough to let them crawl in. The hinges did not squeal and the chamber inside was dark and silent.

Bellator ducked inside first and stood with his axe ready. The others followed and stood in the cool darkness. Xan silently lofted a ball of white light from the palm of his hand into the air above them. They were in a long hall studded with empty rusted sconces. Xan's magical light didn't penetrate to the far end, but the empty room appeared to be about fifty to sixty feet in length. The walls were bare, though the stone was blackened above by old smoke and below by mold where water had seeped inside. The stone floor was well worn, scratched and scarred by countless booted feet, and a gaping arch opened within the wall across from the great iron doors to their right.

"You were right," Kryger whispered to Domo and pointed at the chains crisscrossing the doors on the inside.

"Now what?" Franco asked.

"We go through the arch," Kryger said, nodding toward the blackness. Cool air swirled into the chamber from the arch like ink in water. "That's the way into the mine."

CHAPTER 4

The next morning came quickly for John Brewer. The group had stayed up well past midnight playing D&D even though John had to be at the gas station by eight.

"How did it go last night?" his mother asked. She sipped her coffee and arched her eyebrows. Evie Brewer didn't just tolerate her son's infatuation with *Dungeons & Dragons* like so many other parents did when it came to their teenaged children and their hobbies; she had sat down with him and played through a short adventure. She'd watched the news reports and heard what people were saying: that D&D was a cult, that it was evil and called forth demons. She was apprehensive but needed to find out on her own. During the game she was surprised how wrong what she had heard was. The game wasn't evil at all. She even had fun playing.

"We got a good start," John answered. He refilled his glass with orange juice and stabbed a link of sausage.

"Hopefully we'll get through it all this summer, but everyone is working. They liked it, though."

"Did anyone get slimed?" She smiled.

John rolled his eyes. "Mom, you only played once; green slimes[1] aren't in every dungeon. And no, they didn't." John took a bite of his toast and waited for the next inevitable round of questions.

"Speaking of slime," Evie said, "guess who I ran into at the grocery store."

John shrugged. It was too early for guessing games.

"Paulette Dickerson. Do you remember her?" Evie smiled and curled her lip.

Paulette Dickerson, an evangelist on steroids, was on a mission to save Weston from the wickedness of anything that became too popular with young impressionable minds: the Rubik's Cube led to psychosis; arcades encouraged drug and alcohol use; cruising Main Street led to prostitution and gambling. She waged her campaigns through angry phone calls, letters to the editor, and spreading rumors.

"Yeah." John nodded. "She's crazy." He shoveled a pile of eggs into his mouth.

Evie nodded and held the warm coffee cup between her hands. Her smile was gone. "Today's the day, right? Are you feeling up to it?"

John nodded and wiped his palms on his thighs. For the past two weeks he'd wanted to ask his boss at the gas station, Earl, for a raise. The actual act of asking though, was proving

---

[1]Green slimes are plant growths that tend to drop onto unsuspecting adventurers. They feed on animal, vegetable, and metallic substances and can turn its victims into green slime. *Monster Manual* (Lake Geneva, WI: TSR, 1979), 49.

to be as difficult as asking out Lisa Martin. He puffed out his cheeks and blew air.

Evie nodded. "You can do it, John. The hard part is getting started. Once it's out there it's just a natural conversation. I know how bad you want to go to college, but I just can't afford it. So, it's now or never, as your dad would say."

Tom Brewer had been killed in a farming accident when John was twelve years old, and Evie was doing her best as a single mother. She often quoted her husband since it helped her find things to say, but also because she wanted to make sure John never forgot.

"I know," he said. "Now or never." He shook his head, tired of hearing about their financial situation.

"I'm sorry, John," Evie said.

"Yeah," John mumbled. He scraped his fork across the plate, hoping they were done talking. Since his father's death, John had felt trapped in the small town. His dad had talked about travel, even had a subscription to *Travel & Leisure*, but had never left Weston. John didn't want the same fate, and college seemed the only avenue of escape, but it was expensive.

"I know you don't want to stay in Weston after you graduate, but it's not as bad as you make it out to be, you know. It just might take a couple more years."

"I can't work at the gas station all my life," John shot back.

"Not your whole life, John. There are plenty of—"

"Mom." John rolled his eyes. "There *aren't* plenty of jobs here. It's a fight at the end of every school year just to get a summer job. And there's nothing to do in Weston; we have to go to Moscow just to see a movie."

Earl Conklin was behind the register at Sam's 76. He wore a clean pair of jeans, a short-sleeve button-up shirt, and his torn, creamsicle-colored cap. John saw his boss through the window and thought something was odd; he'd never seen Earl at the gas station without his overalls on.

The tiny brass bell above the door tinkled when John walked in. "Hi. Earl," he said. His heart was bouncing against his chest like it was on a trampoline. "Hey, uh, could I talk to you about something?"

Earl slid the cash drawer shut and looked at his watch. "Sure, we've got a few minutes. I need to talk to you too. Go ahead."

John swallowed hard. *Now or never. Now or never.* "Well, since I've been working here for a year now, I was, er... Well, I was wondering if I might be able to get a raise." There. It was out.

Earl came around the counter and sat on one of the plastic chairs by the window. Its spidery chrome legs scraped the floor as he leaned back. He waved at the other chair and John sat down. Negotiation time.

"Hell, John," Earl said, "I wish I could give you a raise, I really do."

"Oh," was all John could croak. His throat was dry. It wasn't the answer he expected. Was that it? *Now or never.*

"I'm not looking for much," he tried. "You know I'm saving for college, so anything would help."

Earl swept his hat off, scratched his head, then pulled the hat on again. He ran a hand over his mouth and sighed. He looked at John and said, "I have some bad news, I'm afraid. I sold the station, John. I told the new owner about you. I told him you're an excellent employee, good with customers, and you know your way around an engine. I asked him to keep you on."

John felt himself shrink and Earl suddenly sounded like he was at the bottom of a well. His boss shook his head and stood up.

"I'm sorry, John. I know how important this job was to you, but he didn't take you on. He said he couldn't use you. I'm sorry, I tried."

John stood up. "Oh," he said. "Oh. So, that's it? Like right now?"

Earl nodded. "Damn, John. I'm sorry. But yes. He'll be here in a few minutes and I'm handing over the keys."

John stood still, his brain processing, his feet not moving. Earl grabbed an envelope next to the register and pushed it into John's hand. It felt thin. "If I hear of any jobs in town, I'll let you know. I promise."

John nodded. "Thanks. I guess." He walked out and got into his car. Started it up and pulled out onto Main Street. He'd only gone a few feet when he felt the tears running down his face and he choked back a sob. *I'm never going to get out of here*, he thought.

CHAPTER 5

"Man, that sucks," Truck said.

It was close to seven p.m. and John had just told his friends in the Council Chamber about no longer having a job at Sam's 76.

"Did he tell you why the new guy wouldn't hire you?" Levi asked.

John shook his head. "Just said he couldn't use me. I don't know why."

"Who bought it?" Charlie asked.

When he was fifteen Charlie helped fix up the old pickup that he would drive once he got his license, but after dropping three new headlamps, he decided to stick to unsmashable parts only, like tires and radiator hoses. It was why his D&D character, Domo, was an elven thief, someone who had superior eyesight and was as agile and quick as a fox.

"Has to be someone from out of town," John said. "There's no way it could have been kept secret if Earl sold it to somebody from Weston."

"Well, I ain't buyin' gas from there anymore!" Nick said. "You can count on that."

The boys all turned to look at Nick.

"Yeah!" said Levi. "Me neither."

"I'll go over to Bill's Exxon," said Truck. "Screw 'em!"

John smiled. "Thanks guys, but it's cool. I just don't know what to do. I went everywhere I could think of today and nobody's hiring anymore. I even went to the Top Notch, and they don't have waiters."

Truck burst out laughing and tipped back his chair. "You didn't go to the Top Notch to get a job, you were hoping you'd see Lisa." He shook his head—his curly black hair jumped and scattered like a flock of crows—and he laughed some more. "Man, you'd love to get a job working next to her."

John smiled and looked down. "Who wouldn't?" Then his smile faded, and he looked at Charlie. "I didn't go in the grocery store, though. It looked packed. Would it be worth it if I stopped by tomorrow morning? Or Monday?"

Charlie shook his head. "Sorry, man. They hired the last kid about two weeks ago; that sophomore, the kid with the stupid hair."

"Randy?" John said. "Seriously? Are they going to let him look like that at work?" Randy Denmont watched MTV like he was in a cult and worshipped a lot of the British pop bands. He shaped his blond hair with enough gel and hair spray that some girls asked him to style their coifs. But instead of curly and big, Randy's hair was flat, combed down over his left eye, and swept back on the sides. He thought he looked cool; everyone else thought he looked desperate for attention.

"No," Charlie said. "He's going to work in the back until he gets it cut. Then they'll let him bag."

"Shit," John mumbled.

"I might be able to get you on at Henley's," Toff said.

John looked at his friend and winced.

"I know you hate farming," Toff went on, "but it's only for the summer, and the pay's good."

John remembered being in the Top Notch trying to decide what to have for a late lunch when the volunteer fire department was called to duty. A passing motorist had seen what he'd reported as something out of a horror movie: a man covered in blood, staggering around and looking like his arm was missing.

The next day, when the first responders could talk about it without choking up, it turned out that's exactly what had happened. Dave Carlson had been repairing an auger, a spinning corkscrew in a tube that carried grain into a silo where it was stored until transported by semi to either the river, where it would be loaded onto a barge, or to Spokane, where it might end up on a train. They figured Dave's shirt or hand got caught in the rotating auger. It must have happened quickly, and the machine's torque was too strong, crushing and twisting and stretching his bones and muscle until it ripped his shoulder out of the socket and tore the whole arm from his body. Nobody could guess how it happened, and Dave couldn't tell them; he was dead when they arrived.

The man who'd called from a nearby farmhouse to report the accident had gone back to help in any way he could, but it was too late. Dave's heart had pumped too much blood out of the ragged hole that was left of his shoulder. The Weston Volunteer Fire Department crew found the would-be good Samaritan in the ditch where he'd thrown up and was crying. They found Dave's twisted arm at the top of the auger where it had jammed in the spout that dropped grain into the silo.

But it was more than that. John's own father had been run over by a combine, crushed and suffocated in the dirt like an insect. John remembered the three wails of the air raid siren from that day five years ago; they'd sounded different. Morose. He wondered if the sirens had sounded different to Dave's family too.

"Brewer? Brewer!" Toff shouted.

"What?" John looked up, startled.

The boys laughed. "Do you want me to see?" Toff asked.

John looked around the table. He knew they were just laughing because they'd caught him remembering a bad time. At least his best friend wasn't laughing.

Truck dropped his chin and patted John on the shoulder. "Just like in D&D, man, you got to roll the bones and see what happens."

John took a deep breath. Held it. Thought about what had happened to his dad. "No," he finally said. He shook his head. "I can't. No way."

Toff nodded, sat back, and held his palms up. No one said anything, didn't try to push. They knew John wanted a job and why, but they were his friends and knew the pain he'd gone through all those years ago. And was still going through.

Truck clapped his hands once and said, "All right, who's hungry?" He reached into a big paper grocery sack and pulled out a bag of Cheetos, a package of Oreo cookies, two bags of Doritos, and a bag of peanuts. He tossed everything into the middle of the table and said, "Who brought drinks?"

"Jesus, where'd all this come from?" Levi asked as he put a plastic two-liter bottle of Coke on the table.

"Charlie gets a discount at the grocery store," Truck explained. "We both got it."

Nick thumped a six-pack of Mountain Dew on the table. "It's a little after eight now," he said, "if we eat and drink all this shit we'll be playing till dawn."

Toff laughed. "We've done it before."

"Okay," John said. He shook out a mound of Cheetos onto the table in front of him and passed the bag to Truck. "Do you guys remember where we left off last night?" he asked. Being the Dungeon Master gave John some sense of control, of order, even when everything else seemed to be out of his hands. He sat forward, the idea of farming already fading as he turned his thoughts to the game.

Truck nodded as he popped a couple of peanuts in his mouth. "Dark empty building, locked doors to the outside on the right, super dark archway to the left," he said.

"Right," confirmed John. "So, what are you going to do?"

"I've still got the *floating sun*," Toff said, referring to the ball of light his magic-user character, Xan, had issued from his ring.

"Let's move toward the arch so we can see what's on the other side," Nick said.

Nobody verbally agreed but they all looked expectantly at their Dungeon Master.

"All right," John said, "as a group you make your way to the arch and Xan's *floating sun*...is where?" John looked at Toff, his eyebrows arched.

Toff said to the rest of the players, "What do you think? Just push it through?"

Levi nodded. "Yeah, it's just a mine, remember? There shouldn't be anything too crazy this early on."

"But it *is* the entrance," said Charlie. As a thief, his character, Domo, was cautious by nature in unknown places. "Entries are where guards are posted, or traps are set. The earlier you get someone before they get into your place, the better, right?"

"We're already at the arch," Nick pointed out. "Guards would have attacked if they were here."

"Unless they *can't* attack until we've passed through," said Truck.

"Which is why we need to see," said Levi.

The boys all nodded in agreement. Toff looked at John and said, "Okay, I push the light into the archway."

"As your ball of light floats under the arch, you can see images or letters carved into the stone," John told the players.

"I hold the light!" Toff said. "What do the carvings look like?"

"Bellator can read them," John said. "They're dwarvish runes."

Nick said, "Cool. Bellator steps forward, cranes his head up, and reads aloud whatever he can."

"From left to right and just over the arc, not down the sides, it says, "*Below the surface, Dumathoin*[1] *protects our mine. Respect the stone.*""

"What's that supposed to mean?" Truck asked no one in particular.

Nick shrugged. "Does Bellator know what it means?" he asked John.

The Dungeon Master nodded. "It's a dwarvish poem for miners. It's known to all dwarves."

"Not much of a poem," Nick said and wrinkled his nose. "It doesn't even rhyme."

John shrugged and looked at the module. "That's what it says."

"Okay, whatever. So, it's nothing magical or dangerous, right?"

"Right."

Toff said, "Okay, I push the light inside. What do we see?"

Reading from the module, John described what his players saw. "It's very dark," he said, "but you see stairs leading down. They're fairly wide, able to handle two or three people side by side. They're stone and covered in dust and dirt, but it's obviously been disturbed by lots of use."

"What about the walls?" Charlie asked. "Anything unusual or obvious?"

---

[1]Dumathoin is the dwarf god of secrets under mountains. *Deities & Demigods* (Lake Geneva, WI: TSR Games, 1980), 91.

"You need to roll," John said. In *Dungeons & Dragons* a roll of the dice determined if a character's attack was successful, if a spell worked or not, or, in this case, if Charlie's thief would be able to detect any traps or hidden doors. According to the description in *Alchemist's Bane*, there was nothing to find, but John wasn't going to just tell Charlie there was nothing there. The players had to think their way through the adventure.

Charlie rolled his ten-sided die twice then looked at John. "Eighty-two percent," he said.

John nodded. "Good roll. You're successful and find there is nothing unusual." He smiled. "Nothing about the walls on either side or on the ceiling makes you suspicious."

"Can we see the bottom?" Truck asked.

"No," John said. "Xan's light only illuminates a radius of about twenty feet."

"Let's stick to what we've been doing," Truck said. "Bellator takes the lead so we can see over his head, plus this is a dwarf mine, so he may be able to spot things we can't. Are you cool with that, Nick?"

Nick nodded and jammed a few Cheetos into his mouth.

"Toff," Truck continued, "you'll need to have Xan follow so he can keep the light above us but not blind us."

"The stairs are wide," Charlie said, "how about we go two and three: Bellator and Domo in front, Kryger, Xan, and Franco just behind?"

"Everybody okay with that?" Truck asked. "Okay," he said, looking at their Dungeon Master, "we're going down the stairs, slowly, quietly, and ready for anything."

CHAPTER 6

The group descended the stone stairs in silence with their weapons at the ready, expecting the unexpected. They'd gone about forty feet when Bellator stopped and held up his free hand, signaling a halt. He leaned to his right and whispered to Xan, "Can you dim the light?"

The elven magic-user shook his head. The magic ring he'd found some time ago issued a ball of light when he called it forth, but the only command he had over it was movement and size. He could push it forward or back, side to side, or up and down; he could make it as big as an ox, or as small as a grape, but try as he might, Xan had never discovered how to alter its illuminative properties.

"Then stop it," Bellator whispered. "There's light ahead."

Xan frowned, unsure if he should douse the light source. "I don't know if the ring's power is limitless," he whispered back. "We may never get the light again."

Bellator shook his head and took a deep breath. Very slowly he said, "There is a light ahead. We won't *need* your ring again if whoever is down there sees your light and we all end up dead."

"Point taken," Xan mouthed silently. He adjusted the ring on his slim finger and the ball of light above them shrank as it lowered itself, dimming, and finally became the size of a grain of sand before disappearing into the opal gem mounted on Xan's magical jewelry.

The darkness closed in on the party like a cloud of ash and smoke, but as their eyes adjusted, the orange glow of firelight could be seen dancing on the lower landing and walls just a few feet from the stairs they stood on. Bellator felt a hand on his shoulder, probably Kryger, and knew it meant the rest of the team was ready to follow.

After a few more steps the adventurers stood at the bottom of the stairwell and faced a left turn. The torchlight was only slightly stronger here—and no voices could be heard. Bellator pointed at Domo and motioned for him to look around the corner.

The elf stepped forward silently, put his finger to his lips to indicate quiet, then stepped up onto Bellator's shoulders. From this height Domo pressed himself against the wall and skillfully peered around the corner, barely revealing any part of his sharp face. He stood upon the dwarf for only a moment before lightly jumping down and landing without so much as a whisper from his soft leather boots.

Bellator glared at the thief who whispered, "Thank you for the boost, my friend. It was my thought that anyone looking in our direction would not expect someone to look from that height, plus any torchlight would help block their sight of me."

That seemed to mollify the burly fighter, and he nodded while the rest of the group gathered round. Domo whispered, "I did not see anyone. The stairwell is only another few feet and opens into a larger corridor. The torches are there."

Kryger stepped down and looked around the corner. "Can anyone hear anything?" he whispered. Everyone froze in place as they strained to listen, then they shook their heads. "Then let's keep moving," Kryger said.

They moved down the small hallway and Domo repeated his spying around the corners—though without standing on Bellator's shoulders—and again reported no enemies in sight.

"Left, or right?" Franco whispered.

"You just said *left* first," Kryger whispered. "Let's see where it leads. Domo, keep watch at the rear. Bellator, lead the way."

Bellator stroked his beard once, hefted his battle axe, and slowly made his way down the hallway, his eyes dancing side to side. Torches illuminated the passage and appeared to be lit throughout the corridor as they could see the glow from other flames up ahead. He and the rest of the party stayed close to the wall on their left, but after only thirty feet made a hard turn to the right. Bellator stopped and Domo moved across the passage to peer around the corner. He stepped back and motioned that it was clear ahead.

As the group came around the corner they stopped. Up ahead another passage opened to the left. Bellator turned and faced the team, his eyebrows arched. "Well?" he whispered.

"Let's take the passage to the left," Kryger whispered. He looked at each member of the party, silently asking if they agreed. They nodded in return.

With torches providing a flickering but constant light, it was tempting for the group of adventurers to simply walk down the passage as if they belonged there. But these were experienced warriors and knew better than to trust anything for what it seemed to be. With an eye on their destination and another farther down the hall, Bellator crept along beneath the torches and tried to keep his shadow directly under him rather than allow it to be thrown across the floor onto the opposite wall where someone, or some*thing*, might see it.

At the passage opening he and the rest of the group stopped. Bellator risked a quick glance into the opening rather than waiting for the thief, but as far as he could tell, nothing awaited them. "It's a big room, *really* big. I saw columns," he whispered.

With torches lighting the way everywhere they went, it was easier to spot traps, waiting guards, or creatures scavenging the empty corridors. This cavernous chamber was no exception. As they stood in the open archway that led into the hall, they could see it had probably once been used for important gatherings. Eight massive columns, four on each side, ran the length of the room. They were intricately carved in a mountain motif: Leaves floated down from majestic trees, waterfalls thundered over rocky outcrops, and vines climbed up towering cliffs. From floor to the shadowed ceiling, the ancient dwarves had decorated the columns to bring the outside world below ground. Each of the torches helped depict a sunrise, while the flickering flames created an illusion on the ceiling of rolling clouds among a moon and stars.

The five men spread out across the expanse of the room but stayed between the entrance and the nearest pillars. "The torches in the far corner are not lit," Kryger whispered. But his deep voice carried in the airiness of the room and came back to him and his fellow compatriots.

From the darkened depths beyond the far column came a shuffling, or a scrape—a movement over the stone floor—and then it was quiet.

Kryger stepped behind a column and looked at the rest of the team.

"We. Are. Not. Alone," Domo whispered.

Kryger shook his head. Something was at the other end of the hall. He turned toward Xan who sheltered behind the same column, but before he could say anything the quiet shuffling transformed into a ragged drumroll of running feet thumping against the dusty stone floor.

Bellator and Kryger leaned out from their respective columns and looked down the center of the room. Three short creatures, hairless with reddish-gray skin, were loping toward them, grunting and carrying heavy clubs. They wore no clothes but for dirty loincloths fastened by belts and strips of cloth, and leather strips wrapped around their feet served as makeshift shoes. But it was the yellowish eyes and teeth the adventurers noticed first. Three-inch fangs protruded from the upper lips of each creature and the deep-set eyes flicked about in search of an enemy to attack.

Kryger stepped out to meet them head on. He stood a full two feet above these creatures. That alone he thought would give them pause, but the vile beings only snarled and fanned out into a wide arc. Kryger brandished his sword, the blade glinting in the torchlight, then Bellator stepped next to his warrior friend. Domo, seeing the three gnarled hobgoblin-like attackers coming up the middle, dashed down the side, darting from column to column until he was behind them. Franco took a step back to guard the doorway should anyone enter during the imminent battle, and Xan prepared his spell to throw fire.

Once the creatures were close enough, Kryger swung his sword in a feigning arc that looked vertical, but he swept it to the side as he came down. This move caught one of the attackers on the left shoulder, but the blow did not cut the creature as deep as Kryger supposed it would. "Armored flesh," he called to his friends.

Bellator took a step forward to gain momentum and swung his axe at the lead attacker. Since these ruddy-gray monsters were closer to his height, Bellator did not try to sweep his axe across the legs, but rather at the belly. If they had protective skin, it was probably weakest where it was forced to often bend and change shape.

The axe blow landed with a tearing *thwack* that made the creature howl in pain, but the wound didn't slow it down. It did force the beast farther to the left though, so when the creature swung its club at the same time it was struck with the axe, it was too far away to land a solid hit. Instead, Bellator suffered a glancing blow to his shoulder, but lost his grip on the axe.

Then the third guard grunted and skidded to the floor on one knee with one of Domo's throwing daggers embedded part way in its lower back.

The three wicked beings spoke in a guttural, gravelly language and seemingly decided on a quick change in their tactics. They all turned toward the dwarf. Of course, the one with Bellator's axe embedded in the side of his stomach had no choice but to face the bearded warrior. But the axe didn't stay. The creature dropped its club, grasped the offending weapon with both hands, and pulled the blade out of its flesh. Dark blood sprayed across the creature's hands and the floor, and it gave a throaty gasp. Then all three leapt at the dwarf warrior.

The one who had only suffered a glancing blow from Kryger's blade struck Bellator on the left hip with its club and then tried to sink its fangs into the dwarf's shoulder.

The creature on the left limped into the melee and raised its club to smash Bellator across the head. Instead, it dropped its suddenly useless club as Kryger's sword slid into its chest.

Bellator's opponent, bleeding profusely from the axe wound, weakly wrestled with Bellator's left arm, trying to keep the dwarf from grappling with the monster trying to bite him, when he simply fell away. Domo had come up from behind and put his short sword through the base of the creature's skull.

Bellator grabbed the creature on top of him with both arms and threw him down to the floor near Franco, who dispatched it quickly by swinging his mace into the beast's face.

Domo bent down, retrieved his dagger from the creature's back, and looked at his comrades. "Are you hurt, Bellator?" he asked.

The dwarf shook his head. "Stupid thing kept biting my shoulder plate." Bellator wore steel plate armor over his shoulders and thighs; the teeth of most creatures, even those with three-inch fangs, would not be able to pierce it. "That hit on my hip might leave a bruise, but I'm fine."

"What are they?" Kryger asked.

Franco and Xan joined their friends and looked at the bodies. "They look like short relations of the hobgoblin race," Xan observed.

"Let's see why they were hiding in the dark," Kryger suggested.

The group made their way to the back corner where the torches were not burning. Xan took a lit torch from a sconce and used it to ignite those in the corners. "Looks like they were sleeping," Franco said. There were blankets and crude pillows made of sacks filled with dirt. "Someone will come looking for them eventually."

"Maybe they were guards," offered Bellator.

Domo was looking at the wall carvings when he said, "There's a latch here."

Everyone looked at him and the elf pointed to an elaborately carved maple leaf on the wall.

"I don't see anything unusual about it," said Kryger.

"It's well disguised," Domo said. "It either opens a hidden door or triggers a snare of some type."

"In a room like this," Bellator said, "it must be a hidden door."

Domo nodded and pushed the leaf.

There was a muffled popping within the stone and the edge of a door opened inward at the center of the wall. "Aye," said Bellator. "Door."

The team moved closer but did not stand in front of the door that now stood ajar. Domo inspected the edges all around and finally shoved it inward to reveal a small room.

"Cleaned out," Kryger said. "Probably full of treasure before Bohz arrived."

"Could it be a passageway?" asked Xan. "Is there, perhaps, another door inside?"

Domo shook his head. "Look at the patterns in the dust on the floor. Someone has been in here, but there is no sweep of a door, or footprints leading into a wall. But to be sure… Franco, please pass a torch to me."

Franco removed a burning torch from a sconce to the side of the door and handed it to the thief. Domo stepped inside the room and carefully inspected the walls, his thin fingers lightly touching the stone and probing the seams for hidden catches or signs of concealed spaces. He shook his head and stepped out. "An empty room."

"Well let's fill it with them," Kryger said and nodded at the three dead guards at the other end of the hall. "No point in leaving them where one of Bohz Grauer's henchmen will find them and raise an alarm."

CHAPTER 7

John told his mother about the possible farming job over a late breakfast. While the group of boys filled the garage the night before, Evie Brewer had invited friends over for a get-together. It had been a late night for everyone, though due to their excessive sugar and caffeine ingestion, the D&D group had lost focus and cruised Main Street while finishing their snacks.

"John," Evie said, her face as white as her plate, "you can't. I know I can't flat out forbid it, but...you just can't."

"I know. Believe me, I don't want it. I'll keep looking."

"I just can't imagine it, John. When we lost your father—"

"Mom, don't worry. I told Toff to forget it. 'Thanks, but no thanks' and all that. It's not like I want to work on a farm after what happened to Dad."

She nodded and nibbled her toast. "It's just—"

"Mom! Seriously!"

"Okay, okay." Evie gave up and focused on her breakfast. "So, what are your plans for today?"

John sighed. "I'm going to go talk to Carl at NAPA then over to the Grange. They know I worked with Earl at least. Maybe that'll help with a job with one of them." NAPA was the local auto parts store that had changed names, owners, and auto parts affiliations four times since 1979. The Grange was a local feed and grain store that sold farming equipment and supplies. It wasn't just farm goods though; the Grange was more of an everyman store. From bags of feed and dog leashes to lightbulbs and paper plates.

Evie nodded. "Okay. I need to go into the office and get caught up on a few things. Call me there if you need anything. You're on your own for lunch." She stood up and put her hand on her son's shoulder. "Don't get discouraged. We'll figure something out one way or another."

After two more rejections, John didn't know where else to look. In such a small town there were only so many places he could ask for work, and the smaller number of summer jobs were usually spoken for before the end of May.

He steered the Bug to the Warhawk's Nest and found an empty booth in the back corner. Truck's parents owned the small café where farmers gathered to gossip and fuel up on nicotine, caffeine, and big breakfasts served on thick platters. Truck stocked food, bussed tables, filled coffee, and flipped burgers during the lunch rush. John had just sat down when he heard Truck call to his mom, "Brewer's here, I'm going to take my break." John looked out the window and bit his lip. Hard.

Truck dropped into the opposite seat and shook his hair out of his eyes. "Brewer!" And then his face fell. "What happened? Did somebody hit you?"

John snatched a paper napkin from the dispenser and pressed it to his mouth. "I bit my lip," he said and wiped his eyes. "Man, that hurt."

"Well don't get blood all over the place, my mom will freak. What's up, anyway?"

John looked out the window again and pushed the napkin harder against his lip. "I don't know what I'm going to do this summer. There aren't any jobs left. I've been everywhere." He took a deep breath. "I'm not going to be able to go to college after graduation."

Truck stared at him. "What about working with Toff?"

"I can't." John looked at the empty table between them and shook his head. "You know I can't do that."

"Yes, you can."

"No, I can't. I don't want any part of it." He crushed the napkin into a ball and threw it on the table.

"I asked Toff how much he makes each summer. It's double what you expected at the gas station."

"What? Seriously?"

"Yeah. And that's with the raise you were hoping for."

"It doesn't matter. I can't." John looked out the window again and shook his head. "My dad…"

"Hey. We're friends, right? Good enough you won't get pissed off if I say something?"

John wasn't sure what Truck was thinking but nodded anyway.

"I know what happened to your dad. Everyone does. And now Dave Carlson. But people are still farming."

"You aren't going to give me the *it's noble work* crap, are you?"

Truck sat back. "You need to stop believing that what happened to your dad will happen to you."

"I don't!"

"Yes you do. Don't try to bullshit me."

John shook his head but didn't say anything.

"You just said there aren't any more jobs in town," Truck went on, "but there's this one with Toff. It's all summer and it'll suck. But Toff will be there, and we'll still play D&D. Just do it. You can't use what happened to your dad as an excuse forever."

John reached for the napkin he'd crumpled and thought about throwing it at Truck. Instead, he tore at it, pulling small chunks from it to hide his shaking hands. He didn't use his dad's death as an excuse. Did he? "I don't know if I can. All my life I've… Plus my mom—"

"Forget about your mom! Just this once. Come on, man. You can do it. If you want a job, you have to. Take a chance. Roll the bones! You would if Lisa Martin wanted you to." He smiled.

John rolled his eyes and shook his head. "Truck, come on."

Truck held up his palms. "Okay, I'm sorry. But seriously, just go for it. If you want money to get to college and out of town, this is it."

John felt his stomach tighten and took a deep breath. He wadded up what remained of the napkin and squeezed it into a ball. "Maybe."

"No maybe!" Truck pointed to the counter by the front door. "Go over there and use our phone. Call Toff right now. Do it!"

John nodded as he thought about it. He could hear the sirens that called the volunteer fire department to his dad's accident. *What happened to Dad won't happen to me.* He pushed himself up and walked slowly to the counter, his feet sliding across the linoleum.

"And don't tell your mom I talked you into it! She'll kill me!" Truck yelled.

CHAPTER 8

"How come you guys didn't play D&D last night?" Evie asked her son.

John had come down to breakfast well after his mom had finished. He'd sat at the table alone and browsed the newspaper while he ate. Then he went into the living room and lazed on the couch and watched TV. He'd barely acknowledged her all morning.

John glanced at his mother. She was leaning against the doorjamb with her arms crossed. He looked back at the TV and shrugged. "Charlie had to work a late shift."

"And?" she prodded. "What did you do? You were out pretty late."

"Just hung out with Truck. Sat on the bridge mostly."

"Uh huh." Evie sat on the edge of the chair next to the couch. Her eyes closed slightly. Focusing. Scrutinizing. "What's going on?" she asked. "Did something happen?"

John sighed and turned off the TV. "Fine. I told Toff I want the job."

"John! I told you no. We agreed."

"There's nothing else. It's the only job out there. It's not like I want to do it, I *have* to."

"No, you don't! We can figure something else out. Just think about this."

John shook his head. "I *have* thought about it, Mom. I need to do this. It pays twice what I was making at the gas station and it's only for the summer."

Evie stared at him. "Doesn't Toff work for Jim Henley?"

John rolled his eyes. He'd hoped she didn't know where Dave Carlson had worked. Why ask the question if she didn't? "It doesn't matter. Farming is farming no matter where you are."

"I asked you a question, Jonathan. Does Toff work for Jim Henley?"

John sighed. "Yes."

Evie nodded. "Right. Which means you'll be doing Dave Carlson's job, won't you?"

"I don't know. Really! Toff didn't tell me exactly what the job was except that it's for harvest. I don't know what Carlson did."

Evie closed her eyes and shook her head. "John…" She took a deep breath, opened her eyes and looked at her son, who slouched much the same as his father had. "I know you're too old for me to forbid it, but I want you to think about this. Really think about this. You've never worked on a farm."

"I know. But I need a job, Mom. I'm going to be a senior

this year and I don't want to work during the school year again if I can help it."

"Do you even know where it is?"

"Nope." John stabbed the remote with his finger and turned on the TV. He was getting tired of his mother's grilling. He'd made the decision to take the job, which was a stretch for him in the first place. The least she could do was just let it be.

Evie ignored the television. "It'll take you a half hour at least to get out there. Maybe more in the Bug." John drove a 1974 Volkswagen Beetle that, even with the gas pedal pressed flat against the floorboard, struggled to maintain a respectable speed. The Palouse hills, with their steep climbs, didn't make it any easier.

"It doesn't matter, Mom. I need a job, and I had to ask for this one. I didn't want to, but I had to. I just gotta do what I gotta do. Okay?" He stood up and left the room. "I need to change the oil in my car," he said over his shoulder.

John went outside to work on the Volkswagen. He had just started to drain the oil when he heard the screen door squeal open. "John!" his mother called. "Telephone. Get those hands clean before you come in." Evie Brewer kept a gritty bar of Lava soap by the outdoor tap for just such occasions. She expected clean hands and shoes in the house, *Otherwise, stay outside*.

John was drying his hands on a shop rag when he came into the kitchen; his mother handed him the phone. He put it to his ear and walked past her, stretching the cord around the doorway and into the pantry. "Hello," he said.

He expected to hear Truck's boisterous voice asking when they were going to get together again for D&D. Instead, he heard a voice he didn't recognize, an older man who sounded like a windy clarinet.

"Is this Mr. John Brewer?" the man asked.

"It is."

"My name is Jim Henley. I believe you're friends with Toff Hansen."

"Hi, Mr. Henley. Yes, Toff and I are friends."

"Then you know he mentioned you to me about a job on my farm?"

"Yes, we talked about it yesterday."

"Most young men your age were asking for these jobs a month ago. How come you're just now looking?"

"I had a job at Sam's 76," John explained, his shoulders sagging, "but Earl Conklin sold it. I just found out the other day that the new owner didn't want to keep me on."

"I see," Henley breathed. "Do you know why not?"

"Nope. I worked there all last year, too, and Earl gave me a good recommendation."

"Okay. Well just so you know, a job like the one I have is no city job. But Toff said you've done some farm work before. Is that right?"

"Yeah. Smaller stuff. I did some rogueing and haying for a friend of ours."

"Uh huh." There was silence on the line, then, "You won't be pullin' weeds or buckin' bales here, John. I've got a big farm, and we use big machines. Do you know what a swather is?"

"Yes."

"Ever operated one?"

"No, but I can learn."

"Okay. But before either one of us agrees to anything, you need to know that if you come work for me, you need to stay all the way through harvest, no matter what. We work long hours; it's hot, it's dirty, and it's tough. But when I hire someone on, I rely on them. My farm is my livelihood, it's how I take care of my family. You can't quit because if someone quits it throws the whole system out of whack and I can't afford to take on someone who may let down the rest of us. We only have a limited time to cut once harvest starts so I need everyone there. Understood?"

"Absolutely," John said.

"Good. I want you to think about it overnight, though, if this is what you want to commit to all summer. If you decide yes, catch a ride out here tomorrow morning with Toff. Now, put your mom back on; my wife will tell her some more about what to expect. Your mom will want to know."

"Okay. Thanks, Mr. Henley."

"Call me Jim."

"Okay. Jim. Thanks."

John unwound from the phone cord and called his mother as he came out of the pantry. He handed her the phone and went back outside. "Yay, I got a job," John mumbled to himself in a deadpan voice. "Whoopee." He shook his head and threw the rag at his car. "I have no idea what I'm doing."

The oil pan in the VW had drained so John screwed the plug back in and put on a new filter. He was pouring the new oil when his mother came outside. "Wow. Do you know what you're getting yourself into with this job?" she asked.

John rolled his eyes. "It's farming. I know it'll be hard."

Evie sat down on the stoop and hugged herself. "I'm not just talking about the work. For now, you'll be driving back and forth, and the hours will be pretty normal. But when harvest starts, they want you to stay there on the farm. They have an old bunkhouse where you and Toff will stay. Every night."

"What?"

Evie nodded. "Yeah. Mrs. Henley wanted to ask me what kind of food you like because she'll be feeding you at that point."

John sat on the bumper and studied the cracks in the concrete driveway.

"What are you thinking?" she asked.

"If I really want to go to college that bad."

She laughed. "It's true, it'll be a new and very different experience. You'll be gone from home probably late July until the first week of September, right before school starts again. She said they usually let everyone go Saturday afternoon and then back Sunday by lunch. That way everyone can go to church. That's not terrible, I suppose. And you have until tomorrow morning to decide, right?"

"No. I have to decide tonight. He wants me there tomorrow if I take it."

"Okay. We'll talk more later." She stood up and opened the screen door. "John..."

"Yeah?"

"You really need to think about this," she said. Her smile was gone. "Farming can be dangerous; we lost your father because of a stupid accident out in the middle of a field." She closed her eyes and shook her head. "I know it's not very rational of me to think that way," she said, looking at her son again. "But if this is what you want, then this is *your* decision alone."

CHAPTER 9

Jim Henley appeared to be in his sixties. His hair was a swirl of storm clouds, his clean-shaven face was littered with crepe paper wrinkles, and he openly admitted that he couldn't see anything beyond three feet in front of him without his glasses. The farmer's voice was high, not helium-inhaling high, but like he was about to sneeze and wanted to finish his sentence first. He was thin and stiff like a clothing store mannequin and his hands were big with wide, flat thumbs. He wore faded jeans and a T-shirt under a green flannel that would find its way onto the seat of a car as soon as the June morning warmed up.

John stood under a giant oak tree in the front yard of the Henley house. Toff had introduced them, and the new employee had shaken hands with his new boss, whose grip alone could crush walnuts if he tried. "It's nice to meet you in person, John," Henley said. "We have you for the summer, yes?"

John nodded. "Yes, sir."

"No need to *sir* me," Jim said, smiling, "but I appreciate a young person with manners. Okay." He clapped his hands and rubbed his palms together. "Toff, take our new man and show him around. Just a quick look—I want you both over at the Bullhead Flat site before nine. We need to get that silo started pronto."

"Got it." Toff turned around and headed toward a group of buildings that looked like small airplane hangars. Jim Henley nodded at them, turned and walked over to a red Ford pickup, and drove down the gravel driveway.

"Where's he going?" John asked.

Toff shrugged. "He's got a lot of land. Probably going to check on things."

"Is he going to be at the silo with us?"

"He'll show up, or meet us there, but he's not going to help build it. Blaine will be there."

"I've never built a silo before."

"Me neither. But we're not there yet. Just check out what's what and where it's at here so he knows I showed you."

The largest building looked like a small aircraft hangar and was built of old timber beams and corrugated metal panels. It looked about two stories tall and was open on one side. The floor was oiled dirt and mourning doves had tucked their nests into the rafters. On the back wall and along the sides, workbenches made of thick old wood were battered and pale, spattered with paint and fuel and oil. Toolboxes lined shelves and wrenches too big for drawers hung from pegs on the walls.

Taking up the most space, though, were three hulking combines, one in each of the bays. They were painted dark green and had massive tires as tall as John and a foot wider. John craned his neck back to look at the glassed-in cabs where he could see the air-cushioned seats and steering wheel columns. The twenty-five-foot headers were missing—they were too long, and it would be like trying to fit three Cessna airplanes in a three-car garage. Take the wings off, though, and they'd fit. Instead, there was a large rectangular pipe where the header would connect. The header, John knew, was what cut the stalks of wheat, barley, rye, or whatever crop was being harvested, and funneled it into the combine's thresher and then into the hopper. It was essentially a giant lawn mower, but instead of a spinning blade, the header cut with a scissoring sickle.

"Where are the headers?" John asked. Even though Toff wasn't his boss, he hoped his knowledge would help him somehow.

"Over there." Toff pointed to a similar but smaller enclosed structure with a big roll-up door on the end. "They have all the headers and their tools and supplies in the shop. Combines are in here."

"Am I going to learn to work on them?"

"No. Don't ask either. The combines are, I don't know, *sacred* or something. Jim doesn't let anyone except the drivers and Blaine near the combines."

"Who's Blaine?" It was the second time John had heard the name.

"He's Jim's farmhand. He does all the mechanical work, drives swather and combine—sometimes—and drives the semi during harvest. You'll meet him when we go over to the silo site." Toff looked at his watch. "We still have a few minutes. Come on. I'll show you the swathers and the bunkhouse."

It was mid-June; the sky was clear and by nine in the morning, the temperature was already pushing eighty degrees. With no rain since May and none in the forecast, it was promising to be a hot summer. As Toff maneuvered his small Datsun pickup off the black-topped two-lane country road and onto the gravel lane, his tires kicked up a cloud of dust and John eyed the scene before him. About a hundred yards from the turn-off, a flat stretch of land spread out between the gravel road and the base of the hills that looked like fat, lazy bubbles; they just stopped at the bottom like they were placed there.

"That's where we're going," Toff said and pointed through the windshield. "Jim calls it Bullhead Flat because, well, there's a ton of bull snakes out here."

John groaned. "Snakes. Why did it have to be snakes?" he said, quoting Indiana Jones. The boys often randomly quoted a movie and made the others guess the film it came from.

"*Raiders of the Lost Ark*," Toff said. "Easy. But at least bull snakes aren't poisonous like asps and cobras. Or rattlers, which are down by the river."

Toff turned off the road and pulled to a stop next to a flatbed pickup truck laden with tools and lugging a hundred-gallon diesel tank used to top off equipment in the field.

"When are you going to get a real pickup, Toff?" a man shouted as the boys got out of the Datsun. They turned around and saw a stocky man with a bushy reddish-brown beard and a matching wreath of hair beneath an oily baseball cap. He wore a black T-shirt with the ZZ Top eliminator car on the front, blue jeans, and dusty boots.

Toff gave him the finger. John raised his eyebrows; he'd never seen Toff give the finger. Or swear for that matter. "That's Blaine," Toff said.

Blaine was in the middle of a wide concrete pad setting up sawhorses and arranging tools. He laughed and went about his work. John guessed Blaine was in his late twenties or early thirties. Hard to tell with the Sasquatch beard. "Is he going to be trouble?" John asked.

Toff said, "No. He's cool, just likes to give me crap about Dot."

Three big grain silos stood near the road with another weedy two-track running around the other side. Their silvery metal skins glinted in the sun, looking like short, fat rockets from a Wile E. Coyote cartoon.

Blaine was working atop a round concrete pad with crisp edges and dry flakes of cast-off cement around the base. "You must be the new guy," Blaine said, walking toward them. "John, right?" he asked and extended his hand.

"Right. John Brewer. Hi."

They shook hands and Blaine smiled. "Hey. I'm Blaine. Glad to have you. Ever done construction of any sort?"

John thought about it. "I helped my uncle build a fence once and did some framing for a family friend who was adding on to their house."

"Perfect." Blaine smiled. "So, you're not a complete rookie. Great. Okay, let me show you guys what we're going to do."

They stepped onto the concrete where, besides the tools and boxes of nuts and bolts, several long, curved sheets of corrugated metal were scattered about. Two stacks of metal sheets sat on the ground a few feet away from the concrete pad like a giant deck of playing cards, cut and ready to be shuffled.

"You guys ready to get to work?" Blaine asked.

"What are we doing?" Toff asked.

"We're going to build one of those," he said and pointed to one of the silos behind him. "We're going to get started anyway. I don't think Jim wants you two out here for the whole build. Honestly, I think he wants to see what Johnny here is made of."

John looked at Toff, who shrugged.

"But look," Blaine continued, "it's not too tough. Line 'em up and bolt 'em together. Right?"

Blaine showed them the panels. Each end had a zigzag pattern of holes that overlapped the corresponding holes on the next panel, and he explained how they'd be bolted together. Between the panels, before bolting them together, the boys were to place a strip of caulking to seal the joint.

"Come on," he said. "I'll do one with you, so you see what I mean."

The three of them stood one panel up on its long edge. While John held it in place, Blaine and Toff brought another panel over and overlapped one end with the first. Blaine unrolled and cut a length of caulking, peeled away one side of the paper backing, and adhered it to one panel. "Okay," he said, "now grab a couple of screwdrivers and once you get the holes in the panels lined up, put the screwdrivers through at the top and bottom to keep them in place. Good. John, grab a couple nuts and bolts and one of those ratchets."

From each box John scooped two bolts and two nuts and grabbed a ratchet and an end wrench. He knew where Blaine was going with the instructions and just asked, "Bolts from the outside or inside?"

"Outside. The trick is to not overtighten, and you'll have to work together—one inside, one outside. See how each bolt has a rubber washer, or gasket? That basically does the same thing as the caulking tape does—it seals the hole—so you have to get the bolt just tight enough to make the rubber squish out a bit, but not so tight it tears. If it tears, take it out and get a new one. If the seal's broken it's no good. Right?"

John and Toff nodded.

"Let's do these. John, you work inside first, and Toff and I will start outside. We'll switch after a few so you can see what I mean with the gaskets."

After about ten successfully tightened bolts, John and Toff switched places. John worked the ratchet and learned the proper amount of squish for the rubber washers. After he'd tightened the rest of the bolts Blaine announced they were to complete the ring on their own.

"Go back and forth with the panels," he instructed. "This one's on the outside, so the next is on the inside; the one after is on the outside. Right? And wear gloves when you're getting a new sheet—the edges are sharp enough you'll take a finger off if you slip. I'll be back in about a half hour."

John and Toff worked steadily, one working the ratchet the other bracing the nuts, then switching with every panel. After two hours, Blaine still hadn't returned, the temperature had risen at least another ten degrees, and they'd taken a couple of water breaks. "Only a few more panels to finish the ring," Toff observed.

"What do we do then?" John asked.

"We'll wait here. They'd be pissed if we left all these tools and stuff out here."

Close to noon, just as the boys were completing the first ring of the silo, Blaine drove up next to the remaining stack of corrugated metal panels trailing a plume of dust. The cloud engulfed him when he got out and he looked around with his hands on his hips, like a dignitary surveying his domain. "Well, look at you two. I didn't think you'd get it done this fast."

He ambled over and walked around the ring, inspecting bolts, running his fingers over the rubber gaskets, twisting a bolt occasionally to check if it was tight. When he got around to John, who was on the outside twisting the ratchet to tighten the final bolt, Blaine smiled and said they'd done a good job.

"I only have one question: How do you boys—and particularly you, John, since you're out here—how do you feel about snakes?"

John and Toff both stood up. "I don't like them at all," John admitted. His eyes were on Blaine, but he couldn't tell why the farmhand would bring up snakes out of the blue. Then he looked at Toff, who was staring at the ground behind John. Toff's eyes were wide, like he'd just been handed a hundred-question pop quiz that had to be completed in the next ten minutes. "What?" John asked.

"Don't move," Blaine instructed.

"I get it," John said uneasily, "you're messing with the new guy. Toff, you even said—"

Blaine bent down quickly and stood back up, the head of a snake in his hand, the four-to-five-foot body hanging down like a thick, rotten noodle. The snake wriggled and hissed.

"Oh...shit," John muttered. He took a step back.

Blaine held the head of the snake high and away from himself as he bent down again and grasped the tail in his other hand. Then, in a single motion, he spun like an Olympic discus thrower, dropped the head of the snake from his hand and flung the beast by its tail away from the concrete pad. It twisted through the air, a black ribbon of muscle against the blue sky, trying to slither on nothingness. Then it *thwump*ed into the tall brown grass at the base of the hill.

"Just a bull snake," Blaine said and patted John on the shoulder. "Big bastard, though, wasn't he?" He grinned.

CHAPTER 10

After their lunch beneath the tree in Henley's yard, John and Toff packed their small Coleman coolers and stashed them in the front seat of the Datsun.

"What do we do now?" John asked.

"There's always work to be done on a farm, John," Jim Henley said loudly from behind.

The boys turned and saw the farmer walking toward them. He must have come out of the house as they were stowing their coolers.

"I hear you had a run-in with a big bull snake," he said in his alto voice.

John couldn't tell if Jim was ribbing him or not, but the man's face was straight if not concerned. "Yeah. It was a big one." John shuddered at the memory.

That made Henley smile. "Good thing those bulls aren't venomous—they'd be big, ugly, *and* deadly." He chuckled, then said, "That's nature, John. When you're out on the farm you don't have a choice but to deal with it. It's not like ridin' bikes in the park. So, you better get used to it."

John wasn't sure if it was the heat, if he was rattled by the snake, or if he just couldn't get past the idea he was being teased because he was the new guy, but Henley's remark rubbed him the wrong way. He wasn't sure what, if anything, he should say. He was from Weston, not some big city. He'd been on a farm, he'd been in the country, he'd experienced nature. Was Jim teasing, or just being a dick?

John frowned, Henley smiled, and Toff shifted his weight from one foot to the other. "Start gettin' the swathers cleaned up," Henley said. "Toff, you know where the hoses are, use the spigot behind the barn. Should take you boys a while, but you can cut outta here at five."

He turned and walked back up and into the house. The screech and slap of the old wooden screen door gave his exit some finality.

"Dude," Toff said and started walking toward the swather barn with the big roll-up door.

"What?" John asked, exasperated. "What was I supposed to do? He basically called me a candy-assed city boy like he was daring me to say something. Was he trying to make me fire myself the first day?"

Toff didn't say anything, just opened the door to the swather barn—which wasn't a barn at all; it wasn't shaped like one, it wasn't red, and there wasn't a bale of hay in sight. *Barns have hay,* John thought.

It was dark inside, though dusty windows filtered light

from outside to provide some murky illumination. The barn was really just a giant garage, a shell to keep equipment out of the elements. In this case the equipment was three swathers. They looked like small combines and were spaced evenly down the middle of the shop. In the dim light they looked like gangly rejects from a parade of military vehicles.

On the wall between the door and the roll-up was a row of six light switches and a box with two large push buttons colored green and red. "Hit the green one," Toff said.

John bopped the green button with the heel of his fist and the big door started to rattle upward. The door was too big to roll up manually, and when John looked above, he saw it was on tracks and being pulled up by a motor and a chain—it was just a big-ass garage door. John wondered why they called it a barn instead of a garage, or even a shop. He frowned. *Farmers*, he thought.

With the big door open, light flooded inside and the swather closest to the boys was revealed. It looked like two green boxes, like a couple of giant Legos—one long and rectangular that housed the diesel engine, with small wheels and tires attached on the back and large fat donut-like tires on the front. Between the front tires, sitting atop the rectangle, was the second box, more squarish and sitting upright—it was the cab, made of mostly glass so the driver could easily see to the front and sides. The rear of the cab featured a window overlooking the long rectangular engine box.

Below the cab were two arms, bent at almost ninety-degree angles like someone carrying a load of firewood. These held the header in place and raised and lowered it.

Toff stepped on the small ladder on the side, took two steps and opened the side of the cab. "I'll bring it around to the back," he said. "You grab the black hose by the other door and meet me out there. Open the other door just like you did this one."

"Are we just going to wash them down?" John asked.

"Yeah, and clean them out. Mice and birds make nests during the winter." He pointed to the underside.

John nodded and backed up as Toff climbed into the cab of the swather and sat behind the steering column. After a few moments the engine coughed, roared to life, then settled into a working rhythm. Toff saluted then the swather moved out of the barn and into the bright sunshine.

John walked the length of the shop, sidestepping the remaining two swathers, found a coil of black hose on a peg, and opened the large door at the other end.

The swather came around the corner as John stepped outside. Toff maneuvered to just beyond the door and stopped, shut down the engine, and climbed out of the cab.

In the sunshine the green paint stood out against the blue sky, a geometric, metallic beast ready to go to battle in the fields. A green dragon. John shook his head and rolled his eyes to himself. *Wow*, he thought. "So, what's the plan?" he asked.

"They've been in storage all winter, so we need to blow out the filters and radiators first. Then we hose them down, clean the cabs, and get rid of any bird or mice nests that we find," Toff answered.

"So, we're detailing swathers."

For the rest of the afternoon John and Toff blew the dust off and out of the machines, dug mouse nests out of the crevices around the axles, cleaned and polished the cabs, hosed them down, and scrubbed and squeegeed the windshields and other glass panes. They finished two by five o'clock and were getting ready to wash down the third when Blaine walked out of the barn and told them to stop.

"Save it for tomorrow," he said. "By the time you're all done, you're going to be experts in cleaning farm equipment." He smiled, turned on his heel, and walked away.

John stared after him and then at Toff. "What's that supposed to mean?"

"Probably that we're going to do the combines next, the tractors, and all of the trucks."

John thought about it and said, "It's warmer every day, but at least the water's cold. Never got to take a shower at the gas station."

"But you sure needed one." Toff smiled.

Toff drove the swathers into the barn then showed John where the keys were kept. They closed the big doors on each end and walked to where the Datsun was parked.

John's jeans were covered in greasy dirt from crawling around under the swathers, his T-shirt was wet and dirty, and his boots were caked with mud. Toff looked the same and as he turned over the engine of his little pickup, John cranked down the passenger window and mumbled, "What did I get myself into?"

CHAPTER 11

Truck leaned back in his chair until his head rested against the wall of the Council Chamber and his feet floated nearly level with the tabletop. "How big was the snake?"

John sat on top of the workbench instead of the chair where he had been presiding as Dungeon Master. Beyond the space where they played D&D was a normal garage. John's dad had only used it for storage and to tinker at the workbench since it had been built in the 1930s to house a Model T, not the 1979 GMC pickup he'd owned and John's mom still drove. Scrap two-by-fours lay across the rafters; sagging cardboard boxes marked XMAS, PAINT, and MISC were stacked near the side door; the shelves above the workbench were littered with coffee cans filled with orphaned nuts, bolts, nails, and screws; a square tin of three-in-one oil, a tray of wire brushes, and several small boxes corralled spare picture hangers, plumbing parts, hooks, rolls of tape, tubes of glue, and other perchance supplies. Nothing had changed since Tom Brewer died.

"Five feet if not six," John said. Then he laughed. "You should have seen it fly through the air. I've never seen anyone fling a snake before."

Truck laughed too. "He was probably thinking, 'Oh shit!'" Truck's eyes and mouth went round and he flailed his arms. "'The city boy has a bodyguard!'"

They laughed at that. Then John said, "It's not horrible," returning to the subject of the job itself, "but it was only the first day." He hopped off the bench and sat in his DM seat. "It's grubby work. Once that's done, they'll teach me how to drive the swather."

Truck nodded and leaned forward so the chair came upright and his feet hit the floor.

"And Henley's weird," John went on. "I get the feeling he was testing me. I mean, I met him in the morning, then at lunch he…"

"What?" Truck pushed.

"He thought it was funny that the snake freaked me out. He said, 'That's nature, John. You have to deal with it on the farm.'" John raised his voice to a higher register and tried to imitate Henley's tone but ended up sounding like an old woman.

Truck laughed. "Does he sound like that, or did you mix him up with his wife?"

"Probably not that high," John conceded, "but kinda. Anyway, I thought it was weird 'cause he knows I've worked on a farm before. I told him I bucked hay bales!"

"What'd your mom say about it?"

John shook his head. "I didn't tell her about that." He looked at the table, then said, "He was probably just giving me shit the first day, you know?"

Truck nodded. "Probably."

"I don't know. On the phone he sounded like a nice guy. In person, not so much."

There was a knock on the door, it opened, and Evie Brewer leaned inside. "Hello, Truck," she said. "How the heck are ya?"

Truck half yelled, "Hey! Ma Brewer! I'm great!"

She smiled and turned to her son. "Charlie called. He wants the two of you to meet him somewhere called the Wet Brick. What in the world is that?"

John chuckled. "It's the car wash next to Dr. D's office." Weston only had one car wash, a three-bay self-service wash that operated by dropping quarters into a box and turning the dial, one stop at a time, to rinse, soap, rinse, wax, rinse. Then a wand attached to a hose sprayed whatever the dial was set to. People raced around their cars during each setting to pay as little as possible; one quarter only supplied one minute's worth of pressure no matter the selection, so the more quarters you added, the longer and more thoroughly you could wash your car. John had only used it a couple of times, preferring to wash the Bug at home for free, but the VW was small enough and he was quick enough to do the job for only $1.25.

"Don't stay out too late," Evie said as the boys stood to

leave. "You promised Toff you'd drive tomorrow."

"Back by ten," John said.

What the boys called the Wet Brick was known to locals and the IRS as the Warhawk Wash-N-Go. It was owned by a former high school teacher and named after the mascot. The walls were painted the school colors, green and white, and featured a Warhawk—something that looked suspiciously like a regular hawk—taking a shower. The bathing bird was painted inside each bay and on the sign facing the street.

Truck turned into the car wash, drove through the unoccupied middle bay, and pulled up alongside another—though slightly newer—Chevy. Charlie Davis drove a 1965 Chevrolet pickup, three-on-the-tree transmission, with metallic emerald-green paint, a white bumper and grill, newly finished cherry wood planks that made up the bed, and new chrome wheels. The interior wasn't done yet, but the bench seat was newly rolled and pleated metallic light-green Naugahyde.

Since everyone's windows were rolled down to help ward off the heat, Truck turned up his stereo so the music he and John were listening to overpowered whatever Charlie had in his tape deck. Truck timed it perfectly so as he pulled up alongside Charlie, all three boys could hear Judas Priest's swaggering tune: "You've got another thing comin'."

Charlie looked over at John in the passenger seat of Truck's '57 Chevy and grinned. The three bobbed their heads to the beat until the chorus finished and then Truck turned it off. "You rang, Charles? What's up?"

"Nothin'. Levi left me hangin'. We were supposed to

go to a movie, but Amy wanted to go—and not bring me."

Truck shook his head sadly. "Chicks, man. Ya know?"

"So, we're your backup?" John smiled.

Charlie smirked. "Sad, isn't it? Let's go to the A&W."

The A&W was at the north end of Main Street and was half sit-down restaurant, half carhop. The boys opted to dine in and parked their trucks to the side. They went in, dove into a booth, and looked over the menu attached to the wall.

"I know what I want," Charlie said.

"Me too," John and Truck said at the same time.

Charlie took the phone off its cradle and waited for the waitress in the back to pick up. When she did, he said he wanted the Papa Burger with fries and a Coke, then he looked at John and Truck, his eyebrows arched.

"I just want an order of fries," John said.

Charlie wrinkled his forehead in dismay.

"Large," John gave in. "And a root beer."

Truck said, "Chili dog, fries, Coke. Wait. Do they have New Coke? I'll have that."

Charlie relayed the orders and hung up. He looked at John. "Just fries?"

John shrugged. "I already had dinner."

"Wuss. Hey, speaking of being a wuss, I heard Lisa Martin is still in town." He smiled wickedly.

Lisa Martin was the girl John had had a crush on since his freshman year in high school. Lisa had been a year ahead and he'd spent three gloriously torturous years dreaming about her and spending money at the Top Notch Café where she'd worked the counter. He'd never been able to really define what it was about Lisa he found so irresistible, probably because he'd never gone out with her, or talked to her in a meaningful way—aside from saying "Hi" and ordering from the Top Notch menu. Of course, she was beautiful, with brown eyes as rich as chocolate, her brunette hair styled like Joan Jett, but not as severe, and she had a smile like she knew what you were thinking. And her body... Well, literally what his dreams were made of. But there was something else about her; she was nice, always friendly to people, never uppity. He couldn't specify why he liked her. He just did. And he was terrified to ask her out. After all, she was a year ahead of him in school, and now she was going to college. John knew he wasn't movie-star material. He was too short for the basketball team, and not bulky enough for football. He was about as average as he could stand, brown hair, brown eyes, crooked smile. He looked like a pair of Buster Brown shoes. He'd never stand a chance with Lisa Martin. It didn't help that his friends teased him mercilessly about her either.

John shook his head. "I'm sure she'll get a boyfriend in college."

"What if she doesn't?"

"Doesn't matter. She's a college girl now."

"But she's *here* for the summer," Charlie insisted, tapping the table with his finger. "If you ask her out now, what difference does it make if she says no? You won't see her again because she graduated, right? So why not?"

John smiled to himself and relished the idea of going out with Lisa Martin. Was Charlie right? Why not ask her out? Now he smiled outright.

Truck gushed, "There ya go! He's gonna do it!"

"I'll think about it," John said. But he knew it would only be wistful imagination. Lisa Martin was simply beyond his reach.

"I bet you will." Charlie laughed and wiggled his eyebrows. "Just don't think yourself *out* of asking her. Come on, you're a senior now, act like it."

"Now, now," John said playfully, "don't upset your Dungeon Master." He smiled.

"Speaking of which," Truck said, "are we going to be able to play this weekend? Friday or Saturday? Or both?"

"I'm up for it," John said. "Either day, or both."

Just then their food arrived, carried over one shoulder on an oval tray by a girl about their age. Her blond hair was pulled into a ponytail and her black-framed glasses gave her a studious look. The brown and orange polyester uniform went unnoticed by the boys as they looked at her name badge: Rebecca.

"Sounds like big plans for the weekend," she said and set the tray down on the end of the table. The boys stared silently so she said, "Okay, who gets the chili dog and New Coke?"

Truck raised his hand like he was in class. "And fries," he said.

She placed his drink and plastic baskets lined with paper and full of food in front of him. Truck smiled at her and never looked to see if what she put in front of him was what he'd ordered.

"And fries," she said. "How about the Papa Burger, fries, and Coke?"

"Here," Charlie said.

Rebecca then looked at John. "And that means 'just fries' and the root beer for you," she said and placed the pile of French fries in front of him. "Ketchup and mustard are there." She pointed at the red and yellow squirt bottles at the end of the booth. "My name's Rebecca if you need anything else."

"Are you new in town?" Truck asked before she could leave. The dreamy smile had taken up permanent residence on his face.

She smiled back. "Yep. I'll be a junior when school starts. How about you three?"

"We're seniors," Truck said.

John swore he saw a twinkle in Rebecca's eye.

"What brought you to Weston?" Charlie asked almost accusingly as he stuffed a fry in his mouth.

"My dad retired from the military and my parents wanted to move to a smaller town. We're from Seattle. Dad bought a gas station here."

Truck and Charlie looked at John. Now they knew who bought Sam's 76. John wanted to ask why her dad wasn't hiring, but before he could, a voice from the kitchen bellowed, "Rebecca! Order up!"

CHAPTER 12

John squealed to a stop in front of Toff's house at seven fifteen the next morning and leaned on the horn. The sky was still deciding if it wanted to stay orange or turn blue even with the sun already up and about its business, and the air was chilly.

Even with the bite in the temperature, John had his window rolled down and waved at Mrs. Hansen when she pulled the curtain aside. He could see the whites of her wide eyes and she made a motion he took to mean *don't honk* as she glanced toward the neighboring houses. John smiled to himself. Toff's mom constantly worried what her neighbors thought about what went on at the Hansen house. They never had a party of any kind, and the one time the group played D&D in the dining room, Truck had bellowed out, *"Kill the goblin scum!"*

Mrs. Hansen had rushed into the room, her hand at her

pale throat, her eyes as round as Viking shields and gasped, "Boys! That is quite enough of that! What will our neighbors think? Oh dear me! Poor Mrs. Winters across the street must be shaking right about now."

Toff had shrunk in his seat like a wallflower at a school dance and the boys never played there again.

Toff was born Kristoff Hansen; he was of Norwegian descent, had blonde hair and skin so white he looked like he was born underwater, but he didn't have a Viking bone in his body. Toff's only athleticism was in the form of mathematical gymnastics during calculus class. His friends thought it was odd that an intellectual giant like Toff would enjoy farming as much as he did instead of being drawn to academic work, but there it was.

The front door opened, and Toff bounded out and down the sidewalk. He stashed his lunch cooler behind the seat and closed the door as he sat down. John put the Bug in gear, gave it some gas, and beeped his horn as Toff waved to his mom. He tried to pop the clutch and get a squeal out of the tires, but the Bug just didn't have the guts.

"Thanks," Toff said as they picked up speed. "I'll hear about that tonight."

John laughed and said, "You pick the tunes." He nodded at the cassette case competing for floor space with his passenger's feet.

Toff put the case on his lap and popped the clasps. Inside were forty cassette tapes arranged alphabetically. Most he knew were bought at the music store at the mall in Moscow, but ten were tapes John had made himself, recording his favorite songs from his album collection. John titled them *Rock!*, *Rock II*, and so on, like movie sequels. Toff selected one he hadn't heard in a while—the title on the spine was *Rock V*.

The back seat of John's car was occupied by a massive boom box his parents had gotten him as a Christmas gift. The Bug wasn't really car-stereo-friendly since the dash was only a few inches deep and there wasn't anywhere to mount speakers; the boom box was a great solution. Instead of spending money on ten D-cell batteries at a time, though, John wired the portable stereo directly to the car battery, which conveniently was under the back seat.

Toff twisted in his seat and slid *Rock V* into the deck and pressed play. As the Bug sped through town, Def Leppard's "Photograph" thumped out the open windows.

On the way to Henley's farm the boys spotted two white-tailed deer, a doe and a fawn, that looked up as the Bug neared. John turned down the music ("Round and Round" by Ratt) and slowed to get a better look. So, when they rolled into the farm the stereo volume was already low. John had the feeling Jim Henley was not a fan of loud rock music, so he was glad the stereo wasn't blaring when they saw Henley outside waiting for them as they pulled up the drive.

"Are we late?" he asked Toff.

Before Toff could answer, Henley was beside the car. His face was unreadable, a blank mask waiting to be painted.

John opened his door as he rolled up the window and said, "Morning, Jim."

"Morning, boys," Henley said. "I'm going up to Spokane for supplies and Mrs. H is coming with me, so we won't be around today. If you need anything, talk to Blaine. Okay?"

John and Toff both nodded and stood near the car.

"Follow me," Henley barked, and turned toward the oldest building on the farm.

The bunkhouse looked like it came off the set of an old black-and-white John Steinbeck movie. The long and low building was clad in boards thick with cracked and peeling brown paint. One door stood in the middle of a long side, its brass knob rubbed black by age. Two windows, one on each side of the door, were rendered blind by decades of dust, and the roof was a standing army of moss-covered, curled, and torn tar shingles.

Jim Henley turned the knob and shouldered the door open. "Come harvest," he said as he went inside, "you boys will be staying in here."

John and Toff followed Jim into the bunkhouse and looked around. The more they saw, the more their shoulders slumped; Toff sighed deeply enough that John knew he wasn't the only one depressed about the thought of cleaning the place.

"We've been using it for storage," Jim went on, ignoring their downtrodden looks. "Your job for the rest of the week is to clean this place up."

The building was deceptively large from the outside, John thought. Or maybe it was because of all the junk piled inside. It was about twenty-five feet long and maybe fifteen feet wide. Four steel-frame bunk beds lined the long walls, two sets on each side. The space in between was filled with cardboard boxes and dust. Mostly dust.

"How did it get so full of stuff? Didn't you stay here last year?" John asked Toff after Jim had gone.

"No, no one stayed overnight last year. We left late and had to be back early, but no one was ever here as early as Jim wanted. He wanted us ready to go as the sun was coming up. He's infatuated with the weather during harvest; inside the house he has thermometers and barometers everywhere. He'll be out in the fields every day in another week or two, checking if the wheat's ready. Then he checks the weather again. Once he decides it's time to cut, that's all we do every day, all day, until it's done."

"Is anyone else going to stay in here with us?"

"I doubt it," Toff said.

John looked around. "Okay, where do we start?"

It took the rest of the week for John and Toff to clean out the bunkhouse. A dining room table leaning on its end against the far wall had blocked a tiny bathroom just big enough for one person to turn around in. There was a shower, toilet, and sink. No shelves, drawers, or storage of any kind. But it had running water and a tiny window as wide as a loaf of bread. The table had been moved and stood on its four legs and used to pile boxes on top of and stacked underneath.

John's duties the first week at his new job on the farm had been…cleaning. Even putting together the first ring of the silo was basically cleaning up the job site to get it ready for the guys who finished building it.

CHAPTER 13

The next night at seven forty-five, Evie Brewer was playing Scrabble at the Burns house on the other side of town and her garage was full of boys preparing for a night of *Dungeons & Dragons*.

"I can't believe everyone made it," John said. "I figured Levi wouldn't be able to." He smiled and snorted back a laugh. The players were in their regular seats and smiled at their map maker.

"What?" Levi asked innocently. "Why wouldn't I be able to?"

Charlie rolled his eyes. "Everyone knows Amy wants to go out, or at least do something, every weekend. I'm amazed you guys aren't already married."

Levi smiled. "You're just jealous. It's cool, though. I told her we were playing tonight and that was that."

"The man put his foot down!" Nick said in a deep voice.

They laughed and John passed around the cookies his mom had made for them. "Levi isn't the only one we'll need to worry about this summer," he said.

"Did you ask out Lisa Martin?" Truck asked expectantly, his eyebrows bouncing up and down.

"I'm not talking about me. I meant *you.*" John pointed a finger at Truck's chest.

"*Me*? What'd I do?"

John looked at Charlie then back at Truck. "We saw you looking at the new waitress at the A&W. What was her name? Rebecca?"

"What?" Truck asked. His smile was as big and bright as a crescent moon, and his face turned pink.

"Ha!" Charlie pointed at Truck. "We knew it! You fell for her as soon as she said 'chili dog.'"

"Who are you guys talking about?" Toff asked. "Who's the new waitress?"

Truck answered him. "Her name is Rebecca; she's a junior this year. New in town." He took a bite of his cookie. "She's a babe," he said and looked at the ceiling, smiling as if in a trance.

"Who *is* she though?" Nick asked.

"Her dad's the one who bought Sam's 76 and took my job," John said.

"Oh, hey!" Truck said. "I forgot—"

"What's with you two and waitresses?" Levi asked, looking at Truck and then John.

Truck turned a deeper shade of pink and smiled. "It's not about her. You guys know who Paul Statler is, right?"

Toff sat up. "Sure. I worked with him last summer; he drives combine for Jim."

"Doesn't he own the tire shop on the other end of town?" Charlie asked.

"Right," answered Truck, nodding. "He talked to the cops; apparently he was there just before Carlson died. Said he was there to change a tire on the auger but when he left Dave Carlson was fine."

All the boys looked at Truck. Dave Carlson's death was still the favorite gossip around town.

"What do you mean?" Toff asked. "How do you know?"

"It's all everyone was talking about down at the diner today."

Nick frowned. "Who cares? Why were people talking about *that*?"

Truck shrugged. "A lot of people don't believe it. They said he was acting weird that day when he got back to town; they think he saw it happen."

"If I saw a guy get his arm ripped off, I'd be weird too," Levi said.

"That's lame," Nick said. "I would have helped somehow. Wrapped a shirt around him and haul ass to the hospital."

"Bullshit," Charlie said. "You would have freaked out."

"No way!"

"Okay, okay," John said, knowing it was up to him as the DM to get things going, "let's not get off track. We have a lot to get through tonight." He set up his DM screen and sat back. The tension in the air deflated and he had their attention. "Do you remember where you were?"

Levi smoothed his map on the table and pointed to the last place he'd drawn. They leaned over the table and nodded to one another to confirm the location. Nick said, "We hid the bodies of those three creatures in the secret room, then we left that big hall."

"Right," John said. "Okay, you're moving back north through the passage you came down the stairs from. Beyond the stairway the hall turns to the left and you see another opening to the north. It appears to be brighter than the surrounding area."

"Is it daylight coming in?" Toff asked.

John shrugged but kept silent. The Dungeon Master didn't just answer questions, it was up to the players to investigate.

"Shall I go look down the passage?" Charlie asked, glancing at the others.

They nodded. "Why not?" Nick answered.

Charlie looked at John and said, "Domo, the thief who apparently cares more for his friends than himself, which is odd for a thief"—he glared at each of the boys around the table—"volunteers *again* to risk his life to see what's down the bright passage."

Nick rolled his eyes, Truck grinned, and Levi said, "Cool! You go, man!"

John sat up straighter and described the scene. "As you look down the passage, you see it opens up after about thirty feet into a larger chamber. The brightness is coming from the chamber, but you can't see what it is. Your elven eyes can tell it's not daylight, though. It flickers slightly like the torches around you, and you see another long passage directly in front of you on the other side of the chamber."

"When he comes back to us," Nick said, "Bellator gives Domo a gold piece. Thanks for risking your life." He smiled.

"Smart ass," Charlie said. "But Domo still takes the gold piece."

Truck said, "Let's go down the passage, what'd you say, thirty feet? But quietly and looking for traps; the bright light might be a trap itself, something to lead us into trouble."

"Same grouping as before?" John asked.

Truck nodded. "Always."

"You emerge unscathed into the large chamber," John said. "It's a square room, about forty-by-forty feet but each corner is popped out, almost like a square four-leaf clover. Inside these corner alcoves are torches, a little higher than normal and situated in front of a mirror. Each alcove is the same, so the light is reflected back and forth and amplified. Below the mirrors are piles of tools, such as shovels, pickaxes, and crowbars. Passages lead out to the north—that's the one Domo saw, and also to the west, east, and the south where you entered from."

"Can we see anything down the other passages?" Levi asked. His head was down as he sketched the area John had described.

John nodded. "The one to the west has a light coming from it, but it's a ways down there. The north and east hallways are dark."

"I have a feeling this is a trap," Truck said. "The piles of tools in the corners and the mirrors seem off. I think we should pick a passage to go down and leave the tools alone. And don't look in the mirrors!"

"Seriously?" Levi asked. He paused, his pencil poised above the paper, and looked at Truck. "What kind of trap?"

"Could be a fake floor; look in the wrong mirror and the floor opens up into a pit. Maybe an alarm—pick up a tool and they all collapse to make noise. Or they're not tools at all..."

"Right," Toff chimed in. "They could be snakes. Once you touch one, they all change form and attack."

Nick leaned back in his chair. "I'm okay not touching the tools or looking in the mirrors if that's what you guys think," he said.

They all agreed, and Truck said, "I say we just keep heading north. It's dark, but dungeons usually are, right?"

"I'm in," Charlie said. "Let's go."

The others agreed with affirmative grunts and nods of their heads as each one had taken that moment to bite into one of their cookies or shovel a handful of chips into their mouth.

Truck mumbled around his mouthful of half-chewed Doritos, "We moo uph da nor pash-eg. Qui-le, und..."

"What was that?" John asked sarcastically. "You're going to bang your swords on the walls?" He smiled.

"No!" Truck said after he swallowed. "We move up the north passage! Quietly, and looking for danger."

"The passage is about twenty feet wide," John told them. "Do you want to change your order?"

Nick looked around at the others and said, "I think we should keep it the same, but spread out a bit to give each other some room."

"Sounds good," Levi said. "Franco has his mace at the ready."

The players all looked at John expectantly and he rolled a die behind the screen so they couldn't see what he was rolling for, or what the result was. Normally the roll would be made to see if there were any random monsters roaming the dungeon, but in this case he only did it to keep the players on their toes. The die rattled to a stop. John looked at it disinterestedly and said, "The passage is stone, similar to everywhere else you've been down here, it's decorated—carved and painted—with the dwarven mountain motifs..."

The collective shoulders of the group sagged just a little after the die roll, but no one mentioned it. Nick asked, "Is there anything unusual about this passage?"

John shook his head. "Nothing out of the ordinary that anyone can see."

"Okay," Truck said, his voice almost a whisper, "let's keep going."

"After almost a hundred feet you see a set of double doors ahead," John said. "It's the end of the passage."

"What are they made of?" Toff asked.

"They look like wood, and they're beautifully carved—obviously the dwarves worked wood as well. But you also see the doors have been mistreated," John cautioned. "There are claw marks raked across the middle where the two doors meet, and some smears of a dark substance."

"Blood?" Levi asked.

"Probably," said Toff.

"From what you can tell," John said, "it's most likely blood, but you can't tell what kind."

"Is it fresh?" Charlie asked.

"How would you like to figure that out?" John asked, his eyebrows arched.

"I'll get close to the door, but I won't touch it or the substance. Just look closely."

John considered this for a moment. Part of being a good Dungeon Master was flexibility with the rules to make the adventure as fun as possible. Too stringent and the players might fail to complete a task, or they may get bored with the entire adventure and stop playing. On the other hand, if he made things too easy and objectives were accomplished without them even trying to figure things out or use their imaginations, that too would become ho-hum. Technically, in the darkness lit by a single flickering torch, no one would really be able to tell if the substance on the door was fresh, but in his mind, John heard a phrase his mother often said: *pick your battles*, and he split the difference.

"Without touching the door, I think Domo's elven eyes can see that what's on the door is blood, and while it isn't so fresh that it's dripping, you can tell there are layers of blood, some older than others, the newest probably hours old."

"Is there any blood on the floor in front of the doors?" Nick asked.

"Why?" Truck asked him.

"If there's blood on the floor it means something was brought in," Nick explained. "If there's not, then whatever is inside got blood on their hands somewhere else." He looked at John, then Truck. "Just thinking."

"Cool," Levi said.

"No blood on the floor," John admitted.

"So now what?" Charlie asked and turned to Nick.

Nick shrugged. "I say we go in fast and swinging swords."

Truck sat back and tossed his pencil on the table. "Why though? What do you think is in there? Rushing in is liable to get us killed."

Nick sat close with his elbows on the table and looked at everyone in turn as he spoke, even John. "This may sound stupid, but I'm thinking about a couple of hunters I know. They're friends of my uncle's and I've been around when they get a deer. They hang it up in the garage, they skin it, then it stays there until all the blood drains out. I know, it's gross, but that's my point. There's blood everywhere. But when they walk away, go into the house, they don't bring the blood with them, they clean up, right?"

"What in the hell are you even talking about?" Charlie asked, his face all screwed up.

"There's no blood on the floor. Whoever or whatever is on the other side of these doors did whatever it was doing somewhere else and then came back here. It's probably a bedroom or something. We go in swords swinging because we'll get the surprise. There's blood on the door, it's not like whatever is in there is a princess, right?"

John kept a neutral face but was impressed with his friend's reasoning.

Truck laughed. "Well, hell, Mr. Detective. You sold me!"

"Let's do it," Toff said. Levi and Charlie both nodded their assent.

Truck looked at John. "We're going to—"

"Wait!" Toff interrupted. "I'm going to ready my magic missile spell."

"All right," John said. "The magic-user is preparing his spell. Anyone else?" None of the others wanted to switch weapons or prepare anything else so John returned his attention to Truck. "You were saying?"

"We'll kick in the doors, with me—I mean Kryger—on the left, Bellator on the right."

"Are you going to move in once the doors open, or just kick them in and stand there?"

"Wait," Toff said. "Maybe we should—"

"It's not a trap," Nick interrupted in exasperation. "Someone already went in."

"What if the blood is from someone coming out?" Levi asked.

Nick shrugged at that. "I'm going to kick and go in with my battle axe in one hand and my throwing axe in the other."

Truck nodded, but John could tell he wasn't completely confident in the plan. "Kryger will step in with his sword in front in case something rushes out."

"Everyone else?" John asked, looking at Charlie, Levi, and Toff.

The three quickly consulted the group and then Charlie said, "We'll stay in the middle, but step inside with Kryger and Bellator. I have my short sword ready."

Toff said, "I'll have to stay put while preparing the spell."

"And Franco is ready with his mace," Levi reported.

John nodded. "When you kick in the doors, they fly open—there were no locks or even latches. All you see is dark, though. Remember, the torch is ruining the elves' and dwarf's infra-vision."

"Do we hear anything?" Charlie asked.

"Maybe some grumbling from straight ahead," John said. "It's incoherent, not a common language."

"I'll throw the torch toward the sounds," Levi said.

"The torch arcs through the darkness and hits the stone floor in an explosion of sparks. About ten feet beyond the torch, just at the edge of the light, you see two large creatures standing up from the floor; their skin is brownish gray as far as you can tell in the dim light. They're wearing dark, rough-textured clothing; they're about six to six-and-a-half feet tall, and when they turn toward the light you see pinkish snouts for noses and beady eyes as they roar in anger."

"Orcs," Truck said, rubbing his hands together, a grin on his face. He squealed.

"Yep," Toff agreed.

"Bellator chucks his throwing axe at the one on the right," Nick said. "Do I get the surprise attack?"

John nodded. "It looks like you woke them up, so you get the initiative. But they're pissed. Roll it."

Just saying your character was doing something didn't make it successful. Everything was based on the level of the character and the armor class—or strength, essentially—of the enemy, for combat; or the difficulty of a task when it came to detecting or discovering a trap, for example. And the roll of the dice, of course.

Nick picked up his twenty-sided die. It was translucent purple with yellow numbers. He tossed it on the table where it hit his can of Coke and spun to a stop near one of the candles. It showed a sixteen.

John had already consulted his tables on the Dungeon Master screen. The orcs had an armor class of six, and Bellator, Nick's dwarf character, was a level-five fighter, which meant Nick needed to roll a ten or better for the axe to strike the intended target.

"You hit him easily," John said. "Roll for damage."

The throwing axe Bellator threw could inflict one to six points of damage to who or whatever it hit, so Nick rolled his six-sided die. This one was crystal clear with midnight-blue numbers. "Four," said Nick and looked at John expectantly.

Because Bellator had the surprise, and the orc could not defend itself, John added a score of one to the roll and checked the hit points of the orc. Hit points determined how much damage a character or a monster could sustain before dying. When zero hit points were met, that character or monster was dead. Each orc had seven hit points.

"Bellator's axe thuds into the chest of the orc on the right," John said, "and it staggers back, howling in pain."

Toff stood up and said, "Xan throws his magic missile spell." He looked at an old rug on the wall, made a wave motion with his hands across his body, and pointed at the medallion pattern in the middle. "Boom!"

The rest of the boys applauded and laughed. "My mom talks about dinner theater a lot," Levi said with a smile. "Is that what this is?"

"Bravo!" Truck said, still clapping. "Bra-*vo*!"

Toff bowed and sat down. "All right," he said, waving them off. "Shut up."

John cleared his throat. "How many do you get?" he asked Toff.

"Xan is level six, so..." Toff was flipping pages in his copy of the *Advanced Dungeons & Dragons Players Handbook*. He found the bookmark he'd placed at the beginning of the magic-user spell explanations and quickly located what he was looking for. "Three! Xan throws three magic missiles!"

"And how are you—" John started but Toff interrupted, knowing the question already.

"One at the orc with the axe in his chest and two at the other one. Boom! Boom-boom!"

It was the nature of the magic missile spell in D&D that they *unerringly strike their target.* John took this literally of course, so Toff didn't have to roll his twenty-sided die to see if he hit the targets. "Xan throws the spell," John said, "and three bright blue glowing bolts of energy fly from his fingertips. They spread out, two going left and the other right, and they slam into the orcs. Boom! Boom-boom!" John said, mimicking Toff with a smile. "Roll for damage. And tell me which orc you're rolling for."

"Let's go for the one with the axe in his chest first," Toff said. He tossed his pyramid-shaped four-sided die. It was gold with black numbers. "Three, and the plus one, so four total. And the other two missiles are..." Toff rolled a one. "Crap," he said. "Just a one, so that's two, and the other missile..."

The next roll resulted in a two. With the added one that made three; the two magic missiles together damaged the orc by five hit points.

John said, "The orc with the axe in his chest gets blown backward without a sound and doesn't move again. The other orc takes the two missiles and roars back at you even as he drops to one knee."

"It's up to you, Levi," Truck said.

"Cool." Levi nodded and looked at John. "Franco runs forward and smashes the orc in the face."

"Roll it," John said.

Levi picked up his translucent dark-green twenty-sided die and tipped his open palm, so the die fell off his hand and rolled to a stop against his pencil. "Eleven," he reported.

John consulted the To Hit tables on his DM screen. Franco, Levi's character, was a sixth-level cleric so he needed a twelve or better to hit the orc. But, John reasoned, the party did have the surprise against the orcs, the one Franco was attacking was already gravely injured, and frankly, he didn't want to ruin the fun. He added a point to the role because of the surprise attack and said, "You hit! Roll for damage."

All of Levi's dice were the same translucent green. They looked like a small collection of emeralds piled in front of him. The mace inflicted two to seven points of damage, so he rolled the six-sided die and added one. It resulted in a three, so he announced to John, "Four!"

"Franco smashes the orc's face like it's a baseball and it flies back and lies still next to the other one, their blood mingling between them on the stone floor. Both are very dead."

"Nice," Truck said. "We all step inside and close the doors. Franco picks the torch back up and we look around."

"It looks like this is where the orcs slept and kept their stuff," John said. "There are a few rumpled blankets and straw mats on the floor. Your torchlight glints off several halberds, spears, and a few swords leaning against the wall in the northeast corner."

"How many mats are there?" Levi asked.

"Four," John reported.

"Does anybody want to look around more, or do we get out of here?" Truck asked.

"Let's take a look at the—" Toff started, but he was cut off when the side door of the garage flew open. The door banged against the wall and rattled the painted-over glass windowpanes.

A woman came inside wearing a lot of pink and stiff-arming a gold cross as if warding off a vampire. "In the name of our Holy Savior, stop what you're doing this instant!"

Chapter 14

Paulette Dickerson strode into the garage holding the cross up in front of her. It was her shield. Her shoulder-length brown hair, streaked with blond highlights, was teased up and away from her face; she looked like she was running into the wind. A neon-pink suit jacket with shoulder pads, the sleeves rolled up to just under her elbows, created a smart square look.

"Hey!" Nick said. "You can't just barge in here."

Paulette stood at the end of the table by the ice chest and kept the cross high and at arm's length. Behind her, a man stepped purposefully into the garage and stood to the side of the door with his arms crossed over a leather-bound Bible.

"We *can* come in here," Paulette said, her voice shrill as if she was in a panic. "We *must* come in here. Your devil worship *must end!*" She robotically turned toward each boy;

the cross held firmly in her straight arm, as if expecting them to burst into flame at the sight.

"We're not—" Charlie began.

"Don't deny it!" Paulette yelled. "*Dungeons & Dragons* has caused the deaths of teenagers across the country. I will *not* allow it to happen here! Like it or not, you're done. Call it a game all you want—I know what it truly is. Now hand over those books."

"No way! We're not giving you our stuff!" Nick yelled. He looked to his friends for support.

"Your books deal with devils and demons and other evils from the underworld; you must hand them over so we can destroy their influence. It must be stopped!"

Truck looked at John. "What the hell?" he mouthed silently. Paulette sounded like she'd memorized a movie script.

Paulette Dickerson was One Vision Bible Church's most enthusiastic congregation member. Her husband rarely ventured from their farm, preferring the company of his three dogs to that of other people. Occasionally, though, he'd be seen at a high school football or basketball game. That left Paulette to raise the alarm to the Weston community when it came to matters of the children. Having no kids of her own, Paulette and her pastor believed God had bestowed upon her a responsibility for all the children and people of Weston. Only a year or two before, she had supported the Tipper Gore campaign to quash rock 'n' roll lyrics and had written twenty-two letters to the local paper admonishing anyone who would allow their children to listen to such trash. And MTV? The devil's cable channel.

So, the boys knew who Paulette was, and the man who came in behind her was Aaron Evans, the cashier and stock boy at Main Street Pharmacy. What John couldn't understand was what they were doing in his garage.

"Why are you here, Mrs. Dickerson?" he asked, a slight quaver in his voice. "Why do you want our D&D stuff?"

"Jonathan Brewer, you know *exactly* why I'm here. All of you do. You just don't want to admit it to yourselves." She looked down at the table and pointed at Toff's *Players Handbook*. "You see? Right there, that book shows men committing evil deeds."

They looked at Toff's book. It was face down; the back cover depicted a man pulling what appeared to be the tail of a green (probably dead) creature, while two others carried a box. The boys frowned and shook their heads.

"Uh…no…" Levi started.

Charlie laughed nervously. "Those men are the good guys," he said.

Nick looked confused. "Who do you think you are?" he shouted at Paulette.

Paulette ignored Nick and made a grab for the books.

"Toff!" Charlie yelled, and Toff quickly snatched the book out of her grasp.

Aaron Evans stepped forward but didn't say a word. His parents owned the pharmacy he worked at, and he didn't say much there either. He was thirty-eight and single. People in Weston wondered about Aaron.

"I will have those books!" Paulette demanded.

"No, you won't!" Levi shouted back. He hugged his *Players Handbook* close to his chest.

"Mrs. Dickerson," John started again, and stood up. "What do you think we're doing here?"

"Don't play coy with me, young man. I saw the report on *60 Minutes* last year. Our whole congregation watched, horrified, as they told us about suicides, murders, and the summoning of demons! Nobody in our church is to have anything to do with it." Her eyes slid toward Levi. "*No one* should," she said, and glared at him.

This was old news to the boys. Most of their parents had talked about *Dungeons & Dragons* after the *60 Minutes* report and other news stories had fueled speculation that the game was somehow making teenagers commit suicide, go mad, and turn to Satanism. Many churches had held D&D book burnings and accused players and the game's creators of devil worship, witchcraft, spell casting, and even calling forth dark creatures from the underworld. All the parents of their group had satisfied their own worries and concerns. John could see Paulette was obviously embracing the panic. "I'd like you to leave," he said and crossed his arms.

"Not without—" she started.

"You're trespassing," Charlie said.

"You didn't even knock!" Truck accused.

"Don't you interrupt me. I am not leaving without fulfilling my mission." She blinked quickly; the thick mascara made her eyes look like tarantulas dancing above her nose.

Nick stood up and walked over to the bench behind John and rummaged through a couple of drawers. Everyone in the garage became quiet and watched him. Nick ignored them and, once he'd found what he wanted, sat back down and rooted among his own books. While Nick had everyone's attention, Aaron Evans took a step forward and seized Toff's dice.

"Hey!" Toff yelled.

As a group, the boys stood up. Talking—or screeching as Paulette was doing—was one thing, stealing was quite another. And from one of their own.

Paulette sensed the tables had turned and she lowered her cross and took a step back. She and Aaron were outnumbered. "Look," she said.

"No," Truck said, "give them back."

"What are they?" Aaron asked, poking at the geometric plastic gems in his hand.

"They're *dice*," Toff said, frowning. "For the game."

"You're all too young to understand," Paulette pleaded. She'd gone from *I'm right* to *I care about your future*.

"That's it," Nick said. He pushed the chip bags, soda cans, pencils, and papers out of the center of the table and popped the top off of a small plastic tube in his fist. He leaned over and tilted his hand until a dark-gray powder poured out of the tube, and with it he drew a triangle on the middle of the table.

"What are you doing?" Paulette demanded, her voice shrill, panicked.

Nick grabbed his copy of the *Players Handbook* and showed her the front cover. It was an artist's rendition of a large statue of a horned creature (yes, probably a demon) holding a bowl of fire, while below were the bodies of two green-skinned creatures (maybe lizard men) and a number of adventurers. To players of the game, this was a group of adventurers who've reached a major milestone in their quest; the evil creatures guarding the statue had been slain and the explorers were collecting the treasure. Under closer inspection, two men were seen trying to dislodge one of the massive jewels set in the statue's eyes, while others in the party consulted a map, and yet another was cleaning his sword, obviously having recently battled the minions of the weird demonic idol.

To an extremist like Paulette Dickerson, a book with that kind of imagery on the cover could only contain incantations and dark magical instructions to call forth evil.

Nick ignored Paulette and poured a second powdery triangle, this one upside down and overlapping the first.

"Answer me!" Paulette yelled. "What are you doing?"

Nick looked at her and said, "I'm going to summon a demon to get you out of here."

"How *dare* you!" Paulette hissed. The fist bearing the cross snapped up again and she stepped backward. "Do you think this is funny?"

"No!" Nick yelled back. "I think you're trespassing." He took one of the candles out of its hurricane glass protector and placed it in the middle of the triangles. He then opened his *Players Handbook* and started mumbling to himself as if he were reading a spell.

The rest of the boys were wide eyed. They didn't know what Nick was doing or how Paulette and Aaron would react.

"God save us!" Paulette whispered. She backed toward the door.

"Give me my dice," Toff demanded and held out his open hand.

Aaron tossed them back and got behind Paulette. "You're going to burn in Hell! All of you!" she said. Once she and Aaron were outside, she yelled, "I'm calling the police!" and they ran to her car.

The boys looked at one another, unsure of what to say or do. After a few seconds John walked around the table and looked out the door. Satisfied the intruders were gone, he shut and locked the door. "What the hell was that?" he asked.

All the boys were standing; they looked back and forth at one another. Then they burst out laughing, an emotional expulsion after the tension.

"I can't believe that just happened!" Truck said. He moved around the table and paced from his chair to the garage door and back again. "What a freak!"

"Why did she come here, though?" John asked, looking around. His hands were shaking, and he sat back down in his chair, dumbfounded. "How'd she even know we were playing?"

"Probably because of me," Levi said.

They looked at him, waiting for an explanation.

"Amy goes to that church," he said. "She must have told someone I was playing D&D tonight instead of going out."

Nobody had anything to say about that.

Then Charlie said, "Nick, what is that?" He pointed at the configuration of triangles.

"It's the Star of David," Nick answered.

"The what?" asked Truck, inching closer.

"The Star of David. It's the symbol of Judaism. It's on the flag of Israel." Nick shrugged. "I have Jewish cousins."

"How did you even think of that?" Truck asked. His eyebrows were arched, and he was pulling his hair with both hands.

"She was *nuts*," Nick said. "I gave her some of her own medicine. I don't know, it just popped in my head. I saw *60 Minutes* last year too."

They laughed. They'd all watched that story.

"What is that stuff anyway?" Toff asked, pointing at the silvery-gray powder Nick had drawn the Star of David with.

"It's Stop-Leak," John answered. He'd recognized the radiator hole repair solution as soon as Nick poured it out.

Nick nodded and held up the tube. It was about the size of a roll of nickels and was a must-have for anyone who fixed up old cars. "I figured your dad would have had something I could use. I was looking for a grease pencil or something, but this was better."

"That was a total dragon move, Nick," Truck said. For years the boys had labeled their acts of self-assuredness as "dragon" because in D&D dragons were supremely badass and confident in themselves. And it sounded cool.

They found their seats again and were quiet. No one made a sound as each played over in his own mind what had just happened.

"That was just too crazy," Levi said.

John shook his head and stared blankly ahead. When they were younger and played *Dungeons & Dragons* more and more, they wanted someplace more permanent to play, not a dining room table at whoever's house they got permission to play at. They also needed somewhere free of siblings and pets. Charlie's dog, Daisy, for instance, was a bear of a poodle mix and barked every time the dice were rolled. She thought the rattle of the dice on the table was a knock at the door and would instantly bark at full volume and run to the front room, then gallop around barking when no one opened it. The games could go on for hours and they wanted to stay up as late as they could without worrying about waking up someone's parents. The Brewer garage was just right. It had become part of the game, part of their friendship. A lot had been discussed and planned there. It had become the Council Chamber.

And now it had been violated by a lunatic.

"I have a feeling this isn't over," John said quietly.

CHAPTER 15

John sat at the head of the table and listened as his friends tried to explain to the police officer in the Council Chamber what had happened in their own words. In one night, their D&D game had been interrupted not once, but twice. First the evangelist, now the law. He shook his head and thought about Paulette's crazy eyes.

"She had on a ton of makeup," he said.

The boys stopped talking and looked at him.

"What was that, John?" Officer Phillips asked.

John looked up. They all knew Paulette Dickerson. In a small town like Weston, everyone knew everyone, like it or not. But for whatever reason, John had focused on how much makeup Paulette had caked onto her face. He was about to lay out his testimony when his mother burst into the garage through the open side door.

All six boys turned to look at the new intruder.

"What's happened?" Evie asked. Her breath came in gasps as if she'd run home. "Is anyone hurt?" She glanced around the table, focused on her son, then turned to the cop.

"Good evening, Mrs. Brewer," Officer Phillips said.

Evie frowned. "Oh Wayne, stop with the missus stuff. What's going on here?"

"You are not going to believe this," John said. He shook his head, but his eyes were bright now that his mom had arrived.

Officer Wayne Phillips waved his hand and said, "Hold on, John. Let me have a word here, then we'll start at the beginning for your mom."

Wayne Phillips had been a cop in Weston since coming back from Vietnam in 1976. He hadn't seen any action, something he told people he was thankful for. He had been a supply clerk and was lucky to have been stationed far from the fighting, but he served his country nonetheless. He was six feet tall, had short-cropped black hair, and was built like a tree, straight up with thick branches for arms. He had a good reputation among the locals and volunteered as a Little League umpire during the summer.

"We got a call earlier from a concerned citizen," Wayne explained. "We were told your son was leading the rest of these boys in a satanic ritual."

"What?" Evie gaped. Her mouth dropped open, and she stared at Wayne.

"Oh yeah," he continued, trying not to smile. "We were advised to show up with a SWAT team." Of course, everyone knew Weston didn't have a SWAT team. Nor was there one within sixty miles.

"All right," Evie said, holding up her hands to stop the jokes. "What happened in my garage tonight?"

Officer Phillips turned to John. "Why don't you tell your mom. It'll do me good to hear it again."

John took a deep breath and composed his thoughts as if he were talking to Principal Jennings, then he went over every detail of the incident. Truck chimed in more than once: He shook his head at the craziness of it all, nodded when John made accurate descriptions, and gave Nick a thumbs up when his impromptu performance was reached. The other boys kept silent and sipped their sodas while John told the tale. When he finished, John sat back and shrugged. "I'm not sure what else we should have done," he said.

Evie had her arms wrapped around her middle as she strode over to look at the Star of David still on the table. "Paulette couldn't even recognize an actual religious symbol." She shook her head. "She's a menace. Always has been."

Wayne Phillips stepped forward. "Just out of curiosity," he said, "can I take a look at these books she was so upset about?"

The boys looked at one another, not trusting the request.

"I just want to look," he assured them. "They'll still be here when we leave."

Toff handed the officer his copy of the *Players Handbook* and John brought around his *Dungeon Masters Guide*. Evie took the opportunity to give her son a quick hug then examined the table. "What is this?" she asked, pushing her finger through the powder on the table.

"Stop-Leak," Nick answered. "I found it in the second drawer."

Levi stifled a laugh. "The candle was a nice touch."

Evie shook her head. "I can*not* believe that woman. Who does she think she is? You boys were right to tell her she was trespassing."

"Do you want to press charges?" Officer Phillips asked, pausing from his page flipping.

"I'll think about it," Evie said. "What an uproar that would cause in this town."

"These are interesting," Phillips said and laid the books on the table. "Lots of detail. How do you remember it all?"

"You have to write it down when you create your character," Truck said.

"And we can use the books too," offered Toff. "We can look everything up if we have to."

"Plus, we don't follow the rules exactly," John said.

"You make up your own rules?" Phillips asked.

"No, but we don't use everything there is. Like we don't use psionics."

"What's that?"

John picked up the *Players Handbook* and flipped to the first appendix. He showed it to Phillips. "Mind powers," he said. "The cool thing about D&D is everything can be altered. Not *everything*, but stuff like this."

"We don't bother with encumbrance, either," said Toff.

"Encumbrance?" Phillips frowned in confusion.

"Weight," said Levi. "We don't go crazy and carry everything our characters have accumulated, but we don't keep track of the weight either. Takes too much time."

The officer looked at Evie, a puzzled frown on his face.

"Their vocabulary has improved quite a lot," she said with a proud smile.

"Okay," Officer Phillips said, "I think we've seen and heard enough. We need to go write this up before I forget. Though I don't know how I'll forget this." He turned to Evie and said, "If you want to press charges, you'll need to call the station Monday. Better yet, come in and bring John; he'll need to make a statement. Have a good night, boys."

The cop left the garage and Evie turned and looked at the boys seated around the plywood table. "I think you all had a much more interesting night than I did," she said. "Are you all okay?"

"Sure," John said. There were nods of agreement all around. "Why wouldn't we be?"

"Well, I might be wrong, but I think this is your first run-in with a whack-job followed up by a visit with the police."

Nick shook his head and raised his hand.

"Oh, I'm sorry, Nick," Evie said. "No offense. Are you okay?"

"Yeah. That was pretty tame, actually," he said.

Nick Meyers lived on a farm with his uncle Mel, but he wasn't from Weston. He came to town the summer before his sophomore year in high school because his parents had been arrested in California on drug trafficking charges. Moving to a tiny rural community like Weston, Washington, from Los Angeles hadn't been just a culture shock for Nick, it was more like an electrocution.

Nick didn't talk about his LA life much, and he didn't have many friends. He'd heard Truck and John talking about D&D in class one day, how they needed another player to have a good-sized party. Nick thought it sounded cool, and he needed to meet people, so he butted in and said, "I'll play."

Over the course of many D&D gaming sessions, parts of Nick's background came to the surface—teenage boys do talk about things other than girls and cars, especially late at night when their characters have survived the perils of a beholder.[1] He swore them to secrecy, though, not wanting to become a subject of high school gossip. The boys didn't tell anyone at school, but their parents insisted on knowing because Nick was a mystery, and a mystery in a small town isn't tolerated.

"You know," Evie said to change the subject, "your bit of performance art there"—she wiggled a finger at the Star of David—"will probably be the subject of tomorrow's sermon at the One Vision Bible Church."

Evie went inside the house after telling the boys not to stay up too late. When she was gone, Charlie said, "If they do talk about us in church tomorrow, you," he said, pointing at Levi, "aren't going to have a girlfriend on Monday."

Levi didn't know what to say to that. He'd already figured it out and wasn't sure how to feel.

---

[1]A beholder has a spherical body, one large eye, and ten smaller eyes, each at the end of a stalk, all of which can cast a different spell. The creature moves by levitation and is hateful, usually attacking first. *Monster Manual* (Lake Geneva, WI: TSR, 1979), 10.

He stared at his dice on the table in front of him and didn't say anything.

"Hey!" Truck threw up his hands. "Don't be a bunch of downers. Let's keep going."

John looked around the table. Everyone still wanted to play; it wasn't even midnight yet. He walked around the table and retrieved his *Dungeon Masters Guide*. When he sat back down everyone scooted their chairs closer to the table, ready to go. "You just killed those two orcs—"

"And repelled a psycho nut-bar from the Council Chamber!" Nick yelled and they all laughed.

"We should get extra experience points for that," Charlie said.

"Yeah, yeah. I'll think about it," John said with a smile. "What's your plan?"

Truck crossed his arms and looked at the other players. "Go back to the chamber with the mirrors and go…east? West?"

"West," Charlie said. "There was light coming down that passage."

The others nodded and Truck told John, "Kryger opens the double doors and looks down the passageway."

CHAPTER 16

Kryger peered down the corridor from whence they'd come, then looked back at the others. "Looks clear," he reported. The chamber was already beginning to smell of death from the beaten orcs and Kryger wrinkled his nose. "The air out there is fresher as well."

Kryger eased open the door and the band of adventurers moved down the passage. They came once again to the crossroads with the mirrors.

"The longer we stay," Kryger said, "the sooner Bohz Grauer will discover our presence. We need to find him—or the amulet—quickly and not dally."

"Are you afraid?" Domo asked with the hint of a smirk.

Kryger stood to his full 6'3" height and glared half-heartedly at the elven thief. "Certainly not. But I *am* wary. Let us not linger and move on."

They followed the western passage and came to another intersection. Franco pointed and whispered, "There are doors up short passages to the north and to the west. Looks like a long passage to the south."

"Bellator," Kryger said and patted the dwarf's shoulder, "you have mining in your blood and your ancestors dug these walls. Which way?"

The dwarf pulled on his beard and said, "I don't know where the artifact may be hidden; dwarves are very cunning when it comes to secrecy. As for the gray one, my guess is he's in the mine. My instincts say south." He turned and looked down the long hallway and into the shrinking darkness.

Kryger motioned to Domo to keep an eye on their backs. The doors at the end of the shortened halls could be open just enough that someone might have been watching and waiting for an opportune moment to attack.

Without stars or a moon, the passage was darker than the blackest night. As they moved forward, all kept watch: glances upward as whisps of cobweb reached down from the ceiling, to the walls where shadows of a carved relief of a tree came to life due to the dancing torch. Mostly, though, they looked ahead, searching the darkness for the reflection from an eye or a gleaming fang.

A passageway opened to their left and Kryger thrust his sword into the darkness as they all passed by. Domo and Xan peered into the passageway, but neither saw anything. Then Franco whispered, "There's something up ahead, watching us."

The group stopped and peered ahead. The torchlight was unable to reach far enough to illuminate the creature, but someone—or some*thing*—appeared to be standing in their path about thirty feet ahead. It was a gray figure, floating and bobbing in the darkness and, as far as the party could tell, it was staring right at them.

"It is ghostly," Xan whispered.

"Could it be a spectre?"[1] Bellator stuttered.

"It would have attacked us already," Kryger said confidently. "Whatever it is, though, it knows we're here."

"A golem,[2] perhaps?" Franco offered. "It might be standing guard."

"Possibly," said Kryger. He took a step forward. "We must get closer," he said. "Come. And be ready." As a group they moved toward the silent figure watching them from out of the darkness.

"Wait," Bellator mumbled. "Wait!"

Everyone stopped. They were twenty feet from the figure. It remained silent and still.

"What is it, Bellator?" Kryger asked. "What do you see?"

"It's Dumathoin," the dwarf warrior said.

"What's a dumathoin?" Franco asked.

"Not a *what*," Bellator replied, annoyed, "a *who*. Dumathoin is our god who keeps and knows all the secrets under mountains. It's a statue of Dumathoin!"

---

[1]A spectre is a powerful undead human whose touch drains the life from the living. *Monster Manual* (Lake Geneva, WI: TSR, 1979), 89.

[2]A golem is a magically created monster that can be made of clay, flesh, iron, or stone. *Monster Manual* (Lake Geneva, WI: TSR, 1979), 47–48.

They approached, and it was indeed a statue of a majestic and powerful-looking dwarf atop a pedestal of stone. "What made it move?" Bellator asked.

"The dancing torchlight, my friend," Kryger said. "The flickering flames made the shadows change direction, making the statue appear to move."

The statue stood inside an alcove where the passageway made a sharp turn to the east. Another alcove to the west appeared to have once held another dwarf statue, but the broken pieces of it lay strewn across the floor and around the pedestal that was now home to a statue of a hideous, fanged creature. It was in the shape of a man with stony muscled arms and legs, and claws extending from each gnarled hand. A single horn protruded from its forehead like a dagger; the ears were large and shaped like those of a bat; wings were folded across its back; and spikes, like thick talons, curved out of the elbows and knees.

Bellator was incensed; he stammered and sputtered. "Who would destroy the statue of a dwarf god only to replace it with an evil-looking beast like that?"

"We are no longer in dwarf territory," Domo ventured. "I'm surprised any statues of your gods have survived."

Bellator grunted.

"The statue moved," Franco whispered urgently.

"I told you," Kryger said, "it's the shadows."

"Not the dwarf," Franco insisted. "The evil-looking beast."

Domo whispered, "No quick movements. Let me look." Without turning his head or body, the thief shifted his gaze to the statue. "Our cleric is quite correct," he said. "The eyes reflect the torchlight. It is alive."

At that moment the creature screamed at the group, a high-pitched shriek as if the winds of a typhoon had just come to life, and it leapt from its perch. The monster landed on Xan's shoulders and knocked the magic-user down then swung its open hand, raking its claws across Franco's shoulder before the cleric could raise his mace.

The beast was quick; it lashed its spade-tipped tail at Domo and struck him across his leg. It screamed again, spun, and punched Bellator in the nose.

Kryger was desperate to swing his sword at the monster, but he risked striking one of his friends as they dodged the attack. As if reading his mind, the ugly brute swung its outstretched hand at the big fighter, trying to rake his eyes out, but Kryger ducked beneath the blow.

While the beast's attention was on Kryger, Bellator took his shot. He swung his battle axe with both hands and the blow smashed the creature in its side.

The beast howled and jumped back. Suddenly its sail-like wings unfurled and, flapping them furiously (*whup-whup-whup*), it tried to rise above the party. The ceiling in the passageway was only about ten feet high and it could not escape.

Domo stepped close and slashed at the beast's leg, opening a deep wound across the monster's calf muscle.

The new gash caused the beast to duck back down and Franco rejoined the fray. With a wide arcing swing, he brought his mace crashing down on the creature's left wing.

He was too slow in his retreat, though, and the monster slashed its claws across the same place it had struck Franco before. The deep ragged cuts in Franco's shoulder spurted crimson blood and he fell to his knees.

The creature paused, looked at the cleric, and seemed to chuckle a raspy, evil laugh, its fangs glistening. That's when Kryger made his move.

The big fighter shifted his weight and swung his heavy broadsword at the beast's exposed shoulder. The wide blade struck home, sinking into the stony flesh, and cut deeper still when Kryger slid the blade free.

With a shriek the monster spun toward Kryger, its thick, dark blood spraying over the statue of Dumathoin. It raised its one good hand to strike at the fighter and whipped its tail around again to smack Domo across the face.

There was a rush of sound in the air then, like a small flock of birds zooming past in the darkness, and the creature was suddenly covered in sticky strands of webbing. The thick spidery fibers slammed the beast against the statue of the dwarven god and trapped it there. It screamed and thrashed but was held fast.

Kryger quickly ran his sword point through the beast's throat. With wide eyes and a broken look on its face, it gurgled and gagged its terrible screech, weakly struggling against the confines of the web.

Bellator stood in front of the creature and with a mighty two-handed chop over his head, sank the blade of his battle axe into the monster's chest, killing it instantly.

"Thank you, Xan," Kryger breathed as he pulled his sword free. "Your web spell was well timed."

Xan stood up from where he'd been knocked out of the way and nodded to Kryger. "I am glad you were able to get clear of the creature for a moment. I was afraid I might catch one of you in the web as well."

Bellator helped Franco to his feet. "You are bleeding from deep wounds, cleric," he said. "We must apply a poultice and bandages. There may be poison."

While Bellator and Xan attended to Franco's injuries, Kryger and Domo examined the body. "Do you recognize it?" Kryger asked the elf.

"I do not. But I have heard tales of such beasts. I am concerned it may have drawn attention with its howls. It was likely a sentry. We must away from this place as soon as our cleric is able, before Bohz Grauer can send reinforcements."

"Our cleric *is* able," Franco said and stepped up beside them. "Though I could use some rest." He held up the torch to look at the face of the beast. "Utterly evil," he whispered.

Bellator pushed through the group and reached for his battle axe, still wedged in the chest of their enemy. "What is this?" he asked, looking down.

Domo leaned over. The statue of the dwarf god had been knocked askew in the battle and it appeared the base was hollow; a glint of gold shone in the torchlight. "Franco, please rid us of these webs with the flame you carry," the thief whispered.

Franco touched the torch to the web and within a few moments the strands had all burned away. Bellator and

Kryger rolled away the dead body of the monster then pushed the statue back a few more inches to give better access to the cavity below.

With the torch, Domo carefully examined the masonry but found no traps. He stood, gave the torch back to Franco, and nodded at the dwarf.

Bellator reached in and withdrew a large hammer. It was forged of a metal unfamiliar to any of them and inlaid with fine gold etchings. "It's an ancient battle hammer," Bellator whispered. "I've never seen the like. It's so light, yet solid." He examined it further, caressing and fussing over the craftsmanship. "There's an inscription," he said. He held the hammer to the light of the torch and read, *May your battles be those of thy choosing, and may they end with thine victory.*

CHAPTER 17

When Monday morning dawned, Charlie Davis's prediction had come true. The Sunday sermon at One Vision Bible Church had been all about the evils of *Dungeons & Dragons.* Parts of Pastor Andy's speech from the previous year were re-hashed, reminders of the teen suicides across the country, and then he'd brought it to a crescendo with the heroic effort of Paulette Dickerson to rid Weston of the satanic scourge posing as a game.

Paulette told her harrowing tale after the service to other members of the church while they enjoyed tea and pastries in the fellowship room. She regaled in describing the garage she'd found herself in, sure that Evie Brewer had no idea what her son was really up to. There were nods all around as the congregation members agreed teenage boys needed to be watched at all times and have ministry properly witnessed upon them.

When Paulette mentioned Nick Meyers, her chin quaked and tears welled up, threatening to damage her carefully layered mascara. "I thought I was about to experience true fire and brimstone!" She shuddered. "Those boys have no idea what they're playing at."

Aaron Evans had stood nearby, nodding, wide eyed. His name was never mentioned during the play-by-play.

Levi's girlfriend, Amy, was taken straight home after the service. Her parents were shocked. Just *shocked!* They didn't realize Levi was such a horrible boy. Amy was to break off the relationship and not see or speak to him again. After dinner Amy called Levi and, through chokes and sobs, with her parents standing nearby, broke up with him. She wasn't allowed to date devil-worshipers.

Levi called Charlie with the news of his sudden singleness; Charlie then called Truck because his prediction had come true; Truck, of course, called John because the situation was just too ridiculous; and Monday morning on their way to Henley's farm, John told it all to Toff.

"This is crazy," Toff said. "What did we do to her?" Meaning Paulette Dickerson.

John shrugged and looked at the grain-covered hills whipping by as Toff sped along the two-lane highway. "Honestly," he said, "I think it's Levi's fault."

"What? Why?"

"I mean, not *really*, but he told Amy he was going to play D&D. Remember? He told us that when we were giving him crap about not already being married. I bet Amy said something to her mom, or *someone*. It got to Paulette one way or another and she just took it in a whole other direction."

"But still, why us?"

"She obviously hates D&D. We're the only ones in town who play. She's like on another mission, I guess. Remember when she wanted to ban Jolly Ranchers from the concession stand at the basketball games?"

Toff looked at John. "We can't be the *only* ones who play."

"Watch the road!" John yelled.

Toff, more interested in the conversation than driving, had drifted dangerously close to the gravel shoulder. He steered sharply back into the center of the lane and John continued.

"You know we're the only ones in town who play. Has anybody else at school ever talked to you about it?"

Toff shook his head.

"And you know they would if they played D&D too. Nerds unite!" He laughed.

"My mom's gonna freak when she hears about it," Toff said.

"You didn't tell them?"

"No way. You know how my mom is. She's so worried what our neighbors think of everything we do." He rolled his eyes.

"She'll know before you get home tonight," John said. "You can't keep something like this from getting around in Weston."

Toff turned off the asphalt and slowed as he went up the Henleys' gravel drive. As they drove up they saw a swather parked beside the barn. Toff came to a stop and pulled the parking brake. "Looks like it's a learning day for you," he said.

The boys got out and looked around. Usually, Jim or Blaine was around to give them an idea of what they'd be doing. But no one was in sight. "Are we late?" John asked.

Toff didn't need to answer; they knew they were still a few minutes early. They looked toward the house, but no lights were on. The swather barn doors were closed, and the combine shed was dark and quiet. "Weird," Toff said.

The gravel crunched under their boots as they walked up the incline toward the swather. The big metal machine looked out of place; the morning light gave it a glossy sheen that didn't belong among the older farm buildings.

"'Bout time you two showed up," Jim Henley growled as he stepped out from behind the swather barn. He held a cup of coffee, the steam of which rose in the morning air and twisted around his red set-in-stone face. He turned and stepped back around the corner, and John and Toff followed.

Jim stood next to his wife. Mrs. Henley had her arms wrapped about herself, huddled against the world like the matriarch of a family that had been led astray and there was nothing she could do about it. Blaine was there too, sitting on a red metal toolbox placed on end. He held a cup of coffee on his knee, and once he saw John and Toff, he looked out toward the hills.

The boys stopped and put their hands in their pockets. "Hi," Toff said. "What's going on?"

Jim frowned, ignored the question, and said, "We heard about you two and your friends. Paulette Dickerson has been telling everyone."

John stuffed his hands into his pockets. "What's she saying?"

"That you are…mixed up in something…un-Christian-like," Mrs. Henley said.

This was too much. John tried to remain respectful—Henley was his boss after all—but now he and his friends were being attacked. Again. And again, by people who hadn't even read the books or played the game. "Did she happen to mention she tried to steal our stuff?"

"Don't talk like that, mister," Jim said. "Paulette is good people."

Out of the corner of his eye John saw Blaine shake his head. Was he disgusted with him or Paulette Dickerson? "We didn't do anything wrong," he said. His face was hot, his hands were shaking.

Jim pointed his cup at John but didn't say anything. He turned and stared at his wife for a moment; they seemed to be agreeing on something, communicating with their looks. "Some crew I have this year, a coward and a couple of devil-worshipers." He turned back to the boys but only looked at John. "I don't wanna hear about it—at all—when you're here. This so-called game you play—when you're on my land it's not mentioned. Understood?"

Toff said, "Yes."

John stared and then nodded.

Jim flicked his wrist, and the rest of his coffee splattered across the gravel. He turned and walked away from the boys and around the opposite corner of the swather barn. His wife scuttered after him and a moment later they heard Jim order, “Blaine.”

Blaine threw out the remainder of his coffee the way Jim had and stood up. The toolbox fell over with a crash. He took off his ratty flannel shirt and dropped it on top of the toolbox.

John had the sudden feeling he was about to get beaten up; the scene before him was playing out like a gangster movie. Blaine was the muscle sent to teach him a lesson.

“All right, John,” Blaine said.

John took a step backward and tensed up.

“Let’s get you up in that cab. You’ll be so good at driving swather, Jim will think you sold your soul to the devil. Right?”

CHAPTER 18

"When does Charlie get back?" John asked Truck.

"Tomorrow, I think."

They were at the A&W, eating burgers and fries while they tried to plan the next D&D session. They hadn't played since Paulette Dickerson had stormed the Council Chamber; work schedules had shifted for Truck and Levi, and Charlie's family had taken a ten-day trip to visit his grandparents in Arizona.

"This might be the last free weekend for me and Toff," John said. "We're done cleaning everything, I think. Henley said it's time to get the lentils. Then we cut wheat after that. I don't know how long we'll be swathing lentils. Then we have to live out there."

"Look at you," Truck said, smiling, "talking all farmer like."

John rolled his eyes and shook his head.

"Speaking of Jim Henley," Truck said, "I have a little information for you."

"What? If you're going to tell me he's nuts, I'm aware."

"I know why he hates you."

John thought that since his first day working for Jim Henley, the farmer had acted very differently than he had during the initial phone call. His face was carved into a scowl, his voice was a just-struck match, and he eyed everyone like a warden. The *Dungeons & Dragons* episode had only amplified the animosity. Henley snapped at, derided, and insulted John every chance he got. John put his burger down and sat back. "Let me guess, it's because I drive a V-dub."

Truck laughed. "Close, but no."

John stuffed a few French fries in his mouth. "Okay, let's hear it."

"He goes to One Vision Bible Church, the same church as Paulette Dickerson."

John sat back. "Oh, that's just perfect. No wonder he knew all about it. But wait a minute, what about Toff? Henley doesn't treat him the same as me. He's a D&D player too."

"But you're the DM and it happened at your house. Plus, Toff's a relative," Truck said with a shrug.

"What? How? He never said anything."

"Toff's mom is like a second cousin or something. I don't know."

"Whatever," John said, frowning. "This is just great. Plus, he thinks of me as a city boy. Why did he even hire me?"

Truck shrugged. "He can only hire city kids. Farm kids are already farming their own family's land."

"Does anyone talk about anything but farming around here?" Rebecca, Truck's first crush that didn't have an engine, stopped by the table to see if they needed anything else.

Truck scooted over on the bench seat and turned so he could face her. He smiled and said, "Hi Rebecca. Yeah, during summer, it's all about farming. That's all anyone does. It won't be so bad once school starts. Everyone's cleaner, too."

"Is that why you're so dirty?" she asked, looking at John.

He nodded and put down his root beer. His jeans were dusty, and his T-shirt had grease spots; his face was streaked from sweat and his ball cap was fading, dirty, and frayed around the edges. "Yep. Lots of jobs during harvest and none of them are clean."

She turned to Truck. "What about you?"

"Truck is one of the lucky ones," John said quickly. "No harvest dirt and dust for him. He works in town."

"Truck?" Rebecca asked disbelievingly. "Is that really your name?"

"It's Eric, actually," he said sheepishly.

"Then why *Truck*?"

"I got this," John said with a smile. "*Eric* was given a toy truck when he was really little—it was a Tonka, right?"

Truck nodded.

"It was his most favorite toy ever. He was obsessed with it, and he still has it. Learned all about it and the real truck it looked like. After that, all he wanted was more toy trucks. Eric, here, has toy trucks—he's built model trucks, he has books and magazines about trucks, and he drives the coolest truck around. Now, do you call someone who knows everything about trucks *Eric*?"

Rebecca shook her head slowly. "I'm guessing no?" she asked.

"Right. Everybody in town calls him *Truck*."

"So that's your old red truck outside?" she asked Truck.

He nodded.

"It *is* pretty," she said.

"You should give her a ride!" John said to his friend with a big smile.

"Oh, that'd be fun," Rebecca almost yelled, her eyes wide.

"How about Friday?" Truck asked her. "Have you seen *Top Gun*?"

She smiled. "Friday is great," she said. She scribbled her phone number on an order pad sheet, tore it off, and handed it to Truck. "Call me tomorrow so we can decide what time."

"Will do."

"Talk to you tomorrow, *Eric*," she said with a smile and strolled away.

"Smooth," John said. "Nice job."

Truck was grinning so hard he couldn't eat. "Thanks for the assist."

CHAPTER 19

JULY

True to his word, Blaine taught John how to drive a swather. He also showed him how to replace a sickle tooth in the field, how far to follow the lead swather, how to use the CB radio, and so on. In between lessons the cleaning continued and by the second week of July the entire Henley farm was as clean and orderly as the county fairgrounds before the carnival rolled into town. Every piece of equipment was washed and waxed, each tool was in its place, hoses were coiled, and the bunkhouse was shipshape.

John wasn't sure if Henley had purposely waited until the washing, scrubbing, and dusting was all done or if it was just a coincidence, but they started cutting lentils with the swathers the day *after* he and Toff had wiped down every window on the main house.

Swathers were smaller, simpler versions of combines. Instead of unloading what it cut from a chute into a truck, though, the swathers left what they cut in a neat row to be gathered later. John, Toff, and Blaine started with lentils, a small legume that grows close to the ground and is used in soups, chilis, salads, or eaten just by themselves.

It was a crystalline morning. John was excited to finally do something other than clean. As much as he knew he didn't want to farm, cleaning someone else's tractors, shops, and windows—and clearing out their junk—had even less appeal.

Blaine and Jim had moved the three swathers to the lentil field over the weekend, and they were lined up, ready for inspection. "Which one's mine?" John asked, even though he knew instinctively that he'd be driving the oldest one. The new guy never gets the new equipment.

"That one," Blaine said, pointing to the swather at the end of the line.

John got out of Blaine's pickup and inhaled deeply, his chest swelling out like a sail. He smelled the waning exhaust from Blaine's truck mixed with the earthy crop of lentils then strode over to the swather that would be his to operate. Its green paint was chalky, and the few shallow dents spoke of a well-used machine. He walked around it, feeling the metal, kicking the tires, examining the sickle blade on the header. A pilot checking his plane before taking off.

"John! Come on. We need to get started," Blaine called.

John trotted over to the middle swather where Blaine and Toff waited. The paint on that one was bright and gleamed in the early-morning sunshine. Same with the other machine. They were both newer models than John's by at least two years.

Blaine said, "This is a fairly small field, and I want to get it all cut today. John, this is really straightforward. I'll go first, then Toff, then you. Right? Just overlap the cut in front of you by a foot or so, just like mowing the lawn."

John nodded and shifted his weight from one foot to the other. He just didn't want to make a fool of himself. "Is that hill over there part of this field?" he asked, pointing.

"Yeah, it is," Blaine answered. "It's steep, too. But don't worry about it. Toff and I have both gone across it before, and we'll make the first two passes, so you'll be lower down. Okay?"

John nodded.

"All right then. Let's go."

They grabbed their water jugs and small coolers with their lunches out of the back of Blaine's truck then climbed into the cabs of their swathers. Once they started them up, Blaine was on his CB radio. "John? Do you copy? CB working?"

John thumbed his mic. "Loud and clear," he answered.

"Toff?"

"I can hear you," Toff said. "John too."

"Good. This ground is pretty flat except for that one hill. We'll do the lower ground first so you can get used to the swather. Okay, John?"

"Got it."

"Just remember what I taught you and follow my lead."

Blaine's swather lurched forward. He lowered the header, set the tines spinning and the sickle bar cutting. Toff followed suit and as soon as he was about fifteen yards ahead, John got going too.

From his vantage point in the cab, John could look down to the front of the header to make sure he overlapped Toff's cut by the right amount. The sickle bar ran the length of the sixteen-foot header and had palm-sized triangular teeth riveted side by side, end to end. They slid back and forth to cut, just like hair clippers. As he drove forward, the sickle bar cut the lentils, and the spinning tines pulled the plants through the header where they fell out in a neat row behind the swather.

Lentils were the first to be cut because they needed to dry out before being picked up and run through a combine. Cutting the plants stopped the growth cycle and allowed the moisture to dissipate. It was early in the season, but the soaring temperature and lack of rain had them out cutting anyway.

Besides the CB there was an air conditioning unit and an AM/FM radio in the swather's cab. John found a rock station out of Spokane and turned up the volume to drown out the thrum of the engine. He went slow, keeping an eye on Toff just ahead, and found it wasn't as monotonous as he thought it would be. He sat high above the ground and was operating equipment that cut while he drove. Kind of fun.

When he got to the corner of the field and needed to make a hard turn, John slowed down so he could perform the maneuver correctly. Swathers turned with the rear wheels so when he got to the end of the cut, he raised the header and drove about ten yards beyond where he needed to turn. Then he braked and turned the wheel, so the back of the machine swung around, and he was lined up in the new direction. That *was* fun. By the third turn John had the confidence not to brake at all and even give it a little gas; it was like spinning donuts in an empty parking lot.

When they stopped for lunch, they'd cut half the field. And, as Blaine had said, it was mostly flat with just a few bumps and rises here and there.

"What do you think of your first day of swathing?" Blaine asked John. They had parked the machines near a creek bed where a stand of giant willow trees leaned over like tired fence posts.

"Not bad," John said. "It's kind of fun driving something big, something other than my car."

"I like seeing that what I'm doing is getting done," Toff said.

John and Blaine both frowned and looked at him. "What?" John asked.

Toff smiled. "You know, what we're doing, cutting lentils, is getting done right now. I can see the difference I'm making as I drive."

"Instead of a desk job," Blaine said, nodding. "With those, whatever you do goes to someone else, and you don't know what happens after."

"Exactly," Toff said. He smiled and took a bite of his sandwich. "Just like that."

"Will we be able to finish this field today?" John asked.

"Should," Blaine said. "Not too much left. We're going to tackle the big hill now," he said, nodding in that direction. "The rest is cake."

After lunch they set off in the same line, Blaine, Toff, then John. The cutting had been easy all day, but as John looked ahead, he saw Blaine's swather going up the spine of the big hill. From a distance he thought the boxy cutting machine looked like an old biplane slowly taking to the sky. When Toff's swather started up the hill, John imagined they were a squadron of WWI fighters taking off from the fields, heading for a skirmish.

Finally, it was his turn to take off.

Not even halfway up the side John looked to his left and saw Blaine's swather already cutting across the face of the hill. He was looking at the top of the cab. On steep hills, the cabs and axles of combines automatically adjusted so the driver was always level as they drove across the face. Swathers didn't have that capability; they were too small. "Holy shit," John said out loud.

He let up on the gas and watched as Toff turned his swather onto the face of the hill. The machine seemed to roll to the left, the airplane banking into a turn. The header was angled across the rows of lentils, a tangent line in a trigonometry story problem.

Why the hell did he even plant up here? John wondered.

John's foot pressed down the brake, he'd stopped and didn't realize it. Toff was already near the other side of the hill's face and Blaine wasn't anywhere to be seen. This had to be how his father died. On steep ground like this, he got out of the combine for some reason, and it just rolled over on top of him. That had to be it. This was insane.

Then John remembered what Truck had said at the diner. *Okay, I gotta do this,* John thought. *I do not believe that what happened to Dad will happen to me.* His heart kicked into a quicker beat. *I do not believe that what happened to Dad will happen to me. Okay, my turn.*

He let up the brake just enough to let the swather move. He followed Toff's cut line, overlapping as he had before, and slowly turned toward the face of the hill.

The swather dipped first then leaned over to the left. *Oh, my God! Oh, my God!* John thought. *Shit!* He pushed down on the brake again and felt the swather slow. He knew the big machine would roll over if he went too fast; a front tire might dip into a rut, or the other tire could go up over a rock and lift it over. *Nope. Slow, slow, slow. Slow and easy.*

The Palouse hills could be deceptively steep the way a massive hundred-foot wave is unrecognizable until it's about to crash down upon you. The soft lines and the way shapes disappeared into one another create a seamless ocean of pillowy rolling hills. But a walk up some of those hills will get the heart pumping and the lungs gasping like the little engine that could *before* it could.

During the winter, kids in Weston hiked to the top of a field near town and sled back down at speeds rivaling an Olympic luge. Parents loved that their kids were outside enjoying the snow, but the games were short lived. The walk up the steep hill wore the kids out after just a couple runs.

Driving across the face of one of these famed beasts was insane. At least to John Brewer. He shook his head like a dog to get the sweat out of his eyes and wiped his palms on his jeans; he wasn't about to lose his grip on the swather's steering wheel.

The CB radio crackled. "John! Move your ass! We're burning daylight." It was Blaine, his voice tinny but still gruff through the small speaker.

John forced his right hand from the steering wheel and grabbed the CB transmitter. "No way! I've already felt this thing slide twice. This is too steep!" He wrapped three fingers around the steering wheel and kept the mic in his hand.

"No, it's not," Blaine said. "You saw me make the first pass. Come on, move it! I'm already behind you."

"My foot is almost flat against the door, Blaine! I'm tilted so far, I'm standing on the door of the cab!" That's all he was going to say. He shoved the mic back into its cradle and grabbed the wheel tight.

Blaine's voice came over the radio again. "You're right, John," he said. His voice calmer. "It *is* steep. But it's not too steep. Two things. One, you're not going to tip over. Look at how far the header sticks out and how low to the ground it is. Right? Even if you did tip a little, which you won't, the header will keep you upright. Two, the slower you go, the longer you're going to be standing on that door, right? Look ahead. You've got about fifty yards of this hill left. At the rate you're going it'll take you at least ten minutes. You're just torturing yourself. Come on, give it some gas and you'll be through this in one minute, then back on flat ground. You can do it, John Boy. I guarantee you'll be fine."

John rolled his eyes. He hated it when people called him John Boy. It was from that show, *The Waltons*, and he was *not* a fan. He hadn't thought about the header holding up the swather though. That made sense.

And Blaine was right about dragging it out.

And yes, he had seen the other swathers make it across already.

All right, he thought. John took a deep breath and eased the gas pedal down. The swather responded by moving quicker and he felt the back end slip down a bit. His eyes were wide, and he shook his head again to keep the sweat from stinging them. The swather had A/C, but he couldn't feel it. John adjusted his steering and pressed the gas pedal a little more. He kept his eyes on the flat ground ahead and was already closer to the end.

"There you go, John," Blaine's voice crackled over the CB. "Just a little farther."

CHAPTER 20

"How was the date with Rebecca?" John asked Truck. It was three o'clock on Saturday and they were preparing the Council Chamber for a long evening of *Dungeons & Dragons*.

"Fine." Truck smiled.

"Come on," John pleaded. "Did you do dinner?"

"No. We went to *Top Gun*, then had ice cream at that place in Moscow."

"She probably kept talking about that stupid volleyball scene, right?"

Truck smirked.

"Thought so." John nodded. "And then…?" He wiggled his eyebrows up and down.

"I took her home."

"All right. No details. I get it. Just tell me this. Will you take her out again?"

Truck looked at his watch and said, "What are we doing for dinner? Are we going to get pizza or burgers from A&W?"

"Dude! Seriously? You won't tell me?"

Truck laughed. "Yes! We're going out again next week."

"Awesome! So, you like her?"

"Yeah. She's pretty cool."

"Good. So, two things. One, you need to find out why her dad wouldn't keep me on, and two, I vote for pizza. If we get burgers from A&W, we'll never get you back here to play."

"Har har," Truck guffawed. "I already know why he didn't hire you back, though."

"Please don't tell me that was the topic of discussion that led to a second date. Talk about a snooze-fest."

"No, but she's new here; she talked a lot about why they moved. Anyway, her dad and his brother went into business together to buy Sam's. They're both car guys, but the brother is a mechanic."

John nodded. "Makes sense, I guess. Still sucks that I'm eatin' dust."

By five thirty in the evening the temperature outside had plateaued at ninety-five degrees and inside the Council Chamber it wasn't much different. Charlie and Toff lost the coin flip to see who'd go pick up two large pizzas while the other boys went about cooling the place down.

When Charlie and Toff returned, holding the hot flat boxes at arm's length, two fans were pulling hot air out of the garage; one was rigged with a wire coat hanger so it wouldn't fall out the window it was mounted on, and the other stood guard and blew air out the open door. Another fan, smaller and oscillating, sat on a garbage can near the front. Just after six and it was still almost ninety-one degrees around the gaming table.

Toff collapsed onto his chair, sweat rolling off his face. "What's to drink?"

John pointed to the big green Coleman cooler on the floor at the end of the table. It was filled with ice and soda pop. He grabbed a slice of pizza and said, "Throw me a root beer, too, will ya?" and sat down behind his Dungeon Masters screen.

Charlie asked Truck about Rebecca, and the date was repeated—again with no details other than what flavors of ice cream they'd had.

"Very 1950s of you," Nick said with a chuckle.

"Yeah?" challenged Levi. He looked up as he unfolded his hand-drawn map on the table. "What do you do in LA?" He didn't wait for an answer but turned his attention back to his map, making sure the tape between the pages was secure.

"Name it," Nick said. "No offense, but Weston's a dinky town, that's all. LA is huge, you can do anything: parties on the beach, surfing, malls all over the place, movies, clubs—"

"You can't get into clubs. Come on." Charlie scoffed.

"It's LA," Nick said. He shrugged. "Most people don't care how old you are as long as you look close to legal and got money."

"What about you, Brewer?" Truck asked.

"What about me?"

"Lisa Martin! Come on, you gotta ask her out!"

"I haven't even seen her." John took a bite of pizza and talked around it. "Besides, we start cutting on Monday and we have to live out there." He looked at Toff. "We won't even be back in Weston for, what, a month?"

Toff rocked back in his chair, a slice of pizza in each hand. "Whenever it rains, we get the whole day off," he said.

"Perfect," John said. He stuck out his thumb and pinky and held them next to his ear like he was talking on the phone. "Hello? Lisa? Hi, this is John Brewer. You probably don't remember me, or even care who I am, but hey, it's raining right now. Wanna get a shake and some fries in 1950s Weston?"

"Seriously, Toff?" Truck asked. "You don't get a day off unless it rains? Even Sunday?"

"Not a full day, anyway. Last year we were able to leave on Saturday afternoons, but we had to be back out there right after church on Sunday so we could start cutting again. It'll probably be the same this year."

"Maybe you can go to church with her," Nick said. "That'd be a cool date." He snorted back a laugh.

"All right," John said. "I think it's obvious I'll never go out with Lisa, okay? She's going to U-Dub where she'll probably meet some guy, never come back to Weston, and I'll never see her again."

"Wow, buddy!" Truck patted John's shoulder. "That's dark."

"And speaking of dark," John said loudly, "I believe your merry band of adventurers is in a very dark passageway. Are you all going to stay there, or do you want to keep going?"

Levi pointed at his map where he'd drawn a circle to mark where they'd ended last time. As he erased it, he said, "We're still at the statue alcove."

"We just killed that bat creature thing," Nick said, "and I scored a sweet battle hammer."

"I think it was a gargoyle,"[1] Charlie said. "I snuck a look at the *Monster Manual* before we left last time."

"I thought gargoyles sat on walls," Levi said.

Charlie shrugged. "It's D&D, gargoyles can do whatever they want."

"I see what you did there," Truck whispered to John. He looked at the group and asked, "Does anybody need to be healed before we keep going?" He took a bite of pizza and mumbled, "A couple of us took some damage."

John remained quiet. As Dungeon Master it wasn't up to him if the players wanted to use a healing spell or potion. He knew none of them had sustained enough hit point damage that they were in danger, but the decision was theirs.

Levi said, "Nothing too serious. I say we keep going."

"Do we still have a lit torch?" Truck asked.

John nodded.

"All right, then. What are our options again? We're at a weird intersection, right?"

[1]A gargoyle is an evil, magical monster that looks like the stone gargoyles found on cathedrals. Attacks first 90 percent of the time. *Monster Manual* (Lake Geneva, WI: TSR, 1979), 42.

"You'd all just come south when you came across the statue alcoves—"

"I just said that," Levi interrupted. "Doesn't anybody listen to me?"

"Right. Sorry," John said. "Anyway, there's one straight ahead to the south, the other to the west. The gargoyle," he verified with a look at Charlie, "was sitting on the base of a broken statue in the west alcove and the passage continues to the east. The floor around you is littered with broken bits and chunks of marble that was once a statue, and of course the body of the gargoyle."

"Okay," Truck said. "I have one thing to say." He guzzled what remained of the New Coke in his hand and held up one finger so everyone would wait. Then with a look of profound concentration, he began to work his stomach muscles in and out, an organic accordion. He took a deep breath, held it, and looked like he was about to throw up. He spread his arms in a circle as if he were giving someone a hug, the muscles in his neck went taut and stood out like the roots of a tree as he opened his mouth wide and erupted a belch that rattled the windows of the small garage. But it wasn't *just* a belch. Truck was famed throughout the county for his ability to recite the alphabet while belching so it sounded like a perverse rendition of the ABCs. As Truck let loose with his carbonated discharge, he also said, "Let's go east." It wasn't a long belch, but there was power behind it.

The boys laughed. Toff had a mouthful of pizza and had to spit it out or choke. Nick slapped his knee a few times, and not ironically.

"Wow," John said. "Are you okay? It sounded like you tore something."

"That actually hurt," Charlie said massaging his ear with his finger.

"Hey, have you ever done the whole alphabet?" Levi asked.

Truck shook his head and slumped his shoulders. "Not yet. I've only ever gotten to S."

John walked around the table and grabbed another slice of pizza. He sat back down and said, "You move east, and you can see up ahead in about twenty feet or so, the passageway makes a ninety-degree turn to the south."

Levi bent over his graph paper and sketched out the lines as John described what they saw.

"Anybody wanna take a peek or should we just go for it?" Truck asked.

"Go for it," Nick shouted, his hands cupped around his mouth.

"Yeah," Levi agreed.

John didn't wait to hear Truck confirm it, he was in a hurry to move the adventure forward since he thought they wouldn't get to play much the rest of the summer. "It's a long passage due south," he said. "No light anywhere except your party's torch."

"We'll keep moving forward," Truck said. "What do we see?"

John sat tall, narrator mode. "The passage is like others you've already traveled," he began, "intricately decorated in the mountain dwarf motif: carved scenes of waterfalls spreading into lazy rivers, trees reaching up to snowy peaks, even some yawning caves and stout dwarf miners. The floor is dusty, and it's apparent you aren't the first group to come this way in a while. There are confused tracks everywhere, enough you cannot make out any singular footprint."

"How about sound?" Charlie asked. "Can we hear anything from up ahead?"

John shook his head. "No, but as you've been moving down the tunnel it's apparent there's an opening ahead. It's still dark, but your passageway leads into a larger space."

"When we get to the opening," Truck said, "we'll stop. I think we should look before we go in."

"At the entrance to the bigger chamber you can see your torchlight is reflected off of something in the middle of the room. Otherwise, it's dark, but you can tell it's a large space from the cooler air and your voices sound hollow coming back out."

"Let's see if two torches help," Truck said. He looked at John and said, "Kryger pulls a torch from his backpack and lights it from the one Franco is carrying."

"You've doubled your light, so you can now see there is a large pool in the middle of the floor."

"A swimming pool?" Nick asked.

"No." John shook his head. "More ornamental by the looks of it. It's square and takes up the center of the room and there's a raised seat, or rim, I guess, that runs around the whole thing like a frame. You can see sconces with unlit torches in the nearest corners of the room."

"There's going to be something in that water," Charlie said.

"Let's light the torches in the corners and get a better look," Nick suggested. He got up and stretched. Got a Coke out of the cooler. When he turned around everyone was looking at him. "What?" he asked. "Did I sit in something?" He twisted around and tried to look at the seat of his pants.

"No," Charlie said. "We're thinking about traps."

"What do you mean?" asked Nick as he sat back down.

"A pool of water can easily hide something," Truck explained. "There could be a monster in there, and it stays in the water—"

"Until it's called forth," Toff interrupted.

"Called forth? What? How?" Nick asked.

"By lighting the torches on the walls," Truck said.

"You guys are paranoid." Nick shook his head.

"A little," Truck admitted. "But that's how your character keeps going, you know?"

"What if we throw something in the water first?" Nick asked. "Maybe whatever's in there will attack if something breaks the surface."

"Like what?" asked Charlie. "A coin?"

"How about that dead gargoyle?" Levi said and pointed his thumb over his shoulder as if they'd all come down the stone passageway.

"Aren't we wasting a lot of time on this?" Nick asked. "Let's all just go in and light the torch. Everybody at the ready and all that."

"Okay," Truck said. "What the hell."

Everybody else nodded and Truck looked at John.

"We'll move as a group to the west. Kryger has his sword in his right hand, the torch in his left."

John smiled. This is what John liked about playing D&D, trying to figure out solutions to problems—even if the players created those problems themselves. After all, he hadn't said anything about a creature in the water, or the torches being trapped. These were things the players had learned from playing before: Be careful, anything that seemed normal probably wasn't. "You all move to the right, west, along the wall. The water's surface is flat and glassy the whole way and after thirty feet you reach the corner where an iron sconce with an unlit torch is attached to the wall about seven feet up and sticking out at a forty-five-degree angle. It's blanketed by cobwebs that flutter in the air you stir up."

"I reach up and light it with my torch," Truck said.

John sat up and rubbed his hands together. "The torch in the sconce is dry and as Kryger touches his flame to it there's a crackle and then..." He looked at each player, then banged his hands on the table and stood up. "It ignites!"

Nick sat back in his chair and shook his head, a smirk on his face.

"Oh, brother," Toff said, rolling his eyes.

John smiled and sat back down. "You see more sconces around the room. The water in the pool is still, maybe a slight ripple or movement, and there's a passageway to the south."

"Anybody want to go for a swim?" Truck asked.

"Maybe we should look first," Charlie offered.

"Always the voice of reason," Levi chided.

Charlie shrugged. "It's always the thief, isn't it? Gotta look out for number one."

"Let's spread out," Truck said. "If we get the other torches, we can have a more even light."

The players described to John what their characters were doing, who had a torch (all of them except Xan the magic-user), and how they were prepared in case of an attack. "What about the south passageway?" Levi asked.

"Charlie or Toff," Truck said, "both of your characters are elves, even with the torchlight you should be able to see better..."

John shook his head. "You now have six torches lighting up the room; the elves' superior vision is shot."

"Fine. Levi, you keep an eye on the south passage."

While Levi directed his cleric Franco to stand back and watch the dark corridor, the rest of the characters surrounded the pool, held their torches high, and peered into the water.

John described a well, about ten feet deep as near as they could fathom, with natural, rough-hewn and rocky walls beneath the fifteen-inch-tall ledge around the floor. "The water is clear," he said, "and you don't see any creatures."

"There has to be water flowing through below," Nick said. "That's why there's a little movement on the surface. Plus, the water would have evaporated if it wasn't supplied."

John caught himself nodding and looked down as if he were reading.

"Can we see anything unusual in the rocks underwater?" Charlie asked.

"Mostly it looks like natural rock below the surface of the water," John said, trying to not just read the given description. There is an overhang of rock below the surface as well that sticks out like a ledge and runs across the width of the pool, though."

"What do you think, guys?" Charlie asked the others. "Something could be under there, right?"

"Definitely," Truck said. "Either something valuable, or something that's going to chop your arm off."

"Or eat it," Levi added.

"Well let's not overthink this too," Toff said. "Besides Xan, Domo has the least amount of armor to get out of. He could check the pool quickly." He looked at Charlie and cocked his head.

Charlie nodded. "I'm in."

"What kind of spells do you have that work through water?" Truck asked Toff.

"I have *Bigby's Interposing Hand*," Toff said. "That might work."

"What's that do?" Nick asked.

"It's basically a hand that blocks the way of something trying to get through," explained Toff. "If Domo gets in the water and something comes up from the bottom, I can throw the spell, and the open hand will stay between the two." He held out his own hand and moved it like he was blocking an unseen force.

"But it's just a hand," Nick said holding out his own hand. "That's like, six inches. What if it's somc giant crcature like a sea dragon or something?"

"I can make the hand really big, too," Toff said with a smile.

"Oh," Nick said and sat back. "Cool."

Truck looked at John and said, "Okay, the thief wants to go for a swim. Kryger and Bellator will have our weapons ready. Kryger will stand at the western side, Bellator on the south along with Xan. That should give you both a good vantage point," he said, looking at Nick and Toff. "Franco is still on the north side. Agreed?"

Everyone nodded.

"How do you wanna do this, Charlie?" John asked. "Are you going to go all Greg Louganis and just dive in?"

Charlie shook his head. "No. Domo leaves his clothes and stuff on the floor and then steps in like a ladder, then down to the ledge with my dagger out front."

"The water is cold and clear," John said. "Domo easily finds places to grab on to in the craggy rocks and makes it to just under the ledge in a few seconds. It's dark but your elf vision is better because the torchlight from above is scattered by the water." John didn't know how accurate that was, but it sounded reasonable.

The outcrop proved to be nothing more than a natural shelf in the rocky wall. Charlie had Domo search beneath it but found nothing of value, and perhaps more importantly, nothing that chopped off—or ate—his arm.

"You need to—" Levi started, but John cut him off.

"You guys can't help him by saying anything. He's underwater and can't hear you."

"I'm going to swim around the sides," Charlie instructed, "checking my surroundings as I go, but mainly looking for anything like secret doors, traps, or man-made objects hidden in the rock."

John rolled a die behind the screen, then said, "Domo's lungs are burning, he's been under water a long time. His strength just isn't there."

Charlie took a deep breath. "Domo swims up and gets a big gulp of air then goes back down." Charlie continued to have his character search the well walls, coming up for air when needed, looking for...anything.

Finally, John said, "On the east wall, about six feet down and in the middle, you see something different. There's another outcrop, not as long as the ledge on the western wall, but deeper, maybe. Something about it catches your eye."

Charlie nodded. "Domo heads to the surface and tells the others he found something." He looked at his teammates. "Can I get some light underwater?"

"What about your ring?" Nick said looking at Toff.

Toff had a mouthful of pizza and held up his finger. He finished chewing, swallowed, and said, "Never tried it underwater." He shrugged. "Let's see if it works." He put his slice of pizza down on the table and wiped his hands on his shirt. "Xan will call forth the ball of light from his ring," he told John. "Make it smallish—the size of an orange, I guess—and send it into the water near Domo."

John didn't see any reason the magic couldn't work underwater so he nodded and said, "It dims slightly, but there's plenty of light."

"Cool." Charlie smiled. "Domo takes a deep breath and goes back under to the spot with the odd *thing*." He used his fingers on both hands to make air quotes when he said "thing."

"Xan lowers the light until he sees Domo stop, then holds it there," Toff said.

"Domo has his dagger ready, remember?" Charlie said. "What do I see?"

"Behind and under the ledge, you see something about the size and shape of the handle of a hammer. But it looks like rock."

"*How much* does it look like rock?" Charlie asked. "Is it the same as the rock around it? Or is it carved to look like rock?"

"With the light you can see tool marks. Very fine and difficult to see, but they're there." John raised his eyebrows in question.

"Tap it with my dagger," Charlie said.

"It feels like stone, makes a hard tapping sound."

"Can Domo detect any traps?"

"Roll it," John said. He knew the lever was safe, but Charlie didn't. Rolling the dice was part of the fun. Charlie rolled his ten-sided die twice and got a result of forty-seven percent. "No traps that you can find," John said with an air of mystery.

Charlie squinted at John and held his breath. He let it out and said, "Okay. Reach in and pull it."

John smiled. "It takes some effort, it doesn't move easily, but it does seem to grind a little when it finally gives and comes toward you. But that's it. Nothing happens."

"Anything around me? On the other walls, or below?"

"Xan's light begins to bounce up and down and is rising to the surface," John said. He looked at Toff and stared at him as if to say, *Don't ask.*

"Follow it up," Charlie said.

"When Domo breaks the surface," John said, "he sees the other party members are pointing or looking toward the east wall, where one of the mountain carvings has swung inward a few inches."

Charlie smiled. "There you go, boys. The thief finds it again!"

"About time," Nick mumbled.

"Let's hope this one isn't empty too," Levi added.

"Domo climbs out of the water and gets dressed," Charlie said. "Let's check this out."

John rolled a die again behind the Dungeon Master screen. "Just as you finish dressing…" he began. He paused and everyone looked at him. "…you hear Bellator scream."

"What the hell?" Nick shouted and threw his pencil on the table.

"Yeah," John said, not missing a beat. "Something like *that.*"

"What happened?" Truck asked. "Everyone looks to Bellator."

"You see something has a hold of the dwarf," John said. "It's a strange-looking creature; it's like a giant brain floating in the air. It's colored like a green olive with streaks of white. Ten long tentacles are kind of swimming below it. Three of those tentacles are wrapped around Bellator and have lifted him off the ground. Two are wrapped around his torso, the other is holding his right arm. The weird thing is the creature has a giant beak and no eyes." John handed Truck a piece of paper with a picture of the creature so they could get a better idea of what they were facing.

"It's a grell,"[2] Truck said. "Shit."

[2]The grell is an eyeless, levitating beast that looks like a giant brain with a large beak and ten poisonous tentacles. A dangerous and fierce monster to contend with. *Fiend Folio* (Lake Geneva, WI: TSR Hobbies, 1981), 46–48.

CHAPTER 21

Kryger ran around the pool toward the hovering grell and watched Bellator, who was entwined in fleshy tentacles, reach out and twist his torch against the side of the beast. The beak of the monster, a vile yellowish white the color of sickness, gaped open and the grell screamed. It was a screeching yowl, a giant house cat that's been kicked and stepped on. Xan, who had been standing next to Bellator when the creature struck, was on the ground scrambling to stand.

Kryger threw his torch at the monster mid-stride, toward the same spot Bellator had struck, but the grell dodged the flame, easily dancing away in the air. Anticipating the move, Kryger brought his sword down like a guillotine, a powerful blow that severed the tentacle holding Bellator's right arm. The muscley rope of flesh flopped to the floor with a spray of blood and convulsed twice before it was still.

The eyeless grell faced Kryger, but instead of attacking, defiantly wrapped another tentacle around Bellator's left arm. With little effort, the grell snapped the dwarf's arm. The bone cracked like a dry oak branch, the torch fell from his grasp, and Bellator stifled a scream when he saw his forearm bent backward below the elbow.

The grell opened its beak and hissed at Kryger. Then Domo struck. He leapt from the ledge around the pool and tore a gash with his dagger into the floating brain-like body.

Above the scream of the grell Franco yelled. "Be ready to run!" he called. "Xan, can you free our dwarf?"

"I have a spell, yes!" the magic-user called back.

"Make ready and let me know when you're prepared."

The grell hissed again and jabbed its beak into Bellator's neck. The dwarf gasped as blood geysered from the gaping wound. He gnashed his teeth, heaved, and blew air to keep his wits but refused to drop his hammer. The grell tightened the grip on its prey; two more tentacles wrapped around Bellator, one around his legs, the other around his neck like a noose. Bellator gagged.

"No!" cried Domo and hacked at the tightening appendage.

Kryger stepped in and thrust his sword upward into the underbody of the creature; the grell moved enough to avoid a mortal wound, but the fighter's blow was not in vain. The beak opened wide, and it screeched again, an agonizing knell as it thrashed its free tentacles.

Xan had retrieved a wad of what looked like pasty gristle from the depths of his robes. He watched the grell while he worked the fatty material in his hands then called to Franco, "I am ready!"

Franco dropped his mace to the floor. Reaching into his pocket, he removed a small sachet and tapped a measure of sulfur into the palm of his hand. "You all must run when Bellator is free," he called. "Get away from the creature as quickly as you can. Now, Xan!"

The magic-user pinched the white gob between his fingers and uttered a series of arcane words that filled the room. As he finished the incantation, he pushed his hands toward the grell as if he were shoving a boulder up a hill.

The grell hammered at Bellator once again with its beak, blood dripping from the tip, then it seemed to stagger in the air. It pitched one way and then the other. Trying to right itself, the grell loosened its grip on Bellator. All the tentacles ensnaring the dwarf fell clumsily away—except the one about his neck.

Franco held the sulfur in the palm of his hand out toward the grell and chanted loudly.

"Domo!" Kryger shouted. "Take Bellator! Into the pool!"

"He is strangling!"

"Now!"

Domo hefted the dwarf over his shoulder and ran. He felt the tentacle around Bellator's throat go taut and pull him back for an instant, then it gave way, snapped, and they were free.

Kryger set his weight and swung his sword with both hands at the stretching arm of the grell. He imagined felling a tree with a single blow, the feel of a blade through butter, the force of a minotaur striking head on.

The tentacle severed and Kryger flung himself toward the pool after his friends.

Once he began the spell, Franco could not alter the inevitable. He saw Kryger beneath the creature just as a column of flame, as wide as a king's carriage, roared out of the stone ceiling and engulfed the grell. The fire slammed into the floor and billowed up again in a roiling ball of hot death.

Kryger felt the heat, and the air around him became bright as he jumped. His feet, legs, and back were aflame as he crashed mid-air into Bellator and Domo. The three tumbled and splashed into the cool waters of the pool…and sank.

As an elf, Domo was light and nimble, but the weight of Bellator, his weapons, his armor, and his pack, pulled them down. Lithe elves may be, but strong as well. Domo swam down, away from the dwarf, then turned swiftly back up toward him. Kryger was conscious and met the thief's eyes in the water; together they hauled Bellator to the surface where Franco and Xan pulled him out.

"Is he alive?" Kryger asked as he pulled himself out of the water. Franco, Xan, and Domo mothered over their comrade near the partially opened secret door they'd discovered moments before the attack.

"Barely," Franco said. "I fear he will not make it through the night."

"Can you do anything for him?" Kryger said loudly as he stepped closer.

Domo looked up at the warrior and put his finger over his lips to indicate quiet. He pointed to the partially open door and again toward the south passage from whence the grell had come. Kryger nodded in understanding.

"I have a small vial that may help," Xan replied, "but it is not much. It may not have the power to save him."

"I can heal him," Franco said. "But I must concentrate. We need someplace quiet and safe."

"Domo," Kryger whispered. "We must search inside." He tilted his head toward the door. "Quickly."

The elf nodded. He retrieved his sword near the dead grell and met Kryger at the secret door. "The smell will attract other creatures soon," Domo said with a nod toward the smoldering beast. "We must hurry."

The big man put his hand on the elf's shoulder. "But not so fast we set off a trap. Neither of us want a blade in the gullet or a poison dart in the leg."

The elf nodded. "We will be careful."

The search beyond the door did not take long. A short thirty-foot corridor made a sharp right turn into a deep pit that was ten feet square with no way around it or over it. The passage beyond the hole was as dark as a night hag's[1] heart, but the risk was worth it. The open pit should protect them from anything that might come from the other direction as well.

[1]Night hags, from the planes of Hades, are dark-blue/violet in color, with glowing red eyes and black hair. They have long, black, talon-like claws. Night hags search for evil people to kill and take their soul. They hate goodness. *Monster Manual* (Lake Geneva, WI: TSR, 1979), 73.

"We will be safe if we stay in the passage before the corner," Domo told the cleric when they returned.

Together the party eased Bellator inside the secret hallway and made him comfortable. The dwarf was unconscious, his breathing ragged and shallow like a bellows full of moth-eaten holes, his face as pale as parchment. His clothing was torn and bloodied, and his limbs flaccid.

Domo collected the belongings they'd dropped around the chamber, and when everyone was inside the passageway, he pulled the door shut. There was a deep hollow thud as if they had just sealed their own tomb and a click as the mechanism that held the door shut locked in place.

"Can we get back out?" Xan asked.

Domo and Kryger looked at one another. They hadn't checked that. Domo pushed the door, but it didn't budge. Nor did the handle turn.

"Never mind that now," Kryger whispered. "Tend to Bellator before it's too late."

Franco nodded and knelt on the stone floor next to the dwarf. Then the door popped open again. Kryger pulled his sword from the scabbard, and they all looked. "Found it," Domo said and pulled the door shut again. He pointed to the floor. "Foot latch."

Kryger slid his sword back into its sheath. "Good," he grumbled. "Now, everyone quiet. Let our good priest work."

Domo crossed his arms and leaned against the wall. He tilted his head and said, "Go on then."

Franco took a deep breath. He clasped his hands, closed his eyes, and prayed. After a few whispered words, he looked down at the dwarf. He placed one hand on Bellator's chest and the other over his own heart. He closed his eyes again and chanted the words to invoke the healing power of the spell.

"Did it work?" Kryger whispered minutes later when the cleric finally sat back against the wall. "Will Bellator live?"

Franco observed the warrior but did not answer. His eyes were drawn, his hands limp by his sides. "I must rest," he said and closed his eyes.

CHAPTER 22

During the last week of swathing lentils for the summer, Henley held an informal meeting in the shade of the oak tree on his front lawn. The whole crew was there to discuss the wheat harvest, who would be doing what, which fields would be cut first, and other expectations. Henley owned twelve hundred acres—about the size of 907 football fields—and they only had a little more than a month to get to them all.

The combine drivers were to be Henley; his brother-in-law from Boise, Dale Kleinert; and his son-in-law, Paul Statler, the last person to see Dave Carlson alive. Dale was staying in the house and had been there for a few days but had been reacquainting himself with the ins and outs of his combine. Paul owned a tire shop in Weston, and Dale was a high school principal, but they helped Jim with the harvest every year.

The truck drivers were to be John, Toff, and Blaine. Blaine would also haul grain to the river in the semi.

Jim's thin, reedy voice was almost a distraction to the fact he was the boss. Not that employers had to have deep voices, John supposed. It shouldn't matter, it just seemed—

"Now there's something I want you to know before we get started," Jim said, interrupting John's thoughts. "While you're here you might think you've discovered a better way of doing something." He paced back and forth beneath the tree, but every time he looked up at the crew, he directed his gaze at John. "There's a lot to do on a farm and if you've come up with a *better* way to do something"—he used his fingers to put air quotes around the word—"to save time, money, and effort, just keep it to yourself." Henley stopped pacing and looked at John. "I have been working this land my entire life and we will do it one way only. My way." The old farmer started his pacing again. "So just keep your new ideas to yourself. I don't want to hear them. It will save us all a lot of time."

John nodded like he was giving the speech a lot of thought.

"Now, there are two things I want to go over," Jim went on. "First is something we all need to remember, and I will remind everyone again as the summer goes on: Beware of sparks. We are working with metal machines, gasoline and diesel engines that get superhot, and we're driving in bone-dry fields that will go up like a piece of tissue paper if we let them. Fire is our enemy here. A spark of any kind is the same as an open flame." He turned and looked at everyone in turn, just long enough to make sure they were listening.

"So, a few things to remember," he went on, "if there's a need to repair something in the field, banging metal against metal can throw a spark. I know sometimes banging metal can't be helped, so every cab of every vehicle will have a jug of water—not for drinking, but for repairs. If you're working on a repair, have the water with you. If a spark flies, even if it doesn't catch, douse it with water.

"When driving in the fields, John and Toff, never drive on or near uncut grain. The combine will make passes first then Blaine will be the first truck in; you then drive where he did. As things go on, it'll get easier and more obvious where the trucks can drive. And John, never drive your truck down the side of a hill. We'll have spots where the trucks can drive to easily, turn around, and get back out of the fields safely. The combines will come to you. Understood?"

John nodded.

"Good. And obviously, no smoking. Anywhere. If you smoke, congratulations, you just quit."

Nobody said anything as Jim looked around the group.

"Second," Jim continued, "I don't want to talk about this, but it absolutely must be brought up, like it or not. Blaine and Toff have done this before; John, you haven't. You three will be driving truck, which means you'll be dumping grain into the silo augers. When we're done here, you two"—he pointed at John and Toff—"are going to get another lesson in how to do it properly and safely."

Toff raised his hand, but Jim stopped him.

"I know you've done it before, Toff. I know you know how to do it. Just remember this: Dave Carlson knew how to do it too." Jim took a deep breath and looked over at his wife. "Dave worked here for three summers," he said, turning back to the boys. "He never had a problem with the augers. Now he's dead." Jim looked at his feet and put his hands on his hips. When he looked up again his face was red and his eyes white behind his glasses. "Do you know how he died?" he asked, looking from Toff to John and back again. "Of course you do. Who couldn't know in this damn town? But I'm going to tell you anyway." Now Jim moved his gaze to Paul. "He bled to death after having his arm ripped off his body! Do you understand that? Can you imagine the pain? Damn it..." His voice trailed off as Paul bolted up out of his seat and everyone watched him stomp to his pickup. As Statler roared down the gravel driveway, Jim took a deep breath and looked back at his two teenage employees. "Just pay attention."

Nobody knew what to say and it was quiet. John stared ahead, the pickup's rumble forgotten, his imagination played over Dave Carlson's final minutes.

Did he scream?

CHAPTER 23

Bellator pushed himself into a sitting position and looked about. "Where are we?" he asked.

Kryger put his hand on his friend's shoulder. "We are just inside the secret door we found. We are safe."

"Who found?" Domo whispered.

Kryger rolled his eyes. Ego was an odd trait in an elf, but not a thief. "I beg your pardon. The secret door Domo, renowned burglar of the realm, found."

Domo smiled in the dark.

"What happened?" Bellator asked. Color had washed away the death pall on his face, and he frowned slightly in confusion.

"You were attacked by a grell," Xan said. "Quite a nasty beast, I must say."

Bellator rubbed his wrist where the grell's tentacle had gripped and snapped his arm in two; the skin was red and purplish. He looked down at his chest; the armor was dented and punctured by the powerful hammer-like strikes from the monster's beak. He nodded. "Yes," he mumbled. "Yes, I remember…some of that."

"You lost a lot of blood," Kryger said, pointing at the dwarf's neck and chest. The deep gouges had been healed, but his skin and clothing were still smeared with blood. "Franco saved your life."

Bellator looked at the cleric, still asleep on the stone floor. "Was he injured as well?" he asked.

"No," Xan replied. "Recalling and casting spells drains one's energy. He is resting."

"Good, good," Bellator said, more to himself than to the others. "Do we have food? Almost dying has made me famished."

Domo stepped forward and patted the dwarf's shoulder. "I know where there is a goodly supply of cooked grell," he smiled. "Though it may be a bit…well done."

After Bellator had his fill from the supplies and Franco awoke refreshed and rejuvenated, the group gathered themselves up and moved farther into the corridor. They had only gone around the corner when they were forced to stop.

"I've been thinking," the elf thief said softly as the party stood in the flickering torchlight, looking at the gaping pit before them. "There must be a way to get to the other side of this hole. Otherwise, what is the point of it? If there is a room ahead, a place this hole is meant to protect, how did anyone coming in this way get there?"

"Your reasoning is sound, Domo," Kryger said, "but I do not see a bridge, nor even the remains of one."

"Perhaps it's at the bottom of this pit," Bellator suggested. "It could have been tossed down during the siege long ago."

Kryger ignited one of the torches they'd kept from the other room and dropped it into the hole. It landed with a hollow *thwunk* but remained lit. The pit appeared to be about fifteen to twenty feet deep with smooth walls. "It doesn't look like *anything* is down there," Kryger said.

Xan inhaled sharply. "Oh, this is quite interesting," he said. "It's almost perfect. It's just wonderful."

"What are you talking about?" grumbled Bellator. "Have you gone mad?"

"Do you see the floor we're standing on, and the floor of this massive hole?" Xan asked.

Everyone leaned over and looked down.

"There's no dust or dirt or dead rats or anything," Xan explained. "Yet look how covered in filth we are up here. This passageway hasn't been traversed for an age. Why is the bottom of this pit so clean?"

"There's another passage below?" Franco suggested. "Is it a shaft with other hallways leading in and out at the bottom?"

"No," Xan said. He bent down and picked up the torch Kryger had tossed to the bottom. The eyes of his companions were wide in shock.

"How did you—" Kryger started but Xan held up his hand.

Xan handed the torch back to the warrior. "Now watch *this*," he said. He turned away from them and lifted his foot to step out over the pit.

Bellator reached out, grabbed the magician, and pulled him back. "He *has* gone mad!" The dwarf whispered as loudly as he could. "What is wrong with you?"

"Trust me," Xan said with a smile. He pried the dwarf's hand away from his clothing and quickly stepped over the pit. He did not fall, but remained standing in midair above the deep trap meant to keep the corridor separated.

"What spell is it that you have cast?" Franco asked.

"It's no spell of mine," Xan replied, "but this"—he pointed down—"is wonderful magic. It's an illusion, my friends! Most excellent and powerful. Even now, with me standing here of my own free will, unenhanced by my own enchantments, your eyes still deceive you."

He turned and walked away from them. He stood on the other side, then he strode across to them again. "You see? It's almost like a painting on the floor."

"But the torch..." Kryger said.

Xan nodded. "Yes. Most excellent magic. It would seem there is a spell cast to create the illusion of something falling away, becoming smaller. I believe it did not work on me as I stepped over the pit because the spell cannot work on a living creature. The brain would not accept seeing one thing, but physically not falling. Do you understand?"

Domo took two quick and lengthy strides to the middle of the hole. He, too, seemed to be standing in midair. He nodded. "Yes," he said, "an excellent trick of the mind. It is an odd sensation, however. Although I know I'm standing upon a stone floor, my mind believes I'm standing—not floating, but standing—above an open pit. Marvelous."

Kryger and Franco walked across while Bellator stared straight ahead and shuffled to where the others waited. He looked back and shook his head while the others stifled their laughs.

The passage continued another twenty feet then turned sharply to the left. After another twenty feet the corridor ended. "I think Xan was right," Kryger whispered. "No one has been through here in an age." A closed door, perhaps four feet tall, stood centered in the wall. It was built of oak and banded together by heavy iron straps and thick bolts. A latch was on the right along with a ring handle.

Domo said, "Don't touch anything. Old it may be, but some traps—especially those unaffected by the elements—stand the test of time."

He took the torch from Franco and carefully inspected the walls and ceiling surrounding the door. He nimbly touched and stared at suspicious nooks in the stone. When he was satisfied, he knelt before the door and made a quick study of each iron stud, flat hinge, and bit of iron. The keyhole was given special attention as he waved the flame across the opening before putting an eye up close to try and look through. Finally, he took his tools—a packet of thin metal picks and oddly shaped instruments—and went to work on the lock. Using a probe and a long pair of tweezers, he pulled a thin needle from a tiny hole.

"I wouldn't want that in my thumb," he said, showing it to the others. "See the barbs? Coated with poison, as well."

He stashed the needle and turned back to the lock. Within a few seconds there was an audible scrape of long-unused metal followed by a *click*. Domo stood up and, putting away his accoutrements, walked to the rear of the group.

"Yours to open if you wish," he said.

Bellator stepped to the door. "My luck seems to have taken a turn for the better today." He depressed the latch and pulled.

The thick door sucked open and stale air seeped into the dark passage. Beyond the threshold was darkness, only a hint of light glinting back as their torchlight reflected off something metallic inside. Bellator looked at his companions. "I'll go first," he said. "It appears I am the only one who can enter while standing."

With his battle hammer in one hand and a torch in the other, he ducked slightly and stepped inside the room. "Oh my," he said. He waved the torch about and said, "Come in. There is much to see."

The others followed on hands and knees, then stood and clustered about the door. The room was twenty-five feet square and, like the passageway before it, was covered in a layer of dust seemingly undisturbed for eons.

"This room is not dwarf-made," Bellator said.

"The size of the door would suggest otherwise, my friend," Domo countered.

Bellator harumphed like an annoyed old man. "Look at the walls. The door and the wall it inhabits, at least most of it, are dwarf-made, but look at the rest. The room was enlarged by others. Dwarf miners would not have left the walls this rough."

The others looked about at the crudely shaped walls with tool marks, gouges, and uneven rock. The ceiling was rounded over, and it looked like a cave except for the door and six feet of finished stone along the walls. Yet opposite from the door, the wall was chopped up, worked over, and rough.

"This room was made bigger by those who came after my kin." Bellator nodded.

"Everywhere else down here has been big enough for all of us to walk through," Franco said, "even bigger in places. Why was this room smaller?"

"The veins of gold and silver, the precious stones," Bellator said, "they follow the rock to heights beyond all creatures. Our miners simply dig where they must, but always with respect to the mountain, to the rock. We leave it with its dignity intact. This room had another purpose for which we'll never know."

"I don't think the dwarves left these, either," Domo said. He stood next to a wooden rack on the south wall. It was prickly with swords, axes, and hammers. "At least not all of them."

Kryger picked up a sword and tested its balance. "An excellent blade," he said. "I am tempted to keep it, but I cannot betray that which has served me so well." He patted the hilt of his own sword and returned the other to its place on the rack.

Franco hefted one of the hammers. It had two round peens rather than the flat striking surface of most war hammers. "Remarkable," the cleric said, smiling. "A true weapon against evil." He swung the hammer, testing its feel. He nodded. "I believe I will keep it. The craftsmanship is extraordinary."

Two suits of armor stood like sentries on each side of the door. The etched design work and gold inlays spoke of pleasantry, ladies cheering their knights in jousting tournaments, and rich kings lauding their power over visitors of the realm. They were beautiful and no doubt worth a fortune, but impractical, heavy, and worse, noisy. Donning a full suit of plate armor to scour a dungeon in secrecy was like wearing sleigh bells to play hide and seek.

A tapestry on the north wall depicted a dwarf, weary and bloodied, holding up an amulet on a chain. A battlefield lay in the distance and an army of dwarves followed the leader with the prize.

"Do you think that's what we're looking for?" Xan asked.

"Must be," Kryger said. "Jovar told us it was an artifact won in battle. The dwarves thought it important enough to pass down in their lore with this." He nodded at the tapestry.

"I thought they wanted to hide where it was," Franco said. "Why would they create this and let anyone who saw it know they had it?"

Bellator stepped closer to the artwork and looked up. "Whoever the dwarves took the artifact from knew they had it, of course. This only shows their victory, not where it's hidden."

"Now that we know what we're looking for," Domo began, "I suggest we start." He stood near the east wall where a long, thin table held four wooden chests. Like the door, the chests were held together with iron bands and locked, no keys in sight.

"These aren't dwarf boxes," Bellator said. "Too plain. They may be formidable, but their craftsmanship is that of humans, I believe."

Domo nodded. He took a torch and looked around each box before touching it, caressing the wood and the cold metal, but never moving it. Once satisfied each chest stood alone and wasn't connected to another mechanism that might trigger a trap, he set about to carefully unlock each one.

The lid was lifted on the first box to reveal an array of bottles, vials, and ampules lining the interior like a standing army. Each vessel was corked or capped, but a few had nevertheless allowed their liquid contents to evaporate. There were fourteen containers in all, eight of which still retained the fluid inside.

"Potions," Xan noted.

"No labels," Franco observed. "No telling what they do, or if they're still potent after so long."

Kryger nodded. "Even if something looks familiar, it may well be poison now."

Domo selected a small vial that held a dram of blood-colored fluid littered with freckles of white. He inspected the seal then slipped it into a pocket. The others looked at him curiously. "For a…friend," he said with a sly smile.

"For study or to imbibe blindly?" Franco asked, suspicion creeping into his tone.

The thief shrugged, the crooked smile still on his face. "We'll see," he said.

The next box was brimming with coins. All denominations of platinum, gold, and silver pieces were present.

"Booty?" Kryger asked. "There's enough here to pay a king's ransom. It must have been won in battle."

"Or paid for protection services," Bellator said. "That mayor said something about the surrounding hamlets asking for patrols. Perhaps the patrols were not given freely."

The third chest was laden with jewelry and the final box was filled with scrolls.

"There's enough here for all of us to live very comfortably for a long time," Kryger whispered.

"These scrolls will be an education unto themselves," Xan said. "There must be a number of spells. They are priceless."

Domo rolled his eyes and deftly slid a ring from the pile of jewelry into a hidden pocket in his boot. "Are you suggesting we take the treasure and leave?" he asked Kryger.

"I'm only saying there is so much here," Kryger said. "And no one found it until us."

Franco tapped his new hammer against the table. "We gave our word we would rid these ruins of he who would enslave or destroy," he said. "I say we complete our task. The riches will be here for us to collect when we're done."

"I agree," Bellator said softly. "We must go on, at least try to find this...gray dwarf."

Domo used his dagger to scrape through the box of bejeweled trinkets. The jewelry clinked and rattled. He looked like a child rooting through a bag of candy. "And what do we have here?" he said out loud and drew out his knife. Hanging on the blade by a thick gold chain was an amulet, a nebulous red gem set in the center. It was made of gold and shaped like a wall of flame, tongues of fire reaching up and out. Intricate designs and ancient runes were carved on the face, and the thumb-sized jewel in the center was the liquid color of a late summer sunset. Domo stepped to the tapestry and lifted the amulet next to the one depicted in the image. He looked at the others.

"It's the same," Franco said.

"No." Kryger shook his head. "No. I don't believe it."

"You don't believe your own eyes?" the thief asked.

Kryger stepped close to the tapestry and looked at the amulet Domo held aloft. "No, I don't. I don't believe the dwarves went to battle to win something of such power, at such expense, then kept it in a box full of trinkets." He pointed at the tapestry. "You don't celebrate a victory with a work of art then throw the prize in among the common loot. No."

Domo handed the amulet to Xan. "As Bellator said, this room was used by the men who took over the mine and built the castle. The amulet may not have been here. Perhaps they found it and, not knowing what it was, put it here for safekeeping."

"It is very old," Xan said. He laid the amulet on the table and spread the chain out. He moved his hands deliberately in the air—a kind of language almost, or signals—and he spoke the incantation of a spell. The others watched, unsure what he was doing. He ended with a flourish, all the fingers on both hands splayed as if counting to ten.

"I can see the dweomer,[1] the enchantments, placed on the items in this room," Xan said. "Franco, the hammer you selected has magic; there are two rings mixed in with the other jewelry—though I cannot tell what power they've been given."

He picked them out of the box and laid them on the table. They were not beautiful works of art, but if they possessed magical abilities, aesthetics was less important.

"This," Xan said, his hand hovering over the amulet magnetically, "has dweomer, but it's not powerful. Whatever this object has been infused with, I do not believe it is worth going to war over."

"How can you be certain?" Bellator asked.

"While I still have much to learn," the magic-user said, his hands open, "I have never heard of magic fading. It is there, and then it is not. Given the tale we were told by Jovar, the artifact he spoke of should have a bold emanation of dweomer. This amulet *is* magic, but it is not overarching power. It is similar to my own floating sun ring, and the two here from the box."

[1]Dweomer is the magical aura emitted by an enchanted item. It also refers to the art or craft of magic. *Advanced Dungeons & Dragons Dungeon Masters Guide* (Lake Geneva, WI: TSR, 1979), 228.

"Let us be off," Kryger said. "Domo, you hold on to the amulet, we may need it later. We'll come back for the rest once we complete our goal. Only we know of this room. It will keep."

CHAPTER 24

"Are you still having nightmares?" Evie Brewer asked her son. Ever since Jim Henley had described Dave Carlson's death before reinforcing how to safely use the grain auger, John's dreams had been overtaken by images of one-armed, blood-spurting, walking zombie farmers. She put a plate of scrambled eggs, crispy bacon, and sourdough toast in front of him.

"Yeah," he yawned. "Not as bad though. Thanks."

"Good," she said. She looked haughtily at John and he swore she was going to say *I told you so*. "I'm *glad* Jim told you what happened and how," she said instead. "Maybe those nightmares will make you think about what you're doing when you're out there by yourself."

"I've already been thinking about it," John said through a mouthful of toast. "I think I shouldn't have taken this job."

"As much as I'd like you to leave, you gave him your word. You started it, now you need to finish it."

"I'm not going to quit," John assured his mother. He could still hear his father's voice: *"The Brewers are not quitters. If you sign up for something, if you join a team, if you make a commitment, you see it through. Simple as that."* "But really," John sighed, "Henley's an ah…um…a…jerk."

Evie got up to grab the coffee pot from the kitchen. "Not every boss is wonderful to work for," she said over her shoulder.

As she went into the kitchen John looked at his plate and whispered, "He's an asshole."

"John," she said as she sat back down, "there's a saying that farmers feed the world. It's true, but some farmers let it go to their head. People in every profession do—doctors and teachers, too. And they're all right. Without them where would we be? It's how they act toward other people, though, that shows their character."

John nodded and ate his bacon. This wasn't his first lecture, but at least it wasn't about something he'd done wrong.

"All of this going around about Paul Statler doesn't help either, I'm sure," Evie finished.

"What stuff?"

"Don't tell me you haven't heard the awful rumors. People don't believe he's telling the truth about what happened with Dave Carlson, or at least not all of the truth. A lot of people think he saw the accident but froze up, didn't help."

"Oh, that. Yeah. Jim's not happy about it either."

"Well, just keep those things in mind. I'm sure Jim Henley is under a lot of pressure, just like all the other farmers around here."

John nodded. "I guess," he said. *He's still an asshole*, he thought.

"Do you have all your clothes ready for the week?" Evie asked, changing the subject.

"Not yet," John said, scraping the last of his eggs onto a bite of toast. "But it's just jeans and T-shirts."

"And underwear," she said.

"Yeah…"

After breakfast John gathered his clothes and shoved them into a duffel bag. He'd add toiletries and pajamas after his morning shower. He didn't know what Toff was going to bring; they hadn't discussed anything about staying in the bunkhouse together. They wouldn't just go to sleep right after dinner; there wasn't a TV, and he sure as hell wasn't going to watch TV with the Henleys (not that they'd ever been invited). Poker with just two players was boring. He looked around his room and grabbed a travel-sized chess set and tossed it into the duffel. A few games of chess over the summer would be good. Better if he won them all.

At eleven John went into the kitchen and used the phone on the wall to call Truck. The phone rang three times before it was answered by Mrs. Pinder.

"Hi, Mom number two," John said. "Is Truck home?"

"He is," she answered, "but first, tell me, are you ready for harvest? Truck told me you're going to sleep in a bunkhouse all week."

"Yeah, it's going to be weird. Different, I guess. But Toff will be there too. Just gotta do what I gotta do, you know?"

"That's true. Well, I hope it works out. Here's Truck."

There was rustling as she passed the phone and then: "Brewer!"

"Hey, man," John said. "I'm going to go over to the mall to get the new AC/DC tape. You wanna go?"

"Yeah! When?"

"Now. We can eat lunch over there."

"Okay. I'll drive. You did last time."

The Palouse Empire Mall was in Moscow, a half-hour drive away and home to the University of Idaho. Moscow wasn't considered a big town by most people, but it was home to the university, had movie theaters, restaurants, and the mall itself. It's where kids from Weston took dates, and it's where John, Truck, and the rest of the group usually bought their tunes and *Dungeons & Dragons* books.

Within a few minutes at the Musicland store, John found the AC/DC cassette, *Who Made Who*, which had been released a couple months earlier. But they still rooted through the racks of albums and cassettes to see if there was anything else worth buying. It was almost an hour later when he and Truck left the store.

"Why didn't you buy any more blanks?" Truck asked.

"I don't have enough new music to make another *Rock!* tape," John said. "I guess I could make one of second-best songs though. Yeah, maybe I should have bought the album instead of the tape."

"You wanna go back?"

They were on their way to Waldenbooks to see if there were any new D&D manuals or adventure modules they weren't aware of. "No," John said after a second, "it's okay. This way we can listen to it on the way home."

"Hey," Truck said and elbowed his best friend in the ribs. "Look what fate has brought upon you." He nodded at the entrance to Waldenbooks where a group of young women were coming out. One of whom was Lisa Martin.

John took two more steps and stopped. Lisa was wearing a purple T-shirt with HUSKIES written on it in gold collegiate block lettering, a pair of white shorts, and white canvas shoes. He hadn't expected to see her all summer.

"Hey, if it isn't John Brewer." John saw Lisa's lips move at the same time he heard the words but still couldn't believe she was talking to him.

"Hi," he said.

Lisa broke away from the group and glided toward him and John had a vague sense that Truck went to talk to the other girls.

"When do you leave for Seattle?" he asked her, pointing at her shirt.

"Trying to get rid of me, are you?" she teased.

"Oh, no! Sorry. I didn't mean..."

Lisa laughed. "I'm kidding, John. I'm not going to Seattle; I decided a long time ago to go to WSU. You'd know that if you talked to me more." She looked at him and smiled. "I want to be a vet. What are you doing this summer?"

"Whoa! Seriously? You're staying here? I mean, WSU? That's...cool! I...uh...what?"

She smiled like she knew what he was thinking (*she's going to be fifteen minutes away!*) and said, "I asked what you're doing this summer."

"Oh. Er, driving truck."

"What happened to the gas station?"

"Earl sold it and the new owner didn't need me."

"Oh, that's a bummer. Who are you driving for?"

"Do you remember in June when Dave Carlson was killed?"

She nodded. "You walked out of the restaurant without ordering."

He smiled. *She remembered I was there!* "Right. Well, I took his place, I guess. Out at Jim Henley's."

"Oh, wow. That's crazy."

"Lisa!" One of her friends from the group called. "Come on, we're on a schedule here. Bon Marché next!"

Lisa turned and nodded. When she looked back at John she said, "I gotta go. Be careful out there." A hand reached from outside John's vision and grabbed her shirt sleeve and pulled her away. "See you in town," she said as her friend spun her around and then she was walking toward the Bon Marché, the big department store at the end of the mall.

"Dude!" Truck exclaimed and slapped John's back. "Did you ask her out? Is that why she said that?"

"I didn't get a chance to. Who were her friends?"

Truck laughed. "You didn't even see them, did you?"

John shook his head.

"Man, you got it bad."

"I know," John admitted.

Truck sighed. "Okay, two things," he said and steered John toward the exit, Waldenbooks now forgotten, "Lisa Martin saw *you* and left her friends to come talk *to you.* Second, they pulled her away, she didn't leave. You have to ask her out. She won't say no. I guarantee it."

John nodded but didn't agree to anything. He just wasn't as positive as Truck was about Lisa.

Once they were outside in the parking lot Truck asked, "What's for lunch?"

"Let's just go to McDonald's," John said. "I probably won't get a burger for a while."

"Did they tell you what kind of food you'll get?"

John shook his head. "But I'm guessing lots of casseroles, stew, and… I don't know, rabbit or something."

Truck laughed. "Mmm. Casserole." He screwed up his face and made a weird voice like a cross between Mickey Mouse and Donald Duck and said, "Hey, Mrs. Farmer Lady, more casserole please. I love me some casserole! Mm, mm! That's good. I don't know what's in this here casserole, but it's the *best* casserole!"

They laughed as Truck drove the three or four blocks, and they said *casserole* another twenty times. Once they had their lunch and sat down in a booth, though, Truck became serious.

"Hey," he said as they unwrapped their burgers, "tell me the truth. Just between you and me, were you trying to kill Bellator with that grell?"

"What?" John dropped the fries he had raised to eat. "No, I wouldn't kill off somebody's character on purpose. Why would I do that?"

Truck shrugged. "To get Nick to quit showing up."

"What? Why? I like Nick."

"Okay. No big deal. I just thought that fight was pretty harsh. It's the only thing I could think of."

John had to swallow before he could answer. "Those were legit rolls. The grell didn't have to see if it hit because Bellator was wrapped up in its tentacles. It couldn't miss and it got ten attacks! You know. It's a tough monster. Why are you asking me this? We all agreed not to talk about the dungeon without the rest of the guys."

"Oh, you know I won't tell. I don't want any inside info anyway." Truck took a long sip of his Coke. "New Coke is better," he said. "Anyway, Levi told me that Nick called him this morning and thanked him for saving Bellator's life."

"Why?" John asked. He frowned and set down his burger.

"He said nobody's done anything like that for him before, even if it's just a game. He thought when you kept taking off hit points it was because you and the rest of us were tired of him playing and wanted him out."

"Seriously? It's just D&D. I mean, that's what we do. I knew Levi would heal him. Didn't you?"

"If he didn't die, sure. But Nick didn't know. I guess he's just amazed. Kept thanking Levi like he did it in real life."

John snorted. "Don't let that get around. If that psycho Paulette Dickerson hears Nick was acting like D&D is real, we'll really be in for it." They both took big bites then John said, "Hey, can you call everyone and get the game lined up for Saturday? We're going to Grandma and Grandpa's for dinner tonight and then I'm going to bed early."

"What time you wanna play?"

"Does seven work? Everyone can eat dinner first, then we won't have to worry too much about chips and stuff."

Truck nodded. "Seven it is. I'm on it."

CHAPTER 25

John watched the combine trundle toward him like a giant wind-up toy and wondered how his father had gotten caught in front of one. It was slow, but maybe the huge header with the rotating forks had something to do with his father's death. It had been five years and John still didn't know the whole story. Wasn't sure if he wanted to know. He sat up, shook the memories out, and waited.

Earlier that morning, John and Toff had arrived separately, each deciding to drive themselves out of some subconscious need or desire to have their own vehicle available during the week. Probably a sort of escape mentality lodged deep in their psyche.

John was the last to arrive, only a few minutes behind Toff, and while he wasn't late, the men were all there, standing in the gravel driveway watching. They drove to Bullhead Flat in the grain trucks and after a windy, uninspired speech from

Henley about doing God's work, they fired up the combines and trucks and moved into the field to get a late start.

It was almost eleven in the morning. John saw Paul reach for his CB and put it in front of his mouth. His own CB squelched and he heard a tinny version of Paul's voice. "Look alive, John. I'm full and headed your way."

John sat up and gave a thumbs up through the windshield. Henley didn't want the truck drivers on the radio unless absolutely necessary or they were asked a direct question. Paul eased out of the field and made a line toward John. The header lifted up and the reel stopped spinning.

Paul slowed down to make sure a rut in the ground or a large rock didn't bump the combine enough to throw it into John's truck. The header was twenty-five feet wide, and the reel and cutter bar were what mowed the stalks of wheat and fed it all into the thrasher and the rest of the machine. It was big but could also be easily damaged by a collision, and the first day of harvest was not the time to have an accident.

When he was about ten yards away, Paul maneuvered the off-loader arm out so he'd be able to better align it over the back of John's truck.

John cranked up his windows and endured the oven the summer heat made of the cab. Jim didn't want the trucks idling in the fields with the A/C cranked up—it wasted gas and heated up the engines and exhaust pipes—but the combines stirred up dust like an octopus scrubbing the ocean floor, so the windows had to be rolled up. Clouds of dirt rose into the air, the Palouse's own version of a desert haboob. The combine drivers stayed in their air-conditioned cabs while cutting and offloading grain, but the truck drivers cooked in their cabs.

Paul nodded to John as he eased up, stopped, then started offloading his harvested grain. As he waited, John could feel the weight of the truck settle lower, its mass growing greater. He felt a bead of sweat roll off his temple and down his cheek.

Offloading the grain didn't take too long, though, and the truck gently buffeted side to side like a boat on the waves as the grain fell and filled up space in the bed. John's mind drifted away, and he wondered if Paul Statler had nightmares about Dave Carlson.

John realized this was his first interaction with Paul. He knew who he was, of course, and saw him around town, but John's mom bought the pickup's tires from Ferman's Tires because that's where her husband had. At the harvest meeting Paul didn't talk to him, but John guessed he was in his thirties, maybe early forties, with a thin face, a shape John associated with villains from the old silent black-and-white movies. Paul's narrow mustache pointed toward his bony nose and pock marks littered his cheeks like divots on a driving range.

The CB radio sputtered to life and Paul's canned voice crackled across the short distance. "You're full up, John. Let me turn around and get back in the field before you go."

John thumbed his transmit button twice so Statler would hear two squelchy clicks instead of him saying "Roger" or "copy" or something else. Two clicks meant you understood when they couldn't see you through the windshield.

Then John's cab was filled with the high, raspy voice of Jim Henley. "We'll break for lunch at noon. We'll circle the rigs and meet at the flat as you enter the field. John, you might beat us there so if you don't know where to park, ask Mrs. Henley; she'll be waiting for us."

John clicked twice and started the truck.

"Be careful and go slow, John," Henley said.

John ran his wipers dry to sweep away the dust on the windshield and looked across the field. He didn't see Henley's combine. He clicked the CB twice, then slowly turned the truck and lumbered off the hill.

Bullhead Flat was less than a ten-minute drive from the field under normal circumstances. But John was driving a two-ton truck fully loaded with poorly behaving grain that shifted and slid and settled. He drove slowly at first, getting used to the added weight and how it reacted to turns. Blaine had warned him that before a sharp turn he needed to slow way down, more than he might think he should, so the grain could slow down too. "The grain is in the truck," the farmhand had said, "but it isn't *part* of the truck. It wants to keep moving forward. It's heavy and once it gets moving it wants to keep moving."

John saw the turn to the silos about two hundred yards ahead and touched the brakes a bit harder than normal just to test things out. He could feel the mass of grain keep moving forward and the truck struggled to react to the mechanics of the brakes. John's eyes widened with surprise and he let up on the brake pedal, shifted down, and gradually slowed to the turn.

He backed up to the auger, set the brake, and shut off the engine. He took a drink of water from the plastic jug on the floorboard then got out of the truck.

And stepped on a snake.

John's brain kicked into gear and recognized the snake for what it was just as he was putting his weight on that foot. A lot happened almost instantly. John shifted his weight to the other foot and screamed, "Oh shit!" The snake's head whipped around, mouth open, hissing a warning. And John, just as he was yelling "shit!" jumped up onto the edge of the truck bed.

Holding on to the wooden sideboards, he cat-walked toward the cab, leaned out, and shut the door so the snake wouldn't slither inside. From his perch the snake looked about five to six feet long, was mostly black with some gray or brown streaks. It seemed to look at him, then lifted its head and caressed the wheel. It didn't seem injured. John curled his lip. *Damn snakes!*

At a family reunion when he was about six years old, John was playing in a field with his two cousins when they found a garter snake. It was small, no thicker than a finger, and only about a foot long. The older cousin, a chubby twelve-year-old boy with hair the color of an old penny and a face like a jack o'lantern, picked the snake up and jammed it down the front of John's pants. "Don't pull out the wrong one!" he yelled and then laughed like a jackhammer.

John screamed—his cousin not only put the snake down the front of his pants, but inside his underwear too. He could feel the snake squirming back and forth where it had no business exploring. "It's going to bite my wee wee!" John yelled over and over as he pulled his pants and underwear off. Still screaming, he threw his clothes aside and ran into the house where twenty-six of his relatives—some familiar, some not—stared at him like he was streaking through a funeral procession. Snakes were henceforth nightmare material for the boy.

John made his way to the back of the truck. He ducked as low as he could and made sure there weren't more of the vile creatures underneath. It was clear. He checked the one he stepped on; it was still near the cab and stretching itself out long again to soak up the sun. John climbed down without looking at anything except the snake. Then a quick glance at the ground—nothing in the way—then back at the snake—still there.

He made sure the gondola where he would dump the grain and the auger were clear—no snakes, mice, weeds, or other debris was inside, and reached for the switch to start the auger spinning…and stopped.

There was something different, something out of place. Like those What Doesn't Belong? pictures. The silos were shining in the morning sun, but still a bit dull. They'd stood in the elements long enough to lose their polished finish. The ground was beaten and dry, powdery dust lifting with each step and clung to the desperate weeds pushing up through the cracks in the earth. The red paint on the auger was dull…

John took a deep breath and felt a shiver trace his spine and the hairs on his arms stood on end. In movies, this was the scene where a character would make the sign of the cross.

But John wasn't particularly religious. He stared. The tires on the portable auger were brand new. The rubber looked like black porcelain, the treads and tire code on the sidewalls stood sharp like they'd been molded that morning.

Paul Statler had put new tires on the auger that killed Dave Carlson. This was it. This was the auger. John looked around then made the sign of the cross.

There was a dark patch on the hard-packed soil. Was it blood? There hadn't been any rain to wash it away. He walked over to the stain and scraped the toe of his boot across the crumbly surface.

John backed away from the spot in the dirt and stopped. He turned and stared at the auger. Then at the snake. Still there. He stood away from the auger controls and stretched his arm out to push the button to start the engine and the screw spinning.

He pulled his hand away and looked at the snake again, seeing if the noise or the vibration of the machine could entice it to move, but it just lay there. John nodded to himself.

He slid open the chute on the back of the truck and raw, golden, freshly harvested wheat grain rushed through, arcing into the gondola like water over a cliff. He watched the screw spin the wheat and move it up to the silo, kept an eye on the flow out of the chute. As it started to slow, he went to the side of the truck, watched the snake, and operated the hydraulic lever to lift the bed just enough to speed up the flow of grain again, just as he'd been taught.

Dust rose into the sky like smoke from a fire. John walked back and forth monitoring the grain, keeping a wary eye on the snake, and raising the bed of the truck. It took about fifteen minutes before the truck bed was finally angled like a playground slide and the last of the grain churned its way into the silo.

He turned off the auger engine and the world was quiet again. John closed the chute on the back of the truck and ducked down to make sure the snake was…gone. The snake was gone. The big fucking snake was gone.

The bed of the truck was tilted at too steep an angle; John couldn't jump up on it to save himself. The ground was hard-packed earth, trampled grass, dusty weeds, and wind-blown chaff; natural camouflage for serpents of the slithery, coiling, nasty variety—of which all snakes were.

John squatted and surveyed the ground beneath and around the truck. As far as he could tell, it was clear, but the shadows, tires, and the undercarriage of the truck was oily-brown-n-black road shit. Perfect for a snake to hide in.

John's rational mind told him bull snakes weren't aggressive, that it wasn't waiting to wrap itself around his ankle and sink its fangs into his calf. It had just wandered off, in its own stealthy, slithery way.

Of course, that would be the case if he hadn't stepped on it when he got out of the truck.

Where was it? Had it crawled up into the wheel well? Maybe somewhere under the hood? The engine itself would be too hot, but not somewhere near the engine. Snakes liked heat. *Oh, crap*. It was somewhere under the truck. Would it be able to find a way into the cab?

John inched his way around to the hydraulics and lowered the bed. It came down slow, like a cheap ride at the county fair. He looked at his feet. He looked around the tires. At his feet again.

Where was the snake?

With the auger engine off, the truck bed down, and the grain chute closed, it was time to go. The crew would be waiting for him. John kept his eyes on the ground as he walked around the truck and checked the wheel wells. He hoped the snake would be curled up next to one of the tires so he could run it over as he drove out, but it wasn't.

John turned onto the two-lane highway, shifted, and gave the truck some gas. He hoped the snake hadn't crawled onto the truck and was hitching a ride in the hope of getting revenge. He shuddered.

At the field, John turned off the road and saw the trucks and combines parked in a circle like a jamboree. He slowed down as he turned onto the flattened stubble and made a wide turn to park next to Toff's truck. Just as he feared, everyone was already there and watching him drive in. He parked, rolled up the windows, hopped out, and quick-walked his way over to the pickup where lunch was being served by Mrs. Henley. He battled the urge to look over his shoulder to see if the snake was following.

"Your cab's going to get hot," Dale said. He had a paper plate in his hand and had just plopped a spoonful of potato salad on it.

"Better it's hot than full of dust and dirt," John replied. *Or a snake*, he thought. "Once you guys leave, I can roll the windows down."

Dale nodded and took a step to the Tupperware container full of baked beans.

"What took you so long?" Henley asked. He came up behind John and wore the face of a cop talking to a group of suspicious teenagers.

John shrugged. He wasn't about to tell Henley about his run-in with the snake. "I just went slow. I didn't want to mess anything up."

Henley chewed that thought then nodded. "Good," he said. "Good. So, no problems?"

"Nope." From where he stood by the pickup John had an unobstructed view of the driver's side of his truck. He glanced at it and, thankfully, didn't see a snake.

"Well, eat up," Henley said. "You're the last one to get your grub. Come sit over here when you've got what you want; we're going to go over the rest of the afternoon."

"Will do," John said. He was hungry and filled his plate with a ham and cheese sandwich, potato salad, chips, an apple, and two chocolate chip cookies.

"There's root beer in the cooler for you, too, John," Mrs. Henley said. She smiled. "Your mother told me you like root beer."

"Thank you. That's great."

Along with the food, Mrs. Henley had also thrown enough camp chairs in the bed of the pickup for everyone, including herself, to sit in a circle in the shade of a combine while they ate. John perched on a low canvas stool that afforded him a view of his truck and he set his paper plate on his knees.

"Now that everyone's here," Henley said, wiping his fingers on a white paper napkin, "I'd like to say how happy I am that we've finally started cutting, and that we're off to a fine start thanks to you all."

What is it with Henley and speeches? John thought. *And bad speeches at that.*

Henley took a bite of his sandwich and said, "We'll stay here for the rest of the day." The white bread in his mouth rolled around his teeth and flashed like a lighthouse as he spoke. "It'll take the rest of the week and probably a few days into the next week to finish this field." He washed his sandwich down with a few gulps of Orange Crush and continued. "We've got some pretty steep ground, and we'll need to slow down when we get to those hills. That won't be for a few days though. Anyway…" He took another bite and looked around the circle. "Does anybody else want to say anything? Dale?"

Dale Kleinert was a big man—not fat big, but football defensive lineman big. John thought he was probably a very intimidating principal, especially after seeing him have to squeeze into the cab of his combine. But he seemed like a nice guy.

Dale chuckled and wiped the corners of his mouth with a napkin. He pointed at Toff and John and said, "I suspect the person these two want to hear from the least during their last summer as high school students is a principal." He smiled and popped the last of his sandwich in his mouth as if to make a point of not speaking.

Henley's son-in-law held up a finger while he finished chewing then gulped Coca-Cola.

Everyone was looking at him, waiting, when Henley said, "Do you intend to tell us all what really happened that day, Paul?"

Statler frowned and he swallowed, but he didn't say anything.

"No?" Henley went on. "Then let's all get back to work. There's a garbage bag in the back of the truck, and don't make my wife pick up your chairs."

As Henley walked away, nobody knew what to say or where to look. Blaine was examining his dusty boots while Dale just shook his head and looked at the sky. As Paul got to his feet and walked away, John and Toff's eyes met. *That was BS*, John mouthed.

CHAPTER 26

The bunkhouse was as black as the inside of the cardboard box John had hidden in when he was eight years old. It had been in the basement of his grandparents' house and was filled with quilts, old clothes, and a few picture albums laden with black-and-white photos of strangers. John had removed it all, stacked it on top of another box nearby, and sat inside, closing the flaps over his head to hide from his cousin.

He'd sat there forever, certainly longer than Mr. Stephenson's math lessons, which were *so* boring, and was rather proud of himself for keeping quiet when someone clomped down the stairs.

Then the lights went out and the inside of his best-ever hiding spot became a void, a nothingness, a black so black it swallowed everything into nonexistence. Just, gone. But he didn't panic. He *was* eight after all. He knew he was in his grandparents' basement.

John had pushed open the cardboard flaps over his head and stood up. Nothing. No light. No sound. He must have died. Or everyone else had.

"Hey!" he'd shouted. Then he screamed, "Heeeeeyyyyyy?!"

The lights popped on and John's mom raced down the stairs. He wasn't dead after all and no one else was either. Just a dark basement and the realization that his cousin (the same one who'd tortured him with the snake) had not even been looking for him.

The bunkhouse at the Henley farm was just as dark, but the childhood fear that had gripped him then hadn't stayed with John as he'd matured. *Something* had woken him up though. He reached over to the plastic milk crate that stood in as an end table and fumbled for his watch. It was a digital Casio his grandparents had given him for his sixteenth birthday. He pressed the tiny button on the side and the LCD numbers were instantly backlit by a murky glow. 1:42 a.m. He and Toff had come to the bunkhouse right after dinner, both beat from the long day. One of them had suggested a game of chess, but neither was awake enough to play. They'd crawled onto their bunks and were asleep without another word.

John could hear Toff snoring, not buzzsaw snoring, but breathing heavily. That wasn't what had woken him, though. It wasn't loud enough, or out of place. He returned his watch to the crate and lay on his back.

Then he heard it again, a shuffling outside, a scratching at the old wood siding of the bunkhouse. John pictured an undead creature lurking in the dark, a hunched-over wight[1] with rotting gray skin, claws raking the rough boards of the bunkhouse, shaggy matted black hair, and a hatred that fueled its existence. He shook his head and smiled to himself. Why couldn't he remember his algebra textbook the way he seemed to digest the D&D *Monster Manual*?

He heard the scratching again, light, searching. *Probably a raccoon*, John thought. *Maybe a coyote. Nothing to worry about.*

When the door crashed open, John bolted upright, a super-fast ninety-degree sitting position that would make a gymnast proud. At the door, Blaine was awash in silvery dawn light. "Up and at 'em, boys!" he said loudly. "Breakfast is on the table and we're cutting by six."

Toff grumbled something about it being too early and sat up, running his hands through his lopsided shaggy hair. John mused that from behind Toff looked like the wight he'd imagined earlier in the night. He looked at his watch. 5:10 a.m. Had he dreamed the whole thing about wights and raccoons or just fallen back asleep?

The boys got dressed, took turns using the toilet, and stepped out the bunkhouse door. The sun was low on the horizon, and it was already almost seventy degrees. It was going to be another sunglasses-required day. They made their way to the picnic table where Mrs. Henley had laid out breakfast.

"You boys coffee drinkers yet?" Dale asked. He was sitting on one side of the table by himself; he looked like a bear in his black flannel shirt and black baseball hat.

---

[1]A wight is an evil undead human who hates sunlight and seeks to destroy any lifeform it encounters. *Monster Manual* (Lake Geneva, WI: TSR, 1979), 100.

John and Toff both shook their heads and reached for the orange juice.

"How was your first night in the bunkhouse?" Mrs. Henley asked. "Did you sleep well?"

Toff nodded. "Yeah. I think I was more tired than I thought. I was out."

John was going to say something about hearing the scratching outside but noticed Henley listening in on the conversation. When Mrs. Henley looked at him questioningly, he shook his head. "No problems. It's nice and quiet out here. Except for Toff's snoring." He laughed when Toff looked hurt. "Just kidding."

"Well, if you boys need anything," Mrs. Henley said, "you just let me know."

"We will," Toff said. "Thank you."

As Toff and John sat down opposite Dale, Henley refilled his coffee cup and walked out to the driveway. Blaine came out of the combine shed and they met on the gravel and talked.

"Where's Paul?" Toff asked.

Dale shook his head. "Not sure where he is. How long does it take to drive out here from Weston?" Dale was staying with the Henleys in their guest room.

"Depends on who's driving." Toff grinned.

"And *what* they're driving," John added. The principal looked at John like he didn't speak the same language. "Even if I could floor it the whole way out here in my Bug, it'd take me just about a half hour."

Toff nodded and swallowed a bite of his maple bar. "If I really push the Dot, I could make it in twenty."

John scoffed. "No way."

"Please don't test your theory," Dale said. "I may not be your principal, but I can find his number and tell him to keep an eye on you two."

The boys laughed, inwardly wondering if high school principals had some sort of secret communications network.

"Oh, never mind," Dale said. "Here's Paul now."

John and Toff twisted to look behind them and saw Paul's pickup coming up the driveway. A magnetic sign on the door panel had *Keep moving with Statler Tires* written in slanted blue letters and the phone number below. "He doesn't look happy," Toff said.

"I don't think Henley is going to cheer him up either," John said.

"Why don't we go over to your trucks and get ready to go?" Dale suggested and stood up. "Grab a donut for the road."

Blaine saw the trio move toward the parked trucks and stepped away from Henley to join them. John and Toff checked that their emergency water was still on the floorboard in front of the passenger-side seat—Blaine had told them to double check every day because Henley might take it out to test them. They added their own jugs of drinking water filled from the tap and placed in the freezer overnight, then stepped out in front of the trucks where Dale and Blaine were talking.

"What's going on?" Toff asked, looking toward Henley and Paul.

Blaine shook his head. "Family stuff, probably. Don't ask." He looked at his watch and walked over to his truck. "Let's mount up, boys."

The three drivers climbed into their trucks, but neither John nor Toff would start theirs before Blaine. If they started the engine too early, Henley would be mad that gas was being wasted and the engines would be too hot when they got to the field. John knew the engines would be superhot regardless of how long they idled; the drive from the farm to the field would get them hot even if it was winter. Earl had taught him that at the gas station. It wasn't how long the engine sat and idled, it was what was going on *inside* the engine: Gas was burning, exploding, to move the pistons. Yeah, things were going to heat up quick. He suspected Henley knew it too but wanted something else to lord over them about.

Dale climbed into the cab next to John and put his water jug on the seat between them. "I don't know what that's all about, but like Blaine said, I wouldn't ask. Family stuff can be tricky."

John nodded.

It didn't look like Henley was yelling, but he was adamant about whatever he was saying. His body looked like a board standing on end and his hands karate-chopped the air to emphasize his point.

John looked at his watch. "He's not even late," he said, but Dale didn't answer.

John watched as Paul drove ahead and parked his truck, the argument over. Henley turned and walked quickly toward Blaine's grain truck and the drivers started their engines.

CHAPTER 27

Domo put his finger to his lips and looked at his friends, motioning for them to remain silent. He pointed first at his ears and then down the stairs. *He'd heard something from below.*

The adventurers stood just on the other side of the still-smoldering grell carcass on the south side of the pool. It smelled like burnt mushrooms, cat piss, and vomit. Domo had brought them all up short just before they'd entered the dark hall the grell had come from.

"What is it?" Kryger whispered.

Domo leaned close and whispered, "Three or four creatures coming up from below."

"How do you know there are stairs?" Kryger asked.

Domo smiled and tapped one of his pointed ears. Kryger nodded. *Always believe an elf's ears.*

Bellator stepped close and lifted his hands. The frown upon his brow betrayed his impatience. "What are we doing?" he whispered.

Kryger pushed him over to the other side of the archway with Xan and Franco. He showed them three fingers, shrugged, then flashed four fingers. Then with another hand signal, bade them wait.

Soon, several individual voices could be heard mumbling as they neared. They were quiet but not whispering—the language was not one any in the party understood, but they all thought it sounded familiar. They gripped their weapons, took deep breaths, and pushed themselves closer to the cold stone wall. They were ready.

When the first creature came into the light from the hallway, it went straight to the stinking grell corpse. The gnarled, granite-colored, hobgoblin-ish beast was followed immediately by two more who skulked behind, but not out of surliness. It seemed to be their nature, for Kryger and the others recognized the creatures as belonging to the same diminutive and tough race they battled earlier, and whose bodies they had hidden in the secret room of the hall.

There was no way the five of them could retreat down the hallway without being discovered. Kryger thought it was amazing the three sentries, or laborers, or whatever they were, hadn't spotted them when they'd come in. Maybe cooked grell wasn't something they saw every day.

The three dungeon denizens crouched around the grell's body, obviously discussing through their peculiar grunts and growly language how it came to be there in its current state when the one in the middle realized something was…off. It stood up straight, its long arms dangling, and looked at the still-fluttering torches in the far corner.

Domo took two long strides and pushed his dagger into the base of the standing creature's skull. The beast made no sound as it stiffened then collapsed, sliding off the steel blade, to land on top of the grell.

Its two companions stared for a moment, perhaps wondering if their friend was really so hungry, but then turned around, their long chunky fangs bared. Neither had a chance.

Franco smashed the skull of one with his mace, while Kryger removed the head of the other with a mighty swing of his sword.

"Well," Bellator chuckled, "it certainly pays to catch them unawares, yes? But what about the bodies?" he asked, growing serious. "The stink of the grell drew them, it's bound to attract others."

Xan looked toward the secret treasure room. "We could—"

"No," Domo cut him off. "We plan to return there, remember? There is no reason we should suffer these foul creatures again."

Kryger tossed the headless corpse of the one he'd killed into the water. "Maybe they'll sink," he said. "The water will absorb the smell." He looked at Xan. "Right?"

Xan shrugged, but it was too late—everyone was pushing bodies and tossing burnt grell meat into the water.

After dousing the torches around the room, they moved into the south passage under the single flickering torch held by Franco. Domo led them quickly, confident there were no traps to concern themselves with; the three sentries had walked straight through, never pausing.

Thirty feet into the passage there was a hallway to the right. Domo whispered, "The creatures did not come from this direction. There is a hollowness straight ahead. I believe it leads to the lower level. That's where the three guards came from."

Xan nodded. "I feel the change as well," he said.

"I agree with our elf friends," said Bellator. "The way ahead will lead us deeper below the earth. Somewhere down there we will find Bohz, the gray one. His kind crave the darkness."

Kryger looked at each member of the party, and they nodded in return. "Okay," he whispered. "Let us go then. Domo, lead on."

The thief didn't go far. After only fifteen feet Franco's torch revealed a wide set of stairs to the right, disappearing into the deep darkness. Domo paused only a moment then nodded to the rest of the group before going down the steps.

They went slowly and quietly, eyes wide, searching; they strained to hear a whisper, a scrape of stone, a breath, anything that would alert them to what may lie ahead. The stairwell stopped at a small landing then continued down, turning again to the right.

Who knew how much earth and rock was above them? Where they'd just come down from was already underground.

How deep would these stairs take them? What kept the earth from falling down on top of them? Bellator was unaffected—he moved down the stairs steadily—but the others, especially Kryger and Franco, kept turning their eyes up into the darkness.

The group made their way down the stairs and emerged in an octagonal room. The eight walls were carved similarly to those of the rooms above, but the stone was different than that of the upper dungeon. Here it was rougher to the touch, dark like molasses, foreboding in its depth. Instead of mountains, streams, and trees carved upon the walls, the imagery depicted mining scenes. Looking at the stairs from inside the room and moving right, the carvings told a story of creating a small city above and how the dwarves found a lode that turned deep into the mountain; and how they followed it down, rather than aimlessly destroy the mountain around them. Intricate details in the reliefs showed dwarves with various gems, some reverently touching a stony wall, others hoisting mugs of ale. The small amount of space above the stairwell was filled with a mountain, a grand peak made to look like the stairs emptied out of it.

An archway opened the west wall to further depths. Domo stood to one side of it and motioned to the others that there were more steps leading down. They joined him and he whispered, "There's a landing just here and then stairs lead down to the left."

"Our friends obviously came up from there," Kryger said quietly. "Be ready in case there are others." He nodded and stepped through the archway and started down.

The stairs were wrought directly from the stone, but precisely cut so there were no variations in height or width, though they were bowled slightly in the middle from thousands of booted feet tramping upon them over the ages. The steps emptied into another flat landing with an archway to the left.

Kryger signaled for silence as Domo and Xan put their elven abilities to use and listened. Both shook their heads and the party stepped through the opening.

They found themselves in another octagonal room, identical in size to the one they'd come from, but this one had large wooden doors in the north and west walls. They were made of wide, rough-hewn planks and held together with iron spikes.

"Sentry post," Bellator said. He pointed to unkempt bedrolls against the walls. Scattered about the room were several cloth sacks, a barrel, two small rickety-looking chairs, and two heavy clubs leaning against a wall. "Bohz Grauer isn't taking chances."

Kryger thumped the barrel with his knuckles and lifted the lid. Sniffed. "Grog," he said, shaking his head. "Or some sort of foul drink. It's not water or ale." He walked over and stood next to the northern door while Bellator took a post at the west exit.

Franco held the torch aloft while Xan and Domo looked through the bedrolls for anything useful or valuable. "Nothing here," Domo said, flicking away a blanket with the toe of his boot.

"Some coins here," Xan said and jingled a small pouch he'd picked up. "Not very heavy," he added and tossed it to the thief.

Domo glanced inside and placed the bag on top of the barrel. He withdrew one coin and said, "Heads we go north, tails west. What do you say?"

Kryger shook his head. "No games, Domo. I think I heard something on the other side of this door."

Everyone turned toward Kryger. Domo wrapped the coin in his palm and grew serious. He stepped next to the warrior and put his ear near the doorjamb.

"What did you hear?" Franco whispered.

Domo held up his hand. "I hear it," he said. "Distant… voices…and…"

"And what?" Bellator whispered, his eyes anxious.

Domo shook his head. "I'm not sure. There's banging. It's muffled."

"Perhaps we should go through *this* door then," Bellator said, cocking his head toward the entry he guarded. "There are no such sounds emanating from the other side of this one."

Xan stepped closer. "I agree with Kryger," he said softly. "The sooner we know what's down here, the better. If the source of those voices isn't just on the other side of the door, then we will have the opportunity to retreat and try the other."

Franco nodded his agreement.

"The door is unlocked," Domo said, his hand on the latch. Franco took a cloth from his pouch, deftly wrapped it around the flame of the torch, and snuffed it out. They didn't want anyone on the other side of the door, distant or not, to see light coming from a place it shouldn't be. Most, if not all the creatures they'd come across, could see in the infrared spectrum and did not require the light of a torch. Many shunned fire unless it was needed for warmth during the icy winter months.

They waited a few moments for their eyes to adjust to the darkness. Then Domo asked, "Ready?"

"Slowly," said Kryger. "We're not sure what's on the other side."

"Or how many," added Franco.

Cool, earthy air slid into the chamber as Domo pulled open the door. The hinges groaned but quieted again without fuss. Domo left the door open just wide enough for them to pass through, but a casual glance from afar probably wouldn't be enough to notice it was open at all.

They slipped out and found themselves in a short corridor that opened into a larger room only thirty feet or so ahead. Domo and Xan, both elves, and the dwarf Bellator, also had the gift of infravision, and could see perfectly well. The humans in the party, Kryger and Franco, could only stumble in the darkness, something that did not help with the claustrophobic sense of being so far beneath the Earth's surface.

"I can't see a bloody thing," Kryger grumbled. "I am defenseless if we are attacked."

Franco nodded reflexively in the void. "I admit, I do not like this feeling."

"Do not worry, my friends," Xan whispered. "Let Domo scout our surroundings. We will have light in an instant if need be."

"Wait," Kryger whispered. "I see a glow up ahead."

"As do I," said Franco. "Dim. Torchlight, perhaps."

"Yes," said Domo, suddenly appearing before them as a black shadow against the distant light. "There's been a cave-in sometime in the past. Part of this room has fallen away. I went to the edge, and I believe Bohz Grauer has prisoners searching the rubble. There are torches down below and people working."

"Down below?" Franco asked. "Another level?"

"There is a great chasm," Domo said. "It's very deep, but there are people down there, humans from the village, I expect. But there are stairs over here," he said and pointed to the chamber's corner.

At the top of the stairs Franco reignited the torch and they squinted against the sudden brightness. "Deeper still," the cleric muttered.

It was a short but steep flight of stairs, lowering the party even deeper into the earth. Another short corridor led them into a triangular intersection. Franco had just set foot on the stone floor when they were startled by four hobgoblins[1] shoving a sickly shadow of a man toward them from the passage ahead.

Everyone stopped. The dim yellow eyes of the hobgoblins looked first at Kryger, the big human warrior, and then

[1]Hobgoblins are brutish monsters with hairy hides brown to grayish black, their faces are bright red with yellow or brown eyes. They wear armor, carry weapons, and are intelligent enough to work together in tribal groups. *Monster Manual* (Lake Geneva, WI: TSR, 1979), 52.

Franco, the second largest of the party. The hobgoblins were all big—six feet of muscle built for fighting, with thick, hairy hides, black armor highlighted with blood red emblems of their tribe, and weapons designed to cut, sever, and maim. But they weren't the smartest of beings and they knew it. They were four against five, two of which were as big—or bigger in Kryger's case—than them.

And then they saw Xan. Hobgoblins are born with an instinctual hatred of elves. They roared angrily, dropped their prisoner, and charged.

The intersection wasn't a large space, and it was instantly crowded with the battle. Kryger raised his heavy broadsword and ran into the onslaught with a cry of his own. Bellator chased after him with his war hammer ready to crush skulls and smash joints. Franco joined the fray, swinging his mace in one hand, the still-flaming torch in the other. Domo skirted to the left, a long dagger in one hand, while his other hand touched the rough stone wall. Being in contact with the wall as he moved gave him a better idea of his surroundings. Xan, the magic-user, took a step back and to the side. Any incantation he started could not be interrupted; if he was struck, be it by a blade or a flung rock, his concentration would be broken, and the spell lost from his consciousness.

The melee clashed like storm-driven waves breaking upon jagged rocks. Kryger drew first blood, his sword slashing open a wound that made his opponent howl. Bellator struck with his war hammer; the knee bones of the hobgoblin he hit crumbled under the powerful blow like wheat millet. Franco swung his mace in an attempt to break the arm of another, but his attack was anticipated, and he only scored a glancing blow as the hobgoblin ducked to the side.

Domo remained in shadow and snuck behind the hideous creatures. In their rage toward Xan, the elf thief had gone unnoticed, his form quiet and quick; as the monsters rushed forward, he went around them and came up behind. He watched his friends attack then made his own move. With a quick step forward, he sank his dagger to the hilt in the back of a hobgoblin just as it was about to strike the dwarf. The bright blade turned dark with fresh blood, but the beast didn't die. It roared, almost more from surprise than pain. How had he been hit from behind when the enemy was in front?

The hobgoblins stepped back. They grunted at one another, raised their weapons, and charged forward again. The biggest of the group seized upon Kryger while the others attacked the dwarf in an attempt to get to Xan. They were still unaware of the other elf in the party.

Domo tossed the forgotten prisoner a dagger. The man was thin, a series of sticks held together by rags, dirt, and black soot. "Fight for your freedom," the elf yelled. The man caught the dagger and jumped on the back of the biggest hobgoblin. He wrapped his free arm around the creature's neck and jabbed the dagger deep into its shoulder. He pulled it out, his face twisted in anger, and stabbed down again and again.

But he didn't have the strength to kill. The man had been taken from his farm in the dead of night, the devil's hour, and had lost sense of how long he'd been below ground, searching through broken stairs, shattered walls, and loose rubble for an unknown trinket. The knife cut, it even pierced the skin enough to wound, but it didn't kill. Already the prisoner had expended what energy he had. His final thrust was a tired release of hope.

The hobgoblin twisted around, grabbed the man by the neck, and threw him away like an annoying rodent.

Kryger took the opportunity to thrust the tip of his sword through the angered beast's lungs. The hobgoblin gasped, a snarling, hissing sigh of a doused bonfire, and fell to the floor, a pile of lifeless bone and flesh.

At the same moment Bellator suffered a skull-rattling blow to his head. The iron helmet he wore twisted around so he was looking with his right eye through where his left eye normally viewed the world from, and his left eye was blocked by the ear flap. Bellator stumbled but instead of righting his headgear, he blindly—or instinctively—swung his mighty hammer around and caved in the chest of his attacker.

Franco blocked a sword thrust and received a long gash across his forearm for the effort. Blood squirted over the face of his hobgoblin, who laughed at the sight like a bully after pushing down his prey. The maniacal laughter was silenced when Franco brought his mace around with his good hand, smashed the hobgoblin's teeth into small shards of ivory, and severed the vertebrae in the creature's neck with the blow.

The final hobgoblin halted his assault on Bellator when he saw his dead comrades on the floor. He turned and sprinted back down the passage from whence they'd appeared.

"Domo!" Kryger shouted. "Quickly! He mustn't be allowed to report our presence."

The elf thief was the swiftest of the party and set off in pursuit while the others gathered their wits, untangled themselves and their weapons from the dead hobgoblins, then joined the pursuit.

The passage was shaped like a funnel lying on its side and they ran into the skinny end. After fifty feet it widened out again into an unfinished chamber. Similar to the intersection in which they'd just battled the hobgoblins, this was a larger, almost circular cavern. A wide column connected the ceiling to the floor in the middle of the chamber and it appeared as though another passage branched off to the right.

Domo stood near the east wall where a small alcove was filled with a boulder the size of a rhinoceros and the color of black dragon scales. It was quite out of place in the otherwise finely finished halls of the dwarves. To make matters even more confusing for the group, the lifeless arm and leg of a hobgoblin were visible between the wall and the boulder. Blood spattered all around as if a waterskin had been thrown and burst against the rock wall.

The party gathered around Domo, all eyes focused on the gory improbable scene before them.

"Domo," Kryger whispered, his voice awestruck, "how did you—"

"I didn't," the thief cut him off. "This is what I found. I do not understand where it came from or how this came to pass."

Bellator stepped closer to the giant stone. "How can this be?" he asked. "This boulder is unlike any I've ever—"

Then the boulder opened its eyes.

CHAPTER 28

"Rocks don't have eyes!" Truck shouted. "How can a rock open eyes it doesn't have?" He was smiling, but he frowned a little in disbelief too.

"Now hold on. Hold on," Charlie said. He went to the cooler and pulled out a Mountain Dew. When he sat down again, he said, "It might be enchanted."

"Does it have googly eyes?" Toff laughed. "Remember the googly eyes we glued onto rocks in second grade?" He looked at John. "It doesn't look stupid like that, does it?"

John shook his head. "No. No googly eyes. They kind of look like rock, too. They're not white and watery like other creatures. They're obviously eyes, but…just made of rock."

"No other colors?" Nick asked.

"Nope. Same as the rest of it. It kind of looks like a giant potato standing on end but not as round; it's maybe nine feet tall."

Nick sat forward and looked at Truck. "I assume since it's alive it killed the hobgoblin, right? We think it somehow moves itself and wasn't thrown, right?"

Truck nodded. "That's what I think, yeah."

"So, it's dangerous."

"To hobgoblins," Levi added. "So far it's only looking at us."

They all turned to John, who shrugged. He wasn't going to say anything. Then they talked among themselves again.

"Should we attack it before it has a chance to start moving again?" Nick asked.

"Maybe," Truck said. "If it's a spell though, it might not really be a rock. What if it's the spirit of someone who's been cast into the boulder?"

"That would be weird," Toff said. "I've never heard of a spell like that."

"You're only sixth level," Truck said.

"Yeah, but I still read ahead. The *Players Handbook* doesn't have anything like that."

"Sometimes they put new spells and monsters in dungeons," Truck said.

"So, it could be a full-on monster," Nick said.

"I think we should attack it," Toff offered. "It could be a guard, set to not allow anyone beyond this point."

"But the hobgoblins came from here," Truck said.

"With a prisoner," Charlie said. His eyes got big. "Maybe the prisoners are this way. It's a prison guard."

"But if that's true, the hobgoblins were taking a prisoner *out*," said Truck. "Why wouldn't the guard have stopped them?"

"It's a rock," argued Nick. "It can't be that smart. Maybe because the hobgoblin was running it thought he was trying to escape. When we met them, they were all walking."

"I think we need a break," John said, interrupting the players. He laid his Dungeon Masters screen over the adventure booklet and stood up. "I need to take a leak. And then I need to talk to Nick."

"Nick's in trouble! Nick's in trouble!" Truck, Charlie, and Levi sang. They all laughed.

When John came back into the garage his friends were tossing ice cubes to one another from the cooler. When he saw John, Charlie said, "We need to put an AC unit in here."

John nodded his agreement, knowing his mom would just shake her head at the expense of an air conditioner. The tiny garage had no insulation and seemed to absorb and retain the outside heat. The fans helped, but it was a phenomenon worthy of a magic-user's help. "Nick," he said and tilted his head. Nick got up and followed him outside.

"What's up?" Nick asked. He crossed his arms and leaned against the corner of the house.

It was just after nine at night and not even twilight. John looked at Nick and remembered what Truck had told him about their Californian refugee. He didn't want Nick to think he was being kicked out of the D&D group. "Er, this is weird because I don't like to pull you guys out one by one, but I need to tell you what the rock is because Bellator is a dwarf, and he knows."

Nick pushed away from the house and put his hands in his pockets. "Oh. Okay. Cool."

John led Nick away from the garage so the others wouldn't hear. They turned at the sidewalk and leaned on the 1971 station wagon Nick's uncle had traded a rifle for so his nephew could drive to and from school. It was originally sky blue but now looked like it had spent its life outside on the run from car washes, Turtle Wax, and mechanics. The radio antenna had been replaced with a clothes hanger held on with tape and wire, and a crack traveled like a river on a map across the length of the windshield.

"So," John started, his heartbeat coming down, "as a dwarf, Bellator will have heard stories about rock creatures."

"Why?"

"Because dwarves are miners. They live under mountains and know all about rock."

Nick nodded and John continued. "Bellator isn't a miner, but he still knows the stories. You believe that the boulder creature is called a *galeb duhr.*[1] To you it's a legend, told around dinner tables and story times. You don't want to attack it. Bellator will be very against fighting it. He thinks he can talk to it, even. Okay?"

There was nothing in the adventure booklet or *Monster Manual II* where galeb duhr and dwarves were described as friends. Nor was there any hint of dwarves being aware of

[1]Galeb duhr are large (8'–12' tall) boulder-like creatures with two appendages that act as both hands and feet. They are highly intelligent and can animate the rocks around them. *Monster Manual II* (Lake Geneva, WI: TSR, 1983), 68.

the rock creatures. John had simply decided the party was too focused on fighting; they just had two battles in a short amount of time and seemed bloodthirsty. The *Alchemist's Bane* booklet did say that if the party tried to communicate, the galeb duhr

was highly intelligent, neutral in its alignment, and depending on what the party wanted, was likely to enter into discussion. John had simply decided to make it easier for dwarves since they dealt with rock as miners. Seemed logical anyway. Plus, as the Dungeon Master, he could do that!

Nick stared at his feet, a frown creasing his forehead. He tilted his head back and forth like he was talking to himself but didn't say anything out loud.

"Dude," John said.

Nick jerked his head up. "Yeah. Okay, I get it. I wanna talk to it. How do I know what to say?"

"Just say something like, 'Hello. Do you speak dwarf? My name is Bellator.' Something like that. Just make sure you tell me you're going to speak in the dwarf language. After you get going, ask Truck what you should talk with the galeb duhr about. They'll all want to get in on it."

"Okay. Yeah. Let's do this."

When everyone was seated around the plywood table again and John had set up the Dungeon Masters screen, Truck said, "I believe we were about to break this big rock in two." He looked at Toff. "Does Xan have any spells that deal with rocks?"

"Wait a minute," Nick said. He pulled his chair closer to the table and drummed a quick beat with his pencil. "I think we should try and talk to it. It's just looking at us, so why not?"

"What?" Levi scoffed. "Diplomacy from Mr. Attack It?"

Nick smiled out the side of his mouth. He always played fighter characters who swung a sword, thrust a dagger, or threw a hammer first, then tried to figure out what was going on. It might be why Bellator was the sixth character he'd created since he started playing.

Truck looked at Nick then at John. The Dungeon Master's face was as blank as a mask, which told him plenty. "Right," Truck said. "What have you got in mind?"

"I just want to say 'Hi' or something."

Truck's eyes narrowed and John decided to step in. "Bellator grew up hearing stories of fabled stone beings," he said. "All dwarves know the stories but few, especially dwarves who aren't miners, have ever seen one. So, Bellator believes this may be one of those."

"Yeah," Nick agreed. "What he said."

Truck smiled. Dungeon Masters didn't usually separate a player from the group unless it was about something unique to the character. "Got it. Do your stuff then. Let's see if this rock can talk."

"I think since dwarves know about the rock people," Nick said, "Bellator will speak dwarvish. He looks at the rock creature and says—in the dwarf language— 'Hello. My name is Bellator. Can you understand me?'"

John took a drink from his can of root beer. He liked to make the players wait for answers. It helped build suspense. Then he said, "Below the eyes of the boulder, a crack opens wider and becomes a mouth." He paused again and passed a photocopy of the *Monster Manual II* picture of a galeb duhr to Truck. To Nick, John asked, "I assume you're going to tell everyone what the creature says if it answers you?"

"Yeah," Nick said. "Obviously."

It was obvious to Nick that he would share the conversation with the other players, but it was one of those situations that needed defining. John remembered a dungeon Truck had run where he'd had to have a lot of private sideline conversations with Charlie because his thief character, Domo, had a few secret ulterior motives the rest of the players couldn't know about. Passing notes to one another like junior high lovebirds created too many distractions so they'd gone outside and basically played through an entire section of the dungeon where Domo was separated from the group and couldn't reveal what had transpired after they came back inside. John and the others didn't like it—neither did Truck—but it's what the circumstances required.

Nick's situation was similar in that the conversation between his character and the creature was in a language only known to them. Nick could make the choice to keep it to himself, but it certainly wouldn't be in the spirit of the game. John had to ask.

"'Yes, I understand,' the rock replies in dwarvish," John said. "Its voice is deep and gurgly. It's like a river of oil, and even deeper than…that singer women like, really deep voice…"

"Barry White," Toff said.

"Yeah," said John. "Him. Super deep voice that kind of gurgles like thick oil." There was nothing in the *Dungeons & Dragons* materials that described the voice of the galeb duhr, but it's how John imagined a big rock creature would sound.

"I ask him if he has a name, and if he is one of the rock creatures dwarves hear about when they grow up," Nick said.

John was on his own and winging the exchange. There wasn't anything in the printed material to guide him except that, depending on the questions, the galeb duhr would inform the party of the best way across the chasm and where they might find Bohz Grauer. It gave a rough idea of how the rock creature felt about the gray dwarf and what was happening now, a little history of the mine, and its name. Everything else was up to the DM and their imagination.

"'My name is Munt,'" John said, speaking for the boulder. "'We call ourselves *galeb duhr* as you call yourself *dwarf*, but I do not know if it is we you learn about as young ones."

"Now what?" Nick asked, looking around the table at his teammates.

"Ask him if he killed the hobgoblin," Levi suggested.

"It's kind of obvious he did," said Charlie. "Why even ask?"

"To see if he's honest. Then we can ask why and what he thinks of us."

"That sounds good," agreed Truck.

So, Nick asked. John thought for a moment and then in a strangled voice said, "'Yes. I ended the hobgoblin.'"

"Dude," Truck admonished. "Seriously, you sound like the Terminator trying to grunt one out."

John feigned hurt feelings with puppy dog eyes while his friends laughed. He never was good at mimicking voices.

Nick got them back on track by telling John, "Bellator asks Munt why he killed the hobgoblin."

"'Was he a friend of yours?'" John returned, his voice his own again.

"No," Nick said.

"'Then why are you concerned?'"

Nick looked uneasily at Truck, but Toff said, "Just like Levi said, tell him we're not sure what he's going to do with us."

Charlie smiled. "I don't think there's a lot a rock can do with anyone *except* squish 'em."

Nick looked at John and said, "I tell him we were just surprised and we're not sure what's going to happen now."

John smiled. He knew Nick would get the hang of it. "Munt tells you that he's lived a long time and is not in the habit of killing for sport. The hobgoblins and others in the mine right now are vile creatures whose evil ways must be stopped."

"Ask him if he knows who Bohz Grauer is," Truck said to Nick. "If he does, ask him how we can find him."

Munt did know the wicked gray dwarf and where he spent most of his time. The rock creature told them it would be difficult to get there though because of the chasm; it separated the two sides with only one way across, a rickety bridge of ancient wooden planks left over from when the dwarves used them for tables. "'Most come from the up-and-down platform,'" John finished.

The players looked at one another. "We must have missed that," Truck said. "I don't know what he means."

"We passed a few rooms and passages," Charlie said. "Probably something we can go back and find or try our luck with the bridge."

"Going back will take too long," Toff said. "We'd have to go to every single spot."

Levi agreed. "It would be like starting over," he said. He pointed to a rough circle he'd drawn on the map and traced his finger along the passage. "The hobgoblins had a prisoner here which means they came over the bridge, right?"

"Let's go for it," Truck said. "I don't want to go back up and look for something that goes up and down."

"That's what she said," Nick snickered.

"Wait a minute," Charlie said loudly. "What Levi just said—there was the prisoner. We forgot about him. Where is he?"

The boys looked at each other like they'd just lost an easy bet. "Shit!" Truck yelled. "I can't believe I forgot about him!"

"You?" Charlie admonished. "I threw him a dagger so he'd fight, and I forgot about him."

"Well, a big talking rock is an attention getter," Levi said.

John was smiling when Truck turned and told him that Kryger was looking around for the forgotten prisoner of the hobgoblins. "Where is he?" he asked.

As Dungeon Master, John had a dilemma. The prisoner had a key piece of information about the artifact. He'd found a clue among the rubble that revealed the secret of the amulet. In the story provided in the dungeon, the prisoner was caught destroying what he'd found and was being taken to the orcs on the upper level to be tortured and questioned. But the party had basically forgotten about him and had focused on the galeb duhr known as Munt. Munt had information for the party as well, but not as valuable as what the prisoner had. The question for John was: Should the prisoner be there, waiting to thank his rescuers, or did he make a break for freedom as soon as the party had dashed after Domo?

John shook his head. "He's nowhere to be seen," he told Truck.

"Shit! You're killin' me, Brewer!"

John smiled and shrugged.

"Nothing we can do about it now," Toff said.

"Maybe we should go back and look for him," Levi suggested.

Truck met John's eyes. "Don't bother," he said with a smirk. "The dude's long gone. Let's just focus on the galeb duhr." He picked up the photocopied picture and waved it at the others.

"Okay," Nick said. "So, what do I ask now?"

"How do we find Bohz Grauer," Toff said.

John, after Nick relayed what his character asked of the very real and alive rock creature, nodded and said, "Munt leans forward and stands up. The crushed remains of the hobgoblin, mostly unrecognizable meat, guts, and blood, slides to the floor and the back of the galeb duhr is gory with the fresh kill."

"Cool," Nick said.

The boys all looked at him like he'd just farted in class.

"What'd I say?" Nick asked

"Munt walks north," John went on. "You can feel each step he takes because the ground shakes. Standing, Munt is about nine feet tall and maybe five feet across at his widest point. He doesn't have separate arms and legs; as he starts around the corner into the eastern passage, he lifts a foot he's been walking on and points. 'The bridge is this way,' he says, and then he disappears around the corner."

"Are we going to trust a rock that sat on a hobgoblin?" Levi asked.

"Do we have a choice?" countered Toff.

"Sure," said Truck. "We could turn around and head back up and look for the *up-and-down platform*. But I think we should follow him. He killed the hobgoblin, not us, and he's obviously intelligent."

"Yeah," said Nick. "Let's keep going."

"We follow him into the passage," Truck told John, "but we're ready. Ya know?"

Levi said, "Wait! What about the torch? Lit or unlit?"

"Good call," said Truck. "Put it out."

John nodded. "Munt is standing about fifteen feet away to one side of the passage. Beyond him is a hollow darkness, and the floor and walls around him seemed to have disappeared."

"Must be the chasm," Charlie said. "Do we see a bridge?"

"You see what you assume to be a bridge," John said. "It's too dark to see any detail."

"We'll go up and stand behind the big rock dude," Truck said to John. "Kryger asks, 'Is this bridge safe?'"

"'Not for Munt,' he says. 'I am too heavy, but others have used it. Not often though. I suggest you cross one at a time.'"

"Once we cross the bridge," Charlie said, "where will we find the gray dwarf warlord?"

John glanced at Charlie to make sure he was asking on behalf of his character and not just talking to the group of players. Then he said, "Munt lifts his foot and points across the chasm. The bridge in front of you goes straight across a narrow point, due east. Munt is pointing to the southeast. At the other end, the two elves and the dwarf see a rock wall. 'Your gray dwarf is on the other side,' Munt tells you."

CHAPTER 29

Truck looked around the table. "Everybody ready to cross the bridge? Who wants to go first?"

"I need to take a leak," Nick said, and stood up.

"Don't piss all over the garage this time," John said. "We can hear you."

Nick snickered and ducked out the door.

"Break time!" Levi said and lunged for the chips.

"Hey, check this out," John said. He laid the Dungeon Masters screen flat, leaned on the table, and told them about Henley and Paul's argument.

"Statler's getting a lot of shit," Charlie said. "People don't believe he left before the accident. They think he was there but he froze up and just let Dave die."

"Well, if he froze, he *couldn't* do anything," John said.

"You know what I mean. Plus, if that's true, he lied about it."

"My dad thinks Statler's a coward," Levi said quietly. "Just won't admit it. My mom thinks he panicked and didn't know what to do. Either way, I don't get why he doesn't say something."

Truck stood and leaned over the table and grabbed a handful of potato chips. "Down at the diner people are saying he's already lost a lot of business."

Nick had returned to his seat and had the chair leaning back. "This Statler is who again? Your farmer guy's son-in-law?"

Toff nodded. "Yeah. He's married to Jim's daughter, Joanna."

"Why don't people believe him?" Nick asked.

"People he works with or saw later that day say he was acting weird, before anyone knew what happened to Dave. That's what I heard anyway," Truck said.

Nick shrugged. "Maybe he's not a coward. Maybe he thought Carlson and his wife were doing the deed."

Charlie snorted. "Who are you now? Magnum, P.I.?"

The garage was quiet as the boys thought about that. Then Levi said, "Do you think he killed Dave?"

"Why are you whispering?" Nick asked. "Look, you guys knew this dude more than me, but where I come from it wouldn't be a big surprise."

John and Toff looked at each other.

"I think we're freaking out Brewer and the Toff-meister," Truck said with a smile. "Back to D&D!" He looked at John. "What do you say, Dungeon Master?"

John nodded. "Good idea." He set the Dungeon Masters screen back up. They refocused on the game and the task at hand, adjusting their chairs and checking the map, their notes, and their character sheets. "You were asking about crossing the bridge."

Truck smiled and nodded. "Yeah! Who wants to go first?"

Charlie leaned over the table and studied the map. "I'll bet there's some secret to get across safely and the prisoner knew it," he said. "Damn. I wish we would have remembered him." He looked at John, who raised his eyebrows but offered no consolation.

"Should we try to rig some sort of safety rope?" Levi asked.

"How far across is it?" Truck asked John.

"Hard to tell accurately in the darkness," John said. "There is some light from the workers' torches below, so you guess thirty to forty feet."

"And everything is rock everywhere, right?" Nick asked.

"Yep. You're talking among yourselves about the bridge," John continued, "when you feel several tremors in the ground. Munt has taken a few steps back. He raises one of his feet-slash-hands and says, 'Good luck.'"

"He's leaving?" Truck asked, his eyes wide. "Kryger asks him why he's leaving."

"He says he can't cross the bridge. You are going to, so this is goodbye."

"Thanks, Munt," Nick said with a wave.

"I think we're just going to have to go for it," Toff said. "The hobgoblins came across it just a while ago and they were bigger than us."

"Hobgoblins!?" a familiar voice screeched. The boys jumped when they heard it and looked up. Paulette Dickerson, wearing a lime-green shoulder-padded blazer, her hair rigid with another can of hairspray, stood in the open doorway of the garage. She stepped inside without an invitation. "I've caught you practicing evil again! Hobgoblins now."

Her toady, Aaron Evans, slinked in and stepped to the side of the door. His face was blank when he looked at the boys, like they were things. When he turned his attention to Paulette, though, his eyes widened and he looked like a party devotee at a political rally, awed by the next candidate promising to save the world. And buying it.

John laid his Dungeon Masters screen over the top of the adventure booklet and his notes. "Now what? I thought the police told you that you weren't allowed to come here."

"What are you hiding?" Paulette asked, ignoring him. "I'll have it, whatever it is. You boys don't understand the power you're messing with. This must stop!"

John stared at Truck, who rolled his eyes. John widened his eyes at his best friend then cocked his head toward the house. Truck nodded and got up.

"Where do you think you're going?" Paulette demanded.

Nick raised a finger and said, "Um…"

"You shut up," Paulette fired at him. "I wasn't speaking to you." She looked back at Truck and demanded, "Don't you know how disrespectful it is to get up and leave when someone is talking?"

"How about when someone barges in uninvited?" Charlie mumbled, but no one heard him except Toff.

"I gotta pee," Truck said and sidestepped past her to the door.

Aaron Evans straightened out of his slouch and moved to block the door. He wiped a rivulet of sweat off his cheek and crossed his arms.

John stood up, followed by the rest of the boys. There was a length of two-by-four between John and Nick that both boys had spotted, but Aaron relented when Truck stood to his full 5'10", lost his usual smile, and didn't back down. Truck went out the door and into the house.

"Do none of you care what you're doing?" Paulette asked. She was shocked at the teenagers' lack of concern. "Why do you tempt fate by calling upon devils and demons?"

John rolled his eyes. "We are not calling upon—"

"What in the hell is going on here?" Evie Brewer's voice rang out from the door. She pronounced *the* as *thee*, and John knew his mom was pissed.

Paulette, who had her back to the door, flinched and whirled around.

Evie's eyes were round, her face was red, and her hands were balled into fists. "Weren't you told to stay away from here?"

Paulette stood proud and pulled down her blazer. "These boys are tempting a power they can't possibly comprehend."

Evie shook her head. "I've asked two questions so far and haven't been answered. This is *my* home, you know."

"If their parents aren't willing to step in," Paulette said with an accusatory stare at Evie, "then I must. Someone needs to save them from themselves and keep them from spreading their evil activities."

Evie's eyes bulged. "You sanctimonious, egotistical..."

All the boys finished Evie's sentence in their own heads with *bitch!* Evie, however, took a deep breath and forced her shaking hands open.

"You need to leave." She said it slowly and quietly, like a volcano taking a slow, deep breath before erupting. "You, too, Aaron. I don't know why you're even here. Neither of you are welcome."

"Not without these books!" Paulette said, waving her hand at the D&D manuals scattered around the table.

The boys all reached protectively for their books, dice, and papers. Truck pushed his way into the garage and stacked his books and character sheet next to John's.

"No, you can't take anything, Paulette," Evie said. "Just leave. Get out."

Paulette's face turned panicky. Her mouth turned down at the corners, her eyebrows arched into a worried frown, and her eyes looked like golf balls under mounds of mascara—not in anger like Evie's, but from fear. "No!" she shouted. "You don't understand!" She turned away from Evie and gripped the edge of the plywood table with both hands. With a guttural scream the boys would later use to describe the sound of the hideous night hag from the first *Monster Manual*, Paulette heaved and threw the table up on its edge.

D&D books, Levi's map, character sheets, note papers, pencils, dice, bowls and bags of chips, soda cans—everything on the table was suddenly scattered about the garage. The table slid off the sawhorses rather than come straight back down and fell on Nick and Levi. Everyone was surprised by Paulette's rampage and the two boys were caught off guard. The sheet of plywood slid into their shins and they both crumpled to the ground.

"Are you insane!?" Evie shouted.

Paulette spun around, her helmet of hair intact but for a few flyaway strands. "*I* am the only one here who is thinking clearly!" she screamed.

"I don't think that's quite true," a deep voice said.

Everyone turned toward the garage door. Officer Wayne Phillips was standing on the threshold.

"Got your call from the station, Truck. I was just a couple blocks away. What's going on here?" He walked into the garage, his thumbs hooked into his belt, a guy over for a beer.

"Paulette Dickerson is trespassing. Again," Evie answered. "She flipped over the table, which hit Nick and Levi. Are you okay, boys?"

They nodded even though they were still pinned on the ground, and nobody had moved the plywood.

Evie looked at Paulette with cold eyes but spoke to the policeman behind her. "I want her off my property and properly punished this time."

Wayne stepped into the garage and looked around. He focused on John. "Is this true?" he asked.

"Yes, sir," John replied. "They just barged in. Again."

"Paulette?" Wayne asked, turning to face her.

Her eyes had gone from wild and enraged to pleading. She was still breathing hard. "These boys must be saved! Don't you see? What they're doing is immoral. It's dangerous. They will spread evil through the school and into our community! It must stop! Don't you watch the news? Doesn't anyone pay attention?"

Wayne told Aaron to stand next to Paulette and then said, "Paulette Dickerson and Aaron Evans, I'm placing you both under arrest for trespassing." He handcuffed Paulette's left wrist to Aaron's right as he said it. "Paulette, you will receive additional charges: destruction of property and assault."

"What?" she asked incredulously. "I didn't hit anyone!"

Wayne looked at Nick and Levi. "Can you other boys get this table off your friends? I'll be back in a second to make sure they're okay."

The boys lifted the table back onto the sawhorses then gathered their scattered gaming materials. Phillips took his prisoners out to the car, and Evie sat in a chair with a worried frown on her face.

"You okay, Mom?" John asked.

"This is going to cause a stir," she said. "You know how small towns are."

"She started it," Charlie said.

"She's a psycho," said Truck. "And what's with that Aaron Evans guy? What a robot."

"I know," John agreed, "he doesn't say a word. I think he's the one with problems."

"You guys need to keep that kind of talk to yourselves," Evie said. "I guarantee you a lot of people are going to be on her side and if they hear you talking like that, it will only encourage them."

"That's not fair," Nick said.

Evie looked at him and nodded. "I know." She took a deep breath and let it out slowly. "It'll work out though."

Officer Phillips stepped back into the garage. "How are you guys doing?" he asked Nick and Levi.

"Just a couple of scrapes," Nick said. "I've had worse."

Levi came around the table and stuck out his left leg. A rivulet of blood ran down his shin and around his ankle. "Do you need to photograph it or anything?" he asked hopefully. "Will she get in more trouble since I'm bleeding?"

"Oh, Levi," Evie said and stood up. "I'll get a bandage." She turned and went back into the house.

Phillips knelt for a closer look at Levi's injury. "Doesn't look serious," he said. "No stitches required. I'll make sure to put it in my report, but I don't think it will make things worse for her."

Levi frowned. "Bummer."

Phillips patted him on the shoulder. "Sorry, Levi. But you and Mr. Meyers here will probably be contacted. John too. Honestly though, I don't know how far this thing will go."

Chapter 30

Breakfast Sunday morning at the Brewers' was quiet. When John came down the stairs, he watched his mom sip her coffee, nibble toast, and poke at the small pile of eggs on her plate. She stared at the newspaper laid out on the table.

When John pulled out a chair and sat down, she blinked. "You're up awfully early. You don't have to be on the road for another couple hours or so."

John yawned and crossed his arms on the table. "I know. We didn't stay up after we found everything. It took forever to find all the dice. Charlie's four-sided was actually in the cooler. I guess the lid never got shut."

"Elbows. Do you want some breakfast?"

John slid his elbows off the table and stood up. "Just toast. I'll get it." He went into the kitchen and dropped two slices of bread in the toaster. "Wait a minute," he said. "I smell bacon."

"In the oven," Evie told him.

"Can I have a cup of coffee too?" John asked.

Evie stared at him and raised an eyebrow. "Um...sure. You might want to put a little milk and sugar in it," she said. "Not too much of either."

"Okay."

John came out of the kitchen with two pieces of buttered toast, eight slices of board-stiff bacon, and a cup of coffee, the color of which matched the fluff inside a 3 Musketeers chocolate bar. He laid four pieces of bacon across each piece of toast, folded one in half, and took a bite.

"You sure you don't want eggs?" Evie asked.

John shook his head. He chewed, swallowed, and slurped his coffee. He looked at the brew in the cup for a moment and then asked, "Have you been thinking about last night?"

"I'm guessing everyone in town is talking about it," Evie said. "Terry and Sandy across the street were probably on the phone before Paulette was in the car. This one isn't going to just fade away."

"What's the big deal?" John asked. "She deserves it."

"You're right, she does deserve it. Between us and Paulette, she committed a crime and she'll be punished. If it was that simple—and it should be—that would be great. But it's going to blow up. It's a small town, you know how things are. Even worse at school, I'm sure. People will take sides. Trespassing isn't a major crime, so—"

"But she flipped the table over onto Nick and Levi!" John said, spraying crumbs.

"True. And people will say, again, not a big deal. Nothing was broken and no one was…seriously hurt. All those people who go to that church are going to side with her. Jim Henley included."

"I know," John said. He wanted to tell her how Henley had been treating him since the last incident but didn't. It wasn't worth getting into because this time was going to be worse. Much worse.

"I'll be honest with you, John. Paulette is not going to spend any time in jail. She'll get a slap on the wrist and be told to stop being a nuisance. What's really going to happen is people in this town are going to judge us for themselves. You're going to see people look at you; some will treat you differently. The same will happen to me and it's going to happen to all the boys who were here last night."

John knew his mom was right. "So what's the point then? If she isn't going to get in trouble, then she'll just do it again."

"And if she does, we'll call the police again."

"Seems stupid," John mumbled around the last bite of his bacon sandwich.

"It is. She'll get in trouble, but not very much. As bad as it sounds, rules and laws get bent all the time, especially in small towns. Believe me, if that table had hit one of those boys in the head and sent them to the hospital, it would be a different story. We're in the right here, John. Remember that, okay? When you know you're doing the right thing, it doesn't matter what anyone else thinks."

It was already eighty-six degrees as John rolled over the top of Round Barn Hill at a quarter to noon. Hot air blew in through the rolled-down windows as he glanced to his right. The old round barn had been built in 1915, and even though it listed to the south and looked like it would collapse in a cloud of dust if a crow landed on the right spot, the flaked white paint and rock foundation were a welcome and pride-inducing sight for anyone from the Palouse.

It was also the place John knew he had to gun it. At the top of the rise, he reached back and turned the volume knob up on his hot-wired boom box and pressed the gas pedal to the floor. Night Ranger's anthem "(You Can Still) Rock in America" easily overpowered the desperate little 1600cc engine.

The Bug gained speed going down the hill over the black-and-gray two-lane highway that undulated among the great mounds of the Palouse. From the air John imagined his car looked like a scarab running over the back of a giant snake in the desert. At the bottom of the hill the speedometer read 68 mph. Halfway up the next rise it had dropped to forty. At the top the Volkswagen was struggling to maintain twenty. John kept the gas pedal jammed to the floor and was bouncing in his seat, forcing himself not to shift down. "Come on!" he shouted. He pounded the steering wheel to the beat. "Come on, baby! We've done it before! Woo!"

The car crawled over the rise just as it started to gutter, and John was forced to push in the clutch and shift down. The Bug had always made the climb—that's what gears were for, after all—but it was fun to see if he could make it without shifting at all. He gave it some gas and sped down the hill. Round Barn Hill was the steepest climb he'd need to make and knew he could now finish the drive to Henley's at a good clip. At least as good a clip as the car could make.

Toff's little Datsun pickup was parked in front of the bunkhouse and John pulled up alongside. He rolled up the windows and took his two duffel bags inside. Toff was sitting on his bed.

"Hey," John said. "What's going on? What are you staring at? Please don't say a snake got inside." He tossed his bags on his bed and looked at the spot on the floor his roommate was staring at.

"Nothing," Toff said. "I just finished putting my stuff away and sat down."

John opened the drawers of his dresser and started to transfer his clothes from the duffels. "Did you tell your mom and dad about last night?"

"They knew about it before I got home," Toff said.

John shook his head and stuffed a handful of underwear wrapped inside a T-shirt into a drawer. He didn't know why he was embarrassed; everyone wore underwear and his wasn't any different than theirs. It was kind of the same with the boy's locker room and bathrooms. Why did everyone think guys were fine showering together? He knew it wasn't that big of a deal, and obviously the school wasn't going to pay for fifty separate shower stalls, but it was the carefree attitude the coaches took. Meanwhile he and his friends were walking around looking at the ceiling so they wouldn't get caught accidentally looking at someone's schlong. "There are no secrets in Weston," John said.

Toff nodded but didn't look at John. "Yeah. My mom was freaking out. Our neighbors know you and I are friends and play D&D. Now she's worried about what they'll think about Paulette getting arrested at your house while I was there."

John frowned. "Why? Who cares what they think?"

Toff shrugged. "I know, but my mom does. I don't know why. You should have seen her, though. She was pacing around the house and talking to herself. She's upset because I was involved even though I wasn't really. You know?"

"It's not like that banshee Paulette is going to go to jail. I just don't get what your mom is freaking out about. Whose side is she on anyway? Did you tell her what happened?"

"Of course. I felt like I was being interrogated. It doesn't matter."

"My mom is worried too," John said. "She told me this morning to expect a lot of crap because it's a small town and people are going to make their own judgment. Henley is going to be pissed again too. It was bad enough the first time. We'll just have to ignore it."

"I can't play anymore."

John turned around and stared at Toff, his mouth open. "What? Are you serious?"

Toff's shoulders were rounded; he hung his head like a sad flower.

"That's bullshit!" John erupted. "How is that fair?"

"You know how she is. Maybe if we don't play for a couple of weeks, she'll forget about it," Toff whined.

"No way! We didn't do anything wrong! Why should we get punished because that Tammy Faye Baker wannabe went bonkers on us? Not cool, Toff. That's *not* cool." John turned away and neither boy said anything while he shoved the rest of his clothes in the drawers and slammed them shut. "What would she do if you just played anyway? What about your dad? What's he say?"

Toff rolled his eyes. "'Best to listen to your mother, Kristoff,'" he said in a deep voice that sounded as close to his father as a VW Bug sounds like a '68 Firebird.

John chuckled. "You're about as good at voices as me. I say you play anyway."

The rumble of Blaine's flatbed killed their talk, and they went outside. Dust hung in the air, kicked up by the truck's tires, and they saw Blaine already walking toward the grain trucks.

"Are we starting a new field today?" Toff asked Blaine as they ran to catch up with the field hand.

Blaine shook his head as he put his water jug in the cab of his truck. "We probably have a couple more hours on the Glenwood acreage. Up to Jim where we go from there. He hasn't told me yet."

Toff frowned. "That's weird. He always tells you first, doesn't he?"

Blaine swung the door of his truck shut. "Yeah, he does. And I heard plenty this morning, but it was about *you two*." He stabbed his finger at both of their chests. "You *know* Jim and Patricia go to One Vision, right?"

John rolled his eyes and nodded. "Yeah. We know."

"That's right," Blaine continued. "So, I'm going to do two favors for you guys. First, I'll go inside and get your water jugs out of the freezer and bring them out. Second, I'm telling you right now, stay out of Jim's way, out of his sight, and don't say anything. Just click your okays on the CB. Right?"

As Blaine strode across the gravel to the main house, John and Toff looked at each other, unsure of what to say. Finally, John said, "This is crazy." He climbed into his truck and sat behind the wheel with the door open.

The Glenwood area fields took the rest of the afternoon and into the early evening to finish cutting, not the couple hours Blaine had predicted. During that time John and Toff were ignored, treated like they didn't belong, as if they didn't exist, were only another part of the truck they were driving. Whenever Henley came close in his combine, he stared ahead as if they were nothing more than weeds among the grain in the field. When he was fully loaded, he'd drive in, drop his grain in the bed of the truck, then move out without a call on the CB. It was up to Toff and John to see if their truck was full or not.

John ended up with the last load of the evening. The sky had passed the fiery glow of sunset and formed a deep ocean of waves and gunmetal breakers among the clouds. The fields on each side of the two-lane highway were a contrast of Mother Nature's whims, the bony stubble on the right and the buttery tufts of uncut grain on the left. The blacktop of Dry Creek Road was the only thing between them.

John drove easy; no rush, but he didn't want to be dumping his grain at Bullhead Flats in the dark, either. It was after nine at night and he had the windows rolled down, washing the cab with the cooler air. It was still light, but if someone reported seeing him driving without headlamps Henley would blow a fuse. John leaned forward and pulled the lights on. The twin beams barely cast a pale aura across the road but caught on something in the middle of John's lane. As he got closer, he could see it was a running shoe, red and blue, that must have fallen or had been thrown out of a pickup bed.

The truck John was driving wasn't a semi, but he still sat high above the road. He wondered if his aim would be thrown off by the height, or if he'd be able to run over the shoe without really trying. The back wheels were duallies so that should make it easier if he missed with the front tire. He was on a straight stretch and there were no cars ahead; he checked his side mirrors, no one behind. He eased the truck over so he was just over the center line and maneuvered to run over the shoe with his right tire.

The truck weighed about two tons unloaded. The grain in the back was at least a ton in weight if not more. John didn't feel anything as he passed over the shoe in the road and eased the truck back into the proper lane. *Missed*, he thought.

However, the image in the side-view mirror was one of carnage. The running shoe, fabric and foam rubber, had been annihilated under the mass and churning force of the big tires. *Annihilated* was probably too much, John thought. From what he could tell the shoe was much flatter and the sole looked like it was flapping freely at one end. He pumped his fist and laughed out loud. "That's a direct hit! Woo!"

It was still light out as John pulled into the Henley farm, but the sky was a deeper blue, a shade of mystery, danger. Magic hour. Toff and Blaine were sitting near the big oak tree; Henley and Dale were at the picnic table along with Mrs. Henley. Paul and his pickup were gone.

John parked his truck, refilled his water jug and put it in the freezer inside the house, then joined the others, sitting with Toff and Blaine. It was a kind of evening ritual to gather in the yard and enjoy the cool air while resting, discussing the day. Leftovers from dinner were on the picnic table and John was hungry, but Blaine's warning still echoed from earlier in the day. It didn't help that Henley had yet to acknowledge his arrival. He was being ignored.

"Has he talked to you today?" John whispered to Toff.

Toff glanced at the picnic table then whispered, "He said my name when I almost ran into him coming out of the house. He sounded like Principal Jennings when he sees you in the hall. You know, *Toff*—like that—and then stares at you until you go into a classroom or around a corner."

John nodded. *Whatever*, he thought. *I can ignore him too.* "How long have you been here?" he asked out loud. "Did I miss anything?"

Toff shook his head and waved his hands at himself. "Haven't even showered yet," he said. He was covered in dust, darker where it had caked near his temples where sweat slid out from underneath his hat. His jeans puffed clouds of dust when he slapped his thighs and his T-shirt belonged in a detergent commercial.

John looked at himself. As far as their clothes were concerned, they could have been twins.

"What took you so long?" Toff asked.

John shrugged. "I didn't know I did. Maybe a bit slower dumping at night, I guess. Oh, but check this out." He described his precision attack on the hapless running shoe in the middle of the road and how it had been mangled beneath the weight of the truck.

Blaine shook his head as the boys laughed. "Wow, you two are easily entertained."

The laughter stopped when Henley stepped in front of them. "You did what?" he asked. "You ran over a shoe?"

John stared at him but didn't answer even though Henley was right there asking a direct question. The boss didn't seem to notice, though.

Henley went on. "You deliberately aimed for it and ran it over? Why?"

"Uh..." was all John could utter. To him it was obvious: If there's something like a shoe in the road and you're driving a big-ass truck, you run it over. Period. It's not like it was a deer or a chair—which he had seen in the middle of the road once. A recliner even.

"What if it had been full of nails?" Henley screeched. His face was red, pinched.

John frowned in confusion. He glanced at the others who were staring, but at whom or what he couldn't tell. "Nails?" he repeated.

"Yes! Nails! What if someone had filled that shoe with nails and left it in the road for someone to come along and..." He trailed off, exasperated.

"Why would anyone...?" John couldn't even finish the sentence. What was Henley thinking?

"Are you stupid? When you drive my trucks," Henley said, shaking a finger at John, "you don't drive like a fool. Save that for your friends in your garage. Do you understand me? Do you?"

John's eyes were wide as he stared up at the farmer. Henley's eyebrows and forehead dipped into a canyon of anger. Finally, John nodded. Henley shook his head one final time and stomped away into the house.

John looked at Toff, then Blaine, then at Dale and Mrs. Henley. They looked back at him, but it had grown too dark for him to see their expressions, and no one said a word.

CHAPTER 31

The rest of the week was the same. Henley didn't speak to either John or Toff and instead relayed instructions through Blaine like a field marshal. He never said why he was angry, but it could only be because Paulette Dickerson had been arrested. How that was anyone's fault but her own, neither John nor Toff could figure out.

Monday the crew moved to flatter ground and the combines were able to cut more quickly. The temperature was a steady ninety-three degrees by one in the afternoon and John had both windows rolled down as he sat in his truck at the field's edge. The heat enveloped him like a blanket; even with the windows down he couldn't escape it.

For all of Jim Henley's speeches about farming being a noble vocation, driving truck for harvest was boring ninety percent of the time. John fought the urge to fall asleep. He took off his cap and pulled up his shirt to wipe the sweat from his face. He'd need to go to the library in town and find something to read. Henley couldn't begrudge him that. What would be the point of just sitting in the truck staring at the field?

The deep silence, a quiet reserved for nature, was broken by the hum and rumble of a big diesel engine. John looked up and saw two combines coming toward him. They were slow, about thirty-five yards to the left. They were giant alien machines mowing down the forests of earth, careful not to miss anything.

There was a flash, a reflection off eyeglasses in the front cab. Henley was in the lead combine. John sat up, erased the images of alien tanks from his mind, and watched dutifully as the combines slowly came nearer, but they were far enough away that he didn't bother rolling up his windows. There was no breeze, and the chaff and dust shooting out the back of the combines wasn't coming toward him.

As Henley went by, he stared straight ahead, ignoring John and concentrating on the field. Dale was another thirty yards or so out and trailed the boss by twenty seconds. He looked over at John and waved. John had his elbow on the window frame and waved back.

Henley's tinny voice cracked over the radio. "I'm going to pull over," he said. "Take the lead, Dale."

John looked over and saw Dale reach toward his CB inside his cab. Two clicks sounded over the radio in response to Henley as Dale thumbed his mic.

John looked in his side-view mirrors but didn't see Henley's combine. *Probably has to take a leak*, he thought and turned his attention back out the windshield; that wasn't something he wanted to see.

Dale's combine was just passing John's peripheral vision and should have been getting quieter. Instead, the roar of the diesel engine was all around him. It filled the cab, bounced off the dash and the bench seat, it punched John in one ear and then the other.

John looked at his passenger-side mirror and saw two colors: gold field on the bottom, blue sky on the top, as if an artist made two quick strokes with two different paint brushes.

Then he looked at the driver's side mirror.

Henley had driven his combine up behind John and was turning around. He was maneuvering donut style like John had in the swather, to spin the rear end of the combine toward the open window of the truck.

John scrambled to crank up the window but wasn't quick enough. He ducked his head as dirt and chaff shot inside the cab. In seconds he was covered in bits of torn-away seed husks, chunks of shredded wheat stalks, dirt, and dust. John looked like he'd just crawled out of a natural disaster area.

"Hang on," Henley's crisp voice came over the CB. "I'm going to offload here. Hey, was your window open? Make sure that truck's clean before tomorrow morning." He didn't use John's name and John didn't respond with the clicks.

"Ass! Hole!" John yelled at the roof of the cab. "Asshole!"

On Tuesday the temperature climbed to ninety-five degrees and stayed there until six thirty when they broke for dinner. Mrs. Henley had prepared a spread of hot dogs, macaroni and cheese, tossed green salad, and chocolate cake. The hot dogs were wrapped in tin foil the way they were at minor league baseball games, the mac and cheese was still in the pot she'd made it in, but the lid was sealed with more aluminum wrap, and everything else was packed into Tupperware. The cake was in a box from Binna's Bakery. "Too hot to use the oven," Mrs. Henley said with a wink.

Wednesday the temperature bumped up another notch to ninety-six and the radiator hose on Blaine's truck burst. He'd just finished dumping his grain and was pulling away from the silo when a jet of hot steam shot out from beneath the hood of his truck. He radioed his problem over the CB and John answered that he was already on his way there with a load of wheat and would give him a ride back.

The next day the sun beat down a sweltering ninety-eight degrees. Toff drank his entire jug of ice water before lunch and took an extra-long time driving back to the house to refill it. Most of that time he was peeing in the bunkhouse bathroom. Dale burned his hand on the engine housing of his combine when he walked around to take a leak of his own and twisted his ankle on a clot of dirt that had been baked into stone. Paul, who was embarrassed by public urination, even out in the middle of a field, overfilled the jug he had in his cab for just such occasions. But he was unable to stop the flow, sloshed warm piss over his seat and the floor, and even sprayed the windshield of the cab.

Lunch consisted of cold cut sandwiches, potato chips, fruit salad, and popsicles. The popsicles were enjoyed first before they melted from the heat then everyone sat in the shade of Henley's combine. Before he took a bite of his sandwich Henley said, "What is that smell? Did someone run over a coyote?" He looked at Paul as he said it; he knew what it was. Paul had been the last to drive into the lunch circle and climb out of his combine. Everyone saw the golden droplets on the inside of his cab sparkling in the sunshine.

Paul ate as if he hadn't heard Henley. "Paul," Henley barked. "You pissed your pants, didn't you?"

"I did no such thing!" Paul shouted, potato chip crumbs spewing from his mouth.

"If you didn't piss *in* your pants, you pissed *on* them," said Henley. He stared at his son-in-law, a tiger about to pounce on its prey. "Damn it, we all saw your windshield and this heat only makes it smell worse."

"What's your problem? Just get off my case!"

Henley pointed behind Paul. "Go sit by your own combine so the rest of us can eat without getting sick." He said it almost in a whisper and the hair on John's neck stood up.

Paul got up and glared at Henley. "You have no right to talk to me like that, *Dad*. I don't care what you think." He shook his head and stomped over to his combine.

Even though it looked like a fight was brewing, the thought of Paul peeing his pants was the funniest thing to have happened since John started to work on the farm. If he laughed, though, Henley would turn his wrath on him. He coughed out a snort and quickly put a napkin over his mouth to hide his smile. He coughed again, higher pitched like whale song and everyone looked at him.

"Wrong pipe," he choked out. "Sorry."

Henley shook his head as he stared after his son-in-law. "I bet he pissed himself while Dave was screaming for help too."

John didn't feel like laughing after that.

Bullhead Flat on a regular day wasn't anything to look at. It was a storage area, an inland dock beaten down by heavy vehicles and was barren but for a few gasping weeds and buzzing insects. But on a searing, arid day like Friday, it was a wasteland, a savage gorge among shining metal silos that magnified the sun, cooked the earth, and turned the air into a swinging baseball bat that hit head on.

John pushed himself out of the cab, choked on the hot air, and hopped down to the ground. A cloud of dust rose lazily, and he stepped back up onto the truck. He'd forgotten to look for snakes. A quick scan revealed a clear path to the back of the truck where he slid open the chute and watched the grain flow into the auger.

With everything humming, John was already sweating; his hair was painted to his temples and his T-shirt clung to his skin like damp paper. Gravel slid in the soft dirt under his boots as he ambled around to the passenger side of the truck. His water jug was on the floorboard by the door, but it was blocked.

A bull snake. Big enough that Blaine would call it a *big bastard*. "Shit," he muttered.

John took a deep breath, coughed on the thickness of it. He maneuvered the hydraulics to raise the bed then took a step toward the snake. *It's just a snake*, he thought. *Blaine chucked one, for chrissake. He probably threw this one. And it's back. And it's pissed.*

John shook his head and squatted down. He was about five feet from the snake, which just lay there. It didn't move at all, not even a flick of its tongue. He scooted closer. The dry gravel scrunched beneath his boots. *Face my fears. Face my fears.*

"Don't worry, I'm not going to touch you," he said out loud, and scooted within three feet. *Believe me, I don't want to touch you*, he thought. The snake was stretched out, almost perfectly straight. Its eyes were open, but John remembered something about snakes not having eyelids. Was it dead? Did it overheat and die out here?

John leaned over to his left to get a better look at the snake's head and that's when it bolted. In the blink of an eye, it turned into a rubbery S and shot under the truck and out the other side.

"Aagh!" John yelled and fell back on his butt. He jumped up even as his shout reverberated back off the surrounding silos. *Damn snake*, he thought.

CHAPTER 32

Toff Hansen was missing. Not from his home or the bunkhouse, his little white truck wasn't found abandoned with the engine running, there were no ransom notes. It was seven on Saturday evening and Toff wasn't at the Council Chamber ready to play *Dungeons & Dragons*.

"How long do we wait?" Charlie asked. He had his bare feet propped up on Toff's chair like he was enjoying a piña colada on a Caribbean beach. "This is weird. No one's ever been this late before."

"It's only been a half hour," Truck said. He was hunched over in his chair flipping through the latest issue of *Truckin'* magazine.

John said, "I don't think he's coming."

"Oh, come on," Levi crowed. "Give the guy a chance." He was bent over the table and *scritch*ed out a length of tape. He carefully applied it over the edges of two sheets of graph paper to connect his ever-growing map. He looked up and said, "His grandma's probably on the phone or something."

"Seriously?" Nick asked. "Do you all have grandmas?"

Charlie looked at him and frowned, unsure if Nick was serious.

John sighed and shook his head. "He's not coming."

"You sound like you know that," Truck said.

"I do," John admitted. "After last weekend, Toff's mom freaked out and told him he can't play anymore."

"What?" Nick yelled. "Seriously?"

"Why didn't you tell us that before?" Charlie asked.

John tossed his pencil on the table. "I thought I'd talked him into playing anyway."

Truck shook his head. "His mom is a deranged Miss Manners. She probably locked him in his room and boarded up his window."

Nick stood up and stretched. He was tall enough to curl his fingers over the crossbeams of the old garage. "Well, I'm outta here if we ain't gonna play."

"Me too," Charlie said. "This blows. And it's too hot in here."

"Dude," Levi said, looking at Charlie. "You gave me a ride."

"Yep. Let's go or you're walkin'."

Levi folded his maps, grabbed his pencils and books, and stood up to follow Charlie.

"Maybe next weekend, guys," John said. "Sorry."

When everyone else was gone, Truck put his feet up on the table and laced his fingers behind his head. "Well, this is a shitty way to spend Saturday night," he said. "What do you wanna do?"

John shook his head. He *wanted* to play D&D. "There's nothing to do around here. I guess we could go over to Pullman and see *Aliens*." He sighed. "We have plenty of time *now*," he added sarcastically.

"No, you should go to that with Lisa. Go in the house and call her right now and ask her for next weekend. If Toff can't play, what else are you gonna do? Hell, ask her for tonight. Like you said, there's plenty of time."

"I'm not in the mood to call her."

"Perfect! When you talk to her, you'll be in a better mood."

"No!" John straightened his papers and stacked his D&D manuals on top.

"Okay," Truck said. "But let's get out of here. It's hot and Paulette might blow us up."

Weston was one of several small towns built around the Palouse River. Main Street was a straight shot through town, a secant over the lazy C-shaped river. A thick concrete balustrade, only four feet tall, with keyhole openings running its length, was the only indication of the bridges. There were sidewalks on each side and passersby often suffered vertigo if they looked down at the flowing river, and even though the rail was shorter than a hobbit, someone had yet to fall over the side. Before they had their driver's licenses, John and Truck would often sit on one end of the railing, the end cap above land, and watch traffic as they talked and ate snacks.

The first bridge was about three blocks from the Brewer house, so they walked. Neither questioned why nor gave a reason for going, it was just the natural thing to do. In the past they'd talked about girls, imagined their future lives, dreamt up cool jobs, and solved the world's problems while sitting on the concrete guardrail.

Early in their bridge-sitting career is when they were first introduced to Officer Wayne Phillips. He'd been dispatched after a concerned citizen reported two teenagers either making mischief or about to. The citizen had actually used the descriptor *hoodlums* but when Phillips was talking to John and Truck, he changed it to *teenagers*.

Officer Phillips had parked down the street and approached the young men from behind. This would give him the opportunity to come up slowly and perhaps hear what juvenile machinations they were plotting. Instead, he heard talk of elves, dungeons, magic spells, and treasure. To him it sounded like they were plotting a movie, unless it was some sort of medieval fantasy mischief. "Good evening, gentlemen," he'd said when he was about four feet behind them.

Both boys, fifteen at the time, jerked as if they'd been jabbed with an electric cattle prod and Truck let out a scaredy-cat "Gaah!" that was heard inside the small grocery store across the street.

Officer Phillips looked at his feet so they wouldn't see him smile and said, "Sorry. I didn't mean to sneak up on you like that."

They spent the next half hour discussing the Weston Warhawk football team (neither John or Truck played), why Truck was called Truck, a couple of the slicker hot rods that were regularly seen going up and down Main Street, and finally why the two young men were sitting on the bridge.

"No driver's license yet" was Truck's quick answer.

John had nodded and added, "Instead of us in somebody else's car, we sit here and let everyone cruise by us. Grocery store's right over there so we can eat. We talk, and see cars and people, and not spend money for someone else's gas."

Officer Phillips had nodded, thinking the logic was sound. The teenagers had shared their sunflower seeds and Doritos with him, and he had surreptitiously looked for signs of beer or liquor, neither of which he found. They were two young guys hanging out. No mischief. "Thanks for the talk, gentlemen," he'd said as he stood to leave. "This is a good spot. Make sure you clean up."

"Always do," John and Truck had said together.

On the walk from his house John dominated the conversation with complaints about Toff. "He should have called and told us he wasn't going to be here," he said.

Truck nodded. "Probably didn't want to get yelled at." He laughed. "You know what I mean. It's not like he didn't want to play. You know that."

"I don't care. He should have let me know."

"I thought you said he told you his mom wouldn't let him."

"Yeah, that's what he said. Doesn't mean he definitely wasn't." In his mind John knew he was probably making a bigger deal out of Toff's absence than it really was. But he was still mad. He shook his head and wiped the sweat from his forehead.

They stopped on the bridge sidewalk and Truck patted the old concrete balustrade where they sat. "Here, you sit and save our spot. I'm going to go get us something to drink. It's still too damn hot."

John took a deep breath as his best friend crossed the street. It *was* too damn hot.

He had been staring at the battered concrete between his feet when Truck hopped up and sat next to him. How long was Truck gone? John didn't even remember what he had been thinking about.

"Deciding how to kill off Toff's magic-user?" Truck asked. He handed John a fountain drink with an extra cup and a bag of sunflower seeds.

"Thanks." John tore open the bag and threw a small handful of seeds in his mouth and maneuvered them into his left cheek while he thought about Truck's question. He slid the extra cup off his soda and spit the empty shells into it as he worked the seeds baseball style. He handed the bag to Truck who followed the same procedure.

John shook his head. "I wouldn't do that. But it's not a bad idea. Maybe I'll give him some sort of disease though. Make Xan's left nut so big he has to put it in a sling, so he doesn't trip over it."

They laughed, tried to keep it down, but the image of a robed elf with a sling holding up a testicle the size of a watermelon was too much. They blew all their sunflower seeds out and let the laughs roll.

Just then a loud *Whoop! Whoop!* interrupted their glee and they looked up to see Officer Phillips cruising by. They lifted their sodas in greeting.

"Hey, what happened to Paulette?" Truck asked as he tracked the police car. He looked back at John. "We never heard."

John rolled his eyes and popped a fresh handful of sunflower seeds into his mouth. "Nothing happened," he said once he'd stashed the seeds in his left cheek. He spat in the cup and said, "Mom dropped the charges."

"What? Why? I've never seen your mom so pissed. Her face was all red. I seriously thought she was going to level that evangelical psycho."

"I know." John shrugged and watched a Subaru BRAT go by, three kids laughing in the small bed. Probably freshmen. "Mom said she didn't want to push it. She met with the judge or a lawyer or somebody, and they made Paulette promise she wouldn't ever set foot on our property again."

"That's just stupid," Truck said. "We get in more trouble for talking in class."

"I know! And now it sounds like she's going to do something else. If she can't come onto our property, what's stopping her from throwing something from the street? You even said she's going to blow us up."

"Dude," Truck said and spit out seeds. "I was kidding. She's not going to blow up your house."

John sighed. *Not the house*, he thought. Paulette believed the devil worship was in the garage.

CHAPTER 33

AUGUST

John got to Henley's farm almost an hour before he needed to. He put away his clean clothes for the week then went out and sat with his book under the tree in the front yard. The bark of the oak was thick and bit into his back, but the shade was cool. No one was there yet and Henley was at church—not that he expected Henley would come out for a chat—so he just sat in the quiet and read.

He read the same paragraph three times. He looked down the driveway at the fields toward Weston. He was still mad at Toff and didn't want to even see him, unsure of how he'd react. Not mad, really. Disappointed. Toff had let him down. He shook his head and focused on the book.

"What're you readin'?"

John flinched and looked up. He hadn't heard a car drive up let alone someone walk over to him. It wasn't Toff's voice though, it was Blaine. The farmhand came out from behind the tree and chuckled. "Must be good, right? You didn't hear me walk across from the swather barn?"

"*Cujo*," John said, showing Blaine the cover of the paperback. He didn't say anything else, not wanting to encourage a conversation.

Blaine nodded. "Oh, yeah," he said. "I saw the movie. Nobody would get a Saint Bernard after that, right? Just like when *Jaws* came out, no one would go swimming."

John nodded. "Yeah. I remember that." He didn't remember anything of the sort, but he didn't want Blaine to stay. It wasn't that he didn't like Blaine—he was a decent guy, and as far as he knew, Blaine wasn't Henley's stooge. But John wasn't in a friendly state of mind. He was mad at Toff and didn't relish the idea of confronting him let alone staying in the bunkhouse all week with him.

John was saved from any more repartee when Henley and his wife arrived. Their pickup roared by and around the drive to the back of the house. "Gotta go," Blaine said. "Going to be hot; you might wanna get some extra water, right?"

"Okay." John opened his book as Blaine walked toward the house but shut it again when he saw another truck turn up the driveway. A small white Datsun.

Toff.

John took a deep breath and put his hand on his chest. He felt hollow. Why was he so mad, or disappointed, or whatever it was, with Toff? He didn't *want* to feel the way he did, but he couldn't help it. His anger was like a giant boulder slowly rolling down a hill—once it got going, there was no stopping it.

Toff parked next to the Bug and got out of his truck as the trailing cloud of dust swallowed the bunkhouse. He cocked his head toward John in a way of greeting, but John pretended he didn't see. Toff hauled his duffel bag into the rickety building and disappeared behind the door.

John stared at the bunkhouse door then turned back to *Cujo*. He started at the top of the page. Again. The bark of the tree felt like a bed of nails, and he finally slapped the book shut and stood up. A diamond glint caught his eye, and he looked out toward the road. Another truck was coming in. Paul. Once he arrived, it would be go time. Henley didn't like to waste daylight.

John walked over to the house and went inside the back door. It opened into a mudroom where the Henleys kept an old refrigerator and a chest freezer. There was a bench with boots standing at attention under the seat, and a row of hooks where work coats, sweatshirts, overalls, and other items that got dirty were hung up.

John lifted the lid of the freezer and found his water jug. It was a plastic gallon-sized milk container that had been washed out, filled with water, and had his name scrawled in black marker. Everyone on the crew had one and each night the jugs were refilled and put in the freezer. The days were hot enough that the block of ice inside started to melt within minutes of being taken out of the freezer. If someone drank it off too fast, they placed the jug somewhere outside their cab and the sun would quickly melt more to drink.

Toff's jug was next to his. The routine had become that one or the other would go into the back porch and retrieve both jugs. Not today. John picked his jug out and closed the lid. Something in his heart told him he was being petty, but just as strongly, he felt he was right. Was it pride? Toff didn't say he wasn't going to show up to play D&D, and John hadn't told the others there may not be a game. They were upset at John, not Toff, when the game crumbled, and the evening was a waste of time for everyone.

As John walked toward his truck this was all on his mind, swirling about like a maelstrom, and he didn't see Toff emerge from the bunkhouse. Didn't see Toff wave. Didn't see the look on his friend's face when he noticed John was only carrying one jug of ice water. John walked blindly to his truck, his eyes open but his mind on a different mission altogether. When he got in the cab it was the heat that finally brought his thoughts to the present.

John took a deep breath and looked through the windshield. Henley and Blaine were standing at the picnic table talking and were joined by Paul. John frowned. He remembered seeing Paul's truck out on the main road. Whatever. Toff and Dale were talking near the back porch. They looked his way and John glanced down. He left his door wide open and looked again at the same page of his book.

When John got out of the shower that evening, Toff was prepared for battle. He stood in the middle of the floor wearing cotton basketball shorts and a tank top. They looked like high school surplus gym clothes from the 1960s but served as pajamas. They were powder blue and hung on him like a blanket, so he looked like the skinny kid in the bodybuilding ads on the backs of comic books.

John almost laughed. But he didn't. It had been a long day filled with stubborn silence, sullen glances, and one-word answers to unavoidable questions. All of it cooking in the heat of the day and finally brought to the boiling point. "What?" John asked defiantly.

"Oh please." Toff snorted. He kept his arms crossed and sat on his bed. "What did I do?"

"What do you mean?"

"Come on, John. You've been treating me like crap all day."

"Fine," John said. He sat on his own bed and faced his roomie. He took a deep, shaky breath. "You didn't show up Saturday and you didn't call to say you weren't going to make it."

Toff opened his mouth, but no sound came out. He blinked. "John, that's BS," he finally said. "I *told* you my mom said I couldn't play."

John shook his head. His heart thumped in his chest. "That doesn't mean you weren't going to play. Jesus, Toff. We're seniors now. We were all waiting for you to show up."

There it was. Even if he danced around his own embarrassment, John admitted the reason he was upset. And in that second he realized it wasn't worth being mad at his friend about. He shifted his gaze to the floor. Why couldn't he just say he was sorry and admit he was wrong?

"That's not fair,"Toff argued. "Just because I'm not Mr. Cool like you or Truck, or anybody else, and don't sneak out of the house when I'm not supposed to—"

"I don't sneak out of my house."

"Well, I obviously don't get to do whatever I want all the time, either."

"I—" John started to protest.

"No,"Toff cut him off. "You do get to do what you want. At least usually. Not everyone does, you know. My mom checks in on me every hour when I'm home. She treats me like I'm five. So no, I can't just sneak out."

"That's on you then," John said. "All I'm saying is you should have called." He lay down on his bed and turned off the small lamp on the table.

It was quiet and John's eyes were closed, but he could feel Toff standing there staring. After almost a minute he heard Toff's bedsprings groan. Toff's light clicked off and John heard his roommate mumble, "Asshole."

John turned onto his side and faced the wall. He knew his friend was right.

CHAPTER 34

It was still early in August, but the mornings were toying with the cooler end of the thermometer each day. Which still didn't mean the heat was going anywhere soon. Cool mornings and bread-baking heat by noon just meant autumn was on the way, not on the doorstep.

The morning after John and Toff's standoff in the bunkhouse they were both wearing long-sleeve work shirts to discourage the chill they hadn't been used to since early spring. The shirts would be thrown on the passenger seat within an hour or two in favor of the ice water jug. They emerged from their quarters one at a time and it didn't go unnoticed by the rest of the crew.

"Trouble in paradise?" Blaine asked quietly when John sat next to him at the picnic table.

John rolled his eyes and poured a glass of orange juice.

"Fine, don't tell me," Blaine said as if his feelings were hurt, and turned back to his plate of eggs.

John stabbed two links of sausage with his fork and scooped hashbrowns onto his plate along with a mound of scrambled eggs. He tucked in and didn't say anything when Dale sat across from him.

"You're quiet this morning," the principal said. "Something wrong?"

"Nope."

Blaine watched Toff go into the back porch to retrieve his water jug and take it back out to his truck. The farmhand met the principal's eyes, and he tilted his head toward Toff. Dale nodded and sipped his coffee. John stood as he shoveled the last of his eggs into his mouth and went to get his own water jug. Then he sat in the cab of his truck until everyone was ready to start the day.

At lunchtime the sun was white hot, and the temperature had already climbed high into the nineties. John and Toff sat apart and ate silently while Paul complained about the weather. "If this heat keeps up, I'm going to go crazy," he said. "We need some rain to break this heat."

"The heat's just fine," Henley barked back with a scowl.

"But would rain be bad?" John asked. He still had no interest in farming—though driving different machines was okay—but he couldn't help being curious.

"Well," Henley said, looking thoughtful, "maybe a little would be okay. It's a game of win some, lose some, now. We want the sun so we can harvest the grain. We can't cut wet grain; it'll clog up the machinery and it'll rot. So, we want the sun." He took a bite of his sandwich and kept talking, and the thick homemade bread muffled his words like a blanket. "A little rain will break the heat but won't oversaturate the grain or bog it down. We can't cut while it's raining, but I'd rather shut down for a day of light rain than risk losing part of the crop to a long heavy downpour."

John nodded and looked around. Everyone was focused on Henley while he gave the lesson. Except Toff. Toff was looking at him, but John couldn't read his face; it was a stare without emotion. What was Toff thinking? He looked thoughtful, as if he was deciding which way to turn at an intersection. John looked away, back at Henley.

"I wouldn't mind a break from this heat, either," Henley was saying. "It just has to be the right amount of rain."

John and Toff avoided each other the rest of the day. That evening the chessboard wasn't touched and neither said a word.

John lay on his bunk, his eyes open but unable to see anything in the utter darkness that was the countryside at night. Toff was there, on his own bed, but he felt alone, like being adrift on the ocean. What would he do if it had been Truck who hadn't shown up to the game?

The next morning mimicked the one before in that they left the bunk house separately and ate their breakfasts in silence. Henley was worried the cool mornings were leading to an early fall season and might bring too much rain too soon. "I've seen it like this before," he said to everyone at the table. "It's not a guarantee, but it's making me nervous. I wish I had two more combines."

John stood up from the table when he saw Toff coming toward the picnic table. He placed his dishes in the plastic tub on the back porch, fished his ice water jug out of the freezer, then sat in his truck.

When Dale climbed in for the ride to the field, John put his book down. "Is that what your teachers recommend for summer reading?" Dale asked with a smile.

"I'm sure they'd rather I read Charles Dickens or John Steinbeck."

Dale nodded. "The fact you know those guys are authors means your teachers are doing something right."

John pulled his door shut when he saw Blaine get in his own truck and leaned forward to start the engine. He didn't say anything else to Dale.

"Look, John," the principal continued, "I know it's none of my business, and the last thing you want during your summer break is a lecture, but there's obviously something going on between you and Toff. Everyone can see it. And frankly, it looks to me like it's bothering the two of you more than just being pissed at each other."

John looked over at Dale as he put the truck in gear. It wasn't everyday a principal cussed.

"So, I'm going to tell you something. This is my story, okay? Personal experience. You do with it whatever you want."

John nodded and let up the clutch. The truck moved forward, and he followed Blaine down the driveway. He agreed with Dale in that he didn't want to be lectured at, but at the same time he was at a loss about what to do about Toff.

"When I was in college," Dale began, "I had a roommate I'd met for the first time just a few days before classes started. We were freshmen, only a year or two older than you are now, and neither one of us knew what to do. It was one of the ways we formed a friendship, you know? We were both lost on campus together.

"We eventually figured things out, how to get around the university, how things worked, the usual, and we were pretty good friends. We hung out, talked girls, classes, stuff like that. We had each other's back.

"Our freshman year was great. We got through it together and the following year we were roommates again. During midterms of that second year, we were both up late studying. We had different majors, but everybody has big exams at midterms. It was probably around eleven o'clock, maybe midnight, and the coffee pot was empty."

John looked at Dale sideways, wondering what in the world he was getting at.

Dale said, "I know, you probably don't drink a lot of coffee now, but you will in college. Next year when you graduate, ask for a coffee maker. You'll thank me. Anyway, I had brewed the last two pots. Yes, we drank a lot of coffee. You have to when you pull an all-nighter. So, I told him the pot was empty. He didn't say anything, so I said it again. He told me he'd had enough. He was done." Dale shrugged and looked out the windshield. "*Okay*, I think, *but I want some more.* So, I brewed the third pot in a row. And guess what? I wasn't even finished with my first cup when he gets up for a refill of his own!"

"That's not cool," John said.

"That's what I thought too," Dale said. "And because of that cup of coffee, he moved out after midterms, and I haven't spoken to him since."

"Seriously?"

"Seriously. Because of that stupid petty thought I had about him getting more coffee, we had a big argument that ended our friendship. He was a good friend too. I still miss him." Dale looked out the passenger window and sighed. "Now, Toff probably isn't your best friend," he went on, "but he's a good friend. Am I right?"

John nodded and kept his eyes on the road.

"Okay," Dale continued. "My guess is that whatever is going on between you two probably isn't as big a deal as one or both of you have made it out to be. I'm also guessing it's pride that's keeping someone from apologizing. I'm not saying this as a principal now; I've been there.

"Here's the thing, John. I know it's difficult to get these words out, I do, but a quick *I'm sorry* will open the conversation and allow you both to talk about it. It's hard to start it, I know. But someone has to be an adult. After *I'm sorry* it's easy to talk, to admit things that went wrong. And it will save your friendship. *That* is worth it, I promise you."

John nodded and looked out the driver's side window. He swallowed the lump in his throat and quickly wiped away the tears that threatened to spill over.

It was still on the cool side when John made his first run to the silo. As he backed the truck up to the auger, he was thinking about coffee pots and Toff. The bull snake wasn't even on his radar. Lining up the truck, starting the screw spinning, opening the grain chute. It had all become muscle memory and he went through each procedure without thinking about it. His mind was a blender of thoughts and questions. How did Dale know the argument was over something stupid? How did Dale know *he* was the asshole? Even though he didn't say it, he knew. John didn't want to be an asshole. When Toff called him that, it hurt. It didn't make him mad, it dug deep in his heart and his soul like a dull shovel. He looked around at the dry hot ground and nodded to any snakes or buzzing insects that might have been paying attention. "Okay," he said out loud. "I can be an adult."

Suddenly his long-sleeve shirt felt tight, and he was pulled backward. *Did Blaine sneak up on me again?* "All right," he said out loud and jerked his arm forward to break Blaine's grip but it didn't work. Then he realized where he was standing. His shirt was caught in the auger. *Oh no!* his brain screamed. John's heart hammered against his ribcage.

The tail of his shirt was being wound up in the auger and it pulled him down and backward.

"No!" John shouted. He dug his heels into the dry earth and leaned forward, but the mechanical screw held tight, relentlessly, mindlessly pulling him down, back and to the right. The shirt seams turned into iron straps and strangled his shoulders, clamping them so he couldn't turn to reach the power switch, and he felt his strength slipping. Images of his mom and dad flashed in his mind, Truck, and Lisa Martin who he had yet to ask out, let alone kiss.

"No!" he shouted again. *Think!* The veins and muscles in his neck stood out as he strained against the force. *Think! Don't fall back!* Sweat poured into his eyes and stung like salt in an open wound. *Don't fall back!*

John let out a medieval roar. He planted his boot against the auger stand and twisted to his left. *Don't let me die, Dad!* With a surge of strength, straining for his life, he reached for the ground.

The shirt split up the back, the cloth ripped apart by angry opposing forces like a sheet of paper torn in two. John fell to his knees, but his right arm was yanked upward as the auger fed on the half of shirt it still had a grip on. He flapped his hand as if waving away an annoying fly, urging the sleeve beyond his wrist. The sleeve worked its way down his arm as it was pulled into the mechanical screw and finally fell away.

On all fours John took deep heaving breaths, filling his lungs and blowing it back out. He realized he hadn't been breathing. Or maybe he had, but the thought of being twisted into hamburger head first was all that had been on his mind.

How long had he been gone? The auger was churning away, there was still grain raining into the hopper from the truck.

John pushed himself up. His legs were wobbly, the muscles saturated with adrenaline. His shoulders felt like he'd been wearing a three-hundred-pound backpack for days and his hands were vibrating like an out-of-time engine. He took a deep breath, held it. Let it out. Inhale. Exhale.

In.

Out.

Slow.

The grain waterfalling from the truck into the hopper was diminishing. John walked around the truck to raise the bed and when he reached for the lever, noticed that he was wearing half a shirt. His left arm was still inside his sleeve while his right arm was bare. He raised the bed of the truck then pulled the sleeve off his arm. The shirt had been torn almost perfectly in half, right up the middle. The collar, the left sleeve, and half of the shirt remained, the ragged edges all there was to remind him of the violent end that might have been.

John opened the passenger-side door of the cab and tossed the remains of his shirt on the seat. He pulled on his T-shirt, grabbed the water jug, and gulped. He slammed the door and saw a six-and-a-half-foot long bull snake slither out from behind the front tire and make for the hill behind the silos. John took a deep breath, eased it out through pursed lips, and watched the snake get on with its life.

CHAPTER 35

It had been a long rough day: a lecture from a high school principal that turned out to be an eye-opener, almost being churned into human sausage by the same grain auger that had ripped Dave Carlson's arm off, and working all day in one-hundred-degree heat in the middle of nowhere hauling grain and feeding it to the very auger that tried to kill him. In the bunkhouse after dinner and after both of them had showered, John asked Toff to sit down. He opened his top drawer and took out what remained of his morning work shirt and tossed it to his roommate.

"What's this?" Toff asked as he held up the rag.

"It's what's left of the shirt I was wearing this morning. I got caught in the auger on my first run."

"Seriously?" Toff's eyes were wide.

"Seriously. I almost died." John pulled his T-shirt off over his head. Between his shoulders and pectoral muscles were deep red welts like permanent, painful backpack straps.

"Jeez," Toff said.

John didn't hesitate. "I thought it would have been really bad if I'd died and never said I'm sorry. I've been an idiot about last weekend. If you can't show up, you can't show up. And you *did* tell me your mom said you couldn't. This whole thing has been my fault and I've been a dickhead. So, I'm sorry."

Toff nodded and handed the torn shirt back. "Thanks."

The next morning, when Dale climbed into the cab for the ride to the field, John had a smile on his face. "Looks like you and Toff got things sorted out," he said.

John smiled as they set off. "Yeah. Thanks for the advice."

"Glad I could help. Well done. It's cool again this morning. What happened to your long-sleeve?"

John shrugged. "I don't know. I can't find it. I might have missed the passenger window when I threw it in and didn't realize it."

At noon on Saturday, John and Toff parked their trucks, refilled and stowed their ice water jugs, and went inside the bunkhouse to gather their laundry. John stuffed his dirty clothes into his duffel and wondered what to tell his mom about the missing shirt. The truth wouldn't do. She would flip out and forbid him from coming back to work on the farm. On one hand, that wouldn't be a terrible thing. He'd learned to drive a swather, driven truck, survived the auger, and still didn't like farming. On the other hand, he had given his word to remain through harvest or until school started, whichever came first. And he needed the money for college. There was still about a month of cutting to do, and every dime helped. Maybe he'd tell her the same thing he'd told Dale: He went to throw it in the rolled-down truck window and missed without realizing it. The shirt wasn't lying on the ground at Bullhead Flat—maybe a coyote ran off with it.

"Hey," Toff said behind him. John turned around and saw his roommate with his own duffel already packed and slung over his shoulder.

"Yeah? What's up?"

"I'm playing tonight."

"Really? You sure?"

Toff's jaw was set, and he nodded like he was going over a plan of action. "Yeah. I'll be there. Tell the guys."

CHAPTER 36

"So, are we actually going to play this time?" Charlie grumbled. He had his feet up on the corner of the table with his hands folded behind his head. After Paula had flipped the tabletop, John found a couple of screws and mounted the plywood directly to the sawhorses. He eyed Charlie's feet but didn't say anything. The table was secure.

"Toff said he'd be here," John said.

"Are you sure?" Nick drawled.

John sighed. "I'm sorry about last time, okay? It was my fault, I know. But Toff told me before we left work that he'd be here."

"I drove this time," Levi offered. "It's cool."

Everyone had shown up by seven. Truck came early, as usual, and spent the time re-coloring his dice. He rubbed a white crayon over his purple twelve-sided die to fill in the numbers sunken into the surfaces. He would then wipe the excess crayon away with a paper towel to reveal crisp white numbers.

"He'll be here in about one minute," Truck said, not looking up from his rubbing.

"How do you know?" Charlie asked. He took his feet off the table and sat up.

"I heard the Dot pull up."

Toff's truck, a small white Datsun 620 that most people on the Palouse didn't consider a real truck, had a peculiar buzz to its engine noise. It sounded like hundreds of decks of playing cards all being shuffled at the same time. The Dot wasn't buzzing exclusively, it was an underlying bonus sound beneath the six-cylinder that no mechanic or weekend tinkerer could figure out.

Toff sidestepped into the garage and said, "Hi, guys. Sorry I'm late but Xan the magic-user is at your service." He bowed like a Chinese ambassador, dropped his books and dice onto the table, and sat down heavily. "Sorry I didn't make it last week."

John looked at Toff and wondered what he'd had to do to get away from his mother. No doubt there had been yelling. John imagined Toff standing his ground, making his case, storming out. Whatever had happened, John silently gave Toff dragon status for it. "Not your problem, dude," John said as he set up his Dungeon Masters screen. "I'm the one who didn't tell everyone you couldn't play. My fault." He tapped his twenty-sided die on the table like a judge after handing down a sentence. "Throw me a root beer, will you, Nick?" he added.

The other boys looked at one another, clearly remembering that John had told them Toff *was* going to play. Charlie shrugged and opened his *Players Handbook*.

"Did you tell them what happened to you?" Toff asked John.

"What happened?" Truck asked.

"He almost got killed," Toff said, his eyes wide. "Same as Dave Carlson."

"Shh!" John waved his hands. "If my mom heard that crap, she'd never let me leave the house."

"Whoa," Charlie said. "Wait a minute, you're serious? What are you talking about?"

"Show them," Toff said.

John looked out the door then pulled his shirt over his head. The welts between his shoulders and pectoral muscles where the shirt had been pulled tight, like ropes holding a ship at the pier, had already grown darker. They almost looked like raw open wounds.

"Jesus, dude," Nick said.

"John," Truck said quietly, his eyes worried, "what the hell happened?"

John put his shirt back on, wincing when he raised his arms, and sat down. He explained what had happened as best he could, but the details were fuzzy. He had no idea how his shirt got caught in the auger, or even how he finally broke free. It had all happened so fast.

"Looks more like you were strung up and tortured," Nick said.

"Does it hurt?" Truck asked.

John nodded and rolled both shoulders. "Yeah."

Nobody knew what to say then. What *do* you say when your friend had a brush with death that everyone in town knew all too well what had happened just a couple months before?

"Brewer, damn..." Truck whispered. He stared at his best friend.

"Hey, don't worry about it," John said.

"You could've died though."

"But I didn't. And it wouldn't have been on you if I had. You didn't force me to call Toff and ask for the job."

"Are you two going to start crying and hug it out?" Nick chided.

"No!" John said. He sat up and clapped his hands. "All right, let's play some D&D." He opened the booklet behind the DM screen. "It's been a couple weeks. Do you remember where we ended?"

"Hold on, hold on," Levi said. He found his notes and compared them to his map spread out on the table in front of him. He pointed at a ladder-like sketch on the graph paper. "The rock creature left us at the bridge," he said.

"Right," John said. He flipped his notebook open and found the reminder he'd written to himself. "You're in the dark; Franco extinguished his torch, but you can see many dots of torchlight at the bottom of the chasm."

"What about across the bridge?" Truck asked.

"All dark over there."

"What about infravision?" Charlie chimed in. "Since it's dark, the elves and dwarf should be able to see better."

"You're right. None of you can see anything on the bridge or across the way."

"Anybody wanna volunteer?" Truck asked.

"It's probably fine," Nick said. "Remember, a bunch of hobgoblins came across it before we killed them."

"True," Toff said. "But it might only be safe on one side, or there might be a weak board as a trap."

"No volunteers?" Truck asked. "I would, but Kryger is bigger than a hobgoblin and the rock creature told us to go across one at a time."

"I'll go across," Nick said. He sat up out of his slouch and looked at John. "Let's do this."

"All right," John said. He sat up too and pulled his chair closer to the table. "What are you going to do?"

"I forget what's in my hand, but I want my axe. If I fall, I can maybe stick it in a board and hold on."

"Okay, axe it is."

Nick took a breath. "Bellator is going to just walk across, right down the middle."

"Yes!" Levi shouted. "Right down the middle!"

According to the dungeon module, there was a ten-percent chance that a character would fall off the bridge because it wasn't perfectly stable. John rolled his ten-sided die twice, got a six and a four. Sixty-four percent. Bellator was safe. John looked at Nick and smiled. "The dwarf warrior makes it to the other side unscathed and on both feet."

"See?" Nick said, looking at the others. "Who's next? Let's get this show on the road."

Each of the boys brought their characters across the bridge and followed Bellator's steps, right down the middle. Truck brought his warrior, Kryger, across last. "Okay," he said with a grin, "let's set a trap in case we're followed."

"No time," Charlie said. "We need to move before we're spotted. Plus, this might be our only way back. And we might be in a hurry, if you know what I mean."

"Where are we?" Toff asked. "What's around and what are our options?"

John described a thin stony ledge, barely five feet wide and with a crumbling lip that fell into the deep chasm below. "The ground where you stand is smooth," he said. "You can tell it was once the floor of a room or hallway before the cave-in. The bridge is at one end of the ledge so you can't go north. The rest of it curves around the rock wall to the southeast."

"And we can't see very well," Truck said.

"True," John agreed. "You can't see crap. Do you want to light a torch?"

"I want to," Levi said. "A ledge like this is something we need to see. Too risky not to have a light."

Truck shook his head. "Too risky *to* light a torch out in the open. Every monster in here can see with infrared. They only use torches so the human slaves can see. If we light one up here they'll think we're escaped prisoners and come after us, or they'll get word to Bohz and he'll run before we can find him."

"What do we do then? You and I are blind."

Truck looked around the table. "Bellator takes the lead," he said, pointing at Nick. "Then Xan in case he needs to cast a spell. Then you, then me, and the master thief can keep us protected at the back. We stick close to the wall and go slow, everyone holding on to each other."

"Works for me," Toff said. Everyone else nodded.

Truck gulped his New Coke and told John, "Weapons in our good hands, holding the shoulder of the guy in front with our other hand. Let's go." Then he belched.

"Going slow, you move along the wall," John narrated. "Parts of the wall are smooth, parts are damaged from the cave-in. It doesn't take long to get around the curve and then Bellator stops."

Nick looked up and stared at John, wondering what was about to happen.

"A flight of broken stairs leads up into the darkness," John finished.

"Broken?" Truck asked. "How do you mean?" He looked at Nick, knowing full well John would tell him that Kryger couldn't see in the darkness.

Nick looked to their dungeon master. "How do I mean?"

"Bellator describes ragged, broken stairs going up about twenty feet, hugging the rock wall. The stairs are of different widths, from a couple feet at the bottom to maybe five or six feet wide at the top."

"We'll be fine," Truck said. He shrugged and waved his hand as if to dismiss any fears. "We just have to go slow, stick close to the wall, and go one step at a time."

"And hope we're not attacked by something coming down the stairs," Levi said.

"Then let's get to the top before something else does and sees us," Charlie said.

"Lead the way, Nick," Truck said.

"I'm going to have a throwing axe in one hand and my battle axe in the other," Nick mused. "If something comes down the stairs, I'll be ready. Okay?"

John nodded.

"I'm going to stay close to the wall the whole way up," Nick said. "Okay, let's go."

"Wait," Toff interrupted. "Just how dark is it? Can the humans see anything at all?"

John knew what Toff was getting at but wasn't sure why. "There's barely a glow," he said. "The torchlight is down below in the chasm, so I'll say Kryger and Franco can barely make out shapes, but they can't tell what's what."

Toff looked thoughtful then said, "Should we go up one step at a time? And before you say, 'We always go up one at a time,' Nick—you smartass—what I mean is, do we literally go up one step, put both feet on that step, then go up one more? Like that?"

"Why?" Truck asked. "It seems too cautious."

Toff shrugged. "Maybe. Just wondering."

Nick said, "First of all, why am *I* the smartass?" He was grinning; everybody knew he wasn't the only wisecracker, but he was the quickest to jump on the obvious. "Second of all, yeah, I think it's a little too careful. Let's just go up. Stick to the wall, Bellator has the front covered." He held up both fists and pretended to throw an axe with his right hand and swung one with his left.

Toff nodded. "Okay. Just a thought."

"That's cool," Truck said. "But yeah, let's just go up these stairs."

Everyone turned toward John expectantly. He rolled his ten-sided die to see if any monsters randomly appeared at the top of the stairs—none did—and said, "You make your way slowly up the stairs." He rolled again to determine if anyone slipped. When the results showed everyone kept their footing, he said, "And you make it to the top safely. The landing was a thirty-foot square, but now it's a triangle with the broken edge running from the northeast corner to the southwest corner. You just came up on the western side. The broken away part is now a cliff that falls into the chasm. There's a big set of double doors made of what appears to be iron on the north side of the landing."

"We're trapped," Levi said. "Go through the doors or go back. We're sitting ducks right now."

"Nobody can see us," Charlie said. "We're above the workers in the chasm and there aren't any other landings. Or platforms. Or whatever." He looked at John. "Are there?"

"Are you looking?" John asked with a smile.

"I am now. Domo will look all around. Carefully."

John's smile widened. "Almost directly south of you is a flat area that looks like the open passage you first saw the chasm from, just before you all ran into the hobgoblins."

Levi pointed it out on the map.

"Is anybody, or anything, there?" Charlie asked.

John rolled a die. "Nope."

Truck said, "We go through the doors, guys. You know we have to. Once we're inside we'll probably be able to light a torch again, then we can figure out next moves."

"Bellator gives them a shove," Nick said.

"Wait!" Charlie held up his hand. "*Do not* just shove on the doors. They're probably locked anyway. Or should be."

John rolled his ten-sided die, giving it a fifty-fifty chance that the dwarf pushed the doors before the thief had a chance to stop him. Besides, Nick said *Bellator* shoved open the doors and Charlie didn't say anything about his character, Domo, telling him to stop. It was Charlie telling Nick not to do something. So, fifty-fifty. John looked up from his die and said, "The doors both open inward."

"Shit," said Truck.

"Everybody, hold on," said Charlie. He looked at John and told him, "Domo works his way around everybody and goes to the doors to check for traps, hidden guards, and to keep Bellator out of trouble."

"You guys worry too much," Nick retorted.

"Says the dwarf who almost died from a grell because he wasn't paying attention," Charlie said.

"Okay, you guys," Truck said, "let's just use our heads here. There's a time for just blindly moving forward and a time to slow down."

Nick nodded. "Right. We know the hobgoblins just came through here; there's no other way." He looked at John and said, "Bellator goes through the doors."

CHAPTER 37

Bellator felt a hand grasp his shoulder and hold him back just as he was stepping beyond the great iron doors at the top of the broken staircase. "Wait," a voice whispered in his ear. It was Domo, the elven thief.

"Do not be too quick, my friend," the elf whispered. "Look." He pointed to a spot on the floor where Bellator's next step would have landed. Something wasn't right.

The dwarf got down on his knees and inspected the floor more closely. Near the edge by the doors, he saw a raised lip. Bellator put the tip of his axe blade under the lip and slowly lifted. The floor was pliable and tented beneath the blade. He lowered the axe and stood back up. He had to admit the elf's eyes were keener than his own. He nodded at Domo. "A trap," he whispered.

"Tell the others," Domo said, patting the dwarf's shoulder. "I'll find a way around it."

It only took the thief a few moments to discover the secret of the trap. He stepped back out onto the ledge and told the others what he'd found. "It's only a tarp made to look like the floor," he said. "A pit lies below. It's newly dug; I suspect it's intended to capture any prisoners who make it this far. Without a torch they'd be unable to see it and fall in."

"Can we get around it?" Kryger asked, his deep voice a whisper.

"Yes," Domo said. "A thin ledge goes all the way around. The tarp is held up by weighted urns in each corner, but there is room to step around them."

"What about light?" Franco asked.

"Once we're inside and the doors are closed, we'll have a torch," Domo said.

The elf led the party members one by one into the chamber and had them stand still with their backs to the wall. Then he softly closed the iron doors and lit a torch.

They squinted against the sudden bright flame and gave their eyes a moment to adjust. Domo passed the torch to Franco then pointed at the floor. "If you look carefully, there's a slight sag in the middle," he said softly.

The others nodded and they sidestepped around the room, their backs scraping the wall, toward the doors on the far side. Domo put his ear to the door and listened while Bellator kept his eye on the iron doors they'd just come through.

The thief shook his head and tried the door latch. It was unlocked. He looked at Kryger. "We must go quickly," the warrior whispered. "Too slow and the light from the torch will give away our presence. Everyone ready? Now!"

Domo pushed the doors open. Kryger and Bellator stepped out first, their weapons raised as they quickly scanned the room before them. Franco stepped out and held his torch aloft.

The room before them was dark and appeared to be made up of several smaller rooms, like cells, but there were no iron bars or doors. Domo held his finger to his lips and pointed toward the room farther ahead on the left.

Kryger lit a torch off Franco's and poked it into the room on the right while the cleric did the same on the left. Both rooms were empty save a few blankets, sacks of straw, chairs, and scattered bits of tarnished armor.

Domo moved ahead and motioned to the others. He pointed at the next room, held his small sword ready. They went through the opening quickly, knowing the glow of the torchlight would give them away, but all they saw were rats.

Seven giant rats, about three feet long, with dirty matted gray and black fur—two were crouched atop a basin on the far wall, the rest skittered about beneath. Their angry eyes and razor-like teeth gleamed in the torchlight as they turned their attention to the party of adventurers.

Without hesitation Kryger thrust his sword and skewered a rat perched on the edge of the basin. It squeaked and shuddered. The other rats tensed and hissed but Franco stepped forward and waved his torch at the big rodents. They backed into the corners, squeaking and jittery. Kryger brought his own torch down in front of their faces and the rats bolted between and around feet and out into the open hallway. Bellator brought down his axe, but it sparked against the stone floor. "Quick buggers aren't they?" he marveled.

Kryger flicked his sword and the body of the rat he had impaled flopped into the dark corner. "Now," he said, "what were these rats crawling all over?"

"It's a fountain," Xan said. The magic-user stood next to the bowl carved from the wall and had his hands just above the water's surface. "It's cool and clean," he said. "There must be a source down here, probably the same water that filled the pool my kinsman went for a swim in." He nodded at Domo.

The bowl of the fountain was carved from the wall and was a half-circle of about two feet wide. A hole above the basin provided water through a clay pipe and the drain below the surface kept it from overfilling.

They each drank freely, filled their water skins, then turned toward the open passage behind them. "Shall we follow the rats?" Bellator asked.

"We must," Kryger said, suppressing a great belch after gulping so much water. "Though I doubt we'll see them again. They have hiding places, tunnels, and holes, even our crafty elf cannot find."

The passage led due east and was decorated with brightly painted scenes of dwarf life, both above and below the surface. Cool, snowy mountain peaks, thundering waterfalls, wide sweeping landscapes, metallurgists shaping jewelry, artisans fashioning baskets, even great battles. The corners were filled with dust and cobwebs; the floor showed several footprints, but it was clear this was not a commonly used path through the lower levels.

The corridor turned north and ended at a set of bronze doors ten feet high and just as wide. They were milky blue with dull brown patches, a patina having taken over the polished gleam ages ago. The handles were shaped like hammers and forged of the same bronze. Etched across the expanse of the two doors was a tall mountain, the peak among clouds at the top. Beneath the surface of the mountain, on the left door, was a maze of tunnels filled with small figures like an ant hill. The right door was filled with the image of a great dwarf, his arms crossed with a hammer in one hand. His feet were spread wide, and he appeared to be wearing a thick leather apron, the kind worn by blacksmiths, as he gazed across the expanse of the doorway toward the tunnels under the mountain.

"Moradin,"[1] Bellator whispered.

"Who?" Franco asked.

"Moradin. He is the Forger of Souls, the maker of all dwarf kind."

"What will we find beyond these doors?" Kryger asked.

The dwarf warrior shook his head. "I do not know. I am not a miner."

Domo listened at the door and shook his head. "I hear nothing."

Bellator and Domo each grasped a handle, and pulled the doors open. Kryger and Franco held their torches high,

[1]Moradin is the greater dwarf god known as "The Soul Forger." *Deities & Demigods* (Lake Geneva, WI: TSR Games, 1980), 91.

and everyone peered into the darkness. They heard nothing, stepped inside, and pulled the doors shut behind them.

The light of two torches was enough for them to see that they were in a very large chamber. Four columns, forming the corners of a square, stood in the middle of the room, their tops lost among the thick cobwebs hiding the dark ceiling. At the far end a statue could be seen atop a platform.

"A shrine?" Franco asked out loud.

"No," Bellator said. "A proper shrine would have a forge in the center, there, among those columns." He pointed toward the middle of the room. "No, this is not a place of worship, but was used perhaps for important gatherings, and celebrations."

The four facing walls were ornately carved with renditions of the natural seasons. Snow-covered evergreens, budding leaves and flowers, full, grand trees in the sunshine, and a storm of leaves falling among a forest of deciduous trees. Kryger ventured farther into the darkness and said, "There are doors." He pointed with his sword. "To the left and right. Something strange about the one on the left. I can't make it out."

"Kryger," Domo said. His tone was commanding, urging everyone to stop what they were doing and look at him. He glanced up and the others followed his gaze. "Webs," he said. "We've seen their like before."

"When?" Bellator demanded. "I would remember such a mess."

"It was before you granted us your company," Kryger said. He stepped back among the group.

Domo pointed toward the ceiling. "See the holes? If they were merely cobwebs catching dust, the canopy would be solid. They drop through the holes."

"They?" Bellator asked, his voice low.

"Spiders," Kryger answered. "And judging by the hatches they've left themselves, big ones."

"Shall I burn them out?" Xan asked.

"Not yet," Kryger answered. He jutted his chin upward and to his right. "We seem to have an impatient one eager for a meal."

Slowly descending through one of the openings in the dusty cobwebs above was a bulbous shape, its features lost in the darkness. When it was clear of the silk ceiling, the jointed legs uncurled and Bellator shuddered. The spider, its shiny black abdomen glinting in the torchlight, was as big, or bigger, than him.

The legs of the massive spider waved, seeking purchase as it lowered itself on its silken string. Bellator reared back and threw his axe, but it sailed passed and clattered in the darkness on the far side of the hall. He looked sheepishly at his compatriots. "Ugly brute, ain't it?"

"Xan," Kryger said, "if you please, before any others drop down. The added light will help us with this one as well. The rest of you, come with me, and watch the fangs."

As Xan prepared a spell to burn away the webs and any other giant spiders lurking in the dark, the rest of the party approached the dwarf-sized arachnid about to touch down on the floor.

Bellator split off to draw the creature's attention in a feigned attack from the rear. He raised his axe and stomped his boots as he made his way around the great pillar, while Kryger, Franco, and Domo stood nearby. The spider alit upon the stone floor and released the web from its spinnerets. Its legs twitched up and down as it skittered around, watching the three who weren't moving and the one who was coming up from behind. The flickering torchlight reflected in its eight eyes like a kaleidoscope.

As the dwarf closed in, the spider finally turned to face the immediate threat. It reared up on its four hind feet and was illuminated by an orange glow from above. Xan had unleashed his spell and set the webs hiding the ceiling on fire. It blinded Bellator and he shielded his eyes. The spider saw its chance, dropped to the ground, and attacked.

Franco was quicker. The cleric rushed forward and brought his heavy mace down upon the back of the spider. The back two legs on the right side of the monster cracked and collapsed. It turned unsteadily, like a wagon with a broken rear wheel.

Bellator moved to swing his axe but was knocked aside as the charred and smoking body of another spider, its legs curled like a great claw beneath its abdomen, fell from the ceiling and hit his shoulder.

The hobbled spider on the floor backed away toward the center of the room, its belly scraping the floor and pushing the broken legs. Kryger and Franco walked slowly toward it, brandishing their torches, pushing it back among the columns. The spider gnashed its fangs and droplets of venom glistened on the sharp tips like pearls.

Domo, unbeknownst to all, had tracked around to the far columns when Xan unleashed his spell. He silently sprang forward as the massive spider braced its good rear legs and brought both of his long daggers down into the thorax of the creature, nearly slicing it in two. Black blood and innards splashed and oozed onto the stone floor and the creature was still.

"Evil bloody things," Bellator mumbled as he joined the group.

"Just the two then?" Kryger asked.

"Our wizarding friend got two others," Domo said, cocking his head backward.

"Too bad they're not edible," Kryger said, smiling. "I'm hungry."

They all chuckled, happy for a respite from the battle. But Franco didn't join in on the mirth. He was standing back from the group, his torch held high, his gaze directed upward.

"Franco, my friend" Kryger said. "Are you all right?"

Franco pointed his mace upward. "Look at that," he whispered.

CHAPTER 38

Suspended from the ceiling were a number of panels, their surfaces brightly painted. "What are they?" Kryger asked. "Paintings of ancient dwarf kings?"

"They're narrative panels," Xan said, gazing up.

"They're what?" Bellator asked.

"Narrative panels. Long ago, most people couldn't read or write. In order to tell an important story to the masses, narrative panels were created to tell the tale visually. Instead of writing books, they carved or painted pictures."

"And what tale do these narrative panels tell?" Bellator grumbled.

"I believe it's the story of the amulet," Xan mused.

Three panels began the story in horrifying clarity. A tall, red-skinned devil-like creature towered over scores of dwarves, fire shooting from its fingers, raking over the frightened dwarf clans.

The next panel was an image of soldiers dressed in the garb of those who dwell in the desert. They marched toward snowcapped mountains with sandy dunes behind them.

The story continued with more scenes of war. These panels represented battles between the two armies, along with images of the desert sultan and the dwarf chieftain. The red fire-throwing giant made more appearances as well. The chapter ended with a portrait of the sultan touching the amulet worn around his neck and a scene of ruined dwarf homesteads, blackened and crumbled, the desert army marching away carrying much gold, gems, and other dwarf riches.

Next was an image of a council among dwarf leaders. This was followed by an army of dwarf warriors marching toward sand dunes. A large panel then depicted a great battle with thousands of soldiers on both sides.

There was an image of a small group of dwarves inside the sultan's palace, then the same troop holding the sultan at sword point.

The next panels were all dwarves, marching out of the desert with the amulet; this was followed by the amulet being taken deep into the earth. Then another band of dwarves taking the artifact farther north into snow-covered country. The last panel depicted the amulet upon an anvil, its golden case and chain glowing as if it had just come from the kiln; a great blacksmith with a massive hammer was poised to bring down a shattering blow.

"Well," Xan sighed. "There you have it."

"Have what?" grumbled Bellator. "I see many pictures of my ancestors being laid waste by that red-skinned devil." He pointed at the first panels.

"That's not a devil, but an efreeti,"[1] Xan said patiently, a teacher to his student.

Bellator stared blankly.

"Do you know what a genie is?" Xan asked the stupefied dwarf.

"Yes, I know what a genie is," Bellator grunted.

"An efreeti is like a genie but comes from the Elemental Plane of Fire. Quite rare to see them here, in fact."

"You seem to have puzzled it out, Xan," Kryger said. "Tell us what you think."

Xan strode beneath the panels, studying them one more time. He removed his cap and turned to his friends. "It seems to me this sultan from the southern lands either had a vendetta against all dwarf kind, or simply wanted their treasures. That is not clear. What is, though, is that he used the amulet to control the efreeti and used its pyrotechnic powers to lay waste to the dwarf armies, villages, and strongholds. Then his army came and easily took what they wanted."

"How can you tell the amulet controls the efreeti?" Franco asked. He looked at the panels, trying to figure it out.

Xan pointed. "You see the sultan touching the amulet in the battle scenes with the efreeti? In the scenes without the efreeti his hands don't touch it."

---

[1] An efreeti is a magical creature from the Elemental Plane of Fire. The efreeti can produce flame at will and may be forced into limited servitude like a genie. *Monster Manual* (Lake Geneva, WI: TSR, 1979), 37.

Franco nodded. "I see. Yes. And here?" He pointed to the panel with the dwarf council. "The clan leaders decide to mount an all-out counterattack?"

"Precisely," Xan agreed. "As the battle raged a small group entered the palace and surprised the sultan. I assume they killed him and recovered the amulet. We don't know if the battle was won, but most importantly, the dwarves brought the amulet north and, presumably, into this very mine."

"So, we did find it," Kryger said.

"No," Xan corrected. "See? They took it north and destroyed it. We have a false amulet."

"But nowhere in this narration does it show them creating another amulet," Bellator stated. "If this is the story, why would they leave that out?"

"The nature of a decoy," Domo said. "If everyone knew a fake existed, they would keep looking for the real one."

"Go on," Kryger urged.

"Our dwarf friend's kin went to war to take from their enemy an item of considerable magical power. They undoubtedly knew that same enemy would come looking for it. Unwilling to go to war again, this enemy would send infiltrators, spies, and—"

"Thieves," Bellator interrupted.

"Yes," Domo agreed. "Thieves. The amulet we found could have been forged to replicate the original, a spell cast upon it in order to radiate its...dweomer, as Xan called it. It could have been hidden, but not too well, so that if the dungeon was penetrated, the thief would find it, believe he found *the* artifact and be off. The dwarves would know they'd been discovered and either move the real item to another location…or maybe it was never actually here."

"But what if *this* is the decoy?" Kryger said, pointing toward the final panels of the narrative. "What if the story of going north and destroying it is the deception?"

Bellator shook his head. "No, our educated wizard is correct," he said. "This is a ceremonial hall of dwarves; no deceptions would be brought here. This is a place of truth. So, instead of lying, they simply left out the creation of the false amulet."

Domo squinted at the statue on the platform. "Bellator," he asked quietly, "the visage before us is the same as we've seen before, is it not? But…different."

A square block pedestal acted as the base of the statue. The dwarf god was carved standing upon a small mound, his booted feet set apart, his wise and craggy face forward, his gaze a mesmerizing and serious countenance. A thick braided beard fell to his belly over a leather smock, and his leggings were covered in ornate designs that made them look covered in fur from a distance. The right hand held a pickaxe, a shovel was in the left.

Bellator looked up at the statue. "Aye," he said. "It is Dumathoin."

"And forgive me, he is who?" the thief pressed.

"The Keeper of Secrets Beneath the Mountain," Bellator said. "He knows where the earth hides her riches."

"The *Keeper of Secrets*," Domo muttered. "In what you called a place of truth. Odd, isn't it?"

The dwarf warrior groused. "No! It's not odd," he said. "The truth may be kept secret. It's not deceitful to keep a secret."

"Exactly." The thief smiled. He strode over to the statue and looked closely at the carving.

"I believe I understand your way of thinking," Kryger said. He moved to the other side of the statue. "Yes, it's worth a look."

"What are you two on about?" Bellator whispered loudly. "I don't know what you're talking about."

"Here!" Kryger said loudly. He was squatted down between the wall and the back of the statue, his hands on its base. "Franco, bring your torch."

The cleric moved around the stone carving, and they all gathered around the big warrior. "Look," Kryger said. "Here." He touched the statue above the pedestal, just under the right heel of the dwarf god.

"What is that?" Bellator whispered.

"Xan?" Kryger said, making space for the wizard. "Can you make it out? Is it what I think it is?"

Xan knelt down so he was closer to the spot Kryger had touched. "Franco," he whispered. "More light, if you please."

Under the heel of the right boot was a carving of the amulet they'd found in the secret room. The very amulet also depicted in the narrative panels above.

"There's no mistake," Xan said as he stood. "It's the same."

"What does it mean?" Franco asked.

Xan rubbed his smooth chin and faced his companions. "The symbolism in statues varies among the people who create them," he said, "but I believe by stepping on the amulet while it's behind him means it's not only to be kept secret, but that it's also not to be used."

"By anyone?" Kryger wondered.

"At least not by dwarf kind," Xan said. "Their god wants it kept secret."

"It's cursed," Bellator whispered. His gaze was directed toward the statue's left leg.

"How do you know this?" Domo asked.

Bellator pointed. "It's here. Hidden words in the carving." He read: "*Whomsoever calls forth the power of this amulet, lead will be your gold and that made by the hands of dwarf kind shall be overly burdensome. May your greed be your downfall.*"

"Well, now we know," Kryger said. He sighed loudly, the secret finally revealed. "All right. We let it be. Domo will keep it safe."

Nobody moved, they were frozen, their quest diminished.

"Let us move on," Kryger said. "We have more to discover."

"The door there is boarded over," Domo said, pointing to the left. "I took the opportunity to explore while Xan read the panels. But I believe we should let it be."

"What did you find, Domo?" Kryger asked and walked to the barricaded door. "It's unlike you to leave a door unopened, even if it is nailed shut."

The others followed and they stood before the large wooden doors. Six thick oak planks covered the frame in a zigzag fashion and were secured to the wall with thick iron spikes on either side. Warning messages were carved into the boards and ancient whitewash still filled the letters. *DANGER! DO NOT OPEN! DANGER!*

"And since when does a thief of your caliber heed the signs of others?" Kryger asked, a smile upon his face.

Domo nodded, accepting the compliment, and said, "I never ignore the signs or the instructions or even the rules, but I take them into account while observing the situation for myself. In this case, my senses tell me to let the door be and go on our way."

"What could be so bad?" Bellator grumbled. "Perhaps it's damaged from the cave-in. Or it's something—"

"Unnatural," Franco finished.

Bellator's face turned ashen, and he shrank away from the door. "Un-unnatural?" he stammered.

Franco stood with his open palm facing the door, his eyes closed. "It's not evil," he said quietly, "but it is a force not to be reckoned with. I believe Domo's instincts are quite correct."

"Let us move on then," Xan said. "Our prize here was knowledge."

They moved across the great chamber to the opposite door. The body of a spider blocked their way, it lay on its back with the legs curled tightly over the belly. Kryger grabbed one of the legs and started to drag it out of the way when Domo suddenly threw up his hand. Everyone froze. Bellator gripped the handle of his axe.

Domo padded across the remaining span of floor and stood with his ear next to the door. He listened a moment, standing as still as if he'd been turned to stone, then nodded.

"How many?" Kryger whispered.

Domo shook his head. He wasn't able to determine the number of enemies on the other side.

"Look then," Bellator whispered.

They scowled at the dwarf. "We're not opening this door without knowing what awaits us," Kryger whispered angrily.

"The peephole," Bellator said and pointed at the door. When they all looked at him confused, he shook his head and said, "I'll do it. Put out your torches."

In the darkness Bellator stepped carefully to the door. The ornate carvings were of flowers, leaves, grasses, and shrubbery. The motif gave one the sense of autumn, of falling leaves onto a forest floor. The dwarf gently rotated the center of a flower up to reveal soft light flowing in from the other side. A covered peephole. At dwarf height, of course.

After he stared into the other room for a minute or so, Bellator carefully slid the peephole cover back into place and stepped away from the door. "Well?" Kryger asked quietly.

"Prisoners, I think," Bellator whispered. "Must be a holding room. I saw six men, looked like farmers. There may be more, there was a corner not too far down the hallway."

"How did you know the peephole was there?" Domo demanded.

Bellator frowned. "It's right there," he said, pointing. "How did you *not* know?"

Domo looked back at the door and shook his head.

"Perhaps one must be a dwarf," Bellator mused.

"Never mind that," Franco whispered. "You saw prisoners; did you see their captors as well?"

"I did not," Bellator said.

"Our quarry lies through these doors," Kryger said. "If prisoners are there, he's either there as well or nearby in order to inspect and strike fear into them. We must move forward, and if we can free a few townspeople along the way, so much the better. Are we in agreement?"

"It's the only way," Xan whispered. "But we need a plan. Who knows how many of the gray one's followers are out there?"

"I *have* a plan," Kryger said, the smile clear in his voice.

CHAPTER 39

John drove the Bug as fast as he could, which wasn't as fast as he wanted it to go. He had *Rock VI, Back for More!* in the cassette player and couldn't hear the engine above the hard driving "Autoblast" by Black 'n Blue.

It had been a good Saturday night. Toff had come to play and the two of them were back on good terms; Paulette Dickerson hadn't made an appearance; and everyone figured out the story behind the amulet, so the D&D campaign was going well too.

He made it to the Henley farm before Paul, who lately was almost always the last to arrive. Before they loaded into the trucks to go to the field they were currently cutting, Toff sat down next to him at the picnic table and said, "Two weeks, do you think we'll get to go?"

He was talking about AC/DC, who had announced a stopover date in Spokane for their *Who Made Who* concert tour. "It's on a Thursday night," John said, keeping his voice low. "Henley won't let us go."

"Maybe I should ask," Toff pushed.

John shook his head. "Think about it. He won't even let us talk about..." He looked around then whispered, "D&D. Do you think he'll let us go to an AC/DC concert? If he saw the cover of the *Highway to Hell* album, he'd have an aneurysm and sic Paulette on us for that too. Besides, we wouldn't get home till one or two in the morning, and he won't have that."

Toff sighed. "Pray for rain."

"No kidding. That would be great."

"What are you two talking about?" Blaine asked. He'd come out of the back porch door and made for the picnic table when he saw them. "You look like you're making plans."

"Evil plans to take over the world!" John said. "You caught us."

The boys liked Blaine just fine, but when it came to rock concerts or D&D, they didn't trust him to not talk to Henley. He probably wouldn't, Blaine wasn't a flunky, but why take the chance?

"Well," he said, "better get your water jugs and get ready. Paul's driving in. Finally, right?"

Sundays were John and Toff's favorite workday because, for starters, it was only a half day, but they also got a big dinner and went back to the bunkhouse feeling good rather than exhausted from working the regular sixteen-hour days in the summer heat. When they were awake enough, they played chess and listened to the radio. Neither John nor Toff was ever going to win a chess tournament, but they enjoyed the game and were good enough to avoid the easy traps. They didn't play most nights because they were too tired, so the same game had been going on for a few weeks.

"How come we always play games that go on forever?" John asked. "D&D. Chess. We should have brought Risk; we could have had the same game going all summer."

"It doesn't help that we only play Sundays," Toff reasoned. "But hey, about D&D—"

"No way, man. You know we can't talk about the dungeon outside the group."

"I don't want in on any secrets. I'm just curious about something. It didn't come up when I was the DM."

John looked across the board at Toff and narrowed his eyes. "We'll see. Lay it on me."

"The way we've always played: We total up experience points at the end, when we're all done. I don't remember if that's a rule or just how we've always done it. What I want to know is, if it's not a rule, can we level up mid game?"

John pushed a rook forward and sat back. "Yeah, we've always played that way. Why? You want some next-level spells?"

"Not just me," Toff said. "I'm just wondering. I know a few of us were close to leveling up before we started playing. No big deal."

John nodded. Changing how they play was something he could do as Dungeon Master; the question was, how much would it change the way the game was developing? It would add some excitement for characters to level up in the middle of the game, but how could Toff's magic-user acquire new spells while he was running around a dwarf mine? Spells weren't just granted; he didn't think they could bend the rules that much. He'd look at the Dungeon Masters guide. "I'll check on it," he said. "Yeah, I have no idea if it's a rule or not."

They each made another move in the chess game and called it a night.

The next morning John, Toff, Dale, and Blaine were sitting at the picnic table. The breakfast wasn't as big on Mondays because they always had a late dinner the night before, but there was still plenty to eat.

Terminally late Paul was the topic of discussion around the table—as long as Henley wasn't there—and it fell just shy of placing bets upon his arrival. Dale mentioned he would be open to creating a pool to see who was closest to guessing Paul's daily arrival times, but it wouldn't be proper for a high school principal to encourage gambling. John and Toff both rolled their eyes and blew raspberries at him. Instead, they all agreed Paul would arrive within a half hour. "Unless he's been arrested," John muttered.

"Hey man," Blaine said. "Not cool. We don't know anything more today than we did a month ago. Paul's getting enough shit in town with the rumors. We don't need it on this crew. Right?"

John nodded. "Sorry," he said, and they went back to eating their breakfast.

In the ensuing silence John thought about Toff's question. He leaned across the table and told Toff, "I don't know if it's a rule or not, but as Dungeon Master, I think leveling up mid game might add too many complications. How would Xan get his new spells? You know?"

"What in the hell is a Dungeon Master?" Blaine drawled, putting down his coffee cup.

"It's a *Dungeons & Dragons* thing," John answered. "The Dungeon Master runs the game."

"John!" It was Henley, that nasally, aristocratic and condescending voice recognizable with just the shouting of one word. "I told you to never speak of that on my property!"

John's back stiffened and his shoulders hunched like a scolded dog. He didn't turn to look at Henley, just said, "Sorry."

John, deliberating Toff's question, hadn't heard his boss come out of the house and didn't know he was standing right behind him when he'd answered Blaine. John glanced at the farmhand sitting next to Toff. Blaine's gaze was directed at the bowl of cereal in front of him, neither looking at John or Henley. *What the hell?* John thought. *Did he ask that just so I'd get in trouble?*

Nobody at the table said anything. John and Toff both sat frozen, each staring at the middle of the table waiting for Henley to either say something or walk away. Dale and Blaine acted like nothing had happened, continued to munch toast and sip their coffee. John could sense Henley standing behind him, his eyes boring into the back of his head like the big round headlights on the Bug. Staring. Frowning. Fuming.

Finally, Henley mumbled, "You'd better be sorry, mister. I won't have that devil worship trash on my farm." Then he walked around the table and over to the waiting trucks.

John pushed his plate away and picked at his fingernails. The silence was like an edict from Henley for everyone to think about what he'd said, but finally Blaine said, "Time to go, right? Paul's here."

They stood and started across the lawn but stopped. Henley and his son-in-law were shouting. At first the crew thought something had happened—a twisted ankle or a dented fender—or something had been seen, a coyote in the yard or a snake slithering from beneath the shed. But it became clear it was personal. The two men were on the far side of Paul's pickup and the cab blocked their words, but volume won out a few times. Henley called Paul a "no-good liar." Paul, his chin pointed at the sky, shouted, "You don't know what you're talking about!"

"Come on, guys," Blaine ordered. "Let's get ready. There's work to do." He set off toward the trucks and the rest followed. But they glanced toward the argument, drawn like rubberneckers passing a crash on the highway.

John saw Henley glance in their direction and say something to Paul. But his son-in-law wasn't having it, whatever it was. "Go to hell, Jimbo!" he yelled and walked away.

Henley disappeared back into the house. The crew waited more than ten minutes before the farmer came out. As John started the engine, he saw Mrs. Henley leaning against the back door, hugging herself the same way she had when Henley had scolded them after the first incident with Paulette. Her face was the reflection of a gray cloud on a shallow pond.

Out in the field Henley went back to snubbing John whenever they met. If John was the next truck in line and Henley's combine was full, he would pull up and start offloading without a call on the CB. He didn't even look in John's direction. John needed the job though, so he was watching, always ready.

Henley's behavior was odd given the blowup between him and Paul. That seemed forgotten. Or was Henley perpetually angry? Maybe he just didn't like certain people. Why didn't Blaine, who asked what a Dungeon Master was, get reprimanded? *Henley just wanted to yell at me*, John thought. The fact that Blaine didn't get told off was probably because they all sat around when John and Toff weren't there and talked about how evil D&D was. *You don't talk about it because you play it, but I can because I don't understand it.* John shook his head. *Hypocrites*, he thought.

At noon Mrs. Henley's voice came over the CB radio and announced lunch was ready. Henley followed up and directed everyone to where they'd entered the field that morning, a wide, flat area with an even road onto the blacktop of the two-lane highway.

John was returning from a silo run when lunch was announced. When he arrived, two combines and the other two grain trucks were parked in a semi-circle in the field. John pulled off the highway and pulled in alongside Blaine's truck. "Where's Paul?" he asked when he joined the others at the pickup Mrs. Henley drove.

"On his way," Blaine said as he shook potato chips out of a bag and onto his paper plate. "He was a lap behind us on that back patch by the cottonwoods."

John loaded his plate, grabbed a root beer, and sat on a camp stool next to Toff. He took a bite of his po'boy sandwich and looked around. The fields were like dunes, rolling mounds of earth that flowed over the Palouse. It was nearing one hundred degrees and the dirt they sat in was baked like pottery, the sky was as blue as a milky sapphire, not a single cloud to block the sun. He took another bite and looked to his left. Paul was driving his combine over the hill, coming in for lunch. Nobody had started a conversation, so they all turned and watched.

The header on the front of the combine was about three feet off the ground and stretched to five or six feet of either side. It was like the wings of a very boxy awkward land-based plane that would never get off the ground. Paul drove the combine straight down the hill and steered toward Mrs. Henley's pickup.

The rest of the crew continued to eat as if bored, their eyes locked on the bright-green combine maneuvering across the golden field. Paul let up on the gas and the big machine slowed as he drove around the pickup, just missing the tailgate laden with Tupperware, napkins, and sodas. He slowed more when the header bounced as he crossed the ruts leading into the field and turned toward the arc created by the other two combines and the three grain trucks.

John took another bite of his sandwich and looked around. Henley, Dale, and Blaine all stared hard at Paul as if they'd never seen a combine before. He looked at Toff, who shrugged, but then he turned his attention back to Paul's combine as well. It was only a few seconds but when John looked back, he saw why everyone was so interested. Paul had spun the great big machine around to face them. The engine was running, the header was still raised, but it was still, like a bull ready to charge. They could see Paul in the cab, but he wasn't looking at them, he was glancing back and forth between his side-view mirrors that were mounted on either side of the cab and about four to five feet away from him. The combine was big, and the mirrors had to be far enough out to see the rear of the machine.

Then Paul started to back up. Straight back.

John dropped his plate on the ground and stood up. He jumped up and down and waved his arms like he was flagging down an airplane. Then he ran toward Paul.

Henley and Blaine had both stood up, but they just yelled. When they saw John sprint past them, they followed, all three waving their arms, shouting, trying to get Paul's attention.

It didn't work. Paul was focused on his right-side mirror, he never looked back to the other on his left, and he never looked out toward the crew. He didn't stop backing up until he felt the jolt that rocked the whole combine.

John stopped short when he heard breaking glass and saw his truck jostle hard when Paul backed his combine into it. He laced his fingers on top of his head and watched Paul finally look into his other side-view mirror.

Henley and Blaine stood on either side of John, then they were joined by Dale and Toff. They all watched as Paul looked out at them, shook his head, then slowly pulled forward. John's truck wobbled again as the combine broke contact.

"Shit," mumbled Blaine.

The windshield of John's truck had a hole in the lower right corner and the glass was cracked in a spider web pattern that spread all the way across it. The side-view mirror on the passenger side was broken and dangled by one of the mounting brackets; the right fender was crumpled, not too bad, but noticeable and enough that the signal light was shattered and bent.

Paul shut down the engine of the combine and climbed down from the cab. He glanced back at the damage, shook his head, then approached Henley with a sheepish look that was more familiar to Dale, the high school principal.

John was the first to step forward. "What the—"

"Damn it, John," Henley shouted.

John stopped and looked at his boss.

"Why did you park there? This wouldn't have happened if you would've parked your rig where you were supposed to."

That brought Paul to a quick stop. He stared between his father-in-law and John.

John's mouth dropped open. "What?!" he gasped. "This is *my* fault? Where was I *supposed* to park that's different than anywhere else?"

"Don't talk back to me," Henley yelled and pointed his finger. "You shouldn't have parked there." He stomped passed Paul and over to the vehicles to inspect the damage.

John looked at Toff and the others, dumbfounded.

"What the fuck, right?" Blaine said.

CHAPTER 40

The next morning, while everyone else ate breakfast, John sealed the hole in his windshield with duct tape. He bent the side-view mirror brackets back into place and used the same tape to reinforce them. The signal light was broken, and he couldn't do anything about the dent in the fender.

After the accident John still drove the truck the rest of the afternoon. Blaine had checked that it was safe to drive and told John to use hand signals if he needed and to be extra careful. Even though they'd bent the side-view mirror back into place, the struts were aluminum and in their weakened state sagged with every bounce and jolt across the field.

Mrs. Henley had gone back to the house and called auto-body shops in the area until she found one with a windshield for a 1979 GMC 6000 in stock. It didn't take long. The GMC was used by hundreds of farmers, and during harvest more than a few windshields were bound to get broken. The body shops ordered them in advance. The problem was timing; they couldn't fit the truck into their schedule for a day or so.

The duct tape would have to do.

During the day John gave Henley the same treatment he received. The first couple of times the farmer saw John as he approached in the combine, Henley looked like he'd swallowed a mouthful of hot peppers, his face was red, his lips a tight line, and he frowned as he stared straight ahead, ignoring John while bottling up the heat.

John scowled right back. He hadn't done anything wrong and Henley blaming him for Paul's mistake was utter bullshit. The rest of the day, when they saw one another, they glared, drove off in opposite directions, didn't talk, and John flipped him off from the bench seat every chance he got.

The duct tape worked for a while, but the constant dust worked its way in, and John had to replace the makeshift patch on the windshield three times throughout the day. Later, once the trucks were parked back at the main house, Henley pulled John aside while everyone else sat down for dinner. "Why don't you head home while there's still a little light."

It wasn't a question and even if it had been, John wasn't sure how to answer.

Henley said, "I'm going to take the truck to the body shop in the morning and they'll have it all day. So, get some sleep in your own bed tonight and come back out day after tomorrow."

John's hands felt numb, and a rock fell into his throat. He stared at Henley and wanted to shout, *This wasn't my fault, and you know it!* But he knew it wouldn't matter. This was Henley's farm, it was Henley's truck, and the decision had been made.

John wanted to look away, to see if Toff had heard, if Dale and Paul and Blaine were watching. But Henley stood there looking him in the eye, challenging him. John stared right back, didn't say a word. Then he turned, walked to the Bug, got in, and drove off the farm.

"Okay, John," Evie Brewer said. "Slow down. What happened again? One more time."

John had the entire drive home to roll his anger around, smack at it, punch it, and roll it out some more like a ball of clay. He burst into the house, slammed the door, and scared his mother half to death. When she asked what was wrong, he had sounded off at a speed only heard during the quick-read legal requirements of a TV commercial.

John took a deep breath and explained to his mother why he was home and would be there again all day tomorrow. He told her about being reprimanded for mentioning D&D, the shouting match between Paul and Henley, the damage to his truck, and finally being sent home.

"Well, that's not right," Evie said. "I agree with you there."

"I know!" John yelled. Reliving the story just made him angrier.

"All right," she said. "Let's sit down a minute."

Evie turned and pulled a chair out from the dining room table. "You're filthy, John," she said when her son didn't follow her. "You're not sitting on the couch like that."

They sat around the table, John careful not to put his arms on it. In a mirror, he saw what his mother did. He looked like a coal miner but covered in brown dust and dirt rather than black soot.

"Jim Henley is, you might say, a bit protective of his family," she said. "Especially that daughter of his."

"Mom," John breathed. "She wasn't even there!"

"I know that, John," she said, holding up her palm to keep her son calm. "What I'm saying is everyone in town is talking about Paul, how he's a coward."

"You don't need to tell me," John said. He knew what his friends were hearing, and Henley didn't keep his opinion secret. "But so what if everyone thinks he's a coward? Why blame me for what he did?"

Evie sighed. "John, this doesn't leave this room. You can't tell Truck or any of your other friends. Got it?"

John nodded.

"I mean it."

"I promise," John said. "I won't."

Satisfied, she said, "Word is, Paul and Joanna—that's Henley's daughter—are having problems, have been for a while. And now this whole thing with Paul is putting a lot more pressure on them. They might even split up."

"So?" John asked.

"Don't be insensitive, Jonathan," she said.

"I don't mean it like that. I mean, so Paul and Joanna might split up. Why does that mean Henley's mad at *me*? If anything, I'd think he'd be even more mad at Paul."

"Maybe he's trying to protect his daughter."

John frowned. "That doesn't make sense."

Evie patted her son's arm. "Paul and Joanna are having problems and now there's talk that Paul might have been able to save Dave Carlson but didn't. They're saying he froze up; people are calling him a coward. That's a lot to put on a couple. If Jim had gotten mad at Paul again, it could have just caused more problems for Joanna. Understand? If Joanna *and* her father are mad at Paul, what is there to keep Paul in the marriage? Jim probably didn't want to be the final straw."

John thought about how Henley had gone in and stayed in the house for a while after his argument with Paul that morning. Mrs. Henley had come out onto the porch hugging herself and watched them leave. She must have told Henley not to get mad at their son-in-law anymore, that their daughter's marriage was on the rocks. And Henley knew just who to take it out on. Great.

"So, what, I'm the whipping boy for Paul all the time now?"

"No! Of course not. What Jim Henley did to you is wrong. You and everyone out there knows it. All I'm telling you—and I don't even know for sure—is that this might be *why* you got blamed. But it still doesn't make it right."

"Why do things that *aren't right* keep happening to me?" John asked. He thought about Paulette Dickerson and her evangelical crusade.

Evie looked at her son. Her face betrayed her sorrow. "I know it seems like that sometimes..." she said.

"Mom! There's no *seems*. First, Paulette Dickerson comes after us because of D&D and all summer it's been like this with Henley."

"You're right. It's been kind of a rotten summer for you. But it hasn't all been bad, right? You haven't let Jim Henley walk all over you. I'm proud of you for that. You've kept your head. You're handling things the way you should. Henley can only respect you for that whether he'll admit it or not. You stick to who you are, what you know is right, and you'll be fine. You've got Truck and I'm always right here for you. Okay?"

John nodded. He was still mad, but he told himself this was the end of it. Henley just lost whatever control he thought he had over him.

"Are you hungry?" Evie asked.

"Yeah."

"Well, you're filthy and you stink. Go take a shower and I'll get you some dinner."

John smiled and got up. On the way to the bathroom, he wondered how much AC/DC tickets cost.

CHAPTER 41

"Are you in?" John asked.

Truck nodded and jammed a couple of fries into his mouth. "Of course I'm in," he said. "How do we do it if he's watching, though?"

"If you drive, Toff and I can sneak out and go around the combine shed. We'll meet you out on the highway just after the turn-off to Henley's place. There's a hill behind the house that blocks the view."

They were sitting in a booth at the Warhawk's Nest. Rebecca, Truck's new girlfriend, wasn't scheduled to work at the A&W until five, otherwise they would have been there.

"Okay," Truck said. "I can do that. What time are we talking?"

John thought about it. He'd called the Spokane Coliseum earlier and knew the opening band would go on at eight. The person he talked to didn't know how long they would play, though. A half hour is what John thought, just like every other concert he'd been to.

The big question was what time Henley would call an end to cutting for the day. If they were close to finishing a field, they might go until nine at night or later. If everyone was hungry or if it had just been a rough day, Henley might stop around seven. There was no telling.

Then there was the drive back to the farm and dinner. And it would take about forty-five minutes to drive to Spokane from there.

John went over all of this with Truck then said, "No matter what, we'll probably miss the opener. If we leave Henley's by eight though, we should be fine for AC/DC."

"No problem," Truck said. "I'll wait a couple hours if I have to. Part of me thinks you should just get in the Bug and go, though. You know?"

"I know." John had thought about that too. Just driving back to the farm after they were through cutting for the day and then driving away in his car. He'd tell them, *No thanks on dinner; I'll be back a little late but ready to go first thing in the morning.* "But I need the money," he told Truck. "I hate that that's the reason, but I need everything I can if I'm going to go to college. And unfortunately, it's 'my farm, my rules.'" John tried to raise his voice and sound like an old man but sounded instead like a wheezy accordion. They laughed.

"Have you considered the military, son?" Truck asked in a heavy drawl. "The G.I. Bill will get you that college education."

"It's not just a job," John said.

"It's an adventure!" they finished together.

"You know I've thought about it," John said, the joviality gone. "I don't think I'm soldier material, though. Four years seems like such a long time too. I'd be old when I finally get to college."

"Hey, whatever," Truck said. He took a bite of his burger. "We're going to go see AC/DC!"

John arrived at the farm early. His grain truck was back from the body shop and parked next to Blaine's. The windshield had been replaced and was so clear it was almost invisible. The side-view mirror had been replaced, or at least the bracket had, and the turn signal was new. The dent in the fender was still there, though it looked shallower, like it had been pushed out from the inside.

He heard the screen door on Henley's back porch screech then smack shut. Mrs. Henley was laying out breakfast on the picnic table. He waved and she smiled. At least she didn't frown as much as her husband.

Toff came out of the bunkhouse, saw the Bug, and looked around until he spotted John. They ate breakfast quickly as Paul drove in and went over to the trucks. "How was your day off?" Toff asked. He smirked as he said it.

John shrugged. "Kind of boring, really. But hey, I talked to Truck; he's going to take us to AC/DC next Thursday. We got it all planned."

Toff smiled but before he said anything Blaine yelled, "Load up!" The boys jogged over to the back porch to retrieve their ice water jugs and passed Henley along the way.

"Morning, Jim," Toff said.

John, for his part, smiled and nodded.

"Gentlemen," Henley said. "Good day off, John?"

"Not bad," John replied. "I hope not having a truck for a day didn't put us too far behind."

"I think we'll be fine. Just make sure you park in a better spot from now on."

"Sure thing," John said. "And hopefully Paul will start checking his mirrors." He smiled and followed Toff into the back porch and let the screen door shut behind him with a *thwack*.

CHAPTER 42

"That's awesome!" Truck said after John told him what he'd said to Henley about Paul checking his mirrors.

"I thought he was going to follow me into the back porch and kick my ass," John said.

"So, what *did* he do?" Levi asked. They were all gathered in the Council Chamber waiting for Nick so they could continue *Alchemist's Bane*. John filled the time with his tale of rebellion.

"Hasn't said a word to me since," John said. He smiled, but he wasn't sure if he was happy about it. He disrespected his boss, which wasn't something that was done. Just not cool. On the other hand, he felt like he'd also let Henley know that he wasn't interested in being a scapegoat. It was both a win and a lose.

Nick walked into the garage. "Hey," he said and sat down.

"Mr. Conversation," Charlie said.

"Just checking in, you know?" Nick said. "You guys look like something happened. Johnny's got a weird grin, so I'm guessing he lost his virginity or something like that."

"Not if Lisa Martin wasn't involved," Truck said. John glared and he changed the subject. "AC/DC concert Thursday. Are you in?"

Nick shook his head. "Naw. I'm broke." He looked at John. "I thought everything you made was going to college?"

"Rock 'n' roll, dude! I got priorities," John said. "Actually, my grandma always gives me money for my birthday and tells me to do something fun with it. So, I do concerts."

"Ah, ain't that sweet," said Nick.

"Don't be messing with my grandma now," John said.

"Your grandma's cool!" Truck yelled. "She makes really good shortbread."

"I know," John agreed. "At Christmas she gave me a box of—"

"Are you two done?" Nick interrupted. "Are we playing D&D or are we going to break out the knitting?"

"Wow," Levi breathed. "*Someone's* a grump!"

"All right, all right," John said. He set up his Dungeon Masters screen and placed his notes in front of him on the table. "But if anybody *wants* to do some knitting or try some shortbread, just say so."

"What the hell is shortbread?" Charlie asked.

Truck gasped. "Seriously?"

John smiled. "It's kind of like a cross between a cookie and a biscuit. It's Scottish, I think."

"Maybe we can cook some up and bribe a dragon with it in our next dungeon," Nick complained.

"Okay," John said, ignoring Nick's quip. He skimmed his notes and then looked around. "You guys are still in the ceremonial hall. Bellator looked through the peephole in the door and saw prisoners from the village on the other side. We stopped before Truck could tell us his plan."

Everyone looked at Truck.

"What?" he asked. "That was a week ago. I gotta remember. Oh yeah! Here it is: We all have extra weapons, right? Bellator didn't see any enemies in there, so I go in first, real quick like, and give the guys weapons to help us fight whoever brought them there."

"And any other nasties around the corner," Levi said. "I like it."

"It's not a spectacular plan," Truck admitted. "But it's something. Unless Toff has a spell up his sleeve that may work better."

Toff looked at the character sheet for his magic-user. It listed all the spells at his disposal—weapons, magical items, everything the character had, as well as attributes such as intelligence, strength, and so on. He shook his head. "I don't think so. I mean I can create a diversion maybe, but that would be pointless until we see what we're up against."

"I think we can handle whatever we find," Nick said. "So far, there's only been orcs and weird little creatures. Nothing too tough."

"Except the grell," Levi reminded him.

John thought Nick was right. The only challenging monsters so far were the gargoyle and the grell. The dungeon wasn't written to be full of different monsters, it was about the amulet and the story behind it. He'd have to think about a monster that would make a good challenge, but make sense in the dungeon too. Just to stir things up.

"I mean the ones that serve this warlord guy. His minions have all been the same," Nick reasoned.

"It's not the type," Charlie said, "but the number. If they're bringing prisoners down, there should be a lot more of them."

Nick shrugged. "Okay. I have a short sword I'll lend out."

"And Kryger has another sword," Truck said. "That should do it."

"Well," Charlie offered, "I have extra daggers. Why stop at arming just a couple of them?"

"Wait a minute," Nick said. He frowned at John and then Toff. "Are you going to the concert, too, Toff?"

Toff nodded.

"I thought you guys were restricted from leaving or something. Didn't you say this Henley guy is paranoid you'll get in an accident and then not be able to work?"

John said, "We didn't ask. We're sneaking out and Truck is going to pick us up."

"What if it rains?" Nick asked. "Will you get the day off?"

"Maybe," Toff said. "Depends on how hard it rains. Dream on, though. That isn't going to happen."

"Wanna bet?" Nick smiled and John and Toff stared at him. "Don't you guys watch the news? It's supposed to rain Thursday and Friday. Probably start late Wednesday night."

"Seriously?"

"Yeah. Seriously. First rain since May. It's not guaranteed—those weather dudes guess most of the time—but there you go."

"Hey," Charlie interrupted. "Are we here to bake cookies, talk about rain, or play some D&D?"

"*Reer!*" Levi said. "Someone else is grumpy. You sound like Nick."

"Hey!" Nick said.

Truck gulped Coke and belched the alphabet to H. "Weak one," he said. "Sorry."

Everyone stared and it was quiet around the table. Toff sighed loudly. "Let's put Truck's plan into motion."

Truck crushed the aluminum soda can and tossed it onto the workbench behind John. "Kryger unsheathes the extra sword on his back and gets Bellator's short sword," he said.

"Do you want a dagger or two?" Charlie asked.

"Might as well," Truck said. "Kryger also gets a couple of daggers from Domo. He'll go to the door, but let's have our dwarf look one more time."

"Why?" Nick asked.

"If there are more men and they've backed up to the door, or if there are a few orcs or whatever rooting around, we don't want to just go barging in."

"Wait a minute," Levi said. "Did we have a torch lit or not?"

John consulted his notes before they all turned and looked at him. He shook his head. "No torch."

"Then Bellator goes back to the peephole and takes a look," Nick said.

"The hallway on the other side of the door," John said, "is empty."

CHAPTER 43

Bellator let the cover slip over the peephole again and Kryger handed back his short sword and Domo's daggers.

"What happened?" Franco whispered.

"They're gone," Bellator said. "The prisoners have already been moved."

"We must continue on," Kryger said. "We'll go through the door and down the hallway to see what's beyond."

The dwarf peeked one more time, nodded, and carefully opened the door. A dull orange glow split the darkness and widened as Bellator pulled the door inward. Two torches, placed higher than even Kryger could reach, flickered on the walls of the passage and blackened the ceiling.

The party stepped out of the ceremonial hall, their eyes searching for danger ahead, above, and even below. If prisoners were brought into this area, it was reasonable to assume there could be snares of some type to keep them from...wandering away.

The opposite end of the hall emptied into a large square room. Low benches carved from the walls lined the perimeter and another hallway led out of the southern wall. The room was empty but smelled of sweat. And fear.

Domo held up his hand, tapped his ear, and pointed ahead. He could hear something beyond the hallway on the opposite side of the chamber.

They hugged the walls and slowly made their way around the room to the mouth of the southern passage. The walls amplified sound and twice an errant sword point scraped stone and once Franco thumped his mace against a low bench. But they went on undiscovered.

At the end of the hallway, they stopped. Domo retrieved a small mirror from his pouch and got down on the floor. The mirror was the size of a coin, and he held it between his fingers as he eased it passed the corner and into the open hallway. He held it there for a moment, the reflective surface facing the floor, then tilted it up with agonizing patience until he had a tiny view of what lay beyond.

A gruff voice shouted something. It was loud, deep, like an out-of-tune bass drum, but didn't sound angry. It was not a language anyone in the party understood. Then another voice, guttural but similar to the first, answered.

Domo slowly withdrew the mirror and stood up. He looked at Xan and held up two fingers, a question upon his face. Xan nodded. Elves had superior hearing to other humanoid races so the thief and wizard often confirmed what they heard with each other.

As a group they stepped away from the hallway and huddled together. "There are at least two creatures in the room beyond this passage," Domo whispered. "Whatever they are, they're big."

Kryger pointed to Xan and waved his hands. Xan thought about it then nodded. He had a spell he could use as either a diversionary tactic like they'd discussed earlier, or to attack. "It would be best if I could see what we're dealing with," he whispered. He looked at Domo.

"I don't know," the thief countered. "They're very big, like orcs, but bigger. Heavier."

"Giants?" Kryger wondered. "Down here?"

Domo shook his head. "Not that big."

"I have an idea," Xan whispered. "It will take only a moment or two to prepare, but if the creatures are too strong for us, I can, at the very least, weaken them."

Kryger and Bellator scoffed.

"No offense, my fierce friends," the magic-user smiled. "I merely offer an option to aid in our assured victory."

"I feel our luck is running thin," Domo said. "We've been too long in this mine without finding our quarry."

Kryger nodded. "We must hurry, I agree." He turned to the wizard. "What's your plan?"

Xan quickly relayed to his friends what he had in mind and began to prepare his spell.

Bellator readied himself with a throwing axe; Domo unsheathed two well balanced daggers; Franco, unburdened by a torch, hefted his new hammer in one hand and a flail in the other. Kryger stood nearby, watching the hallway, his thick arms crossed but still holding his heavy broadsword at the ready, so it looked like the weapon grew straight up out of his chest.

Xan then stood tall and held his staff, so it leaned forward, he nodded to the group and walked into the hallway. The others fell in line behind him, their weapons poised for battle, their eyes searching for movement up ahead.

The passage between the rooms was short, maybe thirty feet at the most. Xan was in the middle of the hall when the opening ahead was blocked by a hulking ogre.[1] It was nine feet tall, dressed in a wild patchwork of animal skins, and held what looked like a small tree trunk capped with iron. The ogre's skin was the color of burnt flesh and its bloodshot eyes narrowed as they took in the unexpected party.

Xan stopped. The others, who were following in a loose single file, spread out behind the magic-user. The ogre grunted, said something in a low growling voice, and moved to the side. Another ogre, this one taller by a foot and the color of rancid bile, stepped into view. It didn't carry a weapon, but its arms were as thick as the club its companion carried and rippled with sinewy muscle.

The bigger ogre roared, slammed the heal of its fist against the stone wall, and stepped into the hall.

Xan struck. He leveled his staff at the oncoming monsters and muttered his incantation. The air crackled for

[1]Ogres are large (9+ feet tall) mean creatures. Their skin varies from blackish brown to an ugly, dead-hued yellow. They have black or dull dark green hair and wear skins and furs. *Monster Manual* (Lake Geneva, WI: TSR, 1979), 75.

an instant and the hair on Bellator's and Domo's arms, who were standing closest to Xan, stood on end. Then a dazzling bolt of bluish-white lightning shot out the end of the staff, split in two and slammed into the massive guards.

The two giant ogres tensed, their muscles spasming as the electricity coursed through their bodies. The lightning bolt danced in the air, snapping and cracking, its power holding the monsters at bay.

Then, as quickly as it had begun, the lightning was gone. It was suddenly much darker and eerily quiet in the passage. The dazed ogres still stood, their flesh smoldering where the electricity had chewed at them; the animal skin garb of the first ogre was on fire.

Bellator was the first to react. He threw his axe at the larger of the two beasts and the blade embedded itself in the ogre's shoulder. The creature, still dazed by Xan's lightning, grunted and stepped back, unsure of what had happened.

Domo was just as quick and let both daggers fly, one after the other, at the smaller ogre. With deadly accuracy the first dagger found purchase in the monster's left eye. Even though weary from the electrical attack, the ogre flinched, dropped its club, and roared in pain, allowing the second dagger to just miss.

Kryger and Franco ran forward, but the ogres had cleared their heads. Just as Kryger drew back his arms to strike, the bigger ogre lashed out and struck the warrior across the face with the back of its hand.

Kryger's feet left the ground and he slammed into the stone wall like a thrown bag of grain. He crumpled to the floor but held his sword point up.

Franco fared better; he ducked the fist that had been clumsily swung at him by the first ogre. Since the beast missed and was off balance, the cleric brought his hammer down with the ferocity of a frost giant.[2] Franco's aim was true, and he crushed the ogre's big toe and several bones in its foot.

Half blind and hobbled, the ogre howled and fell back into the room it had come from. But Franco swung his flail around and smashed it against the ogre's other foot before it could roll away.

The bigger ogre stood tall when he saw he was alone. He pulled the axe out of his shoulder and looked at it. It was tiny in his hand, but it had bit hard and brackish blood seeped from the wound. The ogre looked down the hallway and roared. He threw the axe at Bellator, but the blade clattered harmlessly against the floor behind the dwarf.

Xan reached Kryger and helped him to his feet. The warrior's nose was bleeding and broken, and the side of his face was scuffed and bruised. "Do you have your wits about you, my friend?" Xan asked.

"I am fine," Kryger said. He drew a deep breath, blew it out, and shook his head. Blood droplets splattered the wall and Xan's tunic. Kryger wiped his nose with the back of his hand and sniffed hard. He eyed the big ogre and said, "I am fine." He stood tall and pushed his shoulders back.

---

[2] Frost giants are 15 feet tall with ivory-colored skin, bluish or yellow hair, and similarly colored eyes. They can hurl rocks and carry large weapons similar to human barbarians. *Monster Manual* (Lake Geneva, WI: TSR, 1979), 44–45.

Bellator stepped close, quickly asked if everything was all right, then bolted away when Xan nodded at him. He threw another axe at the ogre, but the beast was ready and dodged it.

The exchange gave Domo the opportunity to slip into the far room unnoticed. He made sure to stay to the left, to remain in the blind spot of the shorter ogre who had fallen inside.

In the hallway the big ogre lifted the club dropped by his companion. He roared and smashed it into the wall. Stone shards exploded from the corner blocks and flew like tiny knives into the hallway.

The show of bravado didn't sway the party. Kryger dragged his broadsword along the wall and drew sparks. Franco tapped his hammer against the opposite wall, and he held the flail loosely in his other hand. Bellator moved up the middle, the battle hammer hefted and ready. Xan prepared another spell but knew by the determined looks on his comrades' faces he wasn't likely to need it.

Bellator double-tapped his battle hammer against the floor and moved forward to force the attack. The enraged ogre took the bait, took a step forward and swung the club down at the dwarf. Bellator dove out of the way and the club's metal cap smashed against the stone floor and sent sparks flying.

The double-tap was the signal and Kryger was ready. The ogre's club, like his broadsword, was a two-handed weapon. As the ogre's attack missed and hit the floor, the beast's sides were unprotected. Kryger lunged forward, the point of his sword held out flat in front of him and he plunged the blade into the tough, yellowish skin of his enemy below the ribs.

The monster bellowed in rage. It turned toward Kryger, whose blade dripped with fresh blood. But ogres, while strong, were not the most intelligent creatures and it failed to learn its lesson. While it focused its wrath on Kryger, Franco swung his flail at the undefended knee he was closest to and landed the blow with bone-crunching satisfaction.

Xan mentally readied his spell, but the ogre stumbled back and fell into the room where Domo and the first ogre had gone. The giant was bleeding profusely from the stab wound in its side, the gash from Bellator's axe, and its right knee sounded like rolling gravel with each step. But their enemy still held the club. The ogre shook with rage, its eyes wide, and it huffed in great breaths. It knew it was wounded, but it also knew it was bigger and stronger than these small foes.

The ogre stood again, its weight on the left leg, and he swung the club in a sweeping arc to stave off the advance of the party.

"Push him straight back," Domo yelled.

They couldn't see their elven thief, but they trusted him. As in the hallway, Kryger and Franco took up flanking positions and Bellator advanced in the center, followed by Xan who looked about the room for Domo.

The ogre brandished the club again as it hobbled backward, swinging it in wide arcs and trying to keep the three attackers in his sight. Then it stopped. It looked at Kryger, roared, and threw the club in the other direction.

Franco and Bellator saw the feint, but Xan was caught looking toward Kryger. The club spun through the air and hit Xan in the shoulder. The impact knocked him over and he lay still beneath the weapon.

The magic-user's companions charged. The ogre bellowed and staggered back again, but its foot, the one below the smashed knee, caught upon something on the floor and the beast fell backward. The giant ogre grunted when it hit the floor, the air knocked from its lungs; its legs up, arms out, blood running free.

From high above in the darkness a great barrel hurtled down, the wind rushed in its wake as the chain of a pully rattled out of control somewhere above. The barrel exploded upon the downed ogre, the iron bands burst, and heavy stones fell about the broken body.

Nobody moved. Nobody said anything. Then Kryger and Bellator stepped toward the crushed ogre. Beneath its legs, what he'd fallen over, was the body of its companion. Domo's dagger was still in the left eye socket and the hilt of a second blade protruded from its neck.

"Domo?" Kryger whispered.

"Here." The elf was a few feet away near a wooden platform and a contraption of gears, levers, and chains. Domo walked over to join the warriors, holding his left arm close to his body. He looked at the first ogre and pulled the two blades from the body of the ogre with his right hand. "This one gave me more trouble than I thought he would. My arm's broken."

Xan arrived with the help of Franco, his arm around the cleric's shoulders. His face was pale, but he wasn't bleeding.

"Are you badly injured?" Kryger asked him.

"I don't know," the magic-user replied. "I feel like I was hit by a mastodon. My knees are still shaking."

"We can't go on in this condition," Franco said.

Kryger shook his head. "No one is in mortal danger. Domo has lost the use of one arm, but we must push on."

"We are weakened," Franco insisted. "And this battle will have surely alerted others to our presence. My healing spells won't take long."

"Agreed," said Bellator. "We cannot fight together in this state."

Kryger nodded reluctantly. "Very well," he said. Then to Franco, "Begin with Domo. I want to see what this contraption is." He walked over to the platform and inspected the chains and levers. He looked up. The ceiling was hidden in shadow, perhaps fifty or more feet above, but he could make out a darker rectangular opening in the ceiling the same shape and size as the platform, along with five more barrels suspended by the chains. "Do you know what this is?" he asked.

Among the ministrations of Franco's spell Domo answered, "It's the up-and-down platform Munt told us about. It's our ride upstairs."

CHAPTER 44

The elevator had no doubt been built and used by the dwarves to haul ore, equipment, and miners between the levels. Now it was being used for something more sinister: the transportation of prisoners enslaved by the evil gray dwarf, Bohz Grauer.

"The amulet we have is a decoy," Domo said. "The original no longer exists and we must assume Jovar doesn't know this. Our mission will be fulfilled once we hand over that artifact. It's the amulet Jovar really wants, not Bohz Grauer's head. We can go up right now and be rid of this place."

Kryger shook his head. "No, we must put an end to this operation as well," he said, waving his hand at the elevator. "This Bohz Grauer," he spat the name, "this *gray one*, is finished. Who's to say he won't continue his raids on the village once Jovar has his prize?"

"To think slaves are being forced to labor in a dwarf mine," Bellator groused. "I stand with Kryger."

"You know my stance on evil," Franco said. "No need to even ask."

Xan nodded. "I won't let my friends down. We'll continue on and put an end to it."

They looked at Domo, the thief of the group, who tended to look after himself first. They had been through many adventures together and while his profession was as a thief, he was trusted among them. Domo shrugged. "I assume there will be rewards to be had afterward," he said.

With their course of action decided and their injuries magically cured by the cleric's healing spells, they searched the large chamber they found themselves in. The elevator platform took up a large area in the middle of the room and the bodies of the two ogres were strewn across one corner of it. It was empty otherwise. The room was roughly triangular, pointing toward the south. They'd entered from the passage at the north, on the bottom of the triangle. Instead of a point at the southern tip, it continued on as a passageway with large double doors at the end. Two torches, like those they'd seen outside the ceremonial hall, lit that far passage.

"Obviously the prisoners were taken through there," Franco said, pointing to the doors at the end of the hallway.

A crash rocked the elevator platform, and instinctively, they looked up. Two shadowy gray faces looked over the edge of the hole in the ceiling. Then a hand appeared and dropped something.

"Look out!" Kryger yelled. They leapt away from the platform just as a heavy stone smashed the spot where Xan had been standing.

"We've been discovered," Domo said. "Time to move on. Quickly."

They ran south to the point of the triangle and into the passage. "It's a bottleneck. They will be waiting for us on the other side," Franco said. "Our fight with the ogres could not have gone unheard from here either."

Kryger nodded. "Agreed. Xan, do you have a spell that may help?"

"Not until we get through the door."

"Is there a hidden peephole? Like at the ceremonial hall?" Franco asked Bellator.

"No," the dwarf said, quickly scanning the door. "Nothing."

"If we go through blindly," Domo said, "we will be met either by a volley of arrows from close range, or swords from the sides. When we go, we go low and high. Not here." He patted his chest.

"Low, I can do," Bellator said. "How do you mean to go high?"

"Xan and I can stand atop the doors and duck down below the casement to attack." He looked at Xan for confirmation.

The magician nodded. "I'll prepare a confusion spell. Once the doors are open, I will throw the enchantment. Do not attack though; stay behind the doors."

"After the spell is cast," Domo said, "I will see what we have to deal with."

"What does a confusion spell do?" Franco asked.

"Anyone it affects becomes unsure of why they are there, what they are supposed to do. Some will simply leave, others might attack who or whatever is nearby, some might flee right out this door. If that happens, let them go."

"Unless it's the gray dwarf," Kryger said. "Him we want."

"I've never seen a gray dwarf," Xan admitted.

"He looks like a dwarf," Bellator sneered. "But he will be gray of skin, very mean looking, and certainly more unkempt!"

Kryger smiled at his friend's disgust. "Quickly now, before we're surprised from behind."

Xan dug into his pockets, retrieved the three small nutshells he needed to prepare his spell, then stepped to the side. It only took a moment and he nodded to his companions.

Kryger and Bellator squatted near the doors, then pulled them open slowly as they backstepped to stay behind them. Domo and Xan leapt up, bracing themselves against the wall as they each perched atop a door, and Franco stood to the side, his eye on the hallway that led out to the elevator room.

Two arrows sailed through the open doorway and clattered harmlessly against the stone wall. "Fools!" someone shouted from within the room. Xan ducked down and cast his confusion spell into the chamber.

Another arrow narrowly missed the magician's head just as he completed the incantation and lifted himself up again.

They heard a sword clang against the floor, some unintelligible mutterings, and the slam of a door. Then it was quiet.

Bellator and Kryger looked at one another then at Domo. The elf quickly ducked down to look through the doorway before showing three fingers to his companions. Domo dropped lithely to the floor and drew his short sword. Kryger and Bellator stood up behind him, both heavily armed and ready for a fight. Then Franco and Xan stepped into the doorway to face the three foes.

Inside the room two orcs stood against the wall opposite the doorway. They both held crossbows, but they looked about the room as if they had suddenly appeared there from somewhere else. The party standing in the doorway appeared as a curiosity only and they didn't raise their weapons. The other occupant in the room was a human, a man dressed in farming clothes and wandering about looking at the walls.

Kryger stepped through the doorway and into the room. He looked about quickly but kept an eye on the orcs. Ahead and to the right was a passageway blocked by a tall gate set in a wall of iron bars. To the left was a short hallway with another door at the end. Like the rest of the rooms, this one featured ornate carvings on the walls depicting sweeping landscapes and mountain vistas.

The orcs blocked the passage, though only because that's where they happened to be standing. Xan's confusion spell had wiped away any sense of duty they may have had just a few moments earlier. The man was near the iron gate; he gazed through the bars, looked toward the orcs, then walked around in a circle to end up back at the gate. The spell had obviously blocked his memory of how he'd arrived there as well.

"Domo," Kryger called. "See if that gate is unlocked. We should see what's beyond it."

"What about these two?" Bellator asked, nodding at the two orcs.

"Depending on what Domo finds on the other side of those bars, we'll put them in there. Xan, how long will your magic last?"

"It affects everyone differently," the magic-user replied. "But we probably have a few more minutes for them. The man, maybe a little less."

"The gate is open now," Domo said as he joined the group. "There is scaffolding leading down into the cave-in. This must be where they bring the prisoners and then send them down."

"We would have saved them but for the two ogres," Franco said.

"We may yet," Kryger said. "Let's disarm the orcs and lock them behind the gate. I believe we're closer now to Bohz Grauer. Maybe beyond that door." He nodded toward the passage.

It wasn't difficult to take the crossbows away from the orcs. In their addled state they didn't even know why they had them. Franco and Bellator then led them to the gate, pushed them through, and Domo locked it behind them. Xan gave the man water, but he was still unsure of his situation and only mumbled his thanks as he gulped.

"What makes you think Bohz is nearby?" Bellator asked.

"When we first opened the doors and the arrows flew," Kryger said, "do you remember hearing those archers being admonished?"

"Someone yelled, 'Fools!'" Xan said.

Kryger nodded. "That had to be the gray one. He probably fled, anticipating something from our wizard. Come. We mustn't delay."

"What about our new friend here?" Franco asked. The man was now standing outside their conversation like a dog, looking curiously at each one and wondering if he was part of the group.

"Bring him along," Bellator said. "He'll snap out of it soon enough."

Kryger looked at Xan and asked, "Will he remember us as his rescuers, or think we're his abductors?"

"He will remember the orcs who brought him here," Xan mused. "He probably won't know us, but I think he won't fear us."

"Keep him out of the way until he has his wits about him," Kryger told Franco. "Let's go."

The door at the far end of the room was thick oak and featured a cacophony of leaves carved into its surface. Some leaves were curled out in relief from the door's face, some falling over the tops of others, all done so there wasn't a flat surface to be seen; the leaves seemed to flutter in the waving torchlight.

"Any peepholes, Bellator?" Kryger asked.

The dwarf eyed the door. "No."

"How does it open?" Franco asked. He looked up and down the door looking for a latch or handle.

"Like any door," Bellator said and rolled his eyes. He grasped two leaves that were curled over one another and tugged enough to pull the door open an inch or so.

"If they led the prisoners down back there, there won't be torches beyond this door," Domo said. "Everywhere prisoners are, is lit. Have you noticed?"

"Less work for them as slave drivers," Franco spat. He pulled the torch out of the sconce on the wall and nodded at the group as if to say, *So, there.*

"That's where he went," the man said.

They all stepped back and looked at their new companion. "Where who went?" Kryger asked.

"The dwarf." He looked at Bellator and corrected himself. "The *bad* dwarf."

"He's no dwarf," Bellator said. "He's a duergar. Evil, and not of the dwarf clans."

The man nodded. "Evil is right."

"Do you know who you are and how you came to be here?" Franco asked.

"Aye. My name is Clavam. Our homes were set upon by a band of wicked creatures sometime after the witching hour. They beat us then brought us here. The others went through the gate. How I came to be with you, or who any of you are, I do not know."

"No need to worry about that," Kryger said. "You're among friends now, and we seek the gray dwarf you saw go through this door. His name is Bohz Grauer."

"To kill, I hope," Clavam said.

"Why do you wish him dead?" Franco asked.

"It is he who ordered us brought here. We fought for our freedom and our families suffered. My wife is dead because of him."

"We hoped to take him to your mayor, Jovar, for justice," Franco told him. Domo looked sideways at Kryger and cocked an eyebrow.

Clavam snorted. "Jovar *hired* this...gray dwarf. Jovar will bring no justice." He spat.

The group looked at one another as this was surprising news to them. "We've been deceived," Kryger growled.

"Then there is no reason for us to stay in this mine," Domo said.

"No," Franco said shaking his head. "We must stay. Jovar lied to us, but what's happening here is still going to continue if we leave. If not here, then elsewhere."

The others nodded. "I for one would like to put an end to Bohz Grauer's...evil deeds," Bellator said.

"And what do we do with the amulet?" Domo asked, his sharp eyebrows arched.

Kryger stood tall and tapped the point of his sword against the stone floor. "We give it to Jovar," he said.

"And share our knowledge as well," Xan asked.

"I think not," Kryger said. "The dwarf curse is not ours to thwart."

Franco inhaled and stepped forward. "Kryger," he started, but footfalls beyond the door they stood near made him stop. Domo held a finger to his lips and put his ear next to the door.

"How many?" Bellator whispered.

"One," Domo replied. "To the left." He pulled the door open and Bellator leapt through, his war hammer raised and ready.

Nothing.

The others followed and, in the torchlight, found themselves in another short hallway. To the right was a door, to the left, a small flight of stairs led to an iron door at the top. That door was ajar.

"It's our man," Kryger said. "Has to be. Up the stairs! Quickly!"

The roughly smelted metal door stood between two iron columns. A gap of about five inches enticed Domo enough that he chanced a quick look. When nothing happened, he looked again and lingered a moment. Then he slipped a dagger from its sheath and rushed through the door.

Kryger and Bellator ran in to offer aid to their elven companion, then Xan, Franco, and Clavam followed. The torchlight created a soft flickering light that revealed an unfinished area of the mine. The walls were rugged, cave-like with tool marks that looked like a red dragon[1] had raked its claws over the rock. The chamber felt closer, the ceiling here was only eight feet above the floor, and the opposite wall, was maybe twenty feet away at the widest point. It was longer though, with three tunnels leading out of the central core.

---

[1]Red dragons are huge (48 feet long) and evil. They are greedy for treasure, generally live in caves and attack with claws, bites, or by breathing fire. *Monster Manual* (Lake Geneva, WI: TSR, 1979), 33–34.

The rest of the party had come through the door in time to see Domo hurl his dagger at a ragged figure just beginning to turn up the passage ahead on the left.

The gray one. Bohz Grauer.

CHAPTER 45

The topic of conversation around Henley's farm was rain. The weather forecast, being the divination it was, continued to call for precipitation beginning late Wednesday night and into Thursday. Henley's wide eyes were as big and white as ping-pong balls behind his glasses when spoke of it. "Did you see the forecast?" he asked the combine drivers at breakfast. "We might get that bit of rain. Hopefully not too much, though."

The crew agreed, a little rain would be nice. The temperature hovered at one hundred degrees and the dust thrown into the air by the combines clung to sweaty skin and put throats in choke holds. The truck drivers stayed in their cabs to sweat it out until any dust had settled. The combine drivers cranked their A/C and did the same.

"Gonna need to check the air filters in the trucks before we go out tomorrow," Blaine said as the crew sat around the picnic table for dinner.

Henley nodded. "What about the combines?"

"Wouldn't hurt. But they can last a bit longer."

"Let's hold off on them a bit more then," Henley suggested.

It was quiet for a few moments as everyone ate, tired and thinking their own thoughts. Then, Mrs. Henley said, "If it rains the way they say it's going to, will you bring the combines back to the shed and work on them there?"

Henley put down his ear of corn and used a napkin to wipe away a yellow nub stuck to the corner of his mouth. He leaned back and looked at his wife. "I'm not sure," he mused. "Like I just said, maybe we'll wait on them more. We're a ways out, but if we're down for a few days, maybe. But otherwise, the basics can be taken care of out there. Blaine?"

The farmhand had been listening and nodded. "No point in wasting gas and risking an accident in the rain, right? I can take care of anything out there, but yeah, if we're down longer, back here is easier."

"It's going to rain a lot," Toff announced. Everyone looked at him as if they hadn't known he was there. "There's a concert in Spokane Thursday night." He glanced at John. "We're hoping to go. If it rains a lot."

Henley pushed his plate away and sat up. He put his elbows on the table and rubbed his dry hands together, so they made a raspy swishing sound. He looked at Toff, then John, then back to Toff. "I don't think so, Toff," he said. "The forecast has been calling for rain to start Wednesday night and probably be finished sometime Thursday morning. We'll need to make up the time by going a little later that night and we'll be up early Friday morning. No, I think a concert is out of the question for you boys."

John glanced at Dale, whose eyebrows were knitted in thought. John knew exactly what was on Dale's mind: The change in the weather forecast was...sudden.

Neither the concert nor the rain was brought up again during dinner. After both boys had showered and they sat across the chess board from one another in the bunkhouse, John couldn't contain himself any longer. "Toff, why did you tell Henley about the concert?"

Toff didn't say anything. He looked at the board and finally moved a knight. He sighed and said, "I don't know. He seemed like he was in a good mood. It just sort of... came out. Sorry."

"He went from thinking we might have three days off because of rain, down to it only raining a bit overnight and us working both days. He's going to make sure we don't go."

"Sorry."

Over the next couple of days, the talk of rain continued, but John and Toff never mentioned the AC/DC concert again (or *Dungeons & Dragons*), and the cutting went on. John wanted to use Henley's phone to call Truck, but they had set their plans, and he didn't want his boss to overhear. He was an undercover agent in enemy territory, and he was on his own. Instead of nukes, though, this Cold War was about standing firm against uninformed opinions. John was still playing D&D. He was going to that concert.

Thursday morning was gray and wet. The TV weathercasters could face the cameras with confidence, and the rain was exactly what Henley wanted: drizzly, not too much, and not heavy enough to knock down the crops.

Breakfast was served on the back porch and was light: toast, cereal, eggs. Paul had been called and told not to come out until later. There'd be no cutting that morning. Henley would see if the rain continued before making a decision about the afternoon.

John and Toff pulled the three trucks into the combine shed and worked on them all morning. Blaine had already changed the air filters, so the boys cleaned the cabs, checked oil levels, refilled the window washer fluid reservoirs, added radiator coolant, made sure the tires were properly inflated, and cleaned out the grain boxes. Inspection of the lift mechanism hydraulics they left for Blaine.

By lunchtime the rain still hadn't stopped. It wasn't a downpour, sometimes just a mist, but it was steady. In John's mind, there was no reason for Henley not to let them go to the concert. If the rain kept up there would be no cutting on Friday. Even if it did stop, the fields needed to dry out enough so the combines wouldn't get clogged.

At two o'clock the rain stopped. By two thirty the clouds were thinning, and the boys started to get nervous. "We're still going," insisted John. "The fields will take a while to dry. Even if they're ready at three in the morning we'll be back by then."

"When's Truck going to be here, again?" Toff asked.

"I don't know for sure. We decided we'd leave here no later than eight. We'll miss the opener, but that's okay. I plan on walking out of here no later than seven fifteen."

Toff nodded. "What about tickets?"

"Truck went up to Spokane the other day and got them for us."

Henley was late for dinner. He'd gone out to inspect how wet the fields were since the rain had stopped. It was six o'clock and the evening meal was served on the back porch again. The grass was still damp, and the rain collected by the oak tree rolled off the leaves in great dollops to splat on someone's head as they walked underneath.

When Henley finally arrived, it had grown dark again and the misty drizzle had resumed.

"Maybe we should just head home and check in on Saturday," Toff suggested as they finished dinner on the back porch.

Henley shook his head. "I don't think so," he said. He waved a hand toward a window. "This is only supposed to last an hour at most. Wind's going to pick up and dry things out. We'll be up and cutting as usual. Sorry, no concert for you boys."

After dinner, John and Toff retired to the bunkhouse. "Sorry," Toff said. "I thought we might get to go."

"I'll bet five bucks we don't cut a damn thing tomorrow," John said. "Henley is doing the same thing as Paulette, except with him it's the concert. He doesn't like the music so we shouldn't either. Where do these people get off?" His face was red, and he paced back and forth between the beds. "Get ready though. We gotta go in about twenty minutes."

"It's not going to be dark. How are you going to get out to the highway without him seeing you?"

"Around back, over and behind the combine shed, then go down and follow the ditch to where Truck is parked. Wait a minute. Don't you mean *we*?"

Toff shook his head. "I'm not going."

"What? Why?"

Toff sat on his bed. "I'm in enough trouble with my parents over D&D. I've never been to a concert so it's not as big a deal to me. Plus, if I had kept my mouth shut the other day, Jim wouldn't even have known about it and would have sent us home hours ago. You wouldn't have to sneak out. So, I'm going to stay. That way if Jim comes out to the bunkhouse, I can open the door and say you went for a walk if he asks."

"Seriously? Come on. Henley doesn't own us. As long as we're ready to go when we cut tomorrow—which we won't—that should be the end of it."

Toff hugged himself and shook his head. "I can't."

John sighed. He wanted to argue, but he and Toff had already been down that road. *Be an adult*, he thought. "Okay. But you're going to owe Truck sixteen bucks."

At seven p.m. the boys went up to the back porch to make sure their ice water jugs were in the freezer. On the way back to the bunkhouse they stopped at the Bug. They walked around to the front and John opened the trunk and lifted out a couple of board games. They left the hood up and went inside the bunkhouse. Then John came out, closed the trunk, and went back inside. He waited two minutes then went back out and around to the back of the building.

The games were a ploy he and Truck had come up with. They reasoned if Henley saw John bring the games into the bunkhouse, it meant he and Toff were settling in for the night. Leave the trunk open, come out and close it, go back in. In for the night. At least that was the idea.

The two minutes was enough time for a snoop to lose interest and turn around. Which would allow plenty of time to slip out the door and around back. John had read that scenario in a mystery novel; two minutes worked there so it would work for him too.

From the back of the bunkhouse John made his way over to the combine shed. There was a narrow point where he might be seen from the house, but someone would have to lean into the windowsill to specifically see that spot.

It was worth the risk.

Behind the combine shed he crossed about fifty yards of uncut wheat field then dropped down into the ditch that bordered the old two-lane highway. The ditch wasn't deep, but the edges were overgrown with tall weeds, and while it was wet from the rain, no water was running through it.

John ducked down and followed the ditch along the property line. After another forty yards he came around to the culvert that allowed water to flow beneath the driveway between the highway and Henley's house. It was five feet in diameter and dark inside, but John could see light at the other end, and nothing was blocking the way. He ducked and walked through.

On the other side he stayed low and checked his watch. Seven forty-five. He walked another twenty yards and chanced a look up onto the road.

A gleaming, bright-red 1957 Chevy pickup was pulled over on the shoulder not ten feet away.

Truck.

John was wet, dirty, and tired, but he was going to see AC/DC with his best friend. He climbed out of the ditch and opened the passenger door.

Truck nodded and smiled as John climbed in. He pushed a cassette into his stereo and turned up the volume. The machine gun snare drums of Sammy Hagar's hit "I Can't Drive 55" attacked the country air and Truck stepped on the gas.

"Woo!" John yelled with a smile. "Rock on!"

CHAPTER 46

Toff shook John awake at six the next morning. "How was it?"

John sat up and rubbed his eyes. He'd only gotten five hours of sleep, but he had a smile on his face. "Awesome! Man, it was so loud. My ears are still ringing. But so cool. They played everything."

"How did you get back? I didn't hear you come in."

"Truck dropped me off at the driveway about one in the morning. I just walked up. It was still raining then too."

Toff nodded. "It's not now, but the ground's still wet."

"See? No cutting today."

"Let's get breakfast and see what's going on."

They wore their sweatshirts against the added chill of the damp morning and sat at the picnic table. John piled scrambled eggs, toast, and bacon on his plate, then poured a cup of coffee. Dale, Blaine, and Mrs. Henley looked at him.

"What?" he asked innocently. "It's cold out here this morning."

"Would you like a cup of hot chocolate?" Mrs. Henley asked.

"No, thanks. This is fine."

"Where's Jim?" Toff asked.

Dale lowered his cup and said, "He went into town early to pick up a few things."

"Think we'll cut today?" John asked. He was ready for a nap as soon as he finished eating.

Blaine shook his head. "Too wet, right?"

"I suppose. What will we be doing today, then?"

"Always something needing to be done," Blaine said. "I'm sure we'll be able to keep you busy." He smiled and slurped his coffee. "I think Jim will probably send us all home for the weekend, though."

"Really?" John asked. He didn't want to sound eager, but maybe they'd get two nights of D&D in.

"It's been known to happen," Blaine said. "Depends on the weather of course. Supposed to warm up later today. But if he does send you home, don't expect to be paid. This ain't no corporation, right?" He laughed and went back to his breakfast.

"You look tired, John," Dale said. "Feeling okay?"

"Oh, yeah. Didn't get much sleep I guess."

"Well, take it from an old teacher, the coffee only helps for so long. Make sure to turn in early tonight."

"Will do," John promised. He was glad Dale didn't press the subject. He didn't like to lie and felt if the principal had asked outright what had kept him up, he would have told him. Maybe in confidence away from the picnic table, but he would have admitted going to the concert. And why not? Dale hadn't told him not to go.

Mrs. Henley excused herself and took two empty serving dishes back into the house. When the screen door slammed behind her, Dale leaned toward the middle of the table and said, "Listen, Jim had some errands to run, but one was to stop by Paul and Joanna's. Not sure why, but the phone call this morning didn't sound happy. Just saying you boys might want to be busy doing something when he gets back."

"Okay," Toff said. "We'll find something to do."

"What time did he leave?" John asked.

"Just before you two came up here for breakfast. He'll be an hour at the very least is my guess."

"I'm going to get the Steiger ready to start cultivating the fields," Blaine said. "You guys can help me with that. Prepare to get dirty."

The Steiger was a big, boxy, lime-green tractor that John had been wanting to drive. It was slow, but it was built for power, to easily pull the cultivator through the packed soil of the fields.

"Can I drive it down to the shed?" John asked before Toff.

"Have you driven it before?" Blaine asked.

"Nope. Want to, though."

Blaine slurped his coffee and studied John over the rim of his cup, conspiratorial and squinty-eyed. "Okay," he finally said. "I'll show you how and ride down with you."

John grinned. "Cool! Is the cab open? I'll meet you up there." Blaine nodded and John got up, patted Toff on the shoulder, and trotted away.

The Steiger was kept in its own shed tucked into an overgrown ravine two hills created where they met but were too steep to farm. It was about two hundred yards behind and above the house, but Henley and Blaine had plans to eventually add another bay to the combine shed and park the tractor there.

While the Steiger was just a tractor, John wanted to drive it more than a combine. It had eight tires, took four ladder steps to climb up into, and just seemed…like a giant tank.

John opened the cab, sat in the air-suspension seat, and looked over the controls. The shift and throttle levers were on a panel to the right, the dashboard was dotted with familiar gauges, and the steering wheel was the same as any car. It was very similar to a swather and John thought he could learn it quickly enough.

Blaine tapped on the door and smiled when John jumped. He opened the door and stepped into the cab, hunching over behind John in the tight space. "Scared ya, right? It's okay, glad you were checking it out before doing anything." Blaine went over how to start the engine and put the tractor in gear. "We're going to go slow so you don't run anything over," he said. "You don't even have to give it any throttle, it's going to go as soon as you let off the brake. Got it?"

John nodded. "We're just going to crawl."

"Right. Nice and slow. Okay. You know where to go; just steer us there."

John eased his foot off the brake and watched the four front tires slowly turn. He grinned and steered the tractor into the path that led down the hill.

As slow as they were going, it took almost five minutes to cover the two hundred yards. As he turned down the gravel loop toward the combine shed, John saw Toff standing in front of the middle bay. "Is that where I'm going?" he asked.

"Yep," Blaine said. "Slow down more before we get to the bottom of the hill and ease it inside. If you hit anything it's both our asses, right?"

John was tempted to ask Blaine if he wanted to take over, but instead said, "Got it. Slower than slow." *Go for it*, thought John.

Toff stepped to the side as John pushed the brake down and double-checked his clearance on both sides. He let up the brake, moved forward, and the cab got darker as it passed under the canopy of the shed. A few more feet and he put the brake down and stopped the tractor.

"Good," said Blaine. "Put 'er in park and shut 'er down."

John leapt down from the cab and got a high five from Toff.

"You liked it, huh?" Blaine asked climbing down after him.

"Well, it's not a Ferrari," John said. "But yeah, it's cool. Different. Fun to drive something big and powerful, even if it was just a crawl."

"Gotta start somewhere, right? You did good."

"John!" Henley appeared just outside the shed. He had an envelope in his hand and waved him over.

"Hey, Jim," John said, trotting out to meet his boss. "Did you see me in the Steiger? That was cool. If you want—"

"You're fired."

John flinched like he'd been slapped. "What? Why? What did I do?"

"You went to that concert last night after I said no."

"It was raining! I was up early and ready!"

"You're done, John. I'm not going to change my mind. Here's what you're owed up to today." He handed John the thick envelope full of bills. "I won't have people who don't do what they're told working for me."

CHAPTER 47

There was no *Dungeons & Dragons* that Saturday night. Toff called from Henley's house phone Friday and reported that he couldn't make it because they had to make up the time they'd lost due to the rain. John called the other guys and told them, "Maybe next weekend." He wasn't in the mood anyway. Henley had fractured the agreement about staying on until the job was done, and without the pay for working the rest of harvest, John would have to find a job during the school year. He'd have to work during his senior year.

The rain had left the area like a ghost, fading into the ether without fanfare. It had come, granted the wishes of a few farmers and a certain rock 'n' roll concertgoer, then eased over to the Rocky Mountains. The sun dominated once again, turned up the heat, and cooked away any moisture left behind by the single seasonal storm. It was still summer, and the sun was king.

John spent the week mowing his neighbors' lawns, washing cars, and running errands for his mom. He made about $35 and was lucky to do so. People knew they were contributing to his college fund, otherwise the work would have only been for a *Thank you, John! You're so sweet!*

On Saturday John and Truck were in the garage early. They opened the doors and turned on the fans in an attempt to cool it down. They filled the ice chest and stocked it with sodas. Then waited.

"When are you going to finish at the café?" John asked.

"I'll stay until the fair," Truck sighed. "That way we can go and have some fun during the day before school starts. Come on, you've just been moping around. You're bringing me down, man."

The Palouse Empire Fair was small, tiny, compared to state fairs or even some county fairs, but it was an annual event that heralded the end of harvest, the beginning of a new school year, and the transition of summer into fall. It held the typical events—a rodeo, animal shows, vegetable growing, and baking competitions—but the kids from all over the Palouse region looked forward to the carnival.

"Okay," John smiled. "You're on. We'll go opening day."

"We have to go Saturday night too," Truck said. "I bet you Lisa Martin will come over just for the fair."

John rolled his eyes. Even though she was now going to a closer university, he'd given up on his dream girl.

Toff walked in and sat down. "Hey," he said. He stared at John, then looked down and picked at his fingernails.

"Hey," John answered after a moment. He looked at Truck and frowned in confusion. "I'm not mad at you, Toff, if that's what you're worried about. It's not your fault I got canned. Henley had it in for me since day one it seemed like. He was just waiting for the right opportunity. Getting fired for going to AC/DC? Totally worth it."

Toff's shoulders sloped, and he shifted in his seat. "Okay. Well, it's been a lot slower without you there. Jim's had us all working past dark to catch up and get it cut before it's too late."

John nodded. "That sucks. Sorry. But I don't feel bad for Henley. He can lose the whole crop for all I care."

Toff nodded. "Yeah, I get that. Dale insisted on the early Saturday, late Sunday hours though. I think he's doing stuff for his school at night. I don't know what principals do to get ready. Actually, I'm surprised he's still here. Maybe they start later in Boise…"

Truck laughed. "Don't worry about it. Get your mind on some magic spells. We got a duergar badass to fight tonight."

"Are we close to finishing?" Toff asked John. "I remember you wanted to finish this dungeon before school started."

John shrugged then smiled. He was excited to see if they'd finish as well. "Yeah. You're close. Depends on what happens though."

"Always does," Truck said.

The rest of the boys arrived and took their seats. Questions were asked about John's status. No, he wasn't in trouble for getting fired. Yes, the concert was awesome. No, he didn't know how he'd make up the money he would have made. It was several hundred dollars he'd missed out on by getting fired. Yes, probably a job during the school year.

"And look at you two." Nick shook his head. "Are you twins now?"

John and Truck both wore their new AC/DC *Who Made Who* tour T-shirts. "Jealous?" Truck asked.

"You should have come, Nick," John said. "It was a great show."

"Whatever," Nick said. "Come on, let's get *this* show on the road." He nodded at the table.

"Can we close the doors?" Levi asked. "I feel like people are watching."

"You mean the traffic jam of two cars going by?" Charlie smiled.

"And the neighbors," Levi added, defending himself.

"Why would anyone want to watch?" Nick asked. "We're just sitting here."

"Everybody already knows what we're doing anyway," Truck said. "Small-town grapevine."

"Go ahead and pull them shut, Levi," John said. "It's not going to get any cooler in here."

"You think it's cool in here *now*?" Nick asked, rolling his eyes.

Levi pulled the garage doors closed and sat down again.

"Where were we?" John asked, ignoring Nick.

"I just threw my dagger at Bohz," Charlie said. "You ended the night without saying whether I hit him or not."

John smirked. "Did I? Me? And then we didn't play last weekend. The anticipation must have been brutal."

"Yeah, it *was* brutal," Nick said. "Let's kick this guy's ass already."

"Okay, okay, okay," John said. He took a deep breath and looked around the table. "It's dark, there are no torches on the walls. Only the torch held by Franco gives any light." John was in storyteller mode, looking over his notes and the dungeon module as he described the room and situation the party found themselves in. "You're in an unfinished chamber—"

"Yeah, we heard the room description last time," Nick interrupted. "Remember? We went in, you described the room, and said everyone saw Domo throw his knife."

John looked at his notes. "Oh, yeah. Sorry." He shuffled a couple of pages and started over. "It's dark, but even by the light of Franco's single torch, you can see the glint of the blade Domo has thrown as it flips end over end before... striking its target."

CHAPTER 48

Domo's aim was true—the blade hit its target—but it struck plate armor, a steel skin the point of a thrown dagger could not penetrate. But the thief's attack served its purpose; it stopped Bohz Grauer in his tracks.

The blade lay at the fuzzy edge of the light given by the torch Franco held over his head. Like an apparition from beyond this world, a gnarled gray hand reached into the light and picked up the knife. Then the gray dwarf stepped forward defiantly. He squinted toward the group, a scowl carved in his wrinkled face. But he wasn't old—the wrinkles were hatred; some scars were there, but his face was lined with the loathing of all things. His hair was long, a weedy mass of grayish brown that fell upon his shoulders like scraps of rotten linen. His skin was the color of campfire ash, and he wore heavy plate armor across his back and shoulders. His black leather pants and boots were rippled with iron studs.

His beard was loosely braided and fell upon his chest like a spent tassel. Atop his head was a round iron cap bordered by studs, like Franco's mace, but cut in half. Bohz Grauer glared at the party, the thief's dagger in one hand, a sinister double-bladed battle axe in the other. He sneered. "Five against one."

Kryger withdrew his extra sword and tossed it to Clavam. "Six against one," the warrior said.

Bohz glared and flipped the dagger casually and caught it by the blade. "So, you mean to kill me?"

"Unless you come peacefully to be judged for your evil deeds," Franco said. "Or you may choose death."

"Then I choose death. For all of *you*." Bohz threw the dagger at Franco and ran forward, his axe held above his head.

The gray dwarf was fast. The move surprised Kryger and Bellator, the two warriors of the group who should have expected the surprise, but Bohz didn't give a hint of his intention to charge. The blade struck Franco in the hip and embedded itself in his thick leather armor, though he felt a sharp pain as the tip nicked his skin.

Kryger and Bellator stepped forward and braced themselves for the attack. The gray dwarf was a little more than four feet tall; Bellator would face him head on, but Kryger had a significant height advantage.

But Bohz went low. He suddenly dropped to one knee and slid toward his enemies. He held his battle axe low and flat, then brought it up sharply and hit Bellator under the chin. Then he swung it down toward Kryger's unguarded leg. He rolled backward and jumped back to his feet.

Kryger leapt away, but not before receiving a gash across his shin from the sharp axe blade. The gray dwarf's quick attack had caught everyone off guard but now they spread out, faced their foe, and advanced.

Clavam swung his sword wildly, clumsily, in front of him. "My wife is dead because of you!" he shouted. He wasn't a trained swordsman, but his anger was real.

Bohz grinned. "You should have cooperated and come willingly."

"Into slavery?"

"Each man has his fate," Bohz sneered.

Clavam screamed, a guttural eruption of anger, hatred, and anguish. He charged the evil gray dwarf. Bohz Grauer was unconcerned; his eyes remained on the party of adventurers. *They* were the threat, not an untrained emotional farmer. He knocked the sword from Clavam's hands and tripped the farmer, so he went sprawling.

Franco had jammed his torch into a crack in the wall and the sputtering flame sent bizarre, elongated shadows over the floor. He rushed forward, his mace held low in his right hand, his flail swinging above his head in his left. He brought the flail down with an exaggerated arc, but the gray dwarf easily blocked it with his upraised battle axe.

Which is what Franco expected.

His right hand swung up and smashed the mace against Bohz Grauer's left side below the armor. It landed with a satisfying *thwack* and Bohz grunted as if he'd been rammed by a bull.

Domo sailed into the fray and swung his short sword but succeeded in only shortening the gray dwarf's stringy hair by an inch.

Bohz fell backward and rolled out of view. "Wiry, isn't he?" Kryger mused. "Be mindful, now."

Suddenly the room was awash in a white glow as a ball of light rose into the air and hovered above. Xan had used his ring to take away the shadows the gray dwarf hoped to hide in.

"There's a bridge behind him!" Bellator shouted. "*Do not* let him get across."

Xan's light revealed a gaping chasm behind Bohz Grauer, presumably part of the cave-in they'd seen earlier, with a crude plank and rope bridge spanning the distance.

Bohz grinned. Obviously familiar with his surroundings, he continued to back up.

Kryger moved to the left and helped Clavam to his feet. He handed him the fallen sword but told him to keep his distance. Then he turned and ran toward Bohz, his broadsword in front of him like a lance.

Bellator saw his friend's attack and began his own assault from the opposite side, but he was slower and farther back.

Bohz Grauer angled himself toward the human warrior but not so much that he couldn't see the dwarf coming as well.

Kryger did not intend to stab with his sword, it was awkward enough to run with the weight held out in front with both hands. Instead, he brought his elbows in and folded the sword down the length of his body then crashed to the ground, rolling like a log. He slammed into Bohz and knocked him over, the gray one falling forward over the top of the big warrior.

Bellator was shocked when he saw Kryger fall. The garish magical light of Xan's floating sun may have somehow hidden something thrown by the gray enemy. But as he drew closer, he saw Kryger's face and knew he wasn't injured. It was a ploy, a taste of Bohz Grauer's own tactics.

But Kryger came to a stop on top of his sword and wasn't able to maneuver it from underneath himself. Bohz swung his axe in a long arc over his body and brought it down on Kryger's back. The blade tore through the leather armor and split Kryger's skin apart. Kryger flinched and rolled away, pulling the axe from Bohz's grip. The blade was black with blood.

Clavam jumped on top of Bohz Grauer before the mercenary had a chance to recover his weapon. He pounded his fist into the gray dwarf's face then raised his sword. Bohz grabbed up his axe and swung it around. The blade thudded deep into the side of the farmer. With no protective armor to block or even weaken the blow, the axe blade sank deep into Clavam's side, smashing bone and splitting vital organs like a cleaver through watermelon. Blood washed over the floor.

Clavam's eyes widened in shock; his mouth opened but no sound escaped. He rolled to the ground, one hand over the gaping wound, desperately trying to hold his lifeblood in, his other arm wrapped protectively around his body.

Bellator smashed his war hammer against Bohz Grauer's shoulder and heard a crack—from broken bone or armor he couldn't tell, but the gray one only grinned all the more.

Domo saw his opportunity and came up behind Bohz as the gray dwarf stood up. He hurdled the curled-up Clavam, landed silently as only he could, and slashed Bohz's left hamstring. The studded leather pants gave way beneath the razor-thin blade and blood ran freely down the gray one's leg.

Bohz Grauer buckled and fell to his knee, his left leg splayed out to the side. He yelled in rage then ducked down, injured but still aware of his attackers. Franco had moved in and swung his flail at Bohz's head, but the duergar had seen it coming and avoided the death blow.

Then it was Franco who collapsed to the ground, writhing in agony with a blade protruding from his leg just above the knee. Bohz Grauer had pulled the knife from its sheath as he ducked Franco's attack.

Then the gray one scuttled back toward the bridge.

"Xan! Do something! Use your magic!" Bellator yelled. "He must not make it across the bridge!"

It grew cold in the chamber like a freak storm racing from the north. The temperature dropped more than forty degrees in seconds, the warm air turned icy, and sleet streaked down from above. It was a powerful squall with thick clouds boiling over the ceiling, and a fierce wind howled among the rocks. The sleet was fierce, it struck the face, stung the skin, and blinded the eyes. Everyone but the magic-user who'd cast the icy spell felt the effects. They shivered and shielded their eyes; they tried to stand but slipped on the ice that had formed on the floor.

The magic-induced storm lasted only two minutes, and when it cleared, a thick sheet of ice covered the floor. Icicles clung to the craggy walls and snowy crystals encrusted the beards and eyelashes of the victims. But Bohz Grauer was nearer to the bridge. He'd stayed on the floor and slid his way closer to his escape route. Kryger took two steps, slid, and fell to the floor. Bellator was steadier on his feet but couldn't advance quickly enough, and Franco had a knife in his leg. Domo was closest to the gray dwarf but still had a span of ice to cross.

"Come on, elf!" Bohz challenged. The gray dwarf was five feet from the bridge. Domo was thirty feet from the evil gray one, but he'd slip and slide too much if he tried to reach him. "I see it in your eyes, elf. You think you can do it. Come on! I will wait for you." Bohz stood unsteadily, his left leg shaky, his right foot sliding back and forth.

"Domo, is Clavam alive?" Kryger asked.

"No," the elf replied.

Relying on the thief's keen hearing, Kryger whispered, "Keep him talking. I have an idea."

Unsure what his friend had in mind but reasoning it must be an attack of some sort, Domo took two steps to his left. He said to Bohz Grauer, "I would enjoy the opportunity to slit the throat of a shriveled gray gnome[1] such as yourself, but I fear you will crawl away like a coward."

Bohz frowned and growled like a bear. "You dare insult me?"

Domo stepped forward slowly, testing his balance on the ice. "Insult you? No. Look at you. You *are* shriveled, you are gray, though now that I think about it, it may be due to

---

[1]Gnomes are similar to dwarves but are only 3 feet tall. *Monster Manual* (Lake Geneva, WI: TSR, 1979), 46.

loss of blood, and you are a gnome. Are you not? And you are a coward, having already crawled away to escape after promising to kill us all."

Bohz shook his head. "If we had met one-on-one, elf, you would already be dead." He slid another dagger from a sheath in his belt. "Are you sure of your footing?" he brandished the blade and drew back to throw it.

The ball of magical light emanating from Xan's ring dove down from above like a silver dragon.[2] It streaked through the chamber, a meteor on a collision course with the gray dwarf. But it stopped before it struck him, the light was not a weapon and it stayed in front of his face radiating its brilliance, blinding the duergar. Bohz screwed his eyes shut and swatted at the light without effect.

Domo heard a grunt behind him and turned to see Kryger and Bellator both fall on their backsides as they heaved Clavam's inanimate form. The body of the dead farmer, splayed out like a starfish, spun across the ice toward the bridge. It knocked the feet out from under Bohz, who fell on top of the speeding corpse, and tumbled over the edge with it into the jagged crevasse.

Domo dove forward, sliding on the ice to the bridge and looked over the side. Bohz Grauer clung to the rock ledge below with his bare hands. "Haul me up, elf," he grunted. "I won't kill you."

Kryger and Bellator waffle-stepped to the edge next to Domo and looked down at their quarry. "Asking for help

---

[2] Silver dragons live on high mountain peaks, clouds, or other lofty locales. They are very large (48 feet) and can breathe frost. *Monster Manual* (Lake Geneva, WI: TSR, 1979), 34.

from one you were about to kill," Kryger mused. "Xan, you're the scholar. That's called irony, is it not?"

Xan and Franco appeared, and they looked down at the angry gray dwarf clinging to the rock face. "Yes," Xan answered. "Quite so."

Franco squatted down and said to Bohz, "You still may be saved and taken to be judged. What say you?"

Bohz growled, "I'd rather—"

"Done!" Kryger shouted. The big fighter swung his blade down and severed the gray dwarf's fingers, chopping them away from the rock.

Bohz Grauer didn't scream. But the scowl turned into surprise as he fell into open air away from the bridge. He swung his arms wildly, trying to grab anything that might stop his fall. But there was nothing. When he hit the bottom of the chasm it echoed like an avalanche of boulders. Kryger winced, the pain from his wound still sharp, and then he smiled.

CHAPTER 49

"Yes!" Truck shouted. He stood up and his chair slid back, crashed against the wall. "*That's* how you do it! Good job you guys, we got that little duergar bastard!"

Charlie was laughing. "I can't believe you guys slid Clavam's body across the ice! That's hilarious!"

"Hey," Truck said and slapped Nick on the back. "We had to think quick. And it worked!"

"I think it's break time," John said. They all grabbed at chip bags and tossed each other sodas.

"Wait!" Levi said. He held up his hand. "Be quiet for a sec. What is that?" He turned his head toward the garage's front doors.

The other boys listened. They heard voices out in the street.

"What the hell?" Charlie said.

John rushed through the side door of the garage; his mind filled with visions of terrorists throwing pipe bombs. He ran across the yard and stopped short on the front lawn where his mother already stood. They watched as five people—Paulette Dickerson, Aaron Evans, and three others, all members of the One Vision Bible Church—marched in a loose oval and chanted, "Keep Weston wicked-free!"

The Brewers were being picketed.

The demonstrators carried hand-painted signs: D&D = DEVILS & DEMONS; JESUS SAVES, SATAN PLAYS GAMES; JUST SAY NO TO D&D; KEEP WESTON SAFE! They carried them over their shoulders and pumped them up and down as they walked.

The rest of the boys came out; Truck stood next to John and the others fanned out. "Now we know what she was planning," Levi said.

Evie looked around at the crowd. "Explains why Nosy Nellie is here," she said. Nellie Carter was the reporter for Weston's local rag, the *Daily Bulletin*. She was barely five feet tall and carried a folding step stool as part of her camera gear so she could get above crowds. Nellie forced her way into situations claiming freedom of the press, but often forgot to take photos, too engulfed in whatever was happening. People took to calling her Nosy Nellie once they realized gossip was number one and reporting the story was farther down on the list of her priorities.

Across the street, neighbors stood on their lawns and driveways gaping at the spectacle. No one, let alone a group of people, had ever staged a protest in Weston before.

"How'd they know we were playing tonight?" Nick asked.

"Small-town grapevine," Truck said.

"Or those two cars that drove by," Charlie said. "Maybe one was her."

"This is ridiculous," Evie said in disgust. "You're crazy, Paulette!" she shouted. "Why can't you leave us alone?"

Paulette told her fellow picketers to keep marching, keep chanting, then strode over to stand on the sidewalk in front of Evie and John. She wore navy-blue polyester shorts that ended at her knees and a Weston Warhawks T-shirt with shoulder pads; her hair was teased and sprayed into a Samurai helmet. She looked like a Go-Go's groupie. "I'll leave you alone when your devil-worshiping son and his friends stop playing *Dungeons & Dragons*." She said the last as if they were made-up words, aberrations of the English language.

"You're on our property," Evie said.

Paulette looked down and pulled her foot back off the grass. "You're bringing evil into this town. We won't stand for it."

"We're not bringing anything in," John said. "We've been playing for years, and nothing has ever happened."

"*Dungeons & Dragons* is satanism!" Paulette said. "It's not a game, it's indoctrination!"

While Evie argued with Paulette, John whispered to Truck, who ran into the garage. Nellie Carter stood to the side like a boxing referee, her camera dangling around her neck, and she scribbled in a small notepad, her eyes dancing between the fighters.

Truck returned and handed John his *Dungeon Masters Guide.* John opened it and cleared his throat loudly. "Ahem!"

The bickering between evangelist and homeowner stopped, onlookers craned their necks, marchers continued their rounds.

John said, "From page nine, under The Game: '*Advanced Dungeons & Dragons* is first and foremost a game for the fun and enjoyment of those who seek to use imagination and creativity.'"

Paulette turned to him. "Don't you spout that garbage to me."

"Page—"

Paulette slapped the book out of John's hands, hitting his wrist in the process. The page tore out of his grip and the book bounced on the sidewalk, flopping open like a slayed accordion.

"Hey!" John and Evie said together.

Paulette stooped, picked up the *Dungeon Masters Guide,* and snapped it shut. "What is that, right there on the front cover, if not a devil?" she shrieked, stabbing her finger at the cover art of a red-skinned creature with horns and sharp teeth.

"We tried to tell you before," Nick said, almost bored, "it's an efreeti."

"Don't get smart with me, city boy. I don't care what you call it, it's a devil. Anyone can see that."

John put out his hand. "Can I have my book back?"

Paulette pulled it back out of his reach and glared. Evie took a step forward, her face set for battle. Paulette reared back and flung the book in an arc over the boys.

Nellie snapped pictures and the neighbors *oohed*.

The hardcover book sailed over the driveway and crashed through one of the painted-over glass panes in the garage door.

The shocked silence that followed the last tinkling of glass was broken by the shutter clicks of Nosy Nellie's camera. Then Officer Wayne Phillips walked up and stood next to Paulette.

"Good evening, folks," he said. "Looks like we have what I like to call…an incident."

Evie started to talk but Phillips held up his hand and cut her off.

"No need to explain anything, Mrs. Brewer. Or you, Mrs. Dickerson. There are plenty of witnesses, including yours truly. I've been standing right over there for the past fifteen minutes. We even have photographic evidence thanks to the dedicated employees of Weston's *Daily Bulletin*."

Nellie smiled and nodded.

"So," Phillips went on, "what do you suppose this incident includes?" He clapped his hands together. "I'm thinking trespassing, assault, destruction of property, and I'm guessing unlawful assembly."

"Assault?" Paulette shrieked. "I never—"

"Oh, I heard the slap to John's wrist from over there," Officer Phillips said.

"I got a really good shot too," Nellie said. "Should make a nice addition to the story." She grinned.

Phillips took the picket sign—D&D = DEVILS & DEMONS—away from Paulette and set it on the ground. "Unless you want to hold it, John?" He smiled.

John shook his head and frowned. "No, thanks."

"Paulette Dickerson," Phillips said as he placed her wrists in handcuffs, "you're under arrest, again, for trespassing and assault. I'm also adding destruction of property and unlawful assembly. That last charge will be dropped if you can prove you obtained a permit for your demonstration." He read off her rights then led her down the street with his hand on her elbow to his car.

The bystanders gaped and stared. It was the most exciting thing to happen on that street since the Jensens, who lived three houses down on the left, added a back deck to their house in 1983. As they walked by the other picketers, Officer Phillips told them all to follow him to the police station for questioning.

"You may not be charged, but if you *don't* show up, I'll charge you with obstruction of justice. And I know where each one of you lives. Got it?"

"Fuckin' A, man," Nick said. "That was cool."

"Nicolas! Watch your mouth!" Evie admonished. "But you're right. That *was* cool."

CHAPTER 50

"It's a good thing you don't work for Henley anymore," Truck said the next day. "He'd probably try to run you over now that Paulette got arrested again because of you." His eyes went wide as he realized what he'd just said. John's dad had died by being run over by a combine. "Oh, shit. Sorry, man."

John shook his head. "Don't worry about it. But you think Henley would be pissed about her arrest because of me? It's not my fault," said John. "She's nuts all on her own. But I guess you're right. If Henley hated me before…" He trailed off. "I don't care though, you know. He's obviously crazy too. He's an ass." He sat back and waved his hand as if erasing the thought of his former boss.

They were eating lunch at the Top Notch Café and already two people had stopped at their booth and asked about the arrest of Paulette Dickerson. The pictures in the

Daily Bulletin that accompanied the story of her seizure were of the five marchers and one of Paulette being led away in cuffs by Officer Phillips. John was only a little disappointed they didn't use the one of him getting his wrist slapped.

"You know people are going to talk about it at school," Truck said. "Man, that's next week!" He shook his head. "We start school on Wednesday. Crap." He took a big bite out of his burger. Then with his mouth full said, "At least we're seniors this year. We're almost done."

"Yeah? And then what?" John asked as he stared at his burger.

"Whatever we want!" Truck looked at the clock on the wall behind the cash register. "I gotta get back to the café, though. Still have a couple—"

The blare of the air raid siren calling the volunteer fire department cut him off. As it wound down, Truck stood and pulled a few crumpled bills out of his pocket to pay for his burger. When the second blast rang out, he sat back down. At the sound of the third blast, they looked at Millie; she and her husband owned the small eatery and she'd been working the counter since Lisa Martin left. Millie knew everyone in town.

Millie hustled to the phone on the wall near the kitchen and dialed. She pulled the cord around the corner and out of sight of her customers. Nobody ate. Nobody spoke.

After a minute Millie reappeared and hung up the phone. She turned and looked at John. "Jim Henley's farm," she said.

John and Truck looked at each other. "Toff!" they both said.

They dropped what money was in their pockets on the table and dashed out the door. Both of their cars were parked on the street, but they went to Truck's '57 Chevy pickup. It had a rebuilt 350 small block V-8. No question which was faster between it and the Bug.

With a roar and squeal of burnt rubber, the pickup jumped from the curb and raced out of town.

It was normally a twenty-to-thirty drive to Henley's place, at least for John. Truck had the gas pedal on the floor and drove like he was on a slot car track. "Truck!" John said, his hands on the dashboard. "We have to get there alive. Slow down!"

They didn't talk for a while; the windows were rolled down and the rush of air awash with the thundering of the engine were the only sounds from the outside world. John's hands were still flat against the dash as he stared ahead, trying to see a sign. Why had a call been made to Weston's Fire Department? Why was it a three-alarmer? Who was hurt?

At Round Barn Hill, the steep one John's Bug had trouble climbing, Truck didn't give it extra gas or even shift down. As they neared the top, John yelled, "Sharp turn." Truck let up on the gas and then John saw it. Black smoke billowing into the blue sky like an oil slick on the ocean. "Shit," he said.

"Toff's okay," Truck said. "Toff's okay."

"Hurry! That's close to the house. Really sharp turn off the highway."

"I know, I know."

Truck sped down the hill, shifted down, and braked hard close to the gravel driveway and took the turn at 30 mph. The truck slid sideways and fishtailed on the gravel until he got it under control and up the driveway.

John pointed at the lawn near the house. "Just park there."

They saw smoke behind the combine shed but they couldn't tell how far away the fire was. John got out and ran up to the house. He went onto the back porch and banged on the inner door, then the windows when no one answered.

Truck was at the bottom of the stairs when John came out. "Mrs. Henley isn't there."

"Maybe she called then went to the fire," Truck said, nodding toward the smoke.

John nodded and they ran.

They were sweating when they reached the combine shed, but on the other side they lost their breath. John and Truck stood in the tall wheat, dumbfounded. A wall of flame and black smoke writhed into the air at the far end of the field, cutting the world in half.

The smoke billowed and roiled. They were half in half out of a hellish storm as the smoke blocked the sun, changing the world to a sepia landscape of muted colors and shapes. "Oh my god," Truck whispered.

At the far end of the field, just at the edge of the fire, was a combine. Its green paint was scorched, the glass of the cab was gone. Crouched by the big front tire was Mrs. Henley. She wore a blue and white flower print dress that stood out against the end-of-the-world background like a white flare. When she saw them, she stood up and waved for them to come to her. She took a step to the side and revealed the prone form of someone lying on the ground, presumably whoever had been driving the combine.

The boys broke into a run, knocking down a path through the wheat. The fire loomed, crackling and whooshing, hungry to get at them; the heat was staggering, like standing inches from the open door of a five-hundred-degree oven then leaning in.

"John!" Mrs. Henley exclaimed. "I'm so glad to see you. Why…? Never mind. Help me get Paul back to the house!"

Paul Statler was recognizable in that what was left of his hair wasn't gray like Jim Henley and he was smaller than Dale Kleinert. His face was black with soot and burns, skin had peeled away and left open weeping sores across the right side of his face and over his head. His jeans were smoking, and his shirt seemed melted to his upper body.

John thought of a campfire hot dog left too long above the coals. "What happened?" He had to yell to be heard above the roar of the fire.

Mrs. Henley shook her head. "I don't know! The combine blew up! I saw a big ball of flame from the house—it doesn't matter! Hurry! We have to get out of here!"

Truck lifted Paul under his arms while John lifted his legs by the cuffs of his jeans. They scuttled back the way they'd come, John backpedaling, Truck bowlegged, Mrs. Henley trying to lift Paul by the waistband.

Before they got too far the scorched jeans in John's fists tore and Paul's legs dropped and dug into the dirt. John fell backward, Truck got backed up behind Paul's dead weight and lost his footing too, pulling Mrs. Henley down as well.

"I'm sorry," John said.

"Come on," Mrs. Henley pleaded. "We're almost there." Ash swirled around them like snowflakes from Hell, and she waved them away as if they were a swarm of insects.

"I can't breathe in this heat," Truck said. He wiped the sweat off his face and looked at his hand. It was covered with blood, but it was...diluted. Paul's burns were weeping plasma as well as blood. "What the hell?" Truck yelled.

"Don't think about it," Mrs. Henley said. "Wipe your hands on your pants. John, turn around this time so you're facing the house. Come on, pick him up!"

They heaved Paul up again. John faced the way they were going, his grip around Paul's ankles, and they set off in an awkward trot, waddling back and forth like a wheelbarrow race in PE class.

After another rest they made it around the combine shed and put Paul on a patch of dry grass by the bunkhouse. They were smeared with blood and sweat, muddied with ash and dirt.

"You," Mrs. Henley said to Truck, "get the water going and bring the hose." She pointed to a pipe near the combine shed that rose out of the ground and had a red hand pump on top. A green garden hose was screwed onto the spigot.

"That's Truck," John told her when Truck ran over to the pump.

"Truck? Okay." She maneuvered Paul into a comfortable position and looked down the driveway.

John followed her gaze. "They should be here any minute. We just beat them out here."

"Hey," Truck said. He trotted to a stop in front of them but didn't have the hose in his hand. "We have a problem."

"What?" John asked.

"Look." Truck pointed back to the fire. The combine was gone, behind the fire that was now moving north. Toward the house.

"Oh my god," Mrs. Henley said. "The wind changed direction."

Chapter 51

It didn't take a strong gale to make the fire change direction. A whisper of a breeze was enough to give the flame a taste of something else and set it on a new path to sate its hunger.

Even without a wind to push the fire, the dry wheat would be consumed like newspaper in a campfire. The combine shed would be next, followed by the bunkhouse, and the Henley home.

"John!" Mrs. Henley yelled. "Can you till the field?"

"What? What do you mean?" He'd never tilled anything.

She pointed up the hill toward the swather barn. The big lime-green tractor was parked next to it. "You drove the Steiger. The cultivator is hooked up to it now."

John went blank, his mind unable to understand what was being asked of him. He shook his head. "I don't know..."

"You can do it, John," Mrs. Henley said. "You have to. Drive it down and stop when you get to the field. Truck and

I will get it ready. Then you need to drive around and turn over the wheat. Understand?"

John shook his head again.

Mrs. Henley stood and pulled John up the driveway to the tractor. "There's no time to think about it, John. It's called a fire break. Okay? I've never driven it. You can do it. Please! This is my home!"

John stared at her. He saw her pleading, her panic, and thought of his own mother. When he thought Paulette Dickerson might torch the garage, he imagined his mom would be in the same state as Mrs. Henley.

He nodded. "Uh…yeah. Okay. Okay." He climbed up into the cab and sat behind the wheel. The key was in the ignition. He remembered what Blaine had shown him and started it up.

"John! Hurry! Please!" Mrs. Henley hopped up and down and pointed toward the fire.

John shoved the tractor into gear and pushed down the gas pedal. It lurched forward and he turned sharply down the hill. Ahead of him was the fire, a wall of destruction rushing toward the combine shed. It had already overtaken the spot where they'd first fallen down with Paul.

He steered into the field and stopped. The cultivator on the back of the tractor was essentially a series of giant blades or forks mounted on a frame with wheels. Dozens of steel C-shaped tines dug into the soil as they were pulled behind the tractor; they turned over weeds and stubble, and aerated the field.

But it was big. To safely transport the cultivator, the sides were folded up, so it looked like an airplane on an aircraft carrier. Truck and Mrs. Henley pulled the locking pins from each wing and then she operated the hydraulics to lower them down. It was torture watching the wings ease down to the ground; Truck wanted to cut the hydraulic lines and let the wings fall. When the tires finally touched down John released the brake and gunned the engine. The tractor heaved into the field of wheat, leaving a track of fresh turned soil in its wake.

The field behind the combine shed was flat, a dog-legged spur that came off the nearby hill and lay along the ditch. John pulled the cultivator behind the corrugated steel wall of the shed and beyond. As he neared the ditch, where not too long ago he'd snuck through to meet Truck, he turned toward the fire. He could tell it was closer, moving fast. It looked alive, jabbing at the sky, pushing forward, roaring like an angry mob. John kept turning the wheel and headed back the way he'd come, doubling the width of the fire break. *It's not enough*, he thought. The flames were high, powerful, lunging forward and throwing burnt embers and ash into the air. The embers would easily reach the combine shed and beyond. He needed a wider fire break.

Truck stood at the spot where John had driven the tractor into the field. He held up his finger—*one more pass should do it*. John had another idea though.

He turned right at the edge of the field but went straight toward the fire. He wanted to cut the flames off before they got closer to the combine shed. If he could turn over a path right in front of the fire first, it would slow it down enough for him to dig a wider break. Then he could go down the far side by the ditch and connect with his original path to create a box.

As John got ready to turn and cut a path in front of the fire, everything went black. The wind, stirred up from the flames themselves, surrounded the oncoming tractor with black smoke. The cab went dark, the smoke covered the windshield like a blanket; John was blinded and he stepped on the brake.

It was hot in the cab; smoke seeped in, and John coughed and coughed, an old man cough that racked his chest. Where was the fire? Should he go forward or just turn here? It was fifteen yards away when he stopped.

It was just smoke. John decided to go forward slowly, count to five and then make the right turn toward the ditch. If the smoke didn't clear before he got to the ditch, though…

He eased up the brake and the Steiger moved forward. John couldn't see anything but ash and black smoke.

One.

More smoke was in the cab. John choked and coughed and squeezed his tearing eyes against the burning.

Two.

The smoke suddenly rushed past the tractor and liquid-like flames lunged and licked at the cab from only a few feet away. John flinched, covered his eyes, and spun the steering wheel. He chanced a quick look to his left. The flames were swirling, at least fifteen feet tall and leaning forward at the top like waves about to crash, trying to reach him in the tractor. Then he was blinded by smoke once more.

John gave it more gas and veered to the right. The fire was racing him, not wanting the tractor to chew up the dry wheat. At a slant, John no longer knew how long he could go before crashing into the ditch. The smoke blocked his view intermittently, like it was playing a game—*now you see it, now you don't.*

The blaze made a move to get in front of him. It reached out in front of the tractor and the wheat stalks he was about to drive over flared up like matchsticks. *Don't brake! Don't brake!* He turned the steering wheel hard, shifted, and gunned the engine again. The cultivator stuck out maybe ten feet on each side, and it went right through the fire, but John avoided it with the tractor.

The cab was hot. Dangerously hot. *Was the tractor on fire? Overheating?* John didn't know. Sweat poured from his head—his arms and hands were slick with it—and he choked on the smoke that had slipped inside. What he did know was that he was no longer driving just to keep the fire from the Henley homestead. The flames wanted him too. The fire wanted the tractor. It wanted the cultivator. It wanted to kill. To eat.

John knew he had to be close to the ditch. The fire was racing him on the left as he slanted toward the edge of the field. The smoke lifted for maybe two seconds, and he thought he saw the black line of the highway above the dry creek bed. He counted—one, two—and then turned straight toward the combine shed. Behind him the fire slowed, he'd cut a wide path in the wheat, but it hadn't given up. Dry stalks and heads of wheat still caught fire as they lay in the turned soil.

In the murky light John saw the first ribbon of dark soil he'd made parallel to the combine shed. He'd done it! He'd made the box. He slowed, made the turn, and added more break line as he drove away from the ditch.

Truck was still at the entrance to the field and waved for John to come out. John held up his finger just like Truck had earlier. "One more pass," he coughed, and turned again toward the fire.

This time he had his previous track to follow. The earth was dug up where he pulled the cultivator through the field, but it wasn't like garden soil. The stalks of wheat were still there, knocked down, lying chaotically like the trees around Mt. St. Helens after the eruption in 1980. John wanted another pass to overlap his previous path enough to turn the soil more and cover the exposed wheat.

John's world was smoke. What light there was, was muted and dead. There was no ground.

Then it attacked. From the right this time, from inside the box John had created, the fire lashed out, surprising and laughing at him. It had jumped the path to eat what wheat it could still find.

John was driving in the fire.

"Shit! Shit! Shit!" he yelled and coughed. Smoke squeezed through the door, and he choked on his words. John turned hard to the left, and the Steiger veered away from the battle.

When John got to the entrance of the field, he spotted a firetruck and Truck was waving at him to stop. He stomped on the brake, shut off the engine, and kicked open the door. Smoke rolled out and he stumbled down the ladder in a fit of coughs and spasms.

He was lifted and carried. By whom, John didn't know. It might have been his friends, but he had the sense they were older men, stronger, maybe the volunteer firefighters. He coughed, sucked in air, coughed some more.

"Okay now?" Truck asked.

Toff was there too, but John had no memory of their friend arriving. They were sitting beneath the oak tree in Henley's yard. John held a clear plastic oxygen mask over his nose and mouth. He nodded.

"You're crazy. You know that, right?" Truck said.

John took the mask away. "I didn't know what else to do. It's not like I'd ever done that before."

"You're a lucky man, John," Toff said. "What a way to end the summer. I'd say harvest is officially over. At least it is here." He looked at Truck. "Dragon worthy?"

Truck nodded. "Oh yeah. That was the most dragon-worthy thing I've ever seen anyone do."

John replaced the mask, breathed deeply, and watched Gary Carter walk across from one of the fire trucks parked along the drive. Gary was the meat department manager at the grocery store where Charlie worked.

"Feeling better now, John?" Gary asked. He'd taken off his heavy fireman's coat but still wore the bulky pants. They were held up by red suspenders over a green Weston Warhawks T-shirt.

"Yeah," John answered and pulled the mask away from his face again. "Not coughing so much anymore."

"Okay. I still want you to go to the hospital and have Dr. D check you out."

"So, we can go?" Truck asked.

Gary nodded. "But Truck, take him right to the hospital, okay? No stops." He turned to John and said, "Your mom will meet you there."

The boys stood to go but Gary stopped them and put his hand on John's shoulder.

"Hey John, listen to me. I knew your dad, you know? We were pretty good friends. What you did here today? Your dad would be very proud of you."

John nodded and swallowed hard. "Thanks."

While Gary packed the oxygen equipment, the boys stepped off the lawn and said goodbye to Toff. Then John looked around. Firemen were moving about the farm, checking the combine shed, looking around the bunkhouse. Smoke was still drifting up from the field behind the combine shed, but it wasn't black and roiling like it had been only minutes before. Blaine had moved the Steiger back up the hill and was looking it over. He glanced up and gave John a thumbs up. Dale Kleinert and Mrs. Henley appeared from behind a fire truck where they had been looking at the field. She waved at John and smiled.

"Come on," Truck said. "Let's go."

They turned and walked down the driveway. At Truck's pickup John stopped and looked back up the small hill. Henley was alone in front of the swather barn, his arms were crossed, and the sun glinted off his glasses as he looked back at John. His jaw was set, and he didn't move as he watched the young man he'd fired. They stared at each other for a moment then Henley turned and walked away. John looked toward the burnt field for just a moment, a quiet smile on his face, then got in his best friend's pickup and closed the door.

Epilogue

The cause of the fire was never determined. However, the remains of a pack of cigarettes was in the cab of the burnt-out combine and a butane lighter was found on the ground near the header. Joanna later identified it as her husband's. The fuel cap was dangling by its chain rather than screwed tight onto the tank. It was plausible that Paul had been smoking outside the combine and somehow ignited the fumes with his cigarette. Or perhaps he'd gotten out of his combine to check the sickle bar, dropped a lit cigarette and it smoldered in the dry wheat until it burst into an open flame. If that had happened near the open fuel tank, it could have ignited the fumes as well. Or dry chaff had been ignited by a hot belt in the engine compartment.

Joanna later found a note scrawled in her husband's hand that read, *Fuck you and your farm, Jimbo*. So, it was also possible

Paul had purposely started the fire, and it had gotten out of hand.

Many situations were mulled over, but none could be corroborated by Paul Statler. He died from his burns and smoke inhalation while en route to the hospital.

The fire had blocked Henley and the others, and they were forced to find a way around. By the time they arrived at the house, it was over. In the end the fire destroyed fifty-seven acres before it burned itself out—with help from the fire department's water trucks and John's scramble to create a fire break.

The first Saturday following the beginning of their senior year in high school, the D&D group gathered in the Brewers' garage to finish the adventure, *Alchemist's Bane*. Toff's magic-user, Xan, cast a spell that showed every creature in the underground dungeons that Bohz Grauer, the gray dwarf mercenary, was dead. They were told the artifact had been found and warned to leave the prisoners and flee the area or suffer a similar fate.

The party led the freed townsfolk back to their village and were given medical attention, feasts, luxury accommodations, and to Domo's delight, the key to the city.

When they presented Jovar with his prize, they did not tell him it was a false amulet or that it meant his ruination if he tried to use it.

Jovar vanished during the night. He abandoned his post as mayor without a note or a word of goodbye to his staff. His belongings were gone, his quarters were empty, and three horses were missing from the town stables.

When citizens worried about his return, Kryger, the mighty warrior, explained the curse any user of the amulet would suffer. "Jovar will not trouble this town, or any other, except, perhaps, as a beggar."

Paulette Dickerson served four days in jail. During that time her husband filed for divorce. The judge also ruled Paulette had to buy—with her own money and in person (she couldn't ask someone to do it for her)—a new *Dungeon Masters Guide* for John. She also had to pay to have the glass in Evie's garage door replaced.

When her divorce was finalized, Paulette moved to South Carolina. She didn't ask Aaron Evans to go with her.

Two weeks after the fire John received a letter. Inside was a check for $2,000 and a handwritten note.

You saved our home! Please accept this as a token of thanks and admiration, as well as a contribution to your college fund. Thank you so much!

It was signed, *Patricia Henley.*

In October Lisa Martin happily accepted John's invitation to return to Weston as his date to the homecoming dance.

Did you enjoy We Be Dragons? If you have a moment, please consider leaving a review on Amazon, Goodreads, or your preferred platform. A quick review can go a long way in supporting independent authors like me and help other readers discover books you've enjoyed.

Thank you so much for reading!

BIBLIOGRAPHY

Gygax, Gary. *Advanced Dungeons & Dragons: Dungeon Masters Guide*. Revised ed. Lake Geneva, WI: TSR Games, 1979.

Gygax, Gary. *Advanced Dungeons & Dragons: Monster Manual II*. Lake Geneva, WI: TSR, 1983.

Gygax, Gary. *Advanced Dungeons & Dragons: Monster Manual*. 4th ed. Lake Geneva, WI: TSR, 1979.

Gygax, Gary. *Advanced Dungeons & Dragons: Players Handbook*. Lake Geneva, WI: TSR Games, 1978.

Turnbull, Don, ed. *Fiend Folio*. Lake Geneva, WI: TSR Hobbies, 1981.

Ward, James M., and Robert J. Kuntz. *Advanced Dungeons & Dragons: Deities & Demigods*. Lake Geneva, WI: TSR Games, 1980.

Tam Thrift's original hand-drawn art in full.

ACKNOWLEDGEMENTS

I would like to express my sincere thanks to those who answered my many questions during the research for this book. My dad, Terry Weitz, who's been to every corner of Whitman County and knows every piece of land, helped with the farming details. My brother, David Weitz, knows more about grain than I thought there was to know and solved my problems in that area. Jim Lyman, who I've known my whole life because he's my dad's best friend, was my 1980s era combine expert, he answered questions and offered alternatives to my ideas. Having lived through a field fire, he also described what it's like to escape one. Jason Pfaff, who not only taught me to play *Dungeons & Dragons* in junior high, but willingly double checked my accuracy on many facts throughout this book. Kristen Hamilton of Kristen Corrects, Inc., a fantastic editor whose suggestions, expertise, and positive feedback helped make *We Be Dragons* a stronger book.

And especially, my wife, Catherine, who is always my first reader, provides honest feedback, love, and support, and is remarkably patient with my inquiries of, "Are you finished reading that yet?"

Thank you all. Really.

About the Author

Michael Weitz grew up in a small farming community where he worked a number of summer jobs including service station attendant, swather driver and truck driver during harvest. A constant diet of fantasy and sci-fi novels in junior high led to *Dungeons & Dragons.* He credits that game along with his love of reading, and an active imagination with helping ignite his passion for writing. Today he reads almost anything and has an eclectic number of interests. He and his wife live in the pacific northwest with their way too cool dog, Watson.

Michael is also the author of the Ray Gordon mysteries. *Even Dead Men Play Chess*, the award-winning best-selling debut, was published in 2007.

More information can be found at
michaelweitzbooks.com

Made in the USA
Monee, IL
24 June 2025

19690935R00256